THE Golden CHILD

A Novel

CHRISTIAN MARK

PAGE PUBLISHING, INC.
New York, NY

First originally published by Page Publishing, Inc. 2017

This book is a work of fiction. The names, characters, places, and incidents are the product of the author's imagination or used fictitiously. Any resemblance to actual events, locales, or persons living or dead is coincidental.

ISBN 978-1-64027-324-5 (Paperback)
ISBN 978-1-64027-325-2 (Digital)

Printed in the United States of America

This book is dedicated to the loyal people who look after our mentally challenged citizens. They include doctors, lawyers, nurses, social workers, aids, and maintenance people. You know who you are.

The *Golden Child* story begins in the 1950s with a family trying to fulfill their dream of having a child and all the love and satisfaction that goes with it.

The McGilverys are having trouble bearing children, and eventually seek out a state adoption service. Their luck is with them when a beautiful, blond-haired 18-month-old little girl becomes available.

The family welcomes her with open arms, and this completes the dream of having a young, healthy, little child to raise as their own. She is a great child, talented, smart, and outgoing. Things couldn't be better.

When adolescence hits, their world begins to crumble. Anne is acting out, and her studies start to deteriorate. There is constant friction in the household, and the parents don't know if it is drugs or something deeper.

The situation gets so bad that the state has to step in and commit Anne to a mental health setting.

The family is heartbroken, and hires a private detective to investigate Anne's past.

This investigation opens up a Pandora's box of deceit, malpractice, and mismanagement that was thrown onto the family and the next generation. The story migrates the twists and turns of a complicated state mental health system.

The McGilvery's son inherits the mess, and decides to take the situation to the next level, not knowing what the ramifications might be. He is caught up in something he does not understand, and the more he learns, his distaste for the state's actions causes him to start a chain reaction of events that will spin out of control.

PART I

WORCESTER, MASS., 1968

The lighting in the hallway was very dim and depressing. As I looked to the ceiling, I noticed the lights were covered with a mesh steel cap to keep anyone or anything from breaking them. To my right and left were two orderlies and two nurses. Their expressions were vague and quiet. They looked like they were sad, serious, or just did not want to be there. We continued at a methodical, slow pace, and every few feet one of the wheels of the gurney would throw off an annoying squeak.

One of the orderlies' left eye twitched every time the wheel threw off that awful noise. The longer we moved down the hallway, the more aggravated the man seemed to get. There was some low-level conversation, but I couldn't understand what they were saying. It was like everything was in slow motion; my mind was numb but mellow.

As we converged down the tunnel, I noticed a light brown painted wall that looked very damp. I could smell the mildew in the air. It reminded me of being in my parents' cellar when I was little. The walls were similar to these walls. I would make a fort with my blankets behind the heating system and play with my dolls. I would pretend to play house and do everything my mother would do with my little brother.

We stopped. I couldn't see what was happening, but I heard the hum of an elevator being beckoned. It sounded old and creaky as it came down the shaft. Then I heard it stop. As the beige painted doors opened, the nurses moved the gurney at a ninety degree angle to push me into the elevator car. I could not see what floor they pushed, but the car started to move upward. The journey took some time; the progress seemed slow.

Once the car stopped the doors opened again. I was moved out onto what looked like a hospital floor. It was not new, but looked more modern than the place I had come from. There seemed to be a lot more activity than what I remembered from my room on the ward. We went by a nurses' station, which was vacant, and moved down another long hallway. My neck hurt from straining to see where I was, but I had no strength. I tried to see where they were taking me, but all I could do was look up at the faces that had concern written across them.

I decided to relax and enjoy the ride. I would wait to see where they delivered me before I would strain my neck again. Every now and then I would see a nurse or doctor walk by me going here and there. The doctors looked old and grouchy. I could tell they were not orderlies because they were wearing stethoscopes around their necks. One stopped and looked at me, and said take Anne to operating room C. He was old and pale looking, and from my angle I could see all his gray nose hairs. This also matched the hair on his head. He was wearing a white lab coat with a pocket protector with many pens stuffed inside.

The gurney seemed to speed up after the doctor gave his order to the staff. We accelerated at a mild speed, and for some reason that annoying squeak went away. We travelled for maybe another thirty seconds, and then took a quick turn into what looked like an operating room. It's not that I had ever been in one, but I remember what they looked like on the soap opera, General Hospital.

This room was large and had a lot of stainless steel racks and cabinets with medical supplies in them. The walls were white, and the sun reflected in a series of small windows at the top of the wall. Inside the glass was wire mesh in a diamond shape pattern. I felt better being in such a sunny room but my head was still fuzzy. All the nurses and doctors were going here and there, but no one said a word to me. It was almost as if I was invisible. I was still not sure why I was here. Besides feeling spaced out, I felt physically fine.

I raised my neck up a little and saw two nurses and a man in a white, short coat who were working on some sort of machine in the corner of the room. It was a big stainless steel box with a few dials and some cords with paddles on the ends. As they were working with the machine, they kept looking back at me with a guilty look. What could this machine be? I never saw one of those in any doctor's office or hospital, and I had been in a lot of them over the years.

Out of my peripheral vision I saw another nurse coming at me. She had a big hypodermic needle in her hand. She was walking right up to me. As she approached, she tilted the needle up, and squirted some liquid out of the end of the needle. At that point I knew what was coming. I jerked my arm up to block her from getting closer, but my arm came to a halt before I could move it. I looked down and noticed a cloth bracelet was wrapped around my wrist and the safely rail of the gurney. I looked over and tried to pull up my left arm, but it was secured down in the same fashion. Panic started to take over my body.

I ran the last 24 hours back in my mind. What had been happening? I had not gotten much sleep because of those voices in my head. They kept me up at night. They took over my body and controlled my mind. They told me to do things I did not want to do. My uncontrolled laughing at inappropriate times was worse than ever. I would be having a conversation and another resident would say "Are you talking to me?" That would snap me out of it for a split second and I would respond that I did not know what they were talking about. They would give me a look and then walk away. It's not like I was the only person acting weird in this place. The nurses would give me medication at various times of the day, and then my doctor or social worker would ask me if I was still hearing the voices. I would always claim it was better because the pills made me feel tired and lethargic and I hated feeling that way.

As I looked back to my right the nurse swabbed my arm with an alcohol pad, and then jabbed the needle into my arm, releasing the contents into my body. I felt a warm flow immediately run through my body. I started to feel relaxed, but with a copper taste in my mouth. I felt helpless now, but almost resigned to the fact that I didn't care what they were going to do to me.

I could see someone pushing that machine towards me. An old gray-haired man, who looked to be a doctor, came towards me, and I noticed he had rubber gloves on his hands. They reminded me of the ones my mother used sometimes when she cleaned the toilets on Saturday morn-

ing. These gloves were black and looked thicker. The doctor looked down at me, and his expression toward me was one of sadness, like he pitied me or himself. He motioned the other man to come closer.

Then from my opposite side, a woman with a stern look on her face opened my mouth, and put in a heavy rubber mouthpiece. It felt like my old retainer after I got my braces off after junior high, but it was bigger and more uncomfortable. It fit very snug, and I couldn't open or close my mouth at all.

The gray-haired man picked up what looked like the paddles with the wires attached to them, and then the orderly started turning the dials. He put one paddle on each side of my temple, gave the other man a head gesture, and that man flipped a switch. I felt a jolt of electricity go through my head. I tried to fight it, but it was no use. My body felt a surge shoot from my head, and down through my toes. I could feel it so clear. Why is this happening? Are these people trying to kill me?

The faces of the people all around me started to fade away. Was this the end of me? Why would my parents have put me in such a place? They loved me! My parents said this place would make me get better. Had my parents lied to me? No! They were the only ones that cared.

* * * * * * *

I opened my eyes. I was looking straight up at the ceiling. This must be my room because I remember the shape of the chipped paint. It looked like a bird I had painted when I was a little girl. I looked down at my wrist, and the restraints were gone. I could move my arms if I wanted, but I did not. I was so tired and relaxed that I did not want to move them. I rolled over on my side, and noticed the back of my roommate lying in her bed. She must have been sleeping. It was daylight because I saw the sun streaming into the room and illuminating the walls. It was so bright, I had to squint. In the background, I could feel the familiar sounds of the ward. I was not dead, I was alive, and the voices had gone out of my head. Tonight I would get a good night's sleep. I hoped the voices wouldn't come back.

WINCHESTER, MASS., 1950

My mother and father walked down Main Street passing time on a Saturday afternoon. The sun was shining and the downtown area was bustling, with people going to and fro attending to their business. Paul McGilvery was trying to do anything to keep his wife happy. She had been so down the last few months; she had no interest in anything.

She had been through her seventh miscarriage. Both of them now doubted that they would ever be able to have another child. There were no little feet around the house and my mother desperately wanted another child. She was in a perfect situation to have a family, and she could not. My father was doing great at work as an accountant at Texaco Oil Company and was moving up the corporate ladder. They had the means to have a family, but for some reason God was not giving my mother the opportunity. They had so much to give to a child, but for some reason it was not to be.

My father went in and out of stores doing his normal Saturday chores, and my mother strolled along, window shopping, trying to forget her troubles. Looking around, everyone looked so happy and fulfilled.

The 1950s were a time of promise in America. The sacrifices of World War II had left people hardened, but confident in their abilities to conquer anything. America was such a great place and it was now reaping the rewards of fighting for the American cause of freeing the world of Nazi Germany and Imperial Japan. Anything was possible in the U.S. People were moving from the cities into the suburbs in record numbers. Suburban neighborhoods were sprouting up all over Massachusetts, and people were rushing to get in on the dream.

My parents were currently renting in a two-family house in West Medford, a working class city just north of Boston. It was a nice unit that had all the comforts of home, but they wanted a single family house in a town with more land and less congestion.

Winchester had it all. It was up-and-coming, with all the things a family would need to prosper. The downtown area was beautiful, with small shops and a variety of nice merchants and a great theater. There were a few cozy places to eat. The schools in town were first rate. The people were so friendly, and all the things my parents had heard about town were so positive.

My father came out of the cleaners and saw my mother staring through a picture window of a real estate office. As my father approached he noticed she was looking at picture board of several properties that were listed for sale in the Winchester area. Each one had a picture with a short description and a price. My father said "Pat, do you see anything you like?" in a half joking manner. She looked back at him with a serious face, and said "I like this one." She pointed to a small, white Cape Cod house with a breezeway and a single car garage. It had a small front yard and looked perfect. My mother had not taken this much interest in something in months. She had been so down after the last miscarriage that nothing he could say or do would snap her out of it. He was scared to ask her any more questions, due to the price, but he knew he had to. "Why do you like this one so much?" he said in a more interested manner. "I like the way it looks, and the rock formation in the front yard would be perfect to plant a nice garden. It says there is a big back yard, perfect for family gatherings and sports."

His heart sank after he heard family gatherings. Did Pat mean her family, or her extended family? He did not know how to answer her, and tried to play along as best he could. "You are right, Pat," he said. "The back yard would be great for entertaining, and it says here it backs up to conservation land. That is great; we would have our privacy in the back."

WINCHESTER, MASS., 1954

I imagined that I was probably looking around the living room from my bassinet, and noticed my sister Anne run by, giving me a quick look and a smile. The room was crowded with neighbors and well-wishers on my baptism. I had come into the world so unexpectedly, and everyone could not believe my mother had taken me to term.

It was all because of my sister. A few years after my parents moved into their new home, they gave up on the thought of having a child. The local priest mentioned that adoption might be a viable alternative. They looked into Catholic Charities and also the state agencies in Boston. They filled out the paperwork and went to all the interviews. The process was grueling, and they put forth an endless amount of energy to make this dream happen.

The pool of children needing homes had dwindled since World War II, and their choice of a little girl was very highly sought after. Countless nights my father would come home from work and ask about any news. The answer was usually the same. If a child was located they would go to the orphanage or agency to visit the child. Most of the children who were available were usually older and male. My mother had her heart set on a girl.

The weeks turned into months, and my father worried that my mother's depression would come back. The new house, her neighbors, and her activities could only keep here distracted for so long. Most of her friends and the families on the street were having children on a regular basis. The families were big, and the place was littered with kids, bikes, and baby carriages.

The Baby Boom generation was being created right before their eyes. My mother had made some good friends on the street, but she wanted what they had: a child to hold and nurture. How she dreamed that that day would finally come.

One day my father came home from work around 6:00 p.m., and walked in the front door. He did not smell dinner cooking, which was very unusual. My mother loved to cook, and always had a fine meal prepared for the two of them every night except on Friday. That day was reserved for fish, pizza, or whatever my mother could dream up that didn't have meat in it. It was their Catholic tradition, and they stuck to it no matter what.

As my father walked into the kitchen area, he didn't see any activity. His heart began to race with a low level of anxiety. My mother was always waiting for him at the front door when she heard his car door shut. The only distraction could be that she was attending to a great meal in the oven.

As my father made his way down the hallway toward the bedroom he had a fleeting moment of doom where he was worried what he might find on the other side of the door. He was so caught up in his emotions that he had not even spoken out my mother's name. Before he could get out any words, his hand reached down to grab the door knob and open the door. The door stuck as it always did, and my father had to push it with more force than usual. The door finally popped open with a little snap and crackle.

On the other side was my mother sitting at the end of the bed; she looked up at my father with tears in her eyes. She was holding a piece of paper in her hand, and a picture which was flipped over, so he could not see who was in the picture.

As my father looked down he could see that the tears running down were not of sorrow, but of joy. My mother stood up, and threw her arms around his neck.

"Paul, our prayers have been answered," she said. "The agency has found us a little girl." My father couldn't believe his ears. Was it true, was this the news they had been waiting for ? Were their dreams finally coming true?

My mother was so excited she was trying to juggle the letter from the adoption agency and the picture, and put the picture in front of my father's face. She dropped both, and was going to pick them up when my father grabbed my mother and planted a big kiss on her lips, and held her so tight that my mother almost lost her breath. She cried out "Paul, you are going to break me before I have a chance to show you the good news." My mother bent down quickly and snapped up the letter and picture in one fell swoop.

"Look at her, Paul. Isn't she beautiful?" she gushed "The letter says we are to call them and meet as soon as possible for an interview and play date to see what we think. Look at her Paul. I know this will be our little girl," my mother said proudly, as if this little girl had just finished first in a contest or a beauty pageant. As my father looked down he could see a little girl, maybe two years old, looking back at him with blond hair, blue eyes, and the face of an angel.

My father was so elated. He could finally see their hopes and dreams coming together. He had grown up with so little, and worked so hard to achieve the American dream, and it was finally on his door step. How he wished this would work out. He could not wait to see what the next day would bring.

As I looked up from my bassinet, all the people at the party were talking to their neighbors and friends. Everyone looked so happy. A new baby in the McGilvery household! The good times were back. My mother's depression had subsided, and she found out how life can suddenly turn from bad to good.

What a change in luck. After the day my parents got the letter that my sister was available for adoption, life had made a 180-degree turn. The spare bedroom had to be prepared for a child's room, the walls needed to be painted, wallpaper decided on, and little girl's furniture purchased. My mother was thrilled with the prospect of doing all the planning and bringing home her baby girl.

Once Anne joined the family, a whole new world was set in motion. How my mother cherished this time. The sound of a little girl prancing from one end of the house to the other. She explored all the nooks and crannies, learning about her new surroundings and getting used to a new home and new people.

My mother took her everywhere with here. She would not leave her side, even for a minute. She fed Anne, read to her, played with her, and watched her sleep, all while trying to keep up with household chores. The bond between them grew stronger every day. On Saturdays my father would take Anne out with him to do his Saturday morning errands. The first stop was always to the dump. My father would see neighbors there for a few minutes, and catch up with the news around town. Then on to the dry cleaners to have his shirts cleaned and pressed. Then on to the coffee shop to get cup of coffee and a doughnut. My sister would always get a honey dip doughnut and a glass of orange juice.

After the chores were done, my father would take Anne down to the pond located in Winchester center. He would bring stale bread with him so they could feed the ducks. My sister got such a thrill watching the family of ducks follow the mother and father around in single file, and then make a turn toward them when the bread was offered. My father thought to himself, Anne can see in animals the way humans cherish their children. Anne would run after the ducks as they made their way down the shoreline, and said goodbye.

After that he would hold her little hand and walk her around the park so she could see all the flowers and interesting things that were so obvious to a child. She would call my father 'Daddy' and put her hands around his shoulders and squeeze him so tight. He felt so blessed to be in this place and time.

The first year Anne was with them was such a whirlwind. My mother enrolled my sister in Farm School. It was a preschool in Winchester that also had animals. She thrived in that environment. The classroom time was instructive, and the teachers were so caring and helpful for her. At recess, they fed the animals and rode the ponies. Anne was truly in heaven.

After the first year my sister joined the family, my mother and father must have felt at ease. My mother became pregnant with me. They were both shocked, due to my mother's advanced age. "It must be a sign," my mother said. After the stress of trying to have a family, when it was the last thing on their mind, my mother was able to conceive a child.

The fear of another miscarriage never really took hold of her. With my sister to distract and entertain her, she went through the pregnancy with no complications, and was elated to start a family.

My mother and father redecorated a small sewing room next to their room. They had so much fun painting and wallpapering, and my sister always wanted to be involved. She too, was excited at the prospect of another playmate around the house.

The blessed day came. I was born on time and with no complications, a healthy baby boy. My mother came through the birth with flying colors. My father was in the waiting room passing out cigars to my uncle and his friends. God had blessed them two times in two years. How much better could things get?

As is customary in a Catholic family, my parents wanted to get me baptized a soon as possible. That way my mother could take my sister and I on carriage rides when the weather was good. She was not superstitious, but they both felt better knowing my soul would go to heaven if anything ever happened.

I imagined that as I looked up from my nap, I could see the people at the party having a good time. My mother and father had finished their entertainment duties and were standing next to the bassinet, looking over me. They looked so happy. My sister was trying to ride our family dog Baron like a horse. My uncle was guiding her around the living room. The other guests were laughing and taking it all in.

Once Anne knew I was awake, she jumped off Baron, and ran over to me. She stood on her toes, and put her little hands on the edge of the bassinet, trying to pull herself up. My father picked her up in his arms, so she could get a better look at me. They looked so happy together. My sister had brought so much happiness into their hearts. She was indeed the golden child.

WINCHESTER, MASS., 1964

I could hear Anne running up the stairs two at a time to make it to her room in record time. She was just entering junior high school, and things were so promising for her. She was a straight-A student, an excellent piano player, and a Girl Scout. My parents would go on and on about what a great daughter she was and what a joy to have.

My relationship with Anne was one any younger brother would have with a sister. We were very close, sharing the good times and the bad ones together. Fortunately the good outweighed the bad. When we fought, it was usually over something stupid like a TV show or what rock band was the best. She was a great sister, and always helped me with my homework if I was stuck and needed guidance.

My parents' lives were cruising along. They were running a household with two energetic kids, socializing with neighbors, and volunteering for coaching duties, the Girl and Boy Scouts, and other civic activities. My father also had a few part-time accounting jobs to help make ends meet. My parents had both come from meager backgrounds and understood the value of a dollar. Since my sister and I were late joining the family, my parents not only had to think of college for us, but also retirement for them.

I heard my sister enter her room, grab a stack of my 45s, and head across the hallway into her room. I went to her door. She was looking into her closet thinking about what outfit she wanted to wear for the next day to school. She was a fashion bug, and fashions were changing so fast.

She looked over, and waved me in. I walked over to the record player, and asked if I could play some records. As always, she said: "Yes." I put on my Rolling Stones and Beatles, and she put on her Bob Dylan, Donovan, The Mamas & the Papas 45s. We loved each other's music, and enjoyed sitting in the room together listening, and catching up with the news of the day. Music was probably the biggest thing we had in common.

My mother knew Anne had a gift in music, and enrolled her in piano lessons at a young age. She excelled, practicing for hours in our living room, both because my parents made her, and because she put a lot of pressure on herself to be the best. She would always be available to help me with my trumpet lessons even though my key was E flat, and hers was C. She was such a driven person, always studying for an extra hour for a test in school, just to make sure she got a good mark. My parents never put pressure on her, but wanted her to have all the opportunities available.

As we listened to the music, the 45s continuing to drop on the stereo, I heard my mother call up the stairs. "Anne, come on down here. Someone is on the phone for you." She raced out of the room and down the stairs. I continued to listen to the music, and flipped through a few of her teen magazines, looking at all the teen Hollywood and music stars of the day. The magazines had little articles on each person or group, and what they were doing recently. This always fascinated Anne.

Suddenly, Anne burst through the door. She looked nervous. "What's the matter?" I asked. She went over to the record player, fumbled with the records, picking up a new stack to be put back on the player. "My tryout for the Ted Mack Amateur Hour is Friday night," she blurted. I said "So what?" Anne told me that she had a Girl Scout sleepover at the camp in town on the same night, and she was looking forward to it. She had been practicing for months to try to make it onto the talent show, which at the time was the one of the biggest shows around for up-and-coming talent. She sat there, looking very pensive, thinking about how to work in both the tryout and the sleepover in the same night.

As usual, my mother figured out a plan. Since the Girl Scout camp was in town, Anne would have dinner at the camp, go to her tryout after diner, and then go back and sleep at the camp overnight. My mother was one of many chaperones, so logistically it would work.

Friday night came quickly. The anticipation had built all week. The Ted Mack Amateur Hour was one of the most popular TV shows and to have the local tryouts at Winchester High School was such an honor. Most of the acts would consist of singing, playing instruments, and dancing. The judges would pick the top three acts, and they would move on to Radio City Music Hall in New Work City where the show was filmed. At the time Ted Mack was to amateur talent what Ed Sullivan was to professional talent.

My mother, my sister, my sister's friend Betty from Girl Scouts, and I walked into the high school auditorium. Betty was there for moral support, and to keep an eye on me. We walked down to the front of the room, and Betty gave me the look, and said let's sit her on the aisle. I agreed to her request, and turned into the row. Mom and Anne went up the stairs to the right of the stage, and disappeared behind the curtain.

I settled into my seat, and took in the whole atmosphere. It was so exciting to be here, and to think three of these contestants were going to New York to be on television. The noise in the room was moderately loud with people milling about, looking for family friends, or looking for the best seat in the house. As I looked around I saw some of my classmates with their family or friends. I gave a few head bobs to some familiar faces; it seemed like half the town was here to root on a family member, friend, or neighbor.

As I turned my head back the other way, I was looking right into Betty's face. She looked kind of mad, and a little scary. "Hey, squirt, I want to give you a suggestion for when we get back to the campfire tonight," she said. "You are going to go inside with your mother in the cabin, and we are staying outside. You get it?" Before I had a chance to think about it, I said, "I get it." I did not cross my sisters or her friends, due to the fact they might be babysitting for me any weekend, and then I would be in big trouble if I didn't go along. After I looked away, I could see Betty had a little smirk on her face.

As I looked up to the stage, I could hear musical instruments behind the stage being tuned up, and short bursts of the songs that were going to be played once the show went live. The pulse of the room was going up, and all of a sudden the last remaining people sat down, and the high school music director came out from behind the curtain, and introduced himself to the audience.

His name was Mr. Enwright. He was a very scary character. He stood about six-three, two hundred and thirty pounds, with slicked back dark hair, and commanded respect wherever he was. There was a rumor going around our school that once when he was talking to some students at a local grammar school to recruit them to play instruments, some rough kids outside were making faces in the window. The students could see the kids outside, and it took every ounce of energy not to laugh. After a few minutes, Mr. Enwright saw what was going on, and said to one of the students to go outside and retrieve the two boys. Once the boys came in, they tried to play it cool, but the music teacher got right in their face. He taunted them, asking if their little escapade was funny. He asked several times, and finally one of the kids smirked, and said "No." To his amazement, Mr. Enwright slapped him across the face, and then told the two boys to march themselves down to the principal, and wait in the office for him. I guess the two tough guys, and all the other students, were flabbergasted. As the two boys slunk off to the office, Mr. Enwright turned to the students, and said "Who wants to be in the band?" The way I heard it, every kid signed up, not because of their love of music, but because they were so scared of Mr. Enwright.

As Mr. Enwright stood at the front of the stage, he introduced Mr. Ted Mack. With his loud, low voice, Enwright was a master of getting great applause from any group he was speaking to. As Ted Mack came out from behind the curtain the applause even got louder. He looked bigger than life, just the way he looked on TV. Once the noise died down, he gave a short speech, laid out the ground rules, and then the competition started.

The first contestant was a young girl who was going to play the flute. She had a music stand in front of her, so she could read the music. I said to myself, she is not going to win anything if she can't memorize the song she is playing. Doesn't she know this is the big leagues? I also said to myself, I'm glad I'm not standing up there, fame or no fame.

As the night wore on we watched a variety of musical instrument performances, singing, dancing, juggling, and some weird stuff that I don't know how the people didn't get dragged off the stage. I felt bad for the kids whose parents put them up to it.

After about an hour and a half, my sister was introduced and she walked over to a beautiful piano that was to the right side of the stage. We were lucky because we were seated on that side also. My mother had joined us as soon as she settled Anne's nerves behind the curtain. My mother looked so nervous, and Anne looked so cool. I could not believe she was up there. My big sister.

The noise in the crowd died down, and then my sister started. She was playing a song by Bach. Her music teacher made everyone play it, but Anne played it the best. I must have heard it a thousand times in my living room at home, and I never got sick of it. As I watched her, she looked to be concentrating on her speed at which she played. Not too fast or too slow, her teacher would always say. The whole song took about three to four minutes. Anne played it so well you could have made a record from it.

After she finished, she walked around to the front of the piano, and curtsied to the crowd, and walked off. The room gave her a polite applause but no one stood except for my mother and Betty who were clapping like we just saw a famous rock band. As I looked over to my mother she had a tear running down her face, and was still clapping. I could tell just how proud she was of Anne.

After about three hours, the competition came to an end. Ted Mack thanked all the contestants, and then he conferred with the three judges who were sitting to the left of the stage. I did not know who they were, but I'm sure their credentials were impeccable. The judges conferred for about five minutes while the murmur in the crowd grew. Ted walked over and picked up three index cards from the judges' table, and moved to the microphone in the center of the stage.

He reminded us again that the top three acts would be off to New York, and would appear on one of his shows the next fall. The sound in the room dropped off. He said "Thank you ladies and gentlemen. What a show of talent from this fair city. The second runner-up in the competition is the O'Maley Irish Step Dancers." The crown roared with applause. It lingered for a minute. "The first runner-up is Katy Reynolds on the harpsichord." The room exploded into applause again. I could see some parents on the other side of the room jump for joy.

I was getting so nervous; my hands were moist and clammy. After a minute Ted Mack said, "And the winner of the Ted Mack Amateur Night is Sally Joplin, who played the folk guitar." The room went crazy with applause, and hooting from Sally's family and neighbors. The crowd was loud and jubilant.

I looked to my right to see my mother's reaction, but she was gone. I asked Betty where she was, and she pointed and mouthed "Behind the stage." I asked her if we could go up there and she said "Yes," and took my hand and led me through the crowd. Behind the curtain it was a different world. The different sets, booms and pulleys, and many instruments, with parents, and teachers all standing around talking about the night's activities, and consoling their child or student the best they could. Betty pulled me to the other side of the stage, and I saw my sister's face was buried in my mother's chest. I could hear her sobbing. My sister's music teacher was rubbing her back, and telling Anne and my mother that she played well enough to be in the top three. I felt sick for my sister. She practiced so hard, and played so well, it was not fair that she did not make it.

That night, the ride back to the Girl Scout camp was very quiet. I sat in the front seat with my mother, and Betty did her best to comfort my sister in the back. My mother just drove, and we sat in silence. When we got back to the camp, my sister's friends came running into the parking lot, and hovered around my sister. She told them in a shy, meek voice that she had not made the cut. They all voiced their displeasure, and then guided her back to the campfire to do their best to cheer her up. My mother and I made our way back to the cabin to see the other mothers, and tell them the highlights of the night. When my mother tucked me in that night, she did not say a word. She just patted my fore head and said, "I love you."

That night was one of the most exciting I had ever had, and probably the saddest, up until that point in my life. Little did I know the worst was still to come.

WINCHESTER, MASS., 1966

◆◆◆◆◆

The past two years had not been good to Anne. Things had begun to change when she turned thirteen years old. She had a hard time making and keeping her friends. School had become so much harder for her, and Anne seemed so much more undisciplined. She would argue with my parents over any little thing. If the sky was blue, she would say it was gray. Up was down and in was out. My parents, according to Anne were squares, and just didn't get it. To me they were just normal parents trying to keep their kids on the straight and narrow. She was always testing the limits, and picking a fight over the simplest things. Dinner time was not convenient, I don't like this food, too many rules, curfew was too strict, you don't like my new friends, you don't understand me. It was one thing after another. We never had any peace; we just went from one fight to the next.

She was even treating me differently. I was not the enemy, but she only talked to me if she wanted to get me on her side against my mother and father. I did not bite. She stopped inviting me into her room to talk and listen to records. She would spend hours in there on the phone or in the bathroom beautifying herself. The things we used to have in common were now not to her liking. I was no walk in the park growing up, but I knew how far I could push my parents. Anne was always testing the upper limits.

27

A lot of my sister's old friends stopped coming over and stopped calling. I never knew who she was talking to on the phone, but I suspected they were hippies or kids that were doing their own thing versus what their parents wanted. My parents were older when they adopted my sister and had me. They were not real strict, and would always go out of their way to help you if you needed it. Anne took all they had to offer, and threw it back in their faces.

During junior high my sister's marks in school started to deteriorate, along with her mood, and the friends she was hanging around with. I overheard my parents' concern from upstairs on a number of occasions, and it would be the basis for disagreement between them on how to approach the situation with Anne. I hated it when they fought, and wished somehow it would all go back to the way it was when Anne was younger.

Over time things kept getting worse. I tried to stay out of the house as much as possible and play with my friends, because whenever I went home there was an upset for some reason, and it usually originated with my sister. The transition she made in just a short time was like night and day.

Finally, at the end of Anne's ninth grade year, my father told my sister he was sending her away to Catholic school in the area, but she would board there. Anne thought that was a good idea, because she said she needed her space. Over the summer the fighting continued, and my parents tried to put a good face on my sister moving away. I was not happy at all because I loved my sister, and would miss her company, as distant as it was. I still knew she was across the hallway if I needed her.

The mood around our house had grown dim in the last year. Anne had been distant from our family, and was very moody. The outbursts had increased over time, and usually over nothing important. I could see the family turmoil weighing on my parents. My father would come home from work, and eat supper with us, and then head downstairs to his cellar office to work on his part-time job doing the books for a few local businesses. My mother would talk to me a little about the day's events after dinner was over, and then clear the dishes. My sister rarely ate with us, and if she did it lead to a verbal disagreement about some nebulous issue. I would overcompensate, and try and be as nice as possible to keep my parents as happy.

Over that summer I got a good idea of the kids she was hanging around with and it wasn't good. She latched on to the kids who weren't going anywhere, and would hang out downtown, and smoke cigarettes, and see how grungy they could look. I knew a few of the crowd because they were older brothers or sisters of my friends or schoolmates. Some of them did not have curfew or any ground rules because their parents were either rich, and didn't care, or were in my parents' situation, and had given up trying to keep them in line.

Over the past few weeks my parents had many serious discussions about Anne, and her future. My mother was upset about sending Anne away, but they had run out of options. My sister was becoming more rebellious, and due to my mother's and father's older age, they had no idea how to control her. They felt a Catholic private school might do the trick to instill discipline in her. The school was not far from home, and Anne could come home on the weekends. It was a good balance, and one that she agreed with.

One weeknight I came downstairs from doing my homework, and my father was sitting on the couch in his usual spot reading and watching the baseball game. I asked him where my mother was, and he said she went out. He did not say anything else. The only reason my mother ever went out at night without my father was to play cards with her old girlfriends in West Medford. I asked him again where she was, and he said out to the movies. I thought that very strange. I felt uneasy with his answer, and sat beside him on the couch watching him smoke cigarettes and watch baseball.

It started to get late, and my sister had already come in, gotten some food, and retreated to her room. My dad was sitting there concentrating on his book, and seemed relaxed. I just had a sick feeling in my stomach about why my mother went out, and where she was. I hoped she was okay. I started asking my father when she would be home, and he kept saying later. Was he really telling me the truth or did he know what movie she went to see? He was being vague, and I was not satisfied with his answers.

Finally I said, "Dad, where is mom? Tell me the truth." He put his book down, put out his cigarette, and looked at me, and it was written all over his face. He said, "Chris, sometimes parents need some space away from each other. Your mother has been upset lately, and needed some time to herself."

My stomach dropped, what was he telling me? Did my mother leave? This kind of thing did not happen, especially in my world. I wanted everything to be like *Leave It to Beaver*. I lived in my own ideal world, and my sister was tearing it all apart. I was not mad, but I was scared. I asked him again when mom would be home, and he said, go up to bed, since it's getting late, and when you wake up she will be here.

As soon as I heard his promise that my mother would be home, I felt relieved, and went upstairs two at a time, and jumped in bed. The relief I felt knowing my mother and father were here for me could be not be measured, but was worth a million dollars to a kid.

WINCHESTER 1967

————— ◆◆◆◆◆◆ —————

The world as we knew it was changing so rapidly. The kids and the counterculture were overtaking everything. Student demonstrations, civil rights, the Vietnam War, and drugs were all pushing the country to an overheated situation. Across the country campus culture was being turned upside down, students were challenging every social norm we were taught growing up. They were taking over college administration buildings and making demands. Education was almost a second-tier event at college. Having your grievances heard was number one. Professors and administrators had all they could do to keep the colleges operating at normal levels of efficiency. Kids morphed from crew cuts khakis, and golf shirts, to long hair, ripped dungarees, and tie-dyed t-shirts. The cry of the day was to challenge establishment authority, and anyone who got in the way was a square or a sellout.

The civil rights movement was picking up steam, fueled by peace marches in Birmingham, Mississippi, and Dr. Martin Luther King. The demonstrations were getting bigger, and the colored people all over America wanted their voices heard. The cities were becoming a breeding ground for poverty and despair. The promises of President Lyndon Johnson and the Great Society had not taken hold, and the major cities were a glaring showcase of the haves and the have-nots. In our little town, the only colored kids were from the Metco program. They were inner-city kids with a chance to go to a suburban school. I looked at them the same as my other class mates. Little did I know that they were the lucky ones. They had a chance to get an education, and get out of the cycle of poverty.

The Vietnam War was raging. The country had been told this was a war to stop communism in its tracks, just like Korea. If we just hang in there, we can drive the Vietcong, and the North Vietnamese, back into China. The Johnson Administration kept telling the American people to give it more time and more young men, and we can win this thing. The best military planners and generals told us this was a fight we had to win. What we didn't fathom was this was a civil war being fueled by the Chinese and the Russians. Every night on the news we heard the body counts. We were making progress. The North Vietnamese and Vietcong deaths were ten times our casualties. The law of large numbers proved we were winning. That is what the American people were told, and it was what all adults believed.

The teenagers on the other hand were more than skeptical. Young soldiers coming home did not tell stories like World War II of fighting for glory, and the cause to save America and the world from the communist curse. They were coming home broken, depressed, and addicted to drugs and alcohol. The stories they told were nothing like what our newscasters were telling us every night. The body count was going up to alarming proportions. Territory was won, then quickly given back in retreat. The good war to stop the plague was coming apart, and the young soldiers' words were filtering down to every college campus across the country. The boys in the senior class at Winchester High were going to the induction center in Woburn to get their draft card when they turned 18. The draft became a feared and hated fate. If you did not go on to college you were at risk of being sent to a place in Southeast Asia where no one wanted to be. The older kids in high school, and the college dropouts, were doing anything to stay out of the war. Some kids took things to drive up their blood pressure, some would put peanut butter on their rear, and then eat it at their induction physical. The last resort was going to Canada to stay with friends or family. The younger generation knew it was getting a raw deal, and it finally stood up against the war and the draft.

This is what propelled the drug culture. All the teenagers and kids in their twenties felt like the establishment was using them as a tool to keep the macho American myth afloat. It was all coming undone, and people escaped from it using booze, pot, heroin, and LSD. The hippies were the first to feed off the counterculture. They would hang outside stores in the downtown area, or over in the Winchester Common. They held their signs showing their displeasure with Washington's Vietnam policies, and marched around and around the Common. On one day of the year, protestors would stand around a college kid reading off all the names of the men who had died since the beginning of the war. Every year the list got longer. The time it took to read the list went from one day to two to three, and the crowds grew bigger. The hippies were joined by jocks, adults, storeowners. Everyone knew after a while there was something rotten in Denmark.

The slogan of the day with the hippies was you can't trust the establishment. Anyone over 30 is the enemy. We are going to do things our way. We are not going to buy into your lies. Their answer was to drop out of society, and get high, and think of things that really mattered like sex, drugs, and rock 'n' roll. They looked different, and unclean, and challenged authority, but they knew before all of us what had been pulled over on the American people, and they would not let it be done to them.

CHRISTMAS 1967

The mood around the house was tense as usual, but everyone was trying to make an effort to be in a good mood to round out the holidays. My sister was home from school for a few weeks, and I wanted to do my best to get reconnected with her. I had missed her so much when she went away to school, and on the weekends when she did come home, she spent it in here room or out with her friends around town.

Anne's clothes had gotten so ratty. They were the normal hippie wear, and my parents did not give her a hard time because she had to wear a school uniform Monday through Friday. It was also not worth the fight. She also took up smoking at home, which my mother could not stand, but my father could not argue with her because he smoked, and wanted to keep peace for my mother's sake.

I tried to engage my sister on a number of occasions to listen to music, and even bought a new Cream album at the record store, not because I wanted it, but because I thought she would enjoy it. It had "Sunshine of your Love" on it, a song I knew she loved. When I brought it up she told me to wrap it up and give it to her for Christmas. Then she dismissively walked off into her room and shut the door.

Before I left school for the holiday break I had heard a bunch of kids who had older brothers and sisters say there was a group that hung out downtown in the Center, and smoked cigarettes, drank, and smoked pot. Their pastime was complaining about their parents, the Vietnam War, and the so-called establishment. When they saw me get closer they abruptly cut off the conversation, and gave each other guilty looks. After a while I knew that my sister was part of that group. I guess my parents had good reason to worry.

With Christmas approaching I enjoyed my school break. I loved being out of school, and playing street or ice hockey with my neighborhood friends and not having homework. I had finished my shopping, and wrapped all my presents for the big day. My mother had been cooking up a storm and baking all the best cookies to make it a great season. My mother and I decorated the Christmas tree, and my father sat in his chair, and had his egg nog and brandy, and listened to Christmas carols. My sister did her usual, "I'm not interested in Christmas. It's just a concocted holiday to keep corporate America making money off the backs of their slave labor." I was horrified. Had she forgotten this was a celebration of the birth of Jesus, and an important time of year to think of others and how lucky we were? My mother and father gave a quick look at each other, and then turned their attention on me, asking me how things were with my friends and anything else they could think of.

The tree was almost finished. It looked so nice with the tinsel and lights glowing. I could not wait to finish, so we could put the wrapped presents under the tree, and everything would be ready for the big day. The house felt so warm and nice and my parents put a good face on so I could enjoy myself. I knew deep down that they were keeping a lot of pain inside for my sake. I tried on several occasions to coax my sister downstairs to join us, but to no avail.

Finally, Christmas morning arrived. My parents and I attended Mass in the morning, which was our family tradition before opening gifts. My sister flatly refused, saying she was tired, and wanted to sleep in. It was just one of the many traditions that had gone by the wayside for her. I was excited to get home to have breakfast and open our gifts.

We walked into the kitchen, and my sister came in the back door smelling like cigarette smoke. My mother had laid down the law, and only let Anne smoke outside in the back of the house. She did not say 'Merry Christmas,' she just said she was hungry.

"I will make you a nice Christmas breakfast, Anne," my mother said.

She just grunted. "Call me when it's ready. I'll be upstairs" I asked her if she wanted to listen to records in the living room for a while.

"Not now," she said and walked out of the room.

My mother intervened, saying "Chris, put on some Christmas music to get us in the mood." I agreed, and did my best to keep a smile on even though I was mad at my sister, and disappointed she could not join the family for one day.

My mother made a fantastic breakfast, and I cleaned up the kitchen to get to the good part. We walked into the living room, and my father called upstairs for my sister. She gave her disgusted "What?" My father said it was time to exchange presents. I was looking under the tree to see if I could make out anything big or unusual. Anne appeared and sat in a chair near me. My parents sat across from us. I volunteered to distribute the presents. My mother had shopped for many more presents for my sister, because she felt guilty about sending her away to school. I kept handing out the presents, and we began to unwrap. I received so many nice things. I always appreciated everything my parents bought for me. They gave me a Rolling Stones album, ice skates, a subscription to *Mad* magazine, and a few Hardy Boys books. I was so happy. I gave my parent their presents, and we all exchanged hugs and kisses, except Anne. She look so distant, and had a look on her face that we were from another planet or something. As she unwrapped her gifts, she would throw the paper in one direction, and the present on a chair next to her.

My mother asked Anne how she liked her presents. She stood up. "This was the shittiest Christmas I ever had. I can't stand you people. You are all part of the problem," she said.

She was going off about some liberal political speak that I could not even understand. My father and mother sat there and took it for a few minutes, and I sat there shocked and in horror. How could she ruin my favorite holiday? This used to be her favorite holiday. What was happening here?

All of a sudden my father got up with fire in his eyes, and put his arm under hers, and lifted her up and said, "You get up to your room until you can change your attitude."

She walked a few feet, and flung off his arm, and shouted "Leave me alone!"

My mother stood up to get in between them, and Anne ran up the stairs into her room, and slammed the door. Then I could hear "Sunshine of Your Love" playing on the record player. My mother turned to my father and burst out crying. He tried to console her, but she was sobbing. I sat next to the tree trying to ignore the whole situation.

WINCHESTER 1968

Anne continued to spin out of control. Her marks in school kept going downhill. The nuns would call from school to say that Jan was absent. Mother and father would question her, but to no avail. She would say she was not interested in school and it was a waste of time. Then she would go off on some hippie-communist diatribe on how the capitalist pigs and the class system were so unfair and she did not want any part of it. I knew her new friends were feeding her this nonsense, and it went against everything my parents stood for. They had worked for everything they had, and this must have been killing them inside.

My father asked her what she wanted to do. She said she wanted to quit school and move to Boston with her friends and get an apartment. At this point, my parents would do anything to please her to try and keep the peace. My father said he would think about it, but to keep attending school, and do her best, since he was paying for it. My mother was not in favor of the move since Anne had fallen in with a strange new crowd, and she worried about her safety.

Once my sister saw they were bending she put a big smile on her face. She raced up to here room to call her friends and listen to music. I could hear Simon and Garfunkel's "Mrs. Robinson" coming loudly through the door. I puttered around my room, goofing off, looking at my posters on the wall while trying to build up enough courage to knock on her door and see if she would invite me in to listen to music. After a while I decided not to because I knew what the answer was going to be.

One day I came home from school with my friend Stephen. We were going to raid the ice chest for something to eat because we had been out playing street hockey. It was the rage at the time, due to the popularity of "Bobby Orr, and the Big Bad Bruins." We had built up quit a hunger and thirst. My mother was one of the people who always believed in having plenty of food on hand to serve the neighborhood kids when they came over. We had the biggest back yard in the area, so the kids migrated to our house on a regular basis. My mother loved it, and it was a good chance to see who I was hanging around with.

As I was holding the ice chest door open, so Stephen could see what we had to eat, I noticed my mother was on the phone with someone. It sounded like one of her card game friends from West Medford where she and dad used to live before I was born. My mother kept up with her old friends, and also loved to play cards with them. They would play once a week and take turns hosting. My mother was concentrating on the conversation at hand, when my sister who was upstairs appeared by my mother's side. Anne was giving her faces and hand gestures to get off the phone. My mother was doing her best to wave her off, and let her know she would be off in a few minutes. My friend Stephen said "Hi," but Anne just ignored him. I was trying to ignore the whole situation because it was embarrassing to see my mother and sister doing this in front of my friend.

I shut the door of the ice chest, and asked Stephen if he would like to go in the living room and play with my dog until my mother got off the phone. Then she would get us something to eat. He was up for that so we left the room. The back-and-forth between my sister and mother continued. I was having fun with my dog when I heard my mother yelp. She yelled, "Anne, what are you doing?" and started to cry. I jumped up from where I was and ran into the kitchen. There I found my mother pulling a hair pin out of her arm, which was bleeding pretty good. My sister was screaming at her that it was all her fault for not listening to her. My mother at this point was sobbing and obviously hurt, both physically and emotionally.

Anne was trying to pry the phone out of my mother's hand, and my mother finally relented. As Anne was walking away coming towards me stretching the phone cord into the living room, I could feel rage coming through my whole body. How dare she do this to our mother? Who did she think she was? I was so mad my animal instincts took over. As she walked by me, I knocked the phone out of her hand, put her in a head lock, and wrestled her to the floor. She was swearing up a storm and trying to fight me off. I was holding her arms down on the floor. She was totally enraged.

We struggled, and I started to lose ground. I yelled to Stephen to help me, so he held down one of my sister's arms. Anne was struggling, and throwing her weight against us; she looked like she was a crazy person. Stephen and I looked at each other, and let out a nervous laugh, not knowing what to do. That only got my sister madder. I could hear my mother in the background saying, "Chris, let your sister up. Don't hurt her." I ignored her, but felt I could not stay like this forever.

When Anne settled down somewhat, I told Stephen to let her up, and we both did it in sequence. As soon as I let go of her, she bolted to her feet, and let out another litany of curses at all of us. My mother was standing behind us sobbing and holding her arm. I stood in front of her in case my sister came back at her.

Anne left the living room quickly, and bolted upstairs to her room. I heard her door slam, and then I could hear things being smashed and thrown around her room. This only made my mother cry harder. I stood there patting her on the back, saying "It will be all right," but not really believing it. Stephen said he had to go home to check in with his mother.

My mother and I stood there for what seemed like forever listening to Anne smash her room to pieces. Then there was a cold silence. Anne ran down the stairs and out the front door, slamming it as she went. I stood by my mother for a few minutes, then walked up to my sister's room. As I walked through the door, it was clear she had done a pretty good job destroying everything. The lamp by her bed was broken, her paint by numbers pictures were strewn on the floor, her makeup from her vanity was all over the place, her record player was smashed, and her records were broken into pieces all over the floor. I looked over the room in despair. All her prize albums and 45s were smashed and strewn about. All her favorite artists that she had collected for years were gone. How could she have done this? I selfishly thought, where am I going to play my music?

Then I heard my mother come up behind me. She said how sorry she was that I had to see this. We each tried to comfort each other the best we could, but we knew this would not be the last encounter like this with Anne in the years to come.

* * * * * * *

I sat on my bed. I was listening to Simon and Garfunkel's "Homeward Bound." I was looking around the room, looking at the ceiling, humming along. School had been another boring day.

I was daydreaming back to my Confirmation day for some reason. It was so much fun wearing my white dress, walking down the aisle and sitting in the pew, listening to the Cardinal talk to us. I remember going up to the altar, with my lit candle, and him blessing me. He was so tall and looked so wise.

As I turned to walk back, I could see my mother and father, aunt and uncle, and my brother looking back at me and smiling. They were so proud of me; I was proud of myself. The church was at capacity that spring day, and was so vibrant. I felt part of a big Catholic family. All the people in our neighborhood who were Catholic were there.

After the ceremony, we went back to our house and had a big party. I would bet there were fifty people there. All of our neighbors and family. My father was running the bar, and my mother and aunt were shuttling food from the refrigerator out to the serving tables. It looked all so nice, like one of my birthday parties, but bigger and better. A lot of my friends from around the neighborhood were there giving me their best wishes and handing me cards. Some of the other girls who had been confirmed were there in their white dresses. We were parading around the yard like a pack of princesses. I felt so special and proud. My parents said I was an official adult in the Catholic Church.

The food was so good. My parents and my little brother kept coming by and saying how proud they were. I knew my little brother looked up to me. We had a special bond, and a shared love for music. When he took up the trumpet, I helped him practice reading music. Even though it was in the key of E, not C, I always tried to help. He would always come into my room, and we would listen to my records together and talk about things. Music was our bond.

As I was lying on my bed, I heard the next 45 drop onto the turntable. It started playing. It was The Doors' "Riders on the Storm." I was singing along in a low voice when a darkness fell over me. I heard voices calling my name. I had had these thoughts and had heard voices recently, but I could always clear my mind and chase them away.

I closed my eyes and thought about happy things to make the voices go away, but they wouldn't. The voices were becoming louder and louder. I put my hands over my ears, and shook my head back and forth to make them go away, but it was no use. They were starting to control me. I was scared. I was confused. What was happening?

The music played on, but the room had a gray, dark hue to it. One voice I heard was a man. He sounded angry. He said things were bad, and I had to get out. I did not know what he meant, but I was starting to feel desperate.

I didn't know what to do. "I need to call one of my girlfriends, and have them snap me out of this feeling," I thought. The voices grew louder. I jumped up from my bed, ran down the stairs, through the living room.

As I drifted through the room, I felt like I was floating in an alternate universe. Things began to feel weird. I went by my little brother and his friend playing with our family dog. They looked at me briefly, and said "Hi," and went back to what they were doing.

I turned the corner into the kitchen, and I saw my mother sitting at her desk, talking on the phone. I could not make out what she was talking about, but I had to take the phone away so I could call my friend. I had no other choice. As I reached out for the phone my mother pulled it away, and said "Anne, I will be off in a minute, and then you can use the phone." The voices were becoming louder and louder. The room started spinning. I had to get that phone. I saw a hair pin next to the pen holder on the desk. I reached over, grabbed the pin, and jabbed into my mother's arm. Then I ripped the phone out of her hand and slapped the cradle to disconnect the call.

I did not hear or care about anything. I'm not even sure where my mother went. I began dialing a number. My finger kept dialing, but no one was coming on the line. Who was going to help rescue me from the evil voices? I was so scared, I felt like I had no one to help me.

Suddenly an arm came around my head and shoulder, and got me into a head lock, and started dragging me to the floor. I could not see who it was. My body went limp and weak. I felt powerless. What was happening to me?

I was thrown to the floor of the living room on my back, and found myself looking up at my brother. He had my arms pinned behind my head; I couldn't move. As I looked up, I saw my brother's friend and my mother standing there looking at me, like I was a caged animal in the zoo.

My mother was crying and holding her arm. She looked so upset and scared. What was happening? Were they trying to hurt me? Why would they do this? The voices grew louder; they told me to fight, to save myself. At this point, it was me or them.

I mustered as much strength at I could to fight off my brother. I could feel him pressing my hands and arms down to the floor as hard as he could. He was yelling at me, "What's wrong with you?" I fought back even harder. My brother called to his friend to come and help. They both had me pinned down by the shoulders. I couldn't move. I fought as hard as I could, but nothing. I spit at my brother. I cursed them, trying to get them off me . . . I could see the nervous smiles being wiped off their faces. There smiles were replaced by a terrified look at each other. My mother was in the background telling the boys to let me up.

Just like that they let go of me, stood up, and backed away. I jumped to my feet like a caged tiger. I let out a barrage of curses, and ran away from them up the stairs to my room. I slammed the door. Why had they attacked me? It was all their fault. I was so mad. I had steam coming out my ears. How could my family turn on me like that?

I stood in the center of my room, trying to catch my breath. The rage and darkness continued to wash over me. My body did not feel like my own. A higher power was in control of me. I began to pick up things in my room and smash them against the wall. All I could hear was loud noise and things breaking. This went on for what seemed like forever. Before I knew it I picked up my record player and bounced it off the wall. I started flinging 45s against the wall also, like Frisbees. Why was I breaking my records? What spirit had taken over my body?

The voices were telling me to escape. I had to make a run for it. I had to get myself out of this hellhole. I dashed down the stairs and swung open the door. It made a loud noise as I pushed open the screen door. I ran across the lawn. I didn't know where I was going or what I was going to do. I kept running and running. I didn't let up until the voices were gone. My mind could finally rest.

* * * * * * *

Anne eventually came back after a few hours. She went up and cleaned her room as best she could. I was scared to get near her, so I retreated to my room until dinner. When my father came home, my mother filled him in, and then called me down to dinner. As I was coming into the dining room, my mother was going the other way with a tray of food. She was heading up to my sister's room.

I sat down at the table, trying not make eye contact with my father. He looked upset, shaken. I'm sure he felt bad for my mother, who had to take the brunt of it by herself. All of a sudden my father said. "Chris, your mother told me what happened this afternoon, and I am very proud of how you acted. I'm sorry you had to see that demonstration by your sister. She has been having some difficulties recently, and sometimes loses her temper, and says things she doesn't mean."

I looked up at him, and shook my head in agreement. I put my face down and ate my dinner in silence. My mother eventually came back to the table. My mother and father tried their best to have some small talk, and pretend everything was normal. I knew that things were never going to be normal again.

WINCHESTER, MASS., 1968

--- ◆◆◆◆◆ ---

My father, mother, and sister had a long talk the next day, and my sister told my parents she wanted to drop out of school and move to Boston and get an apartment with her new friends. She was 18, and according to Anne, she could do what she wanted and live her own life. My parents were out of ideas and energy to deal with the endless bickering and family disputes. They said they begrudgingly agreed with her, and they would let her try things on her own.

The next few days were a flurry of activity, with my father going to Boston to meet Anne's new roommates, and my mother shopping for Anne and packing for her as if she was going to summer camp. Anne would hardly pay any attention to me as she was clearly focused on getting out of our house as soon as possible. I was feeling bad about the whole situation, but I pretended she was kind of going to college and she would be home for the holidays.

After Anne moved to Boston, the house got very quiet. The record player was never replaced, so the only music I had was my mother's transistor radio. I would listen to WMEX, which played a lot of hit songs. When I heard certain songs, it would remind me of my sister, and being in her room hanging out. How I wished those days could come back. I missed her guidance and energy. She was so focused and always went after things with reckless abandon. I looked up to her in so many ways and hoped this moving out thing would pass.

At dinner that night my parents were having there little chitchat about the goings on of the day, and watching the six o'clock news. Our television was over in the adjoining room and in full view of us. It was very big, enclosed in a nice mahogany cabinet. I could hear the newscaster talking about the Vietnam War, and showing video tape of soldiers getting off helicopters and running across rice paddies in full battle gear. Then the dead and wounded figures were flashed on the screen. It always looked like the North Vietnamese and Viet Cong took a beating compared to the U.S. servicemen.

The next news story to come up was about student demonstrations at our nation's colleges. There were sit-ins on campuses, administrative buildings taken over, and even full scale-riots that had to be put down by police in helmets, swinging batons, and throwing tear gas at the demonstrator's. The reason for all the upheaval was the disapproval of the Vietnam War. It was tearing the country apart, and turning the young people against the adults. On the news I could see a group of students on the front steps of some college building burning their draft cards and lighting up a joint at the same time. The kids on TV looked so proud that they were standing up to the 'man,' and letting their voices be heard.

The lazy days of the 50s were all gone, and the radical 60s were in full bloom, with all the characters that went along with them. I was caught in the middle. I knew this war was wrong, but I figured the leaders of this country knew what they were doing. I was hoping it would all end and those great days of my childhood would come back to stay.

BOSTON, MASS., 1968

◆◆◆◆◆◆◆

My sister and father were making their way down way down Storrow Drive in light midafternoon traffic. My sister reached over and hit the button to the radio to switch it to a local rock station. A Rolling Stones song came on. My parents had decided to let my sister move into Boston with her new friends. They hoped the family turmoil and the back-and-forth would finally come to an end. My parents felt it was better to let Anne find herself in the world and experience all the responsibility it would bring. I'm not sure what Anne thought, since she never discussed it with me. She said our parents were smothering her right to free expression and she should be able to make her own decisions.

I felt sad that Anne was leaving, but pretended she was going off to college in Boston. She would still be able to visit and come home anytime to have a free meal or do laundry. Anne vowed she would never be back, but I assumed she was talking tough and really did not mean it.

My father weaved his red 1963 Chevrolet Impala onto the exit ramp with the sign saying The Fenway Greenway. The car blended into merging traffic and followed what was a big rotary working its way around by Northeastern University. He then took a quick right onto Hemingway Street and looked for number 197. My sister and father strained to check the numbers and soon they pulled up in front of the correct number.

The apartment building was an old brownstone, with a hippie art gallery down under. It displayed what passed for the art of the day, which looked like someone had thrown paint at a blank canvas, and then called it art. It all looked the same, and I would not give you ten cents for it. The hippies all admired it. They said it was beautiful and had so much meaning.

As my father pulled the car up Anne spotted one of her new roommates standing on the front stoop. It was a young man with a tie-dyed t-shirt, dirty bell-bottom jeans, and Indian moccasins on his feet. His long dark hair was halfway down his back. He had a very white complexion, which indicated he did not get outside much.

My sister raced out of the car as soon as it came to a stop. She walked up to the young man and gave him a weird handshake and then a hug. He talked to Anne in some foreign-sounding hippie beatnik language. My father tried to play it cool, but was burning inside. He put some change in the meter, and made his way over to ask Anne's roommate to introduce himself.

The young man was giving my sister some fun facts about the building, and all the stores and businesses around, when my Father approached him. He said "Hey man, my name is Richard. Nice to meet you. You have a real cool daughter here." My father extended his hand to shake it, and the guy gave him the peace sign, and stepped back. My father made a mental note that Mr. Wonderful had flunked test number one.

After some chitchat, Anne and my Dad started unloading the car and bringing things up to the second floor apartment. My mother had packed enough clothes and supplies to keep Anne in business for a least a few months. Once the shuttle service started back and forth up and down the stairs, Mr. Wonderful did his best to disappear. I'm sure doing some honest work went against his rules of railing in the face of capitalism.

After the fifth and final trip up the stairs, my sister was joined in the middle of the living room by a young woman who was playing the part of the welcome committee, and doing her best to sound cool. As my father came up to her, she said "Hey, Mr. McGilvery. I'm so glad you let Anne come and live with us. We have a real good thing going here, and she can be part of it."

She directed my father to a small room with two single mattresses on the floor. The room had a lot of posters on the wall declaring a disdain for normal society, Washington, D.C., and America in general. I believe she introduced herself as Heather, and pointed to one of the mattresses and said this was Anne's. My father's stomach dropped. He did not say a thing, and continued following Heather around on a tour through the kitchen and the bathrooms. It did not look like much, but Anne seemed pleased with the accommodations. The faint smell of incense and marijuana filled the air.

After the tour, and answering all my father's questions, Anne walked him down to the car. She tried to convince him that this was for the best and everything would be okay. Anne had already given my father a thousand reasons why dropping out of school and this living arrangement was what was best for both of them. She also told my father her roommates were going to hook her up with a waitress job at a local luncheonette in the area. It all sounded so good to Anne, but my father had his doubts. My sister had been coddled all her life, and even though she thought she was grown up, she did not have the survival skills to make it in the big city.

My father was trying to be as optimistic as possible, but growing up during the Depression era, he knew what sacrifices had to be made to make everything work out. By what he had just witnessed, these kids looked like they were just floating through life, and whichever way the wind blew was fine with them.

As they walked back to the car, my father turned to Anne, and said, "You be careful now, and don't talk to strangers. Also call us if you need anything or you want to come home and visit. You know your mother would like that."

Anne gave him a short "Okay, okay, Dad, I get it. Don't worry about me." She reached over and gave him a half-hearted hug and a peck on the cheek, and disappeared up the stairs into her new home. My father did a three-sixty of the neighborhood, jumped in his car, and pulled out into rush hour traffic.

How he wished the situation would work out for Anne and she would grow as a young adult. But, he had his reservations. Hopefully everything he had taught her would help her with her new life. Heck, he was only eight miles away if she needed any help or advice. The rush hour traffic was horrible but it gave him a chance to look over the skyline. As he drove he looked across the Charles River to Cambridge. It looked so beautiful with the sail boats meandering back and forth, contrasted with the crew shells jockeying for position.

As my father moved slowly down the road, he could only hope the future would be bright for his young daughter.

BOSTON, MASS., 1968

woke up, startled from a bad dream I was having. I looked over at the dim light coming from the lava lamp on the bedside table. I looked around trying to get my bearings. The posters on the wall all jumped out at me with a message of anarchy, railing against the establishment. The faint smell of marijuana drifted from the other room under the door. I looked over at my clock on the table. It was 12:30 a.m.

I had been trying to find myself for the past year. I was feeling some despair; I was working but giving what I earned to the community apartment folks. It was part of the rules of the living arrangement. I was waitressing down the street at a breakfast/luncheonette counter, making a low hourly salary plus tips. My days of shopping for clothes and music albums were over. The money I made went to food and paying the rent. Some days Barry, the head of the house, would tell us we didn't have enough food for dinner. He would send out a few of us to the Park Street Station after hours to rummage through the discards from the fruit and vegetable stand when it was closed for the night. If we were lucky we would find some good stuff mixed in with all the rotted inventory.

People would always steer clear of us as they waited for their train on the Green Line. The establishment thought all hippies were dope-smoking, crazy people. Didn't they know, we just didn't want any part of their world? We were happy to be left alone. We had a good group of people

51

who were either working, going to school, or volunteering for the cause of their choice.

On weekends, a group of us would go to the Boston Common and listen to speakers who denounced the Vietnam War and the U.S. government policies around the world. A lot of the people who talked to us were from Berkeley. The peace movement and the awakening had started there and was spreading across the country. People were turning on and tuning out. The Students for a Democratic Society had grown stronger on college campuses across the country. They were spreading the message of civil unrest until the government listened to what we had to say. The message was growing louder every day and public opinion was turning against the war. Too many young people, especially minorities, were being killed in a war that the U.S. government really didn't know how to win. The Rolling Stones' "Street Fighting Man" was playing on the radio. It was getting me worked up inside.

I hadn't heard from my parents or brother in a while. My father had been occasionally stopping by on his way home from work. I would meet him down the street from the apartment, because I didn't want to be seen by my roommates. I wanted to come off as cool and unattached to my family. I missed my mother and brother, but they were squares, and really didn't understand what I wanted, and the direction my life was going. My father and I would talk for a few minutes, smoke a cigarette, and then he would offer me money, or ask if I needed anything. I always turned him down, even though I could have used the help.

As I looked over at the door to my room I could see a dim light shining through. I started to hear voices. I thought they were coming from the living room. They got louder and louder. Then I realized they were coming from in my head. I put my hands over my ears and tried to make them stop. This had been happening more and more over the past year. It caused me to talk in front of people, and they would ask me "Anne, what did you say?" I would make up an excuse, and say I was not talking to anyone. It was embarrassing at times. Sometimes they thought I was on an LSD trip and it was all part of the experience. The only drugs I did were marijuana and some wine from time to time.

The noise in my head was getting louder and louder. Voices kept calling me to come. I got out of my bed, and walked through the living room, out the front door, and out into the street. The neighborhood was quiet this time of night. I was walking down the street; it was warm. The few people going by me on the sidewalk looked at me as if I was from another planet. What were they looking at? Why was I the weird person who was being viewed like an animal in the zoo?

I felt the voices in my head growing louder. I was walking faster and faster. I saw people cross the street when I approached them. No one wanted to be near me. I was getting mad. I started to lash out like a drunk begging for money but who was being ignored. I could hear myself saying mean things to people, but it was like I was watching myself in a movie, and could not control the next scene. I was being propelled through the streets of Boston but I didn't know why.

Where was I going? The voices were commanding me to keep going. What direction did they want me to go? As I was walking it started to rain. It was light at first, but soon came down harder and harder. I could feel the drops running down my face and off of my nose. It felt warm and I was not cold at all. No stores were open, and the city had a dark, depressing texture to it. I went by some homeless people in front of the Boston Public Library, and even they snickered at me. What was wrong with me? What were they looking at?

I turned and started walking down a highway ramp. I kept hearing car horns blaring as they drove by me. I was not scared or alarmed, I was just floating down the street with not a care in the world. As I walked the cars continued to speed by. The rain came down harder, and all I could see was headlights and taillights coming and going past me. The voices were calling me to keep going. I would get to my destination at some point. Who were they? What did they want with me?

After a while I saw a police car with its lights flashing; it pulled over and a pig got out of the car. He walked briskly towards me and grabbed me. What did he want? I was not bothering anyone. He was saying things to me, but the voices in my head were so loud I couldn't tell what he was saying. He opened the back door of his car, pulled out a blanket, threw it around my neck, and wrapped it around me. What was he doing? I wasn't cold. His face had a look of concern. His expression was one I had seen on my father's face many times before.

He grabbed my arm gently, walked me back to the car, and placed me in the back seat. I looked up through the shield and could see him on his radio speaking to someone. I could not make out what he was saying. It sounded very official, though. The voices had suddenly left my head. Now I could understand what he was saying. It sounded like he thought I was high on some drugs and he was taking me in to custody for my own protection. What was this all about? I had done nothing wrong. The guy was trying to hassle me for no good reason. I started to chirp at him, but he was ignoring me.

For some reason, I started to feel cold all over. The blanket was not keeping me warm anymore. My whole body was trembling. Why was I so cold all of a sudden? I opened the blanket and looked down at myself. I was bare chested, and had on only purple stockings over the lower part of my body, covering my underwear. The dye in the stockings had run into my skin. I felt cold and ashamed. What was happening to me? Who had I become? My plan of being free and independent was melting away.

The police car accelerated quickly to merge with traffic. I sat back in my seat and drifted into a deep sleep.

* * * * * * *

My father walked into the police station and walked up to the front desk. A stern looking officer stared back down at my father, and didn't look to be in a good mood. As I looked around the quiet station I could see the beige paint of the walls was chipped and tired-looking.

That Sunday night when my father got the phone call to come and pick up his daughter would change our lives forever. As the desk officer looked at him, my father said he was here to see Anne McGilvery. The officer gave no reply, but hit a buzzer on his desk. After a few awkward minutes waiting for something to happen, another officer appeared who seemed a lot more amicable. He shook my father's hand and said "How are you tonight, Mr. McGilvery? I'm sorry we had to bother you. Unfortunately children never pick a convenient time to get in trouble."

54

"I'm sorry we had to put you through this trouble," my father said. "I am very upset that she would get herself in this state and cause such a commotion."

The officer said to follow him to the back of the building where several holding rooms were located. He passed by a few employees who looked up as he went by, obviously knowing why my father was there. The officer opened a door to one room and we entered. My sister was seated at a table in the center of the room. Anne looked up at my father with an angry look in her eyes. Her beautiful hair was wet and stringy, and she had on a hospital johnnie to cover up the purple tights that had stained her skin.

My father was horrified. What had happened to Anne? What could have possessed her to walk out of her apartment and onto the Mass Pike in a rainstorm? "Anne, what have you got to say for yourself?" my father asked. "Can you say how sorry you are to this young officer for the trouble you caused?"

Anne started spewing some misguided talk about how the pigs are out to get us because we oppose the Vietnam War. They think we are a bunch of pinkos. My father's jaw dropped, and it was all he could do to restrain himself from slapping Anne across the face. How dare she speak to me that way? What was going on with her?

The officer got up, and told Anne to sit tight, and we would be right back. He led my father to another office with a young woman sitting behind a desk. She was about 35 years old, neatly dressed in civilian clothes, with long brunette hair. She jumped up to shake hands with my father, introduced herself as a social worker, and asked him to be seated. Then the young woman sat back and began to tell my father what had happened.

When the police found my sister she was walking on the west-bound breakdown lane of the Mass Pike with her thumb out looking for a ride. The visibility was so bad in the rain, many cars just missed hitting her. The young woman said she was lucky she was not killed. Once she was brought to the station, she was given a field sobriety test, which she passed.

"I have seen many cases like this, and it is usually a powerful mix of drugs and alcohol that would create such behavior," she said.

"When we found her, she had no idea where she was, or that she was in any danger." The woman stopped for a minute collecting her thoughts. She looked at my father with a concerned expression. "I feel Mr. McGilvery, there is something else going on here. To be on the safe side I would like to transfer Anne to Worcester State Hospital, where she can be evaluated by a qualified psychiatrist. "

My father could not fathom what this person meant. What did she mean Anne might have a psychiatric disorder? The woman and officer were exchanging glances, and looked as concerned as my father felt. What had happened to the young girl he dropped off at her new apartment that bright sunny day? The clouds had come over Anne's life, and despair was setting in. My father tried to play it cool, but inside his stomach was in a knot. He was thinking about what my mother would think if he did not come home with Anne. "Are you sure this referral to Worcester State is needed? It seems like a little harsh based on my daughter's history."

The social worker began reciting all the criteria that would point to a medical disorder with Anne. She claimed to have dealt with many adolescents, and this behavior and interaction with Anne was steering her to a concern of a significant medical issue versus a drug overdose. "I think it is better to err on the side of caution."

My father sat back in his chair, shaken by the thought that this could be much more serious than what he had originally thought. What was happening to his little girl? He felt guilty that she was in this state, and he had not seen it coming. My father's perfect sub-urban world was falling apart and he felt powerless. How was he going to explain this to my mother? She was already feeling guilty about letting Anne move out of the house to Boston. The past few months had been filled with anxiety and sleepless nights about Anne's well-being. This news was going to push her over the edge.

My father gave his ascent, and told them to proceed with their evaluation. He didn't have the stomach to say good-bye to Anne. The social worker felt it would not end well if he told her she was not getting out or going home. He agreed, and left the building to go home and break the bad news to my mother.

As he drove back home that rainy Sunday night, my father flashed back to when my sister was young and they were playing in the yard on a sunny Sunday afternoon. He had picked her up and twirled her around, and Anne was giving out that infectious laugh. How he wished those days would return. It seemed like only yesterday, his life had been so simple, yet complete. As my father drove, he was turning the radio dial to distract himself. Simon and Garfunkel's "Mrs. Robinson" was playing. He heard the line "Jesus loves you more than you will know." But now he felt that Jesus had given up on his family. He would go home tonight, kneel down, and pray harder than he ever had.

WORCESTER, MASS., 1968

◆◆◆◆◆

A month had gone by since that fateful night. My home life was distant. Mom and dad were going through the motions, trying to keep up a good front that everything was normal. I tried hard to be extra good so I wouldn't cause them any undue anxiety. I missed my sister, and wished I could see her. My parents did not explain to me what was going on with her, but just kept saying she was okay and needed to rest for a while. I was not sure what that meant, but I did not want to delve deeper for more details.

As we entered the gates of the State Hospital, I was struck by how dark and dreary this place was. The buildings were all red brick, with gray slate roofs. The windows all had bars, and I did not see anyone walking around. I had told my parents I did not want to go on this visit. All the buildings looked to me in bad repair, which contributed to the depressing atmosphere. I had heard bad stories from my friends, and remembered a few scary movies which had to do with mental hospitals. My parents had said they could not leave me alone, and bribed me with the promise of ice cream after we visited. I would have rather been playing with my friends, but I tried to make the best of it.

As we rounded the top of the hill, we pulled up in front of a building named after some dead state official. We walked through the lobby and checked in with security. There were a couple of guys sitting at the front desk; they looked as though they would rather be doing anything else. I saw one guy trying to solve a crossword puzzle in the daily newspaper. My father identified who he was, and who he was here to visit. The older man directed us to the second floor. He motioned to us to take the stairs as the elevator was out of order.

As we entered the stairwell, an older man was coming down the stairs. He looked very upset; he was disheveled and talking to himself. I immediately got panicked, and my mother pulled me close as we climbed the stairs and passed by him. My father got in between the man and my mother just in case. On to the second floor a sign pointed to the Adolescent Locked Unit. We walked to the end of the hall, up to the door, and rang the bell. We waited a few moments. Nothing. My father rang the bell again. We waited for what seemed like forever. We could hear footsteps coming down the hallway and then a younger man appeared. He had long hair, a big nose, and was dressed in a blue t-shirt and dungarees. A large set of keys was clipped to his belt. He picked through a number of keys before he found the right one, and inserted it into the door lock. It made a loud click and the heavy door opened.

My father tried to tell the orderly who he was here to see, but the man interrupted, and just said "Follow me." We followed him down the long hallway to a desk that was situated at the end as part of an L-shaped floor. All of a sudden I began to get nervous. The residents passing me by looked like they came out of a horror movie. They were dressed like homeless people, and some gave me a blank stare or muttered weird things as they passed by. As we made our way down the hallway, we passed several rooms that were sparsely furnished, with just a bed and bureau. Most of the people in the rooms were either sleeping or staring out the windows.

We walked up to the desk and asked to see the doctor in charge. One girl started yelling into a room adjacent to the counter, asking where the doctor was. A nurse walked out of the back, and said he would page him. The other two girls at the desk looked very uninterested, giving us blank stares. We stood there for a few minutes until a young man appeared. He introduced himself as Dr. Sherman. He said he was the on-call doctor, since it was the weekend.

He introduced himself in a cold, official way and patted me on the head instead of shaking my hand. I flashed him a quick smile, and then we were led down the continuation of the long corridor to what looked like a bank of offices and a conference room. As we turned into the doctor's office, he pulled a chair out, and placed it in the hallway. He advised my parents it would be better to have me sit there, since what he was going to be discussing was confidential and could be potentially upsetting. I looked up at my mother for sympathy, but she instructed me to wait in the hallway. "Don't leave that chair," she ordered. Before I could object the door shut and I was all alone in the hallway.

I sat myself down, and then started taking in all what was going on around me. I must have insulated myself to what I had just passed in the hallway, because now I noticed it was bustling with residents, social workers, and attendants. Why had I not seen this? Did I have my eyes closed? I pondered the thought for a moment. I looked up, and stared into the room directly across from me. I was face to face with a man who was sitting on the edge of his bed. He was mumbling something that I could not make out. He looked disheveled, confused, and upset. Our eyes locked for a split second before I looked away quickly. I started to look down at the floor, and then I heard it. "What are you looking at?" he said in a bellowing voice. I almost fell out of my chair I was so scared. "Why are you sitting there looking at me? Do you think I am some sort of circus animal?" he demanded. My pulse started to increase as I began to think of my next move. Why had the doctor put me right across from this guy? I started to look up to respond to him, but before I could get the words out of my mouth, he jumped up and slammed his bedroom door in my face. The industrial strength door smashed shut with a loud thud.

I was startled and relieved at the same time. Then I looked toward the nurses' station some 70 feet away. I noticed many residents coming and going, talking to themselves, swearing, and looking very upset. My anxiety level started to rise, and my bladder began to feel full and started to hurt. I sat up and crossed my legs to make the urge go away. I squirmed in the chair but it was no use, I had to go. I pondered what my mother said before she went in the doctor's

office about staying put. She did not tell me I couldn't go the bathroom though.

I jumped up from my chair, and looked for anyone official
walking around. The orderlies seemed to all be congregating at the
nurses' station, and looked like they could care less in what I was
doing. I began to meander down the hallway in the opposite direction from where they were sitting. I took my time, trying to not draw
any attention. As I made my way to the end of the hallway I saw a
sign for a ladies' room on the left, and a men's room on the right.
I quickly turned into the bathroom and made my way to a urinal.
As I started to relieve myself, I heard a faint moaning. What could
that be? I pushed hard to finish my business, because the noise had
piqued my curiosity. I zipped up my pants and turned to find the
source of the noise.

As I made my way deeper into the room, I could see what looked
like a large showering area, similar to our gym showers in school. It
had gray tiles with mildew-stained grout, and had the sharp smell of
chlorine. My heart began to race as I made my way to the edge of the
shower room and looked in. As I turned the corner, the smell of feces
overcame me. I tried to hold my breath, but then I saw a naked man
rolling around on the shower floor wiping the excrement all over his
body, like it was playtime. I could not believe my eyes. What was
going on? Wasn't a shower where people came to get clean? Just then,
a hand grabbed me from behind and spun me around.

"What are you doing in here son?" the man said. As I looked
up, I saw it was one of the attendants from the nurses' station. "This
area is off limits," he instructed. Before I could get any words out of
my mouth, he planted his hand firmly on my shoulder and guided
me out of the mens room and back to my lonely seat in the hallway.
He gave me a stern warning, and then went back to his usual duties.
I thought to myself, Why isn't he going back to help that man clean
himself up?

I sat in my chair for what seemed like an eternity, when all of a
sudden the doctor's door opened and my parents were led out into
the hallway. I looked at my father. He seemed upset. As I gazed up
into my mother's eyes, I could see tears running down her face. She

turned her head quickly away and brushed her hand over her eyes to wipe away the tears. I pretended I did not notice since I knew it would upset her more. She always tried to shelter me from any upset or bad news, as I would learn more and more as the years rolled on.

An attendant walked us to the locked door and sent us on our way. As we walked out the front of the building to our car, I asked my mother why we had not seen Anne. My father spoke up and said Anne was not feeling well and would have to stay here for a while to get better. I was just ready to hit my father with more questions, and then looking over at my mother I decided it was in my best interest to keep my mouth shut.

It was such a beautiful day. Residents and attendants were walking around to enjoy the day and get some fresh air. Except for the run-down buildings and the bars on the windows, you would think you were on a college campus. I settled into the back seat, but suddenly the door on the other side was yanked open and this crazy girl jumped into our car. She slid over towards me. I put my hands up to shield my face. She was mumbling all sorts of incoherent blather, and I was petrified. She threw her hands around my neck and began kissing me all over the top of my head. The smell coming off her body hit me like a freight train. I immediately held my breath, hoping she was finished with me. I looked to the front seat for help from my parents, but they didn't know what to make of the situation.

Before I could say anything to the girl or my parents, an attendant reached in and guided the girl out of the back seat and on her way. My parents looked at me and let out a good chuckle. I was so mad and gave them a disgusted look. Why did I have to come today? This place was right out of a horror movie. I thought I was going to see my sister, and instead I was led into the Twilight Zone.

What was wrong with my sister? Why was she at this place? When she left for Boston she promised me that she would visit and she never did. I was confused by everything that was happening. It seemed like a bad dream. From my parents' expressions, I could tell it was no dream. This was real.

On the way back home my parents took me out for my promised ice cream. I pretended that I felt better, but that was not the case.

WINCHESTER 1968

✦✦✦✦✦

A few weeks after our visit to Worcester State Hospital, I was up in my room doing my homework when I heard my parents downstairs arguing in the family room. My parents never fought, so I was concerned with the suddenly raised voices. I walked out of my room to the head of the stairs, but could only make out a word here and there. I decided to go on a commando mission and go down stairs and get closer so I could hear what they were saying.

As I descended down the stairs, I moved carefully, remembering where every creak was on the stairs and arm rail. I moved like a cat not making a sound. As I turned the corner, and moved through the living room, the voices got louder. I hid behind a big easy chair that was close to the family room. I sat down cross-legged to be more comfortable. Then I focused.

"Pat, she has to stay there and be thoroughly evaluated by the psychiatrist," my father said with a commanding voice. "They have their methods of diagnosing these types of conditions."

"I don't care what they are doing, Paul. I want her home," my mother pleaded, trying to be forceful but not really selling it. "I want her home here where I can keep an eye on her and look after her."

"Pat, don't you understand, the doctors are not sure what they're dealing with at this point. Anne is acting very strange, and they claim she told them she is hearing voices. The doctors don't think it's drugs that are causing these symptoms. They feel it a more deep-seated problem that will take some time to monitor and diagnose."

My mother and father kept going back and forth; they both stuck to their positions, and neither one was giving in. They both seemed exasperated, and they kept repeating their points. But the bottom line was Anne was going to stay at that hospital until they had a better diagnosis.

I did not understand what was going on. Anne seemed okay to me when she left for Boston. She was giving my parents a hard time, but I kept thinking it was normal for a teenager to rebel against their parents. Anne had proven to be a free spirit, but putting her in a hospital to see what was wrong with her seemed to be a little overkill. What was going on with her seemed like a bad dream to me. I just wanted her home and to have things go back to the way they were before. I'm sure my parents wanted to get the situation resolved one way or the other.

Anne did not look sick, according to them. She had been acting out the last few years, but deep down, I did not think she was sick or acting weird. She was anti- establishment, and joined forces with the hippies against the Vietnam War. She attended demonstrations and helped distribute literature in Boston Common to the locals. I kept thinking, if that can get you thrown in a mental hospital, I don't want anything to do with it.

I had heard enough. I had to get back upstairs before my mother or father came upstairs to see what I was doing. I crawled across the living room around the corner, and onto the stairs, then stood up and tiptoed up the rest of the stairs. I got on my bed and grabbed the latest issue of *Mad Magazine*. I propped myself up in bed, and tried to look like I had not a care in the world. At this point, *Mad* was making more sense than my household.

I read through the comic strips. I had no idea how sick my sister was or when I was going to see her again. The good times we had together seemed just like yesterday. In reality, it had been a few years since things were what you would have considered normal. I was half reading and half dreaming about listening to our 45s together, talking about music and anything else. The latest Beatles song started bouncing around in my head, and I began to wonder if Anne had a transistor radio where she was and what songs she might be listening to.

* * * * * * *

I walked quickly through the living room making sure I did not leave any dirt on my mother's rugs. That room was my mother's shrine. It was reserved for relatives, company, and my mother's friends when they played cards. I should have come in the back door, but I was hungry and felt lazy. I tiptoed into the kitchen to not make any noise so I could raid the fridge. I stepped up to the door, opened it, and started scanning the shelves.

There were a lot of choices. My family always bought a lot of food, and my mother entertained the neighborhood kids with snacks and drinks when they were playing in my backyard. She always said it was worth it knowing where I was. As I narrowed my selections, I heard my mother's bed squeak. I froze for a minute, knowing she would scold me if she caught me, since dinner hour was coming up soon. I decided to go scope out what the noise was, and see if the coast was clear. I told myself if my mother was there, I would tell her I was using the bathroom.

I went down the hallway by my parent's bedroom and quickly glanced in. I saw my mother lying on her side facing the other direction. I thought to myself, she must be having one of her world-famous migraine headaches. They had been plaguing her for years and kept her off her feet for hours when they hit. She even had sinus surgery at one time, since a specialist thought that could be the cause.

I turned my body ever so slightly to head back the other way towards the kitchen when I heard a whimpering coming from the bedroom. I was thinking to myself, I thought she was sleeping. Is that my mother crying? Now I had to go in to see what was wrong. My curiosity got the best of me. I turned around again, and walked into the bedroom, and around the front of the bed to the other side. My mother did not hear or see me coming.

I said "Mom, what's the matter? Why are you crying?"

She opened her eyes somewhat startled and tried to wipe her eyes off. She did not answer me immediately. She was getting her bearings. She sat up and hung her legs over the edge of the bed. "Chris, I thought you were out playing. I was just taking a rest before I start cooking."

My mother was doing her best to avoid what had brought her to tears. She kept looking at me, contemplating her thoughts. From the look on her face I knew it was not good.

"Mom, are you okay," I asked meekly. "I don't like to see you upset. Did I do something wrong?" I said holding my breath hoping I was not in the doghouse. My father was still at work, so I knew it could not be him who caused this upset. Then I thought to myself, I hoped no neighbors or relatives were sick, or worse, passed away. "Mom, tell me what's bothering you. I don't like seeing you this way."

She looked at me and motioned for me to sit beside her on the bed. She put her arm around my shoulder and let it all out. She said my sister was a very sick girl and the hospital said she had a lot of issues. Initially they thought her problems were being caused by drugs. I suspected the same thing, even though I would never have suggested that to my parents. My sister and I had been great friends growing up, and you would never rat out a sibling to their parents. It was against the sibling code.

My sister had been in the hospital for two months since the Turnpike incident. My mother said after many tests and interviews, they felt she had mental health issues that were causing all this strange behavior. It could come out of the blue at any time and cause all sorts of problems. I kept nodding my head as my mother spoke, but did not really understand what this was all about. All I knew was she was my sister one minute, and living across the hallway from me, and now she was in a mental hospital being evaluated for some unknown condition.

As my mother spoke, she chose her words carefully, slowing her delivery. I knew that was not a good sign. Was my sister coming home to recuperate, or did she have to stay at the hospital until she was better? I did not want to ask too many questions, but I had to know. I kept looking at my mother as she spoke, and my mother would look down or up, as if she really did not want to get to the point.

"Mom, when is Anne coming home?" I finally said in as firm a voice as a little kid could come up with. I felt her arm drop off my shoulder and she grabbed my hand. She enclosed it with both of her hands, and then she looked into my eyes. "Chris, Anne is not coming home. She has to live at the hospital to get better," she said. She paused for a moment to let the statement to sink in. Before I could process what she just said, my mother added, "Anne is a very sick girl, Chris, and she needs to stay where she is so the doctors can try and help her."

I looked to my mother, and really tried to focus on what she was trying to say. What did she mean, Anne was not coming home? What had happened to her? I had no knowledge of mental illness, the different kinds, the causes, or how it could affect your life.

My mother finished telling me Anne was not coming home, since the doctors were unsure if she could leave the hospital for a very long time. I was so mad and upset after my mother finished, but I did not let on, because she was so upset just telling me about it. All I could do was give her a big hug and tell her it would be okay. How could such a promising young girl end up in the hospital all of a sudden? My mother did her best to calm me down. She stood up and walked towards the hallway, saying she had to prepare dinner before my father got home. I tagged after her to offer any help I could give. I was relegated to setting the table and staying out of the way until the meal was prepared.

That night after diner, I laid in my bed dreaming about going into Boston, and really finding out the truth. Did they give my sister drugs that messed her up, or did she have some problem that the drugs made worse? All these thoughts were swirling about my head, and I wanted the easy answer to come so I could blame someone. I drifted in and out of my thoughts, knowing I would never go to Boston to find the truth.

CAMBRIDGE, MASS., 1971

M y father walked into Middlesex County Courthouse, out of breath from climbing the granite stairs. His lawyer accompanied him. The lobby was buzzing with all sorts of people from lawyers, to court clerks, to security people, and any number people who were seeking a legal outcome in family, civil, or criminal court. The shiny, highly polished granite floor reflected the granite posts and the solemn portraits that hung on the walls. Many of the paintings depicted the forefathers of Massachusetts as well as famous lawyers and politicians. The building was relatively new, but had old-style architecture mixed in with modern conveniences of a contemporary structure.

The two of them made their way up the large stairs to the second floor where many of the courtrooms were. Once they got to that level they sat down on a wooden bench to go over some last-minute strategy before they went into family court. The lawyer advised my father on what to say and what not to say. He also advised my father to only answer the judge's questions directly and don't editorialize. This proceeding today would be the difference between my sister being my parents' child, a ward of the state, or being in shared custody.

The previous three years had been hell for my parents. Anne had been in and out of hospitals, seen numerous doctors, psychiatrists, and social workers. They had tried therapy, medications, changes in facilities and wards, but nothing had worked. Anne was not getting better, and was too uncooperative to live at home. No one could figure out what was going on with her, but my father was getting too old to have the energy to keep up with Anne. She was unpredictable and could be abusive if she was in a really bad mood. There was no rhyme or reason on how or why her moods changed. I know my parents felt so guilty about ending up in this place, but they were running out of energy and money to try and get a handle on the situation. The court proceeding today was to protect both Anne and my parents.

My father sat in the family court with his lawyer, waiting for the judge to appear. There was no one else in the courtroom except for the bailiff standing to the side. You could hear the faint murmur of the people outside in the lobby. This proceeding today was going to be private, due to the confidential nature of the information that would be transacted. As my father looked around to become more familiar with his surroundings, he looked over at his lawyer.

Mr. Buckley was looking down, reading over some legal briefs before the judge entered the room. He was a nice old man in his 60s who was an expert in family law, and had worked for the state mental health department as a lawyer representing the state itself. He was recommended by a lawyer friend of my father's in our hometown. He was very expensive, but also very good at his job, and knew exactly what my parents were up against. As he scanned through the piles of paper, the judge entered the room. A stenographer came from the other side of the room, along with a court assistant. They sat up front to the right of the judge. The count helper called out the official notice that court was now in session, and the honorable Judge Volpe was going to listen to my father's case.

Just as the judge said, "Be seated," the door to the hallway flew open and a man in his 30s rushed in and threw his briefcase on the desk across from my father. The man was dressed in a suit that looked like he had gotten it from the Salvation Army Thrift Store. It was very well worn, faded, and was wrinkled from lack of pressing. He was obviously the state-appointed lawyer representing the mental health department . . . He had broken the first rule of presenting a case to the judge. As my father looked back at the judge, he said "I'm glad you could join us today, Mr. Saviano," in a sarcastic tone.

The lawyer looked embarrassed and said "I'm sorry, your honor, but the traffic on Storrow Drive was horrible."

The judge looked back, and waved him off, and said "Sit down, sir, and let's get these proceedings started. My time is valuable, and you are wasting it."

The other lawyer opened his briefcase and pulled out a pile of paper that would equal my father's lawyer's pile. Once each lawyer started presenting their cases, my father realized they were on the same page and trying to do the same thing. This was making sure my sister was safe and being cared for. After about an hour the judge asked my father a series of questions, basically asking if he was aware that he would be giving up custody of his daughter to the state of Massachusetts. He wanted to be sure my father understood my parents would have limited guardianship, would have visitation rights, and would have limited, basic financial responsibility to pay for cigarettes, soda, or any extra niceties Anne might want. Anne would be transferred to Metropolitan State Mental Health Facility in Waltham to be closer to the family. The State would be responsible for her room and board, clothes, and all medical needs.

My father agreed to all of the conditions but had an empty feeling in his stomach knowing he would have to go home and tell my mother that Anne would be hospitalized for the foreseeable future. My mother's heart was already broken from the past eight years of turmoil, but this would stick the final dagger in it.

Mr. Buckley walked my father out of the building to his car; the lawyer tried to be consoling and supportive as best he could. He mentioned that some important documents would be coming via certified mail, and he would have to sign them with my mother. My father's mind was elsewhere, and he just nodded his head as he fumbled with his car keys.

My father felt relieved that my sister would be taken care of, under the care of trained professionals in mental health. In reality, his troubles were just starting.

BOSTON, MASS., 1974

The school buses pulled up in front of South Boston High School. There was a large crowd made up of Boston police, demonstrators, and concerned parents. This was a daily routine for everyone since the start of the school year, and the beginning of forced busing in Boston. It stemmed from a federal court-mandated action that sent some Irish south Boston kids to Roxbury High, and predominantly black Roxbury kids to South Boston High.

The order was handed down by federal judge Wendell Arthur Garrity, Jr. to enforce a 1965 law known as the Racial Imbalance Law, which ordered school districts to desegregate their schools or risk losing education funding. This consisted of providing a racial balance in the Boston schools any time school enrollment was more than fifty percent nonwhite. The Boston school committee had disobeyed the state board of education up until that point. Judge Garrity upheld the ruling, and the school committee had no other choice but to comply.

No one was happy, especially the parents of those high school children who had to switch schools and go to another neighborhood far across town in a place they knew they were not wanted. The turmoil was high every school day and racial tensions mounted. The local news crews were on the scene constantly, and only helped fan the flames of racial turmoil.

Racially motivated incidents took place regularly. In one a south Boston resident coming out of city hall attacked a black lawyer with an American flag. In another incident, a group of black teenagers threw rocks at a white man's, car causing him to crash. The violence spilled over into the hallways of the high schools. At one point school had to be shut down for a time, and then reopened with metal detectors installed at the front door, and guarded by 500 police officers.

W. Arthur Garrity was public enemy number one. Residents of Boston hated what he had done to the city. Boston was stigmatized as a racially charged city and not tolerant of minorities.

In a lesser-known ruling, Judge Garrity also ruled on using a court-ordered mandate due to deteriorating conditions at the state mental hospitals. Over the last decade the state hospitals that dealt with mental health care had become run down and overcrowded. Rumors swirled that patients were not cared for, were abused, or were experimented on like animals. Complaints mounted from concerned parents, visitors, and caring healthcare professionals. Articles started appearing in the newspapers, and the public started asking questions.

Rumors swirled that residents had disappeared with no explanation, that mental health workers vanished on the properties, that patients had run away and no one knew where they were, and patients had been left in state custody after their parents died, even though their IQ was normal. Violent patients were mixed in with the docile residents, and only the strong could survive. The medication of choice was Thorazine and the preferred treatment was shock therapy. These calmed people down for a while, but then the demons would come back.

There was a constant churn of staff, who really did not provide much healthcare, but were professional baby sitters. People would come and people would go. The pay was low and the risk of harm was high. The committed healthcare workers were overwhelmed by the work, long hours, and lack of caring by most of the staff.

This was an explosive combination, and left the residents at the bottom of the food chain.

WALTHAM, MASS., 1974

My father's Ford sedan was bumping along Pleasant Street as we headed over to Met State Hospital. The roads were in disrepair, and the town department looked like it was in no hurry to fix them. I wished I had stock in an auto repair garage or a shock absorber company. I had the front seat for the ride over, and my mother was relegated to the back seat. I pushed a button on the AM dial, and the newest Elton John song came on. It was "Bennie and the Jets." I started humming the tune to distract everyone about the mission at hand.

All of a sudden this hand came flying off the steering wheel, and with pinpoint accuracy hit the correct radio button, turning the radio back to news and talk all the time. I looked over at my father to make my displeasure known, but decided to back off, after I got that glare that was more than a 500-foot stare. My father was in no mood for any baloney. These past few years had been hell for my mother and father. My sister's illness had taken a toll on our family. Anne had been confined to a mental hospital in Worcester, with no improvement in sight. My parents had dealt with doctors, lawyers, administrators, advocates, and you name it. They were all out to help, but no one could give them answers on how a healthy young girl, with her whole life ahead of her, could end up like this.

I felt the tension at home. My parents, once very close, and who did everything together, were very distant. They were living separate lives under one roof. They did not fight, but dinner conversation was very limited, mostly me talking about my day. Sometimes my father would tell us what went on at the office, but those times were few and far between. I was the main source of excitement. They would always pepper me with questions, and I tried hard to keep up my end of the conversation to keep the dead spots at a minimum.

After dinner everyone would go back to their corners. Dad would go downstairs to his cellar office to do paperwork, mom would clean up the dishes, and then read or watch television. I would go back upstairs to my room to do my homework or read. As I went by my sister's room, I would always have a sinking feeling in my stomach about what had happened and the void in my life. It was like she had been killed in a car accident.

The only good news that happened lately was Anne was transferred from Worcester State hospital to Met State Hospital, which was much closer to our house. It would make visiting my sister much easier for all. Today was my first visit since the transfer, and I was looking forward to seeing Anne. I was twenty years old now, and felt I could be more support now that I was an adult. My parents had not said anything good or bad about her new home, so I was keeping an open mind. The last time I had seen my sister was a few months ago. It had not gone well. The floor where she lived was disorganized, with little care, and my sister was not in a good mood. She would be distant one minute, and lashing out the next. I hoped for a better outcome today.

As we pulled off Trapelo Road and headed up the driveway everything looked nice. Beautiful grounds, freshly mowed grass, and the sun was shining. Could this be a better place for Anne? As we crested the top of the hill, I got a look at the various buildings, and the bars on the windows, and then I knew it was the same kind of place. This was a warehouse for broken toys and broken members of society. My heart sank as the car came to a stop, and my father's door opened. My mother got out, carrying an armload of clothes. She was always bringing new clothes to Anne. They seemed to always disappear, so my mother wrote Anne's name on the tag on each piece. My mother was under the silly impression that this would help.

As we walked into the main lobby, a young man was sitting behind a desk, looking like he was completely bored, and couldn't wait for his shift to end. My father stated his name and who he was here to see. He checked us in, and then told us to ring the doorbell on the locked door just ahead of us. We proceeded to ring the bell. Another man with a heavy French accent opened the door and let us in. We advised the man on who we were here to see, and then we walked into a dayroom. It was a total wake-up call. The place was out of control. The room was filled with residents and staff of all sizes and shapes. No one was dressed nicely. They all looked like slobs. The only way you could tell them apart was the social workers and health aides had a set of keys on their belts to open any door in the place.

The noise was loud, and the residents sitting around were either talking to themselves, yelling at the help, or arguing with the television set at the other end of the room. My parents and I had to cross this room to get to the nurses' station on the other side. We all walked very quickly to the other side, and my father and I kept looking over our shoulders to make sure no one came up behind us. As we approached the nurses' station, I saw an old grouchy nurse cussing out this nice black man.

"How many times have I told you to stop speaking French around the residents?" she snapped. "You know they get paranoid, and I don't want them taking it out on me for your mistake. The next time I hear any French, I'm going to write you up."

The young fellow skulked away. The nurse immediately turned to us, and said "Can I help you?"

My father said "Yes." He advised the woman that we were there to visit Anne. She got up from her station, walked us out of the crazy room, and down a long hallway that had bedrooms on both sides. As we meandered down the long hall, I peered into each room. Most residents were either sleeping or looking out the barred windows, talking to themselves. They all looked like homeless people and were very dirty. The noise level was dropping the further way we got from the dayroom.

As we turned the corner, I saw my sister lying on her bed with her back to us. The nurse said "Anne, look who's here to see you?"

My mother chirped in, "Anne, it's mom and dad, and we brought Chris with us. How are you?"

Anne rolled over, adjusting her eyes. She looked at us like we were from outer space. She looked at me, and I thought I would get a rise out of her, but nothing. She was obviously on some pretty strong medication. The nurse coaxed her up, and we all walked to a visitors' room that was really a bedroom furnished with old chairs made of steel, and which would be heavy to move or throw.

We all sat there looking at each other. From what I could hear and see it was medication time. Residents were flowing out of their rooms to go see the nurse and get their dose of happy pills. My mother and father tried to engage Anne.

* * * * * *

I'm lying in my bed looking at the window with the moonlight streaming in. I'm not sure how long I have been here, but it looks and feels like the other place. The rooms are the same, the halls are the same, and the help is all the same. The orderlies, nurses, and doctors either ignore me or ask me twenty questions. I have been feeling so tired all day every day. I only feel like sleeping all day. I wish I could just stay in my room and away from the crazy people in here.

I hate the dayroom. It is so scary with all these people in it. The noise is too loud, and it hurts my head. I keep telling the nurse I don't belong in here because I'm not crazy. They keep telling me I will get better someday, and might be able to go home. I sure hope so. I make sure I never mention the voices. That would kill my chances of leaving this place.

As I look out the window, I dream about riding the moonlight beam right out the window, high in the sky. It looks so nice to be out there. I wasn't scared out in the world. I could take care of myself. I'm not even sure why people feel I should be here.

I roll over, and notice the door is open, and the light from the attendant station is beaming down the hallway. I feel better when I hear the voices of the orderlies. It makes me feel safe. I am still shaken by the crazy man who rushed into my room the other night. He forced himself on me, and I used all my strength to fight him off. It took two people to drag him off me and send him to his room. He was nice to me in the dayroom, but now I know he wants something else.

I go in and out of sleep for a few hours. The social worker comes in and sits in a chair across from my bed. "Anne," she says, "your family is coming today to see you. Isn't that great?" She smiles. I had to think for a moment who were they. Then I remembered my father. He was my savior. I always trusted him to do the right thing. I am still mad he put me here. He said it was for my own good.

"Anne, we are going to get you up to shower, then we will give you breakfast. That way you will be ready when your family arrives." She had this happy smile on her face all the time. Who could be happy in a place like this? It was horrible.

I went through my paces with the orderlies, and ended back in my room to pass the time. I was glad to avoid the chaos outside and down the hall. People coming and going with no rhyme or reason where they were going and what they were going to do when they got there. I stayed on the bed and dreamed of how things used to be. My thoughts were misty, but I had a good feelings and bad. They kept intersecting in my head. I could not remember when I was little, but I felt at peace about where I came from.

The voices in my head were coming and going. I hadn't taken my morning meds. The voices were getting louder. I put the pillow over my head to make them stop. Suddenly, someone took the pillow away from my face There is my father looking down at me. I think I see my mother and brother. The voices are telling me that my mother was evil and trying to hurt me. She was telling the doctors I was crazy. I would get her back in due time.

I heard the social worker coax me to sit up and welcome my visitors. I was happy and sad. Happy someone different came to see me, and sad because people were happy and trying to make me feel happy. I did not feel happy. How could anyone feel happy or secure in this place? My *mother stepped up and hugged me. She flashed new clothes in my face, and said I would feel better if I dressed in my new clothes. My clothes were fine. I felt comfortable.*

My brother stood in the corner and looked like he was looking into the tiger cage at the zoo. He was uncomfortable. I felt bad for him. Not that bad, though. He could leave after our visit and I would still be here. He looked much older than when I saw him last. How much time had gone by? Why hadn't he come sooner?

After a little chitchat with everyone in the room, the social worker directed us to another room down the hall. I did not feel like going, but she took my arm, and guided me along, telling me how nice this was going to be. I walked along. My mother and father kept touching me and saying how happy they were to see me. We entered the room and all took our seats. The social worker left and the four of us are sitting there looking at each other.

* * * * * * *

My mother, father, and I were led into a visitors' room and we all took a seat. The social worker put Anne in a chair and left the room. We were all sitting there looking at Anne, and she burst out "What are you looking at?!" in a possessed voice.

The outburst really put my mother back on her heels. "Now, Anne, don't be like that," she said. "We came all this way to visit, and catch up with you."

Anne had a disgusted look on her face that said it all. She stood up and paraded around the room in a circle, coming nearer every time she did a lap.

My father continued the conversation to bail my mother out. He kept it to basic small talk to avoid any more explosions. As he asked the questions, my sister gave him one-word answers. He asked how the new hospital was, how the help was, how the food was, and how the residents were.

She blurted out, "These people are crazy," with a stern voice that exempted her from that category. "I can't deal with this. Every day, I'm dealing with crazy people," in a louder voice to get her point across. She looked at me like she was selling me a car and trying to close the sale. She began to pace again.

I tried to intervene to get her off the subject. It had been a few years since Anne lived with us, but I felt like our bond should still be there. I started telling her about the top forty music I was listening to on the radio, and asked her if she had a radio in her room. She turned to me with a pissed-off blank stare, and said "Who are you anyway? Are you with them or do you work here?"

It was like a dagger was plunged through my heart. Was she kidding, or was she serious? I looked at her expression to see if she changed her facial look. After a few seconds I knew she was serious. She really didn't know who I was. All the years living across the hall from her and all our brother-sister interactions. Had she really forgotten me? That was impossible.

"Anne," I said in a surprised tone. "I 'm your brother. Don't you remember me? I came over to see you today. Are you just kidding us," I said in a perplexed voice.

Anne looked back at me like she was sizing me up, and let out a forced laugh. "Of course I remember you," she said. "What was your name again?"

My mother spoke. "Anne, this is Chris, your brother," she said. "He wanted to come with us today because he missed you."

Anne looked back at me, and nodded that she knew me. I felt relieved, but I wasn't entirely sold that she knew who I was. She paced back and forth nervously as my parents continued to pepper her with questions. We quickly ran out of things to talk about. Then there began to be too much space in between responses. Finally, Anne looked at us and said, "I'm tired. I am going back to my room to lie down."

My mother tried to interest Anne in looking at the clothes she brought, but Anne just waved her off and left. I looked over at my parents and felt there was nothing to add to the conversation. My sister had made the transition to being institutionalized in a few short years, and she looked the part. How could such a vibrant young girl turn into a resident at a state mental hospital in such a short time? I felt bad for her being in this place, but felt she could never cut it in the outside world at this time.

We tracked down the social worker to give her Anne's clothes. My parents talked about how she was getting along and then we left to go home. I was happy to be going. The hospital gave me the creeps. I still had nightmares from my experience at Worcester State Hospital. The only good thing about Met State was it was close to where we lived. I felt better that my parents would not have to drive so far to see my sister.

All the way home my father and I just listened to the radio. There was no conversation. I could hear my mother whimpering in the back seat. I tried to pretend I didn't hear her. I knew there would be many days like this in the future.

* * * * * * *

The dayroom was crowded as usual at this time of the day. People were coming and going with their everyday rituals. I woke up late. I didn't sleep well last night because a lot of my fellow residents were upset and didn't settle down as usual. I heard the day nurse say it was due to the full moon. I could not reason that, but I was so tired, I wished I could go back to my room for a nap. The staff tried not to let residents do that for fear they would not sleep during the night when there were fewer staff.

I was in a gruff mood today. It seemed everyone was wearing on my nerves more than usual. The nurses were yelling at the social workers and attendants for no good reason. The doctors were yelling at the nurses. More residents were more confused than usual. I looked over at the television. An episode of Star Trek was on. Half the people in the room were zoned out to it, and all of a sudden the front desk nurse stuck her head through the hole in the wall and yelled at an orderly to change the channel. She was visibly upset. Last week a patient had to be restrained—put in a straitjacket—and put in isolation for a few days because he thought messages were coming though the TV show to make people crazy and do weird things. Once he started ranting, many of the others joined in. Some residents who were not that bad would always start cheering when someone was restrained, and you could see they were trying to get a riot going.

Most people on the unit were either schizophrenic, bipolar, drug addicted, or a severe alcoholic who were homeless. We were all lumped in together and treated alike. Everyone looked the same and acted the same. The medication we got was all the same. They gave you uppers or downers depending on your mood. I overheard some people talking in the dayroom that they came in here faking a mental illness to avoid serious jail time for some crime they committed to feed their drug or alcohol habits. They would make deals with other residents to buy their pills if they could avoid the nurse inspecting their mouth. Normally, you had to drink water with your pill, and then the nurse would look in your mouth. You had to wait for a big line or a distraction, and then someone could hide the pill and give it to the drug addict to feed their habit. The nurses never caught on since the druggies would pick different people so that no one would get their dosage screwed up too much. Then the resident would use the money for cigarettes or soda in the commissary in the lobby of the building. The black market was alive and well on our floor.

A lot of residents thought they were someone else. They believed they were famous politicians, sports stars, or Hollywood actors or actresses. Some people tried to pass themselves off as an eccentric scientist who had invented something important, and the government had stolen the idea, then put them in the hospital to hide the truth. Mostly men, but some woman would either parade around and act the part or saddle up beside you and pretend you were the only one that knew the truth. After a while, one story ran into the next story, you would have trouble keeping the people straight.

We had our share of Vietnam veterans who had come back from the war broken people. They either saw so much war, or had to kill so many people, they could not face life in the outside world. Some had seen their buddies blown up or shot, or had seen local woman and children get mowed down by their own troops. Once the body count stacked up, some of the troops turned to LSD, heroin, or pot to make them feel better. They either became addicted or went on one too many acid trips and burned out. Then they were shipped out on a mental disability. The VA hospitals treated them for a while, but then the soldier would slip away to the city, until he got picked up on a petty criminal charge or brought to the hospital because police thought they were homeless and mentally ill.

They were usually the ones who stayed up and did not want to go to sleep. They knew when their eyes closed those bad dreams and flashbacks would reappear and shock them awake in a cold sweat. Their minds were like a tape recorder replaying all the bad memories over and over in their heads.

One of the veterans would regularly flip out and barricade himself in his room. He would turn over his bed and desk and stack chairs on top to make a fort. He believed the orderlies were Viet Cong and were out to get him. We called him Big Jim. He was way over six feet tall and at least three hundred pounds. He had seen his share of action, and it had damaged him in more ways than you could imagine. He had been at Met State since he came back to the states after he was dishonorably discharged for hitting a superior officer. The story goes that his commander wanted his men to sweep through a Vietnamese village where they suspected Viet Cong were hiding so they could do hit and run operations. Big Jim's squad had taken some serious casualties the past few weeks, and their sergeant was sick of it. He gave the order to kill everyone in the village, and that meant woman and children too. Big Jim was a great soldier, and brave as they came, but he would not kill innocent people for anyone. He stood up to his superior officer, who said he would put Big Jim in the brig if he disobeyed his orders. Jim was so infuriated at the order he punched him in the face and knocked him down. Jim was arrested and shipped back to base to be court-martialed. He was later discharged from the Army and sent home. He didn't get any jail time since the military was nervous that he would go to the press and tell his story. Unfortunately, he was not eligible for VA benefits due to his dismissal from the service, so he ended up at Met State after his parents kicked him out of the house. The one thing the parents did was get a doctor and the state to put him here so he could get his medication and be looked after.

On most days Jim stuck to himself, mumbling to himself as he paraded around the floor. Every once in a while he would get those flashbacks from all the fire fights, and then he would become enraged and no one could control him. He would barricade himself in his room and rant and rave about the gooks, saying they were walking around the floor. "Why can't you people see them? Is anybody going to help me," he would shout in a scary voice.

As usual, all the orderlies who weren't Asian would draw straws to see who was going to play his soldier buddy and help him fight off the enemy. Once one of the workers was picked, he would stand outside Jim's door, and start yelling that he had killed a lot of the Viet Cong, and would ask permission to come in and fight with Jim. Big Jim would give permission, and the orderly would grab a broom handle and jump over the pile of furniture; He would talk to Jim until he calmed down and was convinced the battle had passed.

Then they would put Jim's room back together, give him a sedative, and have him rest. Most of the time this plan worked. If it did not the straitjacket came out until Jim calmed down. He would fight it, but with a shot of muscle relaxer he would become easier to deal with.

I looked down the hall. I saw Mr. Peavy coming toward me doing his usual dance. He looked like a combination of a ballet dancer and a drunk working his way through the Boston Common. He would mumble unintelligible things and then chuckle. He was about 70 years old, with gray hair, and very thin. He always had a good appetite at dinner, but for some reason he never gained any weight. The orderlies and nurses liked him because he was entertaining and never gave anyone trouble.

The rumor was he had come to Met State decades ago from another institution when he turned 18. Apparently, he had spent most of his childhood in state custody after his parents were killed in a car accident. The story goes he had no extended family and had learning disabilities and was deaf, which combined to give the impression he was not right. I never knew him when he was young, but some of the other lifers said he was actually very smart. But after being in the system for decades, and being on daily medication all those years, he became like all the rest. Now his days were spent dancing, mumbling, eating, and sleeping.

The nurses' station was where all the action was. The orderlies, social workers, and doctors would congregate there, and if they were not in the mood would go into the back room off the station to disappear for a few minutes.

If you had a complaint you stepped up and stated your case. The personnel would listen to you, or at least make it look like they were listening. For the most part no one ever got their grievance acted on. If you kept talking or arguing with them, the orderlies would come up behind *you and escort you back to your room. Sometimes, medication helped change your mood.*

At some point the nurse at the front desk would say, "The complaint window is now closed." Everyone would grouse, but then return back to where they came from.

The floor had two dayrooms. One was used for watching television, and one for playing cards and just to have a quiet place to go. If two people in one room were not getting along, they would split you up, put one of you in the other dayroom, and then watch you to make sure you did not go back to cause more trouble.

I knew I was sane, and I wasn't really sure why I was here,. I would tell anyone who would listen. But then out of nowhere the voices would come back and get me mad. Then I would go off on whoever was standing near me. It did not matter if it was a nurse or orderly or resident. After I was finished I would look around and people would be looking at me with a bewildered expression.

I would get frustrated that no one was listening or sympathizing with my plight. Then I would stomp back to my room for some quiet time. I would sit on the edge of my bed and try to calm down. Sometimes I would have a flashback to my childhood and wish I could take a time machine back. The voices mixed me up, but I remembered the good times and the music. If I heard a song on the radio, I could recite all the words. I never stopped loving music.

The orderlies were told to keep everyone in the dayrooms or walking around, so when night came everyone would sleep. For the most part that is what happened. If someone was very lethargic from the level of medication they were taking they would let the patient rest or sleep. It was not worth the trouble to keep someone awake if he was dead on his feet. The attendants' mantra was to do whatever was easiest to keep peace and tranquility.

My life was one of confusion and hopelessness. One day would blend in with the next. No one knew the day of the week or cared. Our wing was one of many that housed mental patients, drug addicts, and alcoholic homeless. No one better than the next, even if they thought so. We were all just a pile of broken toys in a little child's toy box. The weeks and months went by with no change in routine. I had no hope that I would ever be leaving this place.

WINCHESTER, MASS., AUGUST 1974

◆◆◆◆◆◆

I raced out the door on my way to school. I was late and the traffic to Boston was going to start to stack up on I-93. My alarm clock had failed me again. I knew my professor would not be happy if I strutted in after the lecture started. I had already tested the waters with that and had come out on the losing end.

As I walked between my parents' car and mine, I noticed what I thought was something under a blanket in the back seat. My curiosity got the better of me, so I took at better look. As I peered in the back window, I saw a blanket covering what looked like a person. I thought to myself, this is great. A homeless person decided to take a pit stop in our car for the night. No one locked their car in our neighborhood, but we were the lucky ones to have an unwelcome guest. I gently opened the back door to see who this vagrant was. I bent over, being oh so careful, so as to not startle this stranger.

As I lifted the corner of the blanket, I saw it was a young woman. I could only see the back of her head, and her face was snuggled into the seat of the car. As I tilted my head ever so slightly, I finally could make out who it was. My sister was sleeping in the car! She had run away from Met State Hospital.

A sinking feeling came over me. How could this have happened? She was in a locked ward, with plenty of people to watch over her and watch out for her well-being.

My sister somehow made it out of her room, out of a locked floor, down a flight of stairs, passed security at the front desk, and then walked a quarter of a mile to get to the front entrance of the main road. Then she had to walk or thumb a ride six miles to our house. I thought to myself, How could this have happened? What kind of security did they have at that hospital? I thought for a moment about all the other residents there, some of whom were pretty dangerous. I wondered, How careful they are watching them?

I headed back inside to let my father and mother know what was waiting for them out front. They were very surprised, and tried to reassure me that Anne was safe and would be fine. I somewhat believed what they were telling me because I wanted to and because I was pressed for time.

Fast forward to that night. I had some late classes that day, and negotiated the rush hour traffic, so I would get home when my father usually arrived home for dinner. It was around six o'clock. I raced in the door and to the kitchen to see my mother. As I walked through the living room, I could hear my father upstairs washing up for dinner. As I entered the kitchen my mother was busy making a salad, and putting the finishing touches on another great meal. My father was very finicky about his food and my mother's dinners never disappointed.

I gave her a quick peck on the cheek, and she greeted me with a big kiss back and a hug. I asked her how Anne was, and she said my father would discuss things at dinner. I kind of got a sick feeling in my stomach from my mother's voice and demeanor, but I just tried to shake it off and wait until we sat down for our nightly meal.

I sat down to watch the nightly news that was on the television. Most of the news was about Watergate and President Nixon. That episode has been raging for two years, but was finally coming to an end. The American public wanted a period of tranquility after Vietnam, and now hopefully the country could heal and move on. As I focused on the news my father breezed into the room and said a brief hello. He sat down at his regular seat at the head of the table. His mood seemed very relaxed, given the circumstances of the morning.

We joined my father and started passing around the food to fill our plates. He asked how both our days went, and we both gave a halfhearted "Okay." I sat there waiting for him to give me an update on my sister, but nothing came. After a few minutes of small talk, I had finally had enough. I turned to my father, and said "Dad, how is Anne doing? Did she get back to the hospital okay?"

My mother and father both looked at each other at the same time, and then back to their food. Then my father said "Anne is doing okay, and I took her back to Met State on my way to work. It seems she was out on a group walk going to a structured workshop in another building, and drifted away from the group."

I looked at my father perplexed, and asked, "Is there something wrong with their security up there? It seems that someone should have noticed a resident drifting off towards the main street."

My father explained because of the casual dress of the staff, sometimes it was tough to know one person from the next. Also, some residents who are deemed mildly ill have passes to leave the property during the day and then come back at night.

I thought to myself, What kind of place was this? People are there because they are crazy, and the staff lets people come and go like some sort of hotel? It did not give me a good feeling at all that my sister was being looked after in the proper way. My father also asked Anne how she got to our house, and she said she thumbed a ride. This was her choice of transportation back in her hippie days. She would thumb everywhere, and it gave my parents fits because Anne was so small and defenseless. She just had no idea how dangerous the world was getting, and she had no perspective because of her illness.

Hopefully, my father had stressed with the staff that Anne needed closer attention, and her group activities should be closely watched over. This drifting away could get her lost, molested, or worse.

Little did I know that the adventure was just beginning.

NOVEMBER 1974

My father pulled the car up in front of Anne's building. It was a clear, cold day in New England, the leaves fading from beaming yellow and orange to brown and brittle. They were falling off in clouds as the late fall wind blew across the open grounds at Met State Hospital.

We had a date to take Anne out to lunch off the grounds. This would be the first time a visit included an off-campus outing. My mother decided to stay in the car. I walked with my father through the outer, bulky glass door, and into the main reception area. My father had been very quiet all the way over, and I could tell he was apprehensive to take Anne off hospital grounds. She was so unpredictable; in her current state, every day was a different experience. I told my parents that I had other things to do, but they insisted I go. They said my sister would be heartbroken if I didn't show up. I knew they just wanted me there for security if things got out of hand.

We stepped up to the secure glass window, told security who we were, and they buzzed us in. We stepped in and my father signed some forms while an orderly went to fetch Anne in her room. Once we completed the legal process necessary for taking Anne off hospital grounds, we stood around with nervous anticipation. After ten long minutes I saw my sister walking toward us. All the beautiful clothes my mother bought her were nowhere to be seen. In their place was a bunch of rag-tag duds that weren't fit for a homeless person in Boston. My father and I looked at each other at the same time, equally disgusted.

Anne left the orderly's side and walked up to us. I put my arms around my sister, gave her a hug, and said "Hi." I couldn't feel her hugging me back. She stood very still and stiff, like a mannequin in a department store window. She released from me and started walking through the front door. As we approached the car, I ran ahead to open her door to the back seat. She totally ignored me and jumped in the front seat. She started to play with the radio to find her favorite music. Anne did not even acknowledge my mother in the back with me. My mother tried to start up a conversation but got a lot of one-word answers back in return. We decided to not talk at all, and rode to the restaurant listening to my sister's music selections.

Once we got to the restaurant, we all got out at the same time and headed for the door. My sister walked ahead, not even looking back to where we were. She had one thing on her mind, and that was food. I'm sure this was going to be nice change of pace from the institutional food she had to eat. Anne's appearance seemed hippie-like and she seemed agitated. My mother and father steered her into a booth and gave her a menu; and my mother tried to interpret for her to speed up the ordering process. I also realized why they came here. This place had counter service and good Italian food.

As my sister looked over the menu she became more agitated, to the point where I was wondering if they gave Anne her dose of medication for the day. My parents struggled to keep Anne in check while not drawing too much attention. Anne picked up the menu, scanned it with her eyes, then put it down. She repeated this for a few minutes, until my mother asked her what she wanted.

Anne looked at her with those sunken crazy eyes and said in a loud voice, "I don't know! I can't read it." She sat and stared at my mother some more.

My father jumped in, opened the menu, and started pointing to the pictures. This got Anne even more disturbed.

"Dad, stop pointing to the pictures. What do you think I am, a fucking retard!" she shouted at him. He pretended he hadn't heard what she said, but everyone in the booths around us heard it. They looked at us, and then looked back at their diner partners, and tried to look unfazed. I knew better though.

Finally, my father said to Anne, "What would you like, and I'll see if they have it."

"I want a hamburger with French fries and a Coke." she said. My father said "Then okay. We are getting somewhere." He continued to take our orders, and then stepped up to the counter some 20 feet away.

Now I had to jump in with some small talk, along with my mother. I talked about music, the weather, school, Boston, and whatever came into my head. Anne's responses were a lot of one-word answers. It was worse when my mother talked to Anne. No matter what the question or comment was, Anne would either curse at my mother or just blow her right off as if she were invisible. The longer this went on, the more people looked at us. I tried to intervene on my mother's behalf. Just when things looked like they were going to spin out of control, my father showed up with the food. He was none too soon.

My father slid each meal in front of us. He sat down and looked at Anne. She had her head down, inhaling her order. I never saw someone eat so fast. It was like she was not chewing the food, just biting it off and then swallowing it. Maybe the food at Met State was not filling Anne up, and she was really hungry. My father tried to get her to slow down, but it was no use. She ate so fast that she finished her meal in under five minutes. As soon as she was done she wanted another Coke. My Father tried to put her off for a few minutes, but it was no use.

I felt bad for him, so I offered to get Anne a drink. He jumped at the chance and tried to give me money, but I shook my head and then walked up to the counter.

I came back a few minutes later to raised voices and arguing. All I could hear was my sister and mother arguing, or it seemed. As I got real close, I realized Anne was doing the arguing and my mother was doing her best to reason with her. This tack was clearly not working, but my soft drink did. As soon as I put it in front of Anne she grabbed the drink and the straw out of my hand and slurped the drink down. She then let out a loud burp. My mother turned around to see if anyone heard this, and of course they all did. She was mortified. My father was getting used to it.

Once she finished the drink Anne wanted a cigarette. My father had forgotten to ask the floor attendant to give her a few cigarettes for the ride over. Anne didn't think about it on the way over. She wanted a cigarette and she wanted it now.

"Anne," my father said in a very cool, passive manner, "I do not have your brand with me, but you may have one of my unfiltered cigarettes if you like." She shook her head and said "No, I want my brand." He followed up with, "This is all I have for now. Would you like one?" She again said "No!" only louder. She pointed, "I want you to go over there, and buy me a pack of my brand."

As I looked back to the front door, I saw a cigarette machine. My father looked over, and then back at my sister. Then he said "No, Anne. You have a carton back at the hospital, and you can either have one of mine, or wait until you get back. Those are the choices," he said with a firm voice.

Anne snatched the cigarette out of his hand and waited for him to light it up for here. He pulled out his lighter and lit the cigarette. She took a big drag and inhaled it, and then blew the smoke in my mother's face. My mother was still in the middle of finishing her meal and started to cough.

"Anne, can you blow that smoke up in the air? People are trying to eat," my father snapped.

Anne kept it up because it was the only thing that made her happy. I could see the glimmer in her eyes. I hadn't seen that look since she left home for Boston.

My father stood up, and gave my mother and myself the high sign that we were done. "Anne, wasn't that good?" he said. I am so glad we had a chance to see you."

I could tell from his body language he did not mean it at all. Anne just looked at him and rolled her eyes. Her target was still my mother. She walked right beside her, and just gave it to her up and down for no good reason. My mother tried to play it cool, but Anne was getting the best of her. I tried to get on the other side of her and distract her, but it was no use. She completely ignored me.

Finally, my father grabbed Anne by the arm and steered her into the front seat. She flicked the cigarette in his direction, but it went over his head. He pretended he didn't see it.

Once we were all in the car, Anne reached over, turned the radio on, and started clicking the buttons, trying to find a song she liked. It took her some time to find anything that suited her taste. As soon as Aerosmith came on she turned up the volume, practically blasting us out of the car. My father reached over, and turned down the volume to a reasonable level. As fast as he put his hand back on the steering wheel, Anne turned up the volume again. This went on for most of the ride until my father finally gave up. The car was rocking and nobody was talking. I suppose my father realized it was a ten-minute drive, and he could stand anything for ten minutes.

As we cruised up the long driveway back to the hospital, we sounded like a bunch of teenagers cruising around the neighborhood with their new eight-track player and playing their first tape. The residents looked at the car as we drove by, and gave us the peace sign or the power sign or nodded in agreement with our choice of music.

As soon as we pulled up Anne was out of the car and into the lobby, my father chasing after her. My mother and I just looked at each other. She was exasperated. Her eyes looked tired, and it seemed despair had seeped into her body. I didn't know what to say, so I said nothing. I just sat there looking out the window waiting for my father to reappear.

THANKSGIVING, NOVEMBER 1974

————— ✦✦✦✦✦ —————

I walked quickly into the house after being at the big Thanksgiving Day game. Winchester had lost to Woburn in a huge upset. I had dreaded this day for a week. My sister was home for the day from the hospital and my Aunt Ollie was coming over, also. The day would have been tense enough with Anne, but my great aunt would tip the Richter Scale well above the red zone.

I looked into the kitchen and saw my mother busily getting Thanksgiving dinner prepared. As I was standing there my father came up behind me and told me we were going to get my aunt. I asked where my sister was. "Up in her room listening to the radio," he said in an exasperated voice. I asked if I could go up and say hi. "No. I want to get over and pick up your great aunt, and bring her over as soon as possible. Today can't go by fast enough," he said nervously.

We walked outside and piled into his '74 Ford. It was a cool car and I loved to ride in it. I always asked my father if I could drive it, and he always said no. He would say, "You have your own car, and you will never drive one of mine."

He must have been referring to my checkered accident history. It was fair at best. I almost got his auto policy canceled for having too many accidents. Now I had my own policy, and my premiums had gone through the roof. As I jumped in the car my father started it, and the radio came to life with a loud rock 'n' roll song on WBCN. It practically blew us out of the car. My father reached over, spun the dial down, and put the radio back on AM. It sounded like all news all the time. I went to switch it back, and he covered his hand over the buttons.

"Don't even try it, Buster," he said with a glare that would kill. "I have to put up with that crap when your sister is in the car, and I don't plan on doing it when you are here." He looked back towards the road and continued his way over to Malden.

I knew better than to press him. He was in no mood to bargain with. I decided to leave it alone, and continue the small talk until we arrived at my great aunt's house.

As we pulled up the street, I could see Aunt Ollie standing on the porch of her three decker house. It was a disgusting green color with cedar shingle siding. It looked old and dreary, just like my great aunt.

As we were pulling up I had a flashback to when my parents left me with her when I was about ten years old. It was the worst weekend of my life. I would have rather go into to a pit of poisonous snakes than relive the weekend from hell I encountered. I will never forget the smell when you walked in. It smelled like witch hazel and it made me gag every time. My parents went to a wedding out of state; I got the death penalty. The whole weekend consisted of me doing all kinds of chores around the house while Aunt Ollie tried to make it sound like we were having fun. She would go from room to room and sit in a chair and order me around. The only time we stopped was for meals. That was worse than the work. She did not cook anything I liked, and so I had to fake eating everything and then put the food in my napkin and drop it in the trash when she was not looking. Of course she had no television. She grew up on a farm and liked to go to bed early. This meant I had to go to bed early because she did. I just counted the hours until my parents came back to pick me up. The only saving grace to the whole weekend was she was addicted to Dr. Pepper and I got to have as many as I liked. That is what I survived on. I stole crackers and drank Dr. Pepper all weekend.

As we pulled up she walked down the walk to the car, hobbling on her cane. My father jumped out to assist her. "You're late. You were supposed to be here ten minutes ago, and I'm freezing to death," she spouted with venom. I'm sure my father wished she would freeze to death, since she was not his favorite person. This was my mother's aunt from Canada. She never seemed to have a good day in her life.

I jumped out to get in the back. She gave me a peck on the check and told me how big I had grown from the last time she had seen me. My mother would come over to take her shopping every other week when I was growing up, and she would always tried to talk me into going. I always conveniently got lost or had to stay late at school when that day arrived.

The ride back was very long; we had to listen to my great aunt telling my father how to drive along with all the news from Canada, her birthplace. For some reason she forgot that we had driven over to her house to pick her up. If I heard one more time "drive dead ahead," I was going to throw up.

I was never so glad to get back to my house, but the real fun was just starting.

I joined my mother in the kitchen after we returned, and watched her wheel around like a well-seasoned short-order cook. She would open the oven, check the bird, and then watch the stuffing. She would pivot back to the stove to stir the potatoes and vegetables. She looked like a woman on a mission, and as she moved she threw some small chores at me, like setting the table and shuttling hors d'oeuvres to the living room where my father and aunt were sitting. I felt like a waiter in a restaurant, but otherwise I would be the one sitting with my aunt instead of my father. As usual, she was droning on about everything that went wrong in her life.

I loved the smell of the house on this day. Thanksgiving was my favorite holiday because you could watch football and eat to your heart's content. The high school football game in the morning was also fun. It gave me a chance to touch base with some of my old friends. I started on my way back to the kitchen, when my mother came out the door. "Dinner is served," she said in a stern military manner. "Go get your sister upstairs, and bring her down for the meal."

I wheeled around and eyeballed my father trying to pry my great aunt out of the living room chair. That was high comedy by itself, but if my father caught my eye he would have been pissed.

I ran up the stairs two at a time to get my sister. I was excited and apprehensive at the same time. Her looks and manners were gone, and her clothes were something straight out of a secondhand shop. For a girl who was so hung up on how she looked as a teenager, she had let herself go through no fault of her own.

I knocked on the door twice. I heard nothing but the low murmur of a transistor radio with her favorite rock station on. I opened the door and stepped in. As I looked to my left and saw her lying on her bed, I had a flashback to years before when we would hang out and listen to music together. The room looked the same and the smell of the room was the same. Those were the best of times; my sister and I were so close then.

As I walked toward the bed, I saw Anne was looking up at the ceiling, not looking at me in the least. "Anne, Thanksgiving dinner is ready, and mom would like you to join us downstairs," I said meekly. She looked at me with a blank stare and started to lift herself off the bed. She came towards me with a stern stare; I held my breath. She then strutted by me and made her way down the stairs to the dining room. I followed closely after to make sure she kept going in the right direction and not out the front door.

My mother greeted her. "Anne, look who is joining us today, your great Aunt Ollie. Isn't that wonderful?" she said with as much cheer as possible.

Anne looked her up and down and then sat, and said nothing. My mother gave us the look to sit, and then said, "We will say a prayer to thank God on how lucky we are to have Anne and Ollie with us today. Chris you can start the prayer."

I looked over at my mother, and started reciting our usual blessing. As I started Anne reached for dishes of food and began serving herself. I tried to ignore her and keep going. I looked at my aunt out of the corner of my eye, and saw her look of disgust at what my sister was doing. I saw her lips start to move, and then looked back at my father. He gave my great aunt a look that could kill, and then pointed his finger and directed her to keep her mouth shut. My aunt's mouth was open, but nothing came out, as she looked back at my father.

I rushed to finish my prayer, and then started passing dishes around the table so everyone could fill their plates. My mother made small talk with my aunt and me, and my father kept an eye out for Anne in case she was going to do something outrageous in front of everyone. The meal was going well, even with my aunt complaining about everything about her life. You would think she lived in a war-torn African country the way she talked about her situation. I did my best to nod once in a while like I understood her plight.

I looked over to my sister sitting next to me. She was eating like a truck driver. I had never seen anyone devour food the way she was going at it. She ate enough for two people and in half the time. I know the food was good, but this was some kind of a world record. All I could think of was she must love this food compared to the hospital food she was used to.

As soon as she finished she stood up and walked to the other end of the room. My mother said, "Anne, don't you want to sit with us until the meal has ended? I made you your favorite desert, bread pudding, from Aunt Ollie's special recipe. Won't that be special?"

My sister continued to the piano, sat on the bench, turning her back to my mother. My aunt gave my mother a look, but saw my father staring at her, so said nothing. We resumed the conversation, pretending Anne was not there. Now I was the lucky one to listen to all my aunt's boring stories of life on a farm, and how hard it was for her. My mother had grown up on the same farm, and she looked pretty good for it. I just went along like I was interested and tried to make the best of it. I knew my parents were on edge but were just trying to make a nice day of it for everyone.

As we were talking, I could hear the faint noise of Anne touching the keys on the piano. It sounded like a little kid tuning up after just having a lesson with their teacher. Gradually, each keystroke became more specific and clear; her playing began sounding like a real song. All of a sudden she stopped. I figured she was bored and would make her way back to her room to listen to music to kill some time until she went back to the hospital.

My mother was just laying out the desert menu to my aunt and father when the piano came to life. Anne pounded the keys with both hands, and the music was clear and concise. The song was so familiar to me, but I could not remember the name. I had heard my sister play it a thousand times and she never played any better than today. By this time everyone was transfixed on Anne; we could not believe what we were hearing. She had not played a piano in over ten years and had not practiced that we knew of in the hospital.

As Anne played my great aunt was transfixed, probably the first time she was speechless in her life. As Anne played, I asked my mother what the name of the song was. She said Beethoven's Moonlight Sonata. It sounded as good as the time Anne tried out for Ted Mack's Amateur Hour when she was younger.

My sister finished the song, and my Aunt clapped in applause. Anne got up and walked up the stairs to her room without even turning around. My great aunt kept clapping as she was so impressed by what she had just witnessed. I was impressed that she was impressed, and decided to try and treat her nicer for the remainder of her time with us. I even offered to drive her home so my father could drive my sister back to Waltham and not have to make two separate trips.

A few hours later we all went our separate ways. My mother stood in the doorway with a look of relief that Anne had not had a meltdown, and my great aunt had not started a fight with my sister. She looked tired but satisfied standing there waving out the door to all of us. So much time had gone by, but the memories of years past kept flooding through my mind.

WALTHAM MA. DECEMBER 20, 1974

◆◆◆◆◆◆◆

I walked through the front door of the Fercello Building and checked in with security. The two guards at the desk looked very bored and very put out that they had to ring in so many people today for the residents' annual Christmas party. Both men at the desk had on wrinkled blue uniforms, worn shoes, and a shiny silver badge on their chest. They were about mid-fifties, and both had a receding hairline. When I told them my sister's name they did not even check a list; they just waved me through and then turned away.

I followed the noise that indicated the gathering was in the main gym. The party was put on every year by the Knights of Columbus of Waltham. They had maybe 20 to 30 volunteers on hand, equally spread between men, women, and teenagers of the members. Some were dressed up in red and white and some as Elves with stocking caps on. They had brought the party favors, food, presents, and even Santa. He was sitting on the stage, all dressed up, and asking each person if they had been good. About ten residents stood in line, some with a friend who came to visit and some who were by themselves. Most of the people looked nervous and antsy, even though they were adults. After Santa spent a few minutes with each person, he would reach into a big red box beside him, pull out a perfectly wrapped present, and hand it to the person. Some residents didn't want to get off Santa's lap, and some would stand in front of him and unwrap their present. The they would drop the wrapping and box and hug whatever was inside. Some just took their present and marched off the stage like they had just won the Academy Award. They all looked so proud and happy.

Some volunteers were running around trying to keep the food coming for the buffet table and trying to keep things organized. Others were organizing the dancing to the Christmas carols in front of the stage, while others helped residents who had severe mental health issues to eat. The lights in the gym had been turned down and colored lights had been hung by the disc jockey playing the music. The atmosphere made it seem like a real party, and helped the shy residents come out of their shells to socialize or dance. If the volunteers saw any wallflowers, they nicely tried to coax them to eat or join the fun.

On the outer ring of the hall were the doctors, nurses, and attendants. They looked very bored, but tried to put their best party face on since management was also involved in the celebration and managers were taking everything in.

After I entered the gym, I waited a minute for my eyes to adjust to the light before I made my way through to locate my sister. My eyes were just coming around when I felt someone take my arm. I looked around quickly, thinking it was a resident, but it was one of the elves. She smiled and asked who I was there to see. I let her know that I was looking for my sister. She greeted me warmly, took my hand, and led me through the gym. We exchanged pleasantries while we walked; then I saw my sister dancing with an older man on the dance floor. I could tell from his demeanor he was a resident. I told the elf that was my sister. We stood there at the edge of the makeshift dance floor and just watched until the song was over.

I watched Anne. She looked like she had aged so much from the time she entered the hospital six years ago. I didn't know if it was the stress of being housed with other mental patients, or the drugs she was given to control her schizophrenia, or being away from her family. As she danced, she showed no affect, but I could tell she had a good rhythm from her years listening to and playing music.

As the song ended, the volunteer grabbed my hand and walked us in between Anne and her dance partner. "Anne, I have a special someone who came to celebrate with you today, she said." Then she kind of nudged me into her. "Merry Christmas, Anne. How are you doing?" I asked with as much cheer as I could muster.

She looked back at me. "Chris, what are you doing here?" she asked with surprise.

"I wanted to come and wish you a merry Christmas, Anne. The social worker told me when the party was, and I wanted to celebrate with you."

Just as Anne was ready to guide me away with her, another girl jumped into the group, babbling about something. I could not understand her at first, and then I made out her saying, "Anne, is this your brother?" As she spoke she gave me a big bear hug. Then she stuck her face into my chest, and kept saying over and over, "Anne, your brother is so cute. How come you never told me about him?"

Anne looked over with a put-off expression, and said "I never thought to," then gave me and the volunteer a dirty look. I tried to play it cool and let the girl have her fun. She kept her arms around me and squeezed me in nice way. Finally, she heard a song come on that she liked, let go, and danced her way back into another circle of people. I breathed a sigh of relief. The volunteer and Anne's dance partner walked away, leaving us standing there looking at each other. I tried to carry on a conversation with her, but it was much too noisy where we were standing. I grabbed her arm and directed her over to the back of the hall. As we walked, Anne said hi to many of her friends and other people were saying hi to her. They all looked like they would be homeless if they were on the outside of this place.

The hall we were in resembled the Boston Tea Party. That was a battle of the bands concert hall that was started in Boston and was the launch pad for some of the biggest rock-and-roll bands to ever hit the national stage. Anne would go every time she could get away from work to listen to new bands play. Her love of music never left her, even in her darkest days.

I pulled out two chairs from the table and we both sat down. I ask Anne if she wanted a drink, and she shook her head no. I asked her if she was glad I came, and she said yes. "Chris, did you bring me any presents?" she then asked.

I said "No, Anne, mom and dad will be over in a few days right before Christmas to give you your presents. They are also going to take you out to lunch to any place you want." As I looked over at her, I could see her contemplating her next question.

"Are you going to be there?" she spouted out nervously. "I want you to be there, and bring my presents."

I told her I could not be there due to a college exam in Boston the same day my parents were coming. Anne gave me a blank stare, taking in what I had just said, and then said, "Are you coming to our New Year's Party? It's going to be here, also. The social workers said it is going to be cool." Then Anne laughed uncontrollably for an uncomfortably long time.

I looked over at her, and shook my head no. I told her I was going skiing in Vermont for the weekend and would miss the party. I said I would be back soon, and would bring her a surprise if she was good. She perked up when I said that. Then she just started looking around at all the excitement, and I could tell she was enjoying herself, even though she had a very low affect.

We both passed the time eating, drinking, smoking, and dancing. The Knights of Columbus did a great job making everyone feel special at this time of year. Many of the residents did not have parents or a special someone to visit, so this was their big day. On Christmas, there would be a special meal up on the floor, but no presents would be distributed by Santa or anyone else. I thought back on all the great holidays we had in the past. Since my sister had been confined, my mother and father tried to make Christmas special, but you could see it wasn't the same. They went through the motions, but they knew their beautiful daughter would not be there to tear the paper off those special presents from under the tree.

After some time, Anne got up and paced nervously. I knew it was time for me to leave. I told her I needed to go and then gave her a big hug. She seemed so fragile and helpless, but then she said an abrupt goodbye and meandered over to her friends on the dance floor. She started moving rhythmically to the music. By now the disc jockey had played all his Christmas music, and was breaking into his top forty rock and roll. All the residents seemed to be having fun in a crazy sort of way.

I walked out the front door of the hall and out to the parking lot, an Elton John song was wafting in the distance. I thought to myself that Anne was enjoying herself. But then I remembered she was in a mental hospital, committed there by a court of law. She would never be coming home to spend a normal Christmas with us.

WALTHAM, MASS.,. MARCH 1975

———————— •‹•◆•›• ————————

I walked through the lobby of our building on my way to my job. The social workers called it a structured workshop. I noticed a few residents from other floors that were not locked. They had privileges to roam the building or the grounds if they chose to. The only rule they had to follow was to not go off hospital grounds unless they had permission. As I walked by them with my group some stared blankly at us, others looked off in to space like we did not exist. Most of them walked around by themselves with no set plan, or stood right outside the front of the lobby, chain-smoking cigarettes, or trying to bum a cigarette from anyone who walked by. The lobby was sparse, and not decorated very well. There was some boring, plain furniture in a yellow and orange color scheme, but no pictures on the walls.

Security barely looked at us since they know the social workers were in charge and responsible for any breakdown in the movement of residents from one building to another. I followed my group out the door into the cool morning air as I looked up at the sunshine.

The voice in my head had grown louder lately, disturbing my sleep. The nurses wondered who I was talking to all the time. My unprovoked laughter was happening more frequently. The voice came and went, but had grown more severe and authoritarian. I kept trying to suppress it, but it was ruling me. It was telling me to do bad things. The voice was becoming angry. I kept telling him to leave me alone, but it wouldn't stop.

104

As we walked over to the recreation building the social workers tried to be cheery while telling us to stay in line and stay together. The winter snow was still melting and my feet were a little cold, since we never really got good winter clothing. Didn't really need it; we hardly ever went out. The social workers kept saying we were going to have so much fun. Most of our work consisted of folding letters, putting them in envelopes, and sealing the envelopes. It was a pretty mundane task, but most people went along with it, and never complained, me included. The best part was the snack they served us at breaks. We usually got coffee or hot chocolate, with a donut or muffin. It all tasted so good; it was worth the trip just for the snack and see something new. The workshop usually took two hours, with a fifteen minute break in the middle. Then we would be back in our building by lunch.

Today, things were going to be different. I noticed myself falling behind the group as they walked along. One of social workers was in a serious conversation with her coworker, and did not notice me drifting away. It was like someone else was ruling my body. The commands were becoming regimented and louder. I put my hands over my ears, but it wouldn't stop. I was heading down a driveway out towards the main street. As I looked back at my group, no one noticed me walking away.

I kept walking for a long time. My feet were cold but the voice said to keep going. I stayed on the edge of the driveway as cars and vans passed. No one even gave me a second look. Before I knew it, I was out on the main street, traffic zooming by in both directions.

I stood on the side of the road, and then almost automatically stuck my thumb out. I was not even sure why. I'm not sure how long I had been waiting when a van pulled over; it was filled with a bunch of kids in their twenties who looked like I used to look. They were hippies, with their hair long and unkempt. The smell of marijuana drifting from the inside of the van.

They asked me where I was going, and I said I did not know. I just hopped in like the voice commanded, and sat in the back. They did not stare at me or ask me a lot of questions. They just let me sit back and enjoy the music on the radio. Harry Chapin's "Cats in the Cradle" was playing. I drifted off to my happy place, and hoped the voice would go away.

* * *

I looked over at the truck driver who was looking attentively at the road. He had picked me up on the side of the road hours ago, and we just sat there in silence. He kept fine-tuning the radio to his favorite country stations as he drove. He kept talking to someone on his radio from time to time. He kept mentioning speed traps and where they were located.

The voice in my head was coming and going. I'm sure it was due to missing my medication since I left the hospital. I had never been gone this long since I arrived there. I kept trying to suppress the urge to talk to my invisible friend, because I did not want to spook the driver. It was a nasty night out, and with the temperature so cold, I would not last long outside this truck cab.

I looked down at my haggard-looking clothes . . . I had old dungarees with holes in them, and a tie-dyed long-sleeve shirt, white socks, and black sneakers. I was wearing an old gray woolen coat that was fairly dirty. I felt a little chill when the driver would open the window a few inches to dispose of a finished cigarette. The coolness would go up my shirt and remind me I had no bra on. That was my normal self since I detested wearing a bra just because that was what was expected. I bummed a cigarette off him from time to time to get my nicotine fix.

It seemed like we had been driving for hours, and as we rolled down the highway, I started to drift off to sleep. I fought it for a time, and then I felt the driver's hand shake my shoulder. "Why don't you get some sleep up in the sleeper compartment, and I will wake you up when I stop," he said in a cheery manner. "Then we can get something to eat, once we get further west."

I took his suggestion and climbed back in the cab. It was a pretty cool compartment with a big mattress, with red sheets and comforter. The walls were covered with naked pinup girls, and over in the corner was a shelf with an ash tray and several porn magazines. I did not think much of it, since I was tired, and could barely keep my eyes open. I put my head on the pillow and drifted off to sleep. Not even the voice in my head could keep me awake at this point. All I could feel was the hum of the diesel engine and the faint sound of country western songs coming from the cab.

I'm not sure how long I slept, but I felt the truck slowing, then going through a series of stops, and starts, and turns. I was in a sleepy state, and really wasn't awake yet. I just lay on my side, going in and out of consciousness. I drifted back to sleep since the music was gone now and the truck remained silent. I was having a happy dream of lying on a beach in California and having all my new friends around me. I had met them in San Francisco, and they were just like me, and believed in what I wanted, too. They had a cool apartment in the city like my old place in Boston. It had all the same posters of 60s rock bands, and all the counterculture décor. Everyone in my dream was so happy and satisfied with their lives. All the strife, pain, and society's pressure were gone. The only thing that existed was a coexistence with the world. Everyone fit into their little place, and were satisfied with the simple things in life.

My dream shifted to a third-story deck of a beautiful old house in Haight-Ashbury, a free-thinking section of San Francisco that was the center of free thinking. Many musical groups and counterculture trends originated in this neighborhood. The people here were trying to change the establishment. I was sitting in a chair with a drink in one hand, and a cigarette in the other, taking in the beautiful view of the harbor. I could see the Golden Gate Bridge to my left, and the Bay Bridge to my right. In the background, I could hear a Joan Baez song playing from inside the house. The folk guitar's distinct chords were wafting through the air out onto the deck. Everything was so serene, and so right, I wished the moment could last forever.

Suddenly, I felt a heavy weight on top of me. I felt a hand between my legs making its way to my groin. Was this part of the dream? I was coming to, but still sort of groggy. What was happening to me? My eyes opened to a man's face inches from mine. He was on top of me, talking dirty. My survival instincts kicked in. I realized what he wanted and I was not going to let him do what he planned. Many people in the hospital had snuck into my room at night for the same thing and I had fought them all off.

It was the truck driver. I could smell stale coffee and Fritos on his breath as he struggled with me. He kept trying to pry my legs open, but I fought to keep them closed. I hit him, and pushed against him, but he kept forcing me back down on the mattress. I started to yell at him to stop, but he just put his free hand over my mouth. He kept saying, "I know you want it little girl. Why don't you just relax, and have some fun." He kept keep saying it over and over in a joking kind of way.

I knew I would really have to fight to get out him off of me. There was no way I could simply throw him off. He had much more strength. I looked from side to side while I wrestled with him to look for an escape route. To my left, through a break in the curtain, I saw a reflection from the passenger side window in the front seat. I had to make my way to the front, no matter what it took. I relaxed for just a second to make him think I was submitting. He became less aggressive for a second, and then I sprang into action. I spit in his face and then poked him in the right eye with my long nails. He yelped in pain. I pushed him as hard as I could. This gave me enough space to slide out from under him while he was clutching his eye. He was swearing up a storm. I bolted to the front and opened the cab door. I felt the cold wind hit my face as I dropped to the ground. I missed every step and fell into some icy slush on the pavement.

I got up as fast as I could and started to run. I did not look back, I did not want to see what was coming, if anything. It seemed like I was stuck in a sea of tractor trailers. As soon as I came around one corner, there were several more trucks blocking my exit route. The slush on the ground was getting into my sneakers, and making my feet wet and cold. I assumed most of these trucks were off the road so the drivers could get some sleep. The parking lot was endless. As I made my way toward the noise of trucks moving, and what looked like bright lights, a truck door opened, and a man put his foot out to jump down. We were both startled, and I ran even faster toward the light. As I came around what seemed like an endless line of heavy machinery, there it was. The light blinked on and off, flashing 'All Night Diner.' As I moved towards it, I could see a lot of people inside. It was a sight for sore eyes.

I went to the side door and walked in slowly. The place was packed with truckers of all sizes and shapes. Old ones, young ones, and every-thing in between. I felt a simmering heat being blown out of a heater fan from the back of the room. It felt so good to be warm. I felt safe for the time being. I sat on a barstool and grabbed a menu. A waitress approached, and asked me what I wanted. I asked for a glass of water, and then looked down at the menu. I knew I didn't have any money.

Everything I had to eat on my journey up until this point I had bummed from people who picked me up.

I had no money, I had no home, I had no one who was looking out for me. I was all alone in the middle of nowhere. As I tried to blend into the background to not draw attention I felt the urge to go the bathroom. I wasn't sure how long it had been since my last bathroom break. I made my way to the back of the diner until I saw a sign for a women's room on an old wooden paneled door. I pushed it open and made my way to the nearest stall. It felt good to relieve myself while I planned my next move. I washed my hands and looked up at the mirror. The person I saw was not the person who I had been many years ago. I looked unkempt, with a white complexion and a chopped hairdo that I didn't even recognize. What had become of me?

As I stared in the mirror, I heard a voice drift in the air. I turned to see where it had come from, but no one was there. I looked back at the mirror again, and the voice started to call my name. How long had it been since I left the hospital? How long had it been since I took my last dose of medication? I had lost all track of time. As my mind raced the voice turned into two voices; they sounded very angry. They were telling me things I didn't want to hear. I had to get out of this place to make them stop. I put my hands over my ears, and shook my head, but it made no difference. They were trapped in my mind.

I raced for the door, and almost slammed it into a woman's face who was coming in. She said something to me in a deep southern drawl, but I could not understand it. I made my way back to my stool, and sat there holding the menu up to my face. By that time a few truckers had settled into the stools on my right, and were chattering away about some storm that might be heading across the Midwest. I could not hear exactly what they were saying because there were so many voices talking at once. It all seemed to be blending into one voice.

The voices in my head were coming back loud and clear. I was getting them mixed up with all the background sound, and tried to keep all the voices straight. I started to feel dizzy. I thought it might be the heat or maybe it was due to lack of food. I picked my glass of water up and drank it down as fast as I could. I waved to the waitress to get me another. As I waited it seemed like everywhere I looked people were star-

ing at me. *What were they looking at? I checked myself up and down, and didn't think I looked that out of place. The waitress came back with my water, and then drifted back down the counter to wait on some other guys. I thought I saw her turn and look at me while she was walking in the other direction. The voices in my head were getting louder. I put the menu up to my face, and told them to stop, but they wouldn't. I started to feel panicked. When I put the menu down, more people were looking at me. I had to get away.*

I got up and moved to an empty booth at the end of the restaurant. The dizziness kept getting worse. The voices were getting louder by the minute. I put my hands over my ears and pressed hard, to see if it would make any difference. It didn't. My ears were ringing and my head started to hurt. I saw some people staring at me. Was I standing out that much? I grabbed a menu and put it up to my face like I was reading it. I wished I could escape this place, I thought, but outside was cold and dark, with the wretched smell of diesel fuel wafting through the air.

As I pretended to look over the menu, I saw a waitress standing over me. She looked very put-out. "Honey, are you going to order something, or are you just going to look at this menu all night?" she said in a Midwestern drawl. I tried to think. What would I have done if a cop had asked me questions while we were rummaging for food at Park Street Station in Boston after hours? We always had an answer. "You can get me a cheese burger, some French fries, and a coke," I said in a semi-confident manner. She looked at me sort of funny, snapping her gum as she wrote down my order. She finished writing without saying a word, and then turned on her heels and walked off.

For a few moments I was relieved and happy with myself because I got this woman to get me some food and also to leave me alone. The voices had subsided a little, probably because I was thinking about how I was going to pay for the meal. I did not have a thing except the clothes on my back. I'm sure I was many, many miles from where I was supposed to be, and didn't have a friend or companion in the world right now. I thought about it for a few minutes, and then my hunger took over. I felt very pleased with my resourcefulness. That thought stayed with me until the food was delivered.

The waitress came strutting to the booth with my order and with a mission in mind. She put the plate in front of me, set down the drink, and pointed to the catsup at the end of the table. The she slapped the check upside down across the table, and blurted out, "I can take that for you any time, dear. No rush." She hustled off to wait on a few truckers who had just sat down in her section. As she parted, I began inhaling the food like I hadn't eaten in a week. Once I thought about it, I could not remember the last time I had a meal. It must have been at the hospital. Who knows how many days ago that was? Since then I had been living on drinks and snacks from any person who picked me up along the way.

The food felt good as it slid down my throat. My hunger pains were subsiding with every bite. The burger was great, and I tried to slow down and chew my food to get the maximum taste. But it was so good, I kept gorging my body with the greasy delight. Before I knew it everything was gone. The voices in my head had diminished for some reason. The hustle and bustle of the diner now had my attention, and I noticed truckers coming and going. On the wall I could see the clock said three o'clock. It must have been the middle of the night, because it was still dark out. People were talking and laughing, and everyone was inhaling coffee and smoking cigarettes. A cloud of smoke hung up on the ceiling. The smell of the cigarettes was enticing. I wanted to go over and bum a smoke from someone, but they were all men, except for the help. I was still afraid my attacker was out there or even right here in the diner.

I sat there for a few minutes building up my guts to go over and ask for one. I had done it back at home a million times, but my ego was at an all-time low after everything that had happened to me. I finally got out of the booth, and went over to two old guys wearing University of Nebraska hats and who didn't look intimidating. I stood in front of them and asked for a smoke. I heard my own words, but it did not sound like me. It sounded like a crazy person. One looked up from their conversation, and said "Darling, how are you doing?" in a deep voice. I put my two fingers up to my mouth without saying a word; they got the hint. One of them pulled a pack of Marlboro's out of his pocket, and banged it on his hand to pop out a cigarette. He handed it to me, and then flicked a gold-plated lighter to light me up. I took a drag and exhaled the smoke out. Then I gave them the head-bob thank you, and retreated to my booth.

I sat back down in my booth puffing on my cigarette, feeling very proud of what I had accomplished. As I puffed away the time, I looked down at the table and noticed the check. My heart began to race. Then I flipped the check over and saw the price. Then my heart really began to race. I could not pay this. I had no money, and the waitress already looked like she hated me. I thought about heading for the door, but as I peered out the window I could see a temperature sign in the distance by the gas pumps that read 22 degrees. The people walking outside all moved quickly and looked cold. I knew if I made it outside my only way out of here was to thumb a ride with another trucker. I had a sinking feeling in my stomach just thinking about it.

I just sat there getting more depressed. My mind was a jumble of ridiculous options that would never work. I had not been in the outside world for years. I had no idea what I was doing. The voices came back. "Leave the diner, Anne, leave the diner," they commanded. I put my hand over my ears again and hummed to drown out the sound. The waitress was very busy, but always kept me in view out of the corner of her eye. As the voices got louder, I put my head down into my arms on the table, and starting singing a Dylan song. "Lay Lady Lay." It was one of my favorites. I hummed it softly; it drowned out all the background noise. I was sailing off into another world dreaming about California again. All my old friends in Boston were heading there, and I wanted to be part of it. I thought to myself, if I could only thumb out there, they would take me in and everything would be okay.

I must have drifted off to sleep. I felt a tap on my shoulder. It shocked me out of my happy place. I looked up and saw two huge Indiana state policemen with their big brimmed hats standing over me. They were saying something to me, but their words were silent to me. I was in another place. The voices had come back, and were commanding me to laugh. I could hear laughter in the background, but thought it was coming from somewhere else. The two cops were staring down at me with stern looks. They put their hands under my armpits and gently pulled me up. They walked me out of the diner. I could see everyone was looking at me, but I didn't know what I had done wrong. I did not give them any resistance since they were not harming me. I just went with them like a puppy dog being taken out by its master.

* * * * * * *

My father turned off I-70, hitting the exit ramp at a high rate of speed. The skyline of Indianapolis was right in front of us. We had been driving about sixteen hours, and covered somewhere around a thousand miles. We had taken turns driving to make the journey faster and less dangerous. The city looked like a beautiful place. My father's face looked drawn and strained from many hours on the road and the gravity of the situation.

The city had been a big fur trading stop in the Midwest going back to the 1820s, according to my driver's atlas. In 1847, railroad service reached the city. Mass migration had set in and the population jumped from 8,000 to 169,000 residents. This was also a stop for the Underground Railroad in the early nineteenth century. The city's nickname was 'The Crossroads of America.' It looked a lot like any other big city, with a combination of high rise buildings, a business district, poor neighborhoods, and middle-class neighborhoods. This was all surrounded by a looping interstate highway system.

As we came off the ramp I read off a few street signs to guide us to our motel. My father was very good at making his way around with limited information, and this was with very little sleep also. I saw the familiar orange roof of Howard Johnson's. It was a sight for sore eyes. I was hungry and tired and I knew my father was the same. Fortunately, the weather had cooperated on our cross-country adventure, and the weather report called for clear weather on the way back.

I asked my dad several hundred miles back why he wanted to come way out here to pick up Anne. She had been arrested a few days before at a truck stop outside the city and brought to a mental institution for safe keeping. The state police had checked their all-points bulletins, and missing person's lists, and Anne had come up as being missing from a Massachusetts mental hospital. The hospital in Waltham said the trip back would involve her being escorted by police from one state line to the next. At each state's border her custody would be transferred until she finally made it back to Met State. The state social worker said it could take up to two weeks to complete the trip, so my father said he would go and get her and bring her back to the hospital. He was none too happy about the whole thing, but my sister's well-being, and safety were the overriding factors.

How my sister could have thumbed a thousand miles in cold weather with no food, warm clothes, or medication was beyond comprehension. For some reason she had a knack for getting picked up, even as a teenager when she lived with us or in Boston. How she had gotten this far without being harmed was a minor miracle. She always looked rag-tag and unkempt, but people picked her up and drove her places. She also was very quiet, so she was not much trouble to a lonely commuter or someone on a long trip across country. My father had warned her a hundred times not to do this because it was dangerous, but it did not matter to Anne.

My father put his blinker on and pulled into a parking space in front of the check-in office of the motel. The lot was very full for a Tuesday night, but my father had a reservation, and they said they would hold it. I glanced at my watch and it said nine o'clock. I sat in the car listening to some country western station while my father checked in. I could see him talking to the front counter person for a few minutes and then he returned. He opened my door and handed me the room key. He said to run the bags up to the room on the second level and meet him at the restaurant. I jumped out and popped the trunk, and then I was on my way with the luggage. As I made my way up the stairs I came across a man and woman in an embrace and who were surprised by my appearance. They broke up their kiss and the man fumbled around for the key to open his door. Both of them had a look of guilt on their faces, and the woman had a wedding ring on. As they disappeared into their room, I passed them and walked a few doors down to room 231. I opened the door quickly, flipped on a light, threw the bags on the bed, and turned and left. I went back down the stairs from where I had come.

As I opened the door to the restaurant I noticed a few people at the counter having pie and ice cream, and a few diners scattered around. My eyes scanned over a few booths, and I saw my father with a menu up to his face studying the selections. I approached him and slid into the booth. He glanced over at me, then looked back at the menu again. I grabbed one and looked it over. I was so hungry I was going to go with my standby: a cheeseburger, French fries, and a black and white frappe.

A waitress approached and asked us for our orders. She was about 30 years old, maybe five foot, five inches tall, with blond hair. She was somewhat attractive, except for snapping a piece of gum while she talked. My father ordered two dropped eggs on toast, and a cup of coffee. That was his standby. The only thing she couldn't figure out was the frappe. I finally realized it was called an ice cream soda in this part of the country. She was very nice and polite in a Midwestern sort of way.

As she walked away, my father gave me the overview of how tomorrow's events would shake out. My role would be to keep my sister entertained and calm. I thought to myself, how bad could it be? She was going to be medicated, and it was only a 16-hour journey. After we went over the particulars, the conversation switched to the Boston Bruins and their hopes for a Stanley Cup berth this season.

I looked out the window and over the parking lot to the pool area. It was cold and dark out, and I could see the blue tarp over the pool at the motel. The diving board had been removed to save on the liability insurance for the motel. I had a flashback to my family travelling down the east coast to visit my aunt in Florida. The journey had taken us three days to go 1,800 miles. My sister and I rode in the back seat reading, playing games, or talking to one another. The most important thing on our minds was where we were stopping for the night and did the place have a pool with a diving board? My mother would consult the travel guide to double check our criteria so we would not be disappointed. I remember being in the south, pulling into a motel after a long day on the road, and then seeing the pool as we pulled into the parking lot. My sister and I would jump up and down, urging my father to check in as fast as he could so we could go swimming.

My father did not mind getting checked in fast because he could get rid of us for a few hours, and sit and relax and have a drink in the room. Once we came back and had dinner we were so tired, we would fall asleep right away. I knew there must have been a method to his madness. Those were the days when we were carefree and happy. How times had changed for all of us.

* * *

The next morning we had a quick breakfast and then checked out. Central State Hospital was only a few minutes from where we had spent the night. It wasn't long before we were headed up the main driveway to the administrative building. This place looked depressingly like Met State. The poorly landscaped grounds looked the same, and the buildings looked the same with their red brick veneer and steel case windows with chipped paint.

The hospital had been built in 1848 on ten acres of land. It consisted of multiple buildings with an elaborate tunnel system that connected them all. At the corner of Tibbs Avenue and Vermont Street was a graveyard where the residents who had died here were buried. Most did not have families and those who had families were simply cast off in some cases like yesterday's news.

As we meandered up the driveway I started to feel a little sick. The realization was setting in that we had to get my sister and drive her halfway across the country to another hospital just like this one. As we came to the top of the hill, an old dilapidated sign with an arrow pointed to the main office. My father parked in a nearby parking space, and he said to wait in the car. He said he would go in and handle all the paperwork and find out where they were holding my sister. As he got out and walked away, I noticed he had left the keys in the car. That was good news since I could listen to the radio while I was waiting.

I switched on the key and turned on the radio. It came to life with a cascade of noise and static. I turned the dial to find a local rock 'n' roll station. The AM stations were not strong, but they would have the best selection of songs. As I slowly turned the dial, I finally locked in on a station one playing the Top 40 of 1975. In about a half hour I listened to "Philadelphia Freedom" by Elton John, "Fame" by David Bowie, "One of these Nights" by the Eagles, "Black Water" by the Doobie Brothers, and "Sister Golden Hair" by America. I was humming along when the driver's side door flew open. My father piled in and threw a folder on the seat between us. He let out a long, exasperated exhale. He started the car and we were on our way across campus to the other side of the property.

We pulled up to another depressing red brick building. Even though it was still late winter, most of the windows were cracked open to let out the heat. All I could think of was they could not control the old heating system, and this was the only way to have the temperature remain comfortable until the heat was turned off at the end of the winter.

As I looked over at my father he gave me the head bob to get out and follow him. As we walked up the small walkway to the entrance I could hear the cat calls and pathetic screams coming from inside. It sounded like a combination of a prison and torture chamber all rolled into one depressing home. We walked into the front door where a security guard in a very official blue looking state uniform, with shined black shoes, and a silver badge clipped on his shirt manned the desk.

My father handed him the folder he took from the car. The guard looked it over. He said to wait there, and unlocked another secure door, and disappeared. I looked over at my father's face; he looked like he had aged many more years than the sixty five he really was. I'm sure he thought to himself, How did I get myself in this predicament? I should be retired and in Florida instead of chasing my daughter half way across the country.

I turned back and looked out the front window. The property was in a beautiful spot on the top of the hill, looking out over the city of Indianapolis. It was hard to believe that this whole enterprise was probably one of the most depressing places in the state. It was a collection of broken buildings, broken people, and state employees who didn't really give a crap. The gray hue in the sky, and the prediction of light rain sometime today, only added to my dreary outlook.

Once my father signed a million pieces of paper and got a two-day dose of my sister's medication, we were on our way. When she came down with the guard and social worker, she looked upset but relieved to see some friendly faces. I gave Anne a big hug, and as usual she pushed her body away from mine. It was nothing new, but it always made me feel bad when it happened.

As we started to get in the car my father said "Chris, you sit in the back, right behind Anne." I was ready to argue, since I wanted to be up front and in charge of the radio. Once I thought about it for a few seconds though, I realized dad didn't want Anne to be able to open the back door of the car, jump out, and make a run for it. He knew it was in her nature and did not want to take a chance with her.

The hospital was near the interstate, and we were on the highway headed east at cruising speed in no time. Anne settled in, chain-smoking her way back to Massachusetts. My father and I both smoked, so it did not really bother us. She acted as though we were not even there. Whenever I asked a question to be friendly, she would either answer with one word, or not at all. Anne was so much more distant than I really could remember. I thought it might be a combination of the mental illness, the medication, and being in the institution for so long.

Her face was starting to look old and drawn, as if she were middle-aged rather than only 24 years old. Her golden blond hair was now a chopped institutional haircut and had turned more dirty blond. Her beauty had started to fade over the years; she looked like any homeless person you might see in a big city. Anne's main interest at the moment was fine-tuning the radio to her favorite 60s and 70s sounds. She liked the folk music and ballads by Bob Dylan, Joan Baez, Jefferson Airplane, and a variety of artists from that era. Anne would listen to one song, and then turn the station until she found something that suited her taste. She was not being very gentle with the radio dial, and I could tell it was aggravating my father. He kept it all inside, though, and just gripped the wheel even tighter to get through the ride.

About halfway home we stopped at a turnpike restaurant to gas up the car and get something to eat. On our stop my father and I took turns watching Anne and going to the men's room for the balance of the long journey home. As I waited for my father to come back from the bathroom, I pitched small talk to Anne to break the ice. I started by asking her about music, figuring this was a favorite subject of hers. I asked her about the bands and groups I knew she liked. As usual, she would give me one-word answers or simply a look of disgust. That was so unlike the Anne I grew up with.

I had a cheeseburger, French fries, and a cola. My father got the same, with coffee. My sister ordered everything on the menu until dad intervened and ordered for her. The waitress look perplexed as to why my father was ordering for an adult. After a few seconds though, she got the message that Anne was a little off. When the food finally came, my sister inhaled everything like it was her last meal. I wished I had a stop watch to time this meal.

Once we were back on the road, Anne had a quick cigarette, found a station she liked, and fell asleep with a full stomach. She was content and so were we. She didn't know my father had put her medication in the cola when she wasn't looking. That way there would be no argument in the restaurant. Over the years he had accumulated a few tricks to keep my sister happy and content so she would not unleash her vengeance on my mother. Anne would always target my mother for some petty gripe, and my mother would take it because she was so guilty about how my sister turned out. She took her misfortune personally and considered it a failure on her part. From my point of view my mother and father were perfect parents, and did a great job raising us and making our home a loving one.

After my sister went to sleep I talked to my father for a while to help keep him sharp and awake. I knew we would not be stopping again. He wanted to get back to the hospital as soon as he could without incident. I did my best to stay awake, but the New York Thruway was very boring with not much to see. After hours of passing by endless repetition of farmland I fell asleep and stayed asleep until we made it to Met State.

I woke up when I felt the car stop to take a left into the Met State Hospital grounds. We meandered up the driveway and pulled up in front of Anne's building. I looked at the clock on the dashboard. It was 3:00 a.m. It was the middle of the night, but we had made good time. The radio was now on a talk show on the AM dial that was more to my father's liking.

He reached over to nudge Anne awake without startling her into a frenzy. He gently put his hand on her shoulder and began to wake her up. She instinctively reached for the radio dial and for a cigarette to light up, but my father said we were home and he had to bring her upstairs. She looked out the window. She knew she was at the hospital and not at our home in Winchester. She started to bark some orders at my father, and he flipped off the radio, and forcefully said "You can finish your cigarette here, and then we are going upstairs. There are people up there who are expecting you."

She looked back at him, and I was getting ready for the blast that never came. I was ready to grab her shoulder from the backseat if it got physical. I sat back in my seat and waited for the smoke break to be finished. Then the door flew open and my sister got out before I had a chance to say goodbye. My father got out and ran after her, knowing that security would be all in a lather over the middle-of-the-night check-in.

Once they both vanished from sight, I jumped into the front seat, turned on the talk radio show my father had on, and lit up a cigarette. Then I sank back into the seat. I could feel my body go into a total state of relaxation. It was a good feeling.

WALTHAM, MASS., 1975

I sat at the mahogany conference table looking across at representatives from the Massachusetts Department of Mental Health. There was an administrative person who was dressed to the nines. He had a legal pad in front of him and a look of confidence in his manner. His pile of legal papers had the State of Massachusetts logo all over them. He kept fidgeting in his chair, waiting for the meeting to start.

Next to him was a man who was not very well dressed, and who looked familiar to me. He had long hair and was smoking a cigarette. He took long, methodical drags in, and exhaled the smoke out of his lungs all over the room. I did not mind since I was a smoker at the time. He had an air of being put off that he was even here.

Next to him was a woman in a nice pants suit, with dark hair, but very plain looking. She smiled across the table. She had a nice leather brown briefcase open, and was pulling out legal documents, which I assumed had to do with my sister's commitment with Met State Hospital. She had her eye glasses down on the edge of her nose, and was running a pen over the documents while she was reading.

I sat back in my chair. To my left my father was looking very serious waiting for the meeting to start. He was in deep thought about what he was going to say and was trying to keep his composure. The last few months had been hell, with Anne running away from the hospital, and ending up at our house, or at neighbor's houses, or landing in other states. The supervision at the facility was poor at best, and she was not getting the supervision or care she needed. Every day was a new adventure, none of which turned out well. Fortunately, when my sister ran away to other states the hospital had to coordinate with state and law enforcement sources to get her home safely. When she ended up in our neighborhood, my father was responsible to bring her back to the hospital. He was sick of the upheaval Anne's behavior created in my mother's and father's lives and sick of the worry for Anne's overall safety.

Anne's health and personal hygiene had deteriorated as the months and years had gone on. Her mental state was unpredictable. Whenever I went to see her, I never knew is she would be up or down. Most of the time I left with a feeling of utter hopelessness. Some days she would hug me with a big smile on her face. Other days she would rant and rave. "What are you doing here?" she would lash out in a curse-laden commentary.

Today, my father said it was all going to come to an end. He could not take it anymore. He was 66 years old and had just started his retirement. His dreams for himself and my mother had been on hold for many years. After working his whole life he wanted some assurance that Anne would be safe and taken care of after he was too old to keep up with her.

The well-dressed man began the meeting. "Welcome, Mr. McGilvery. I hope we can answer any question you might have for us. We feel terrible that you are unhappy with how Anne has been progressing here at Met State," he said in a confident manner. "This is John Bryer, and Rosalie Prince, our social worker and state legal counsel, and they will help me answer any questions you have today."

My father looked back at them. "First of all, I am very upset with the way my daughter is being looked after, and you people are going to change her care plan and supervision," he said in a harsh voice. "Her health is getting worse and mentally she has had too many setbacks."

"Mr. McGilvery," the hippie-looking man commented, "We are doing the best we can with what we have to work with. Our facility has been overrun with people in your daughter's circumstance, and many other people with all kinds of issues." He sat back in his chair with a pompous look on his face.

Mrs. Briefcase spoke up. "Mr. McGilvery, we are sorry you are unhappy with the care your daughter is getting, and we feel terrible about it. Anne is a nice girl, and we are trying to balance her needs with the resources we have." She sat there for a second to let the statement sink in. "What would you like to see for your daughter, sir," she asked with a sympathetic tone in her voice.

Dad looked at her with a stern look. "I want Anne moved out of this place to another facility where I can get guarantees she will be looked after in a manner that is satisfactory. Right now that care has not been met in my eyes," he said forcefully. He sat back and stared at the head administrator. "What do you think of that?"

The head man looked at the social worker and then to the woman at the end of the table, and said, "What did you have in mind?"

The woman, who certainly looked and talked like a lawyer, looked at me and dad. "We can arrange that, Mr. McGilvery, but it might not be as convenient to get to if you would like to visit. There is a facility in Westborough that has an excellent reputation, and has all the medical staff and services Anne would need to thrive," she said in a confident way.

I looked at my father and gave him a smile in agreement. "That is exactly what I want," he said. "I think my daughter needs a new start in a facility that can give her what she needs. I think it would be best for all concerned."

The administrative person looked at the other two, and then he murmured," As much as we will miss taking care of Anne, if this is your wish we would be able to transfer her to Westborough, and if you are in agreement, we can make that happen within a few weeks. I can make all the arrangements, and let you know when she has been moved." He sat back in his chair and let the statement drift in the air.

We agreed.

After some handshakes the two men left. The lawyer said she wanted to talk to both of us. I could tell from her demeanor that she was a nice person who really cared about residents and the care they were getting.

She looked at me. "You must be Anne's brother. She speaks of you a lot, and really looks up to you. I'm sure you two must have been close growing up," she said in a serious, but considerate manner.

"Yes, we did grow up together, and we always got along well'" I replied "I was very close with my sister until she got sick and left home. Since then things have never been the same, but I still miss her and want her to be cared for."

"I think you are making a good decision, and one that is in Anne's best interests," she said "While I am a legal counsel for the state, I still represent Anne and I am here on her behalf today. I have a lot of friends who work at Westborough, and I feel she will get good care there. I will have my sources to check in to make sure she is getting what she needs to have a good quality of life. I have many families who are in your position, Mr. McGilvery. We sincerely do our best to match the concerns of each resident's family with the proper facility and care plan."

After some chit-chat the meeting broke up. My father and I left the hospital, which I hoped would be the last time. The attorney had made a good impression on me, and I felt she cared about Anne. I could tell from my father's body language he was pleased with the outcome. Hopefully, this would be a new, better chapter in my sister's life.

WESTBOROUGH, MASS., 1976

✦✦✦✦✦✦

I entered the gray, dark stairwell on my way up to the unit that housed my sister. The door clanged shut with a thud from the weight of the steel. The light strained to come through the stairwell window, what with its wire mesh and cloudy reflection from years of never being cleaned. As I rounded the corner, a family of three—with looks of disbelief on their faces—were coming down the stairs. They obviously had either been to my sister's unit or the adolescent unit on the other side of the building. No matter which side, the outcome was the same, pain and despair.

As I passed through the next steel door at the top of the stairs, I stepped into a long hallway. In the center of the hall there was an elevator bank. I looked both ways, and then walked to my sister's side of the floor to a locked door. There were a few residents meandering about, seemingly with no particular mission in mind. As I approached them, they looked me up and down, and then asked for a cigarette. I told them I did not smoke, and as fast as I said it, they turned their backs and moved on. They were not a threat to leave the grounds, so they could roam around during daytime hours. If they got hungry, they knew when and where to report for food.

As I got further down the hall, I looked to my left, and saw the social workers' office. There was a sign with a few names on it. I assumed that one of these days I would meet Anne's social worker and check to see how Anne was progressing. Anne had been here several months. The commute to see her was longer, so my parents were not able to come as much. They had delegated me to fill the void, and said Anne loved to see me and was always asking about me. I half believed what they said. I wanted to believe that my sister missed me and the great home that we grew up in.

As I approached the steel double doors, I saw a door bell on the left wall. I pushed it twice but didn't hear a ring. I looked through the glass and saw the nursing station was all the way at the end of the floor to the right. I waited about thirty seconds, then pushed it again. A few residents saw me standing at the door and one started to yell to the other end of the floor. A short guy of about fifty with a very gray face started waving his hands in a wild manner.

After a few minutes, I heard the sound of feet and jingling keys approaching. The sound got closer and closer until a woman in her thirties appeared. She looked at me with a bland stare. After she was convinced I wasn't a resident, she pulled a big key out of her chain of keys and shoved it in the door and turned the tumblers. I heard the bolt unlock, and backed away from the door so I wouldn't get hit when she opened it. As the door opened, she said nothing. "I am here to see Anne McGilvery," I said in a weak voice that I wished I could have taken back. The woman turned as if I had said nothing, and began to walk to the other end of the floor. I tagged along to see what I needed to do to visit my sister.

The ward was in full gear; a lot of residents were walking around, ranting and raving, and the staff was going about their daily routine, barely noticing them. As I ventured deeper into the ward, the residents' radar turned on and they realized I was not one of them. They descended on me, like seagulls at the dump. I was not nervous because they looked harmless, but I am sure my blood pressure must have gone up a few points. The residents were mostly older and middle-aged, and all they were after was cigarettes or money. I kept my pace steady and let them follow me to the end of the hallway.

As I neared the nursing station my new friends started peeling off one by one and going back to what they had been doing before, which was probably nothing. As I stepped up to the counter, I saw a few staff members doing paperwork, some other people in a back room, and doctors and nurses coming and going. Most staff members were dressed alike in street clothes, and the only way to tell who was who was their name badge and title. I stood there for what seemed an eternity before someone addressed me. One of the women at the desk looked up from her crossword puzzle. "Can I help you?" she asked in a very monotone voice.

I looked at her. "Yes. I am here to see my sister Anne," I said. "I told her social worker, Bill, that I was coming."

The woman looked down at a clipboard and responded "He is not working today. He is here Monday through Friday. What did you say your name was?" I told the woman my name, and she looked down, and started shaking her head. Then she yelled to the people in the back room, "Did you know anything about Anne's brother coming to take her out?" Everyone at the front desk and in the back looked at us with the same blank stare, and shakes of their heads.

Finally a nice woman in her forties with blond hair and a medium build came up behind us. "What seems to be the problem?" she asked in an authoritative manner.

Before any of the staff could interject I blurted out that I was here to see my sister, and take her out to lunch, and I had come a long way to do so. She could tell I was getting impatient, She reached over and grabbed the chart from the woman behind the desk, who immediately put her head down and continued doodling with her crossword puzzle. The woman with the chart looked it over very carefully, flipping pages, and looking concerned. Then she looked up, and said "Mr. McGilvery, I'm sorry, but your sister's social worker gave no instructions or a pass to take Anne out anywhere. I'm sure it was an oversight on his part. He is usually very attentive to detail."

I shot her a look that showed my displeasure. "If I cannot take her out, can I see her for a few minutes?" I asked. "It has been a while since I have seen Anne, and I would like to see how she is adjusting to her new environment." I tried to look like I was serious, so hopefully I would get somewhere.

The woman looked back. "Of course. I will get Anne, and you can go in an empty room to catch up with her," she said.

As soon as she said it was okay to see Anne, she turned and started walking around the floor looking for Anne. She checked the dayroom. Then the bathroom, then the sitting area at the end of the hallway, and then Anne's bedroom. Soon enough, I saw Anne coming towards me, walking behind the woman. She had a determined look on her face. As she approached, her affect turned to a slight smile with a surprised expression. I walked toward her. "Hi, Anne, how have you been?" I greeted her. She threw her arms around my neck and hugged me in her guarded way. I held her momentarily, and then she pulled away. Her problem with affection had been with her since she was very young. Nothing had changed.

"Hi, Chris, what are you doing here?" Anne asked in a confused way. "Are we going somewhere?"

I looked back at the social worker, then at the staff, then back at Anne. "No, Anne, we will go out another day," I replied. "This is my first time here, and I do not know the area very well." I tried to be as forthright as possible, but firm. Otherwise, she might get upset.

She looked back at me with a concerned look. At the same time, many of the residents started clustering, asking the staff to get them a cigarette. The staff had to hustle to fill all the requests. The residents each had their own separate pack and brand, and the correct brand had to be matched with each resident. They got their cigarettes, and then lined up at a door in the middle of the floor. Anne abruptly turned away from me and stepped up to the counter. The staff person had her correct filtered cigarette ready and handed it to her. She then got in line with the group.

I turned back to the social worker. "Where are they going?" I asked, looking perplexed. She said they were going outside to a special area where they would smoke their cigarettes and get some fresh air. She said this happens several times a day and the residents really look forward to it. She said I could tag along if I liked or I could wait up on the floor for Anne to return. I decided to accompany Anne outside.

I walked over to the line of people, and stood beside Anne. A staff member unlocked the door and the group proceeded down two flights of stairs. There was very little talking; another staff person brought up the rear. The people in line looked determine to get to their destination. We came out to a little patio area in the back of two connecting buildings. It was a dismal place and gave me the creeps. As soon as we got to our destination all the residents lined up to have their cigarettes lit. Then most went to their regular sitting areas, some stood around muttering to themselves. There was no interaction. I just looked around and took it all in. I know all these people had families who had a heartbreaking story about how their child had ended up here.

As I sat next to Anne, I tried to make small talk, but she was focused on her cigarette, giving me one-word answers. One staff member opened a cupboard that was to the side of the patio, and lo and behold he started handing out soft drinks and coffee. This was a real hit, and it made me feel good that the hospital was trying to give the residents a few perks to make this place bearable.

After about twenty minutes, we all went back to the floor. After we got back upstairs, Anne turned to me, thanked me for coming, and asked me to come back again. That made me feel good. She walked down the hall, and disappeared back into her room. I said my goodbyes to the social worker, and then she assigned a staff member to let me out. As I was walked down the hallway I could hear the faint sound of Boz Scaggs on the radio singing "Lowdown." I continued the song in my car as I pulled out of the parking lot.

* * * * * * *

I stood in the shower with the warm water pouring down on me. I had a feeling of foreboding come over me. The last few days on the floor had been turbulent, with many residents acting up and giving the staff a hard time. My mood was off, and I heard voices in my mind here and there. I told the nurse and doctor in my group meeting, but they said I was fine and that they would monitor my condition. I tried the best I could to overcome this feeling, by trying to eat well and get some rest, but my mind was racing with thoughts. Some good, but most were bad and evil.

Just before I came into the ladies room, two patients had gotten into an argument about what to watch on TV. They almost started fighting.

129

The staff took both of them back to their rooms to calm down. Of course, this happened regularly. The reason could be anything from TV, food, cigarettes, turf, a staff member being unreasonable, or just the resident's mood. When this happened, I tried to stay as far away as possible so I didn't get involved.

From the shower, I could hear two residents arguing. Through a slit in the shower curtain, I could see them standing at separate sinks, combing their hair. It sounded like they were having a disagreement about something. With the water running, I couldn't hear what the argument was about. They were gesturing and waving their arms and I could tell it was getting heated.

I went back to doing my hair while the water was still hot. I heard a scream. I pulled the shower curtain aside just slightly, so they would not see me. The bigger girl was pulling the other girl's hair. She was trying to swing her around with it. The smaller girl was getting hurt, and was yelling louder and louder for the bigger girl to stop it. Her screams seemed to be going unanswered.

I got nervous. The more the screaming continued, the louder the voices got. I put my hands over my ears to make the voices stop. I pressed as hard as I could and tried to think of good things to make the noise go away. My hands did not make a difference. One voice was telling me to go help beat up the small girl because she was evil. I tried to ignore the voice, but it was loud and grew harsher with every word. It kept saying, "What are you afraid of? That girl hates you and always has. You need to show her who's boss of this floor."

Just as I reached my breaking point, two orderlies came running in yelling at the girls to break it up. They had on white outfits and looked like medical personal, but I knew they weren't. They were the resident security, and only came when there was a big problem. The men tried to separate the two girls, but they were going at it pretty good. Finally they each grabbed one girl and pulled them in opposite directions. They were yelling out to the hallway for back-up because the girls' robes were falling off, and they wanted some female orderlies to help them.

My legs got weaker as the noise got louder. The voice got louder and louder. I slid down the wall to the shower floor. I put my hands over my ears and started humming to myself to make it stop. I started singing my favorite *Fleetwood Mac* song in my head to drown out the screaming and noise.

I sang and sang. The shower curtain was ripped open, and two female orderlies were standing there. "Anne, you need to get out of the shower and dry off," one said in a very stern manner. I looked up at their faces, and they looked like they were all business. I did not see a hint of a smile or a comforting affect.

I was scared. The voice got louder and louder. "Are you going to let these two dopes give you a hard time? They don't care about you, and when you are not around, they make fun of you." I kept trying to block it out, but the voice wouldn't give up. My body was paralyzed, I Just sat there. I could see both girls talking and giving me orders, but I could not hear what they were saying.

One of them reached in and shut off the shower. My body immediately went cold. Then they both reached in and put one arm under each of mine, and pulled me off the floor. A wave of paranoia came over me and then the voice said "Defend yourself you stupid little girl. You do not have to take that." I lashed out at one of the orderlies and caught her with my fingernail by the side of her eye. The scratch started bleeding immediately, and the woman jerked her hand up to her face. She gave me a look of disgust, but kept her grip under my arm, dragged me out of the shower, and started drying me off. I was really struggling, which made their job a lot harder.

The voice kept demanding that I fight them and not let them tell me what to do or physically direct me. I could hear my voice start to say things to them in an angry fashion, but I could not make any sense of the words. I could tell by the expression on their faces that whatever I was saying was not good. We kept jostling back and forth and they were getting the better of me. Once they finished putting my bathrobe on they walked me out of the ladies room into the hallway. I looked down the hallway, and everyone was looking at me like an alien, even the residents. Their faces and body language said they thought I was evil.

I looked down at my feet, I wasn't walking. I had been lifted off the ground and my slippers were just barely dragging across the checkerboard linoleum floor. The orderlies took a quick right into my room. My roommate was not there, she must have been out in the dayroom. My body came to a rest on my back, lying on my bed. I tried to raise my hand to scratch an itch on my nose, but my arms would not move. The girls had my arms pinned. I pulled with all my might to break free, but it was no use. I was their prisoner. The voice was commanding me to fight for my freedom, but the harder I fought, the weaker I felt.

I gave up and settled down, I focused on all the faces in the room looking at me. What were they looking at? I was not an animal in the zoo, I was a human being, too. I saw them discussing things, but it all seemed like a jumbled up mess of voices. I knew they were talking about me, but the voice was mad and was drowning out what they were saying.

I saw Dr. Patel come into the room, looking right at me. He had a hypodermic needle in his hand. The voice said 'Get out of there!" He was going to hurt me. I started to struggle as hard as I could, but I discovered my wrists were tied to the bedrails. I started to kick my feet, to squirm away. The two orderlies held my feet down. I felt a pinch in my left arm. I looked up at Dr. Patel. He was standing there guiding the needle into my left arm; then pulled it out and backed away. He began talking to the people in the room, but after a few seconds things started to get hazy. The voice began to fade, and my eyes got droopy. A wave of relaxation started to wash over my body. My head melted into my pillow, and then there was nothing.

WESTBOROUGH, MASS., 1981

It was a beautiful fall day. I had promised my sister that I would take her out for something to eat. She was becoming accustomed to being at the hospital and going about her life as best she could. The reports I got from staff and social workers were that Anne would never be able survive in the outside world because of her schizophrenia, but she would be safe and taken care of in a hospital setting. The state of Massachusetts had been getting a lot of pressure over the last ten years to improve living and medical conditions at all state facilities, and little by little conditions were improving. The facilities had been a dumping ground for state employees, but they were now hiring people who genuinely cared about the mentally ill. The programs were better and the day-to-day operations were smoother.

After I got off the elevator onto the second floor, I walked by the social workers' office. As I passed a middle-aged man got up from his desk and walked towards me. "Can I help you?" he asked in an official voice. I was a little taken aback because I had never seen the office door open. Most social workers were in the office from Monday to Friday. Never on weekends, unless there was a special occasion. The man stretched out his hand to shake mine. I extended my hand, and said "I am here to take my sister to lunch," in a half-hearted manner.

"Are you Anne's brother?" he shot back. I nodded my head, and said "Yes."

"My name is Bill, I am one of your sister's social workers," he said. "It is so nice to see you. I know we have talked many times on the phone."

"It is nice to meet you also," I replied. Usually I don't see any social workers here on the weekend."

He pondered the statement for a few seconds. "I had some paperwork to catch up with, and Saturday is quiet around here, and I am more efficient," he said. Then he gave me a quick smile, like I would know what he meant. I nodded my head.

After a few minutes sitting in his office, and going over some particulars of my sister's care and the hospital in general, he unlocked the door to the ward and let me go through. I walked the long corridor down to the end where the staff and orderlies were sitting. I checked in, and advised them that I was authorized to take my sister off the grounds for three hours.

They looked up like they had no idea what I was talking about. It seemed like sometimes they were not on the same page with the nurses, doctors, or social workers who authorized these activities. I stood at the counter while they flipped through charts, went in the back room to confer with coworkers, and then come out saying they did not have an order from the doctor for me to take Anne off hospital grounds. I knew she was looking forward to our field trip, and would be very disappointed if it didn't happen.

I asked the girl who I thought was in charge to call someone to see if the paperwork had been lost or not finished yet. They looked at each other like I was asking them to move heaven and earth. They picked up the phone and made a call. After a few minutes of back and forth, they advised me that someone would come up to try and solve the problem. They suggested I wait in the visitor's room. I thanked them for their help, walked across the hallway into the room across from them, and sat down.

The room was a little brighter than most, with newer furniture and cleaner windows to look out. It was a beautiful view because the hospital was on a hill, and looking to the east you could see for miles.

It was a peaceful setting, and I'm sure the residents felt more at ease being out of the city. As I sat there you could hear the murmur of patients and staff going up and down the hall talking, mumbling, or getting upset about nothing. Some patients would look in to see who I was, and if I would talk to them. I did my best to look out the window and pretend not to be looking.

After several minutes had passed a scruffy guy in his early forties came in. He was dressed in tattered, hand-me-down clothes and had a beard and long brown hair. He was wearing a pair of gray slippers that he shuffled in. He sat in a chair across from me, and I could feel his eyes burning a hole right through me. He made me nervous. He slightly resembled Charles Manson. I did my best to pretend he was not there, when he called out, "Hey man, who are you here to see?"

I looked back at him, and answered "Anne McGilvery. She is my sister." I tried to be as forceful as possible to fend off a question and answer session. He pondered my response for a few seconds and then said, "I know Anne. She's a cool cat." He sat back in his chair very pleased with himself.

I gazed out the window again, hoping for no more questions. I could feel him fidgeting in his chair getting ready for his next question, when an Indian man entered the room and walked over to me. He stuck out his hand. "Mr. McGilvery, so nice to meet you. It's been way too long," he said in broken English. "My name is Dr. Patel. I look after your sister." I jumped right up, shook his hand and said how happy I was to meet him. As I rose, the scruffy guy got up and made his way out of the room.

I told Dr. Patel about the problem with the pass to take my sister out, and he filled me in on my sister's progress and her life at the hospital through his eyes. He reviewed her day-to-day activity and her medications. His most important statement – at least to me – was that Anne was doing better and the new drugs she was taking were helping with the voices in her head. He then said to wait where I was, and he would fill out the pass for my sister.

I sat back down in my chair thinking about what the Doctor had told me. I felt pretty good about how things were going. As I sat there I hoped Charles Manson would not come back. Soon, Dr.

Patel came into the room with my sister. She looked as good as she could be under the circumstances. She gave me a big hug and asked where we were going. She asked the doctor for two cigarettes for the ride. She always wanted one for the way to where we were going and one for the way back. Dr. Patel left the room for what seemed like a minute and came back with two cigarettes. I thanked the doctor for his time, and also for taking care of my sister.

Anne and I made our way out of the building, and got in the car. Anne immediately pushed the lighter in my dash board to light her cigarette. Then she drew in a big drag, and blew out towards the window. She leaned forward to turn on the radio and turned up the volume once she found a song that suited her. Anne sang along; she knew all the words. This amazed me, since she had such poor short-term memory. But she knew all the words to every top forty song. I knew she had a radio in her room, but even I did not know every word to every song on the radio. We made our way down the street to the main drag and drove to a restaurant.

We went to a seafood restaurant that specialized in fried clams. The staff at the hospital said it was good, and from the looks of the crowd, it must have been. Every seat was filled and so was the counter. The waitresses were coming and going and the cooks were yelling for plates of food to be picked up and served. Fortunately, we were the next party in line and we got seated in a reasonable period of time. The hostess handed us a couple of menu's and then said a waitress would be with us in a few moments. I looked over the menu, and then I looked up, and Anne was just staring at the menu, not really knowing what she was looking at. I felt bad for her as I thought back on what a great student she was and how she loved to read books as a child. "Anne, what would you like for lunch?" I asked in a cheery voice. She looked up, exasperated, and told me to read her the menu. I started at the top, but could see the information was not penetrating the gray matter. I then decided to give her a highlight review of the menu. After a few minutes of this, I asked, "Would you like a clam roll with fries and a cola?" She looked back at me with a questionable expression, and nodded her head in agreement.

The waitress came over, asked what we wanted to drink, and immediately sized up Anne as being from the hospital. I'm sure everyone in the area was aware there were mentally ill patients right down the street. The hospital had been there for many years, and many visitors would take their children or siblings out for day trips. She came back with the drinks in a few minutes and took our order. After she left, I heard a slurping sound, and saw my sister sucking the cola up through the straw like she had not had a drink in twenty years. It looked something like a spoof on an advertisement or a *Saturday Night Live* skit. As fast as the drink was gone Anne started belching, and told me her chest hurt. I tried to tell her to drink more slowly, but it was futile. I looked around for the waitress to order more drinks, but she was waiting on other customers.

Anne started laughing, and winking to someone. I didn't think anything about it at first, and then I realized she was looking at the two small children who were seated in the booth behind me. She had always been infatuated with children since she had been sick. It always made me think that she could identify with them better than adults.

I was sitting there waiting for our food while Anne was entertaining the kids in the next booth, when I felt the father of the children get out of the booth abruptly. I could hear him muttering under his breath, but I could not make out what he was saying. I assumed the children were acting up, or had spilled a drink, and he needed some napkins. But suddenly I found him standing over me while glaring at Anne. He was in his late twenties, and was very big and filled out. He was wearing construction clothes with work boots. He was red in the face, and had an angry look in his eyes. A bad feeling came over me that this was not going to end well, so I stood up and asked the man if I could help him. I got up to block his path towards my sister; I came up to about the middle of his chest.

"What the hell is she looking at? She is bothering my kids," he growled. He stood there staring at me, waiting for a response. I could feel the whole restaurant come to a halt. The murmur of the crowd turned into silence. You could hear a pin drop. I knew I could not go one-on-one with this guy, so I had to talk my way out of this. I looked up to him in an official manner. "Sir, this is my sister, and she lives down the street at the mental hospital, and I am taking her out to lunch. She is harmless, and just loves kids," I reassured him.

He stood there thinking, figuring out his next move. I could tell what I told him did not impress him. I looked back at Anne, and she was oblivious as to what was happening. Just as the guy was ready to blast me, the waitress stepped in between us with our food, and said to the guy, "Bobby sit down, and finish your lunch. Kelsey and Stephen want to try the chocolate cake they saw on the counter. I will bring them some, on the house." He must have been a regular. He thought about what she said for a few seconds, and then went back to his seat. The waitress placed the food on the table, I told her "Thank you," and she went to fetch another cola for Anne. I switched seats with my sister so she would not be looking at the kids. As fast as all this happened, the mood in the restaurant went back to normal.

I ate my food as quickly as possible, as did Anne. She normally inhaled her food and drink. She looked like she enjoyed it, and I gave the waitress an extra big tip, since she had probably saved my life. On the way home, I pulled down a dirt road near the hospital; it brought us to a lake that was next to the hospital grounds. I opened Anne's door, and we walked to the edge of the lake and sat on a big rock. We looked over the water as she finished her cigarette. There were a few fishing boats in the middle and people on the other side enjoying the day as well. The water brought us some serenity. I could tell looking at my sister's face that she felt at ease. I wished she could come home with me, and live a normal life, but I knew her life would never be normal.

PART II

WINCHESTER MA. 1982

I was careful going down the stairs to my father's office. The wood was old and creaky, and there were containers of paint and cleaning fluid lined up on a cinder wall shelf. My father had had his office in the basement for as long as I could remember, running his second and third businesses in accounting and tax preparation. His normal routine was to come home from his day job as an accountant, wash up, have dinner with my mother, talk over the day's events, and then retire to the cellar for the rest of the evening. He would get changed into his pajamas about eleven o'clock, and then read a paperback novel until one in the morning.

I had never seen anyone work so hard on such a sustained basis. He seemed to have an unlimited amount of energy. I'm sure it was because he grew up during the Depression and World War II, when most people did not have much, and had to sacrifice for anything of value they achieved.

I remember my mother telling me a story of when my father was 18 years old he had received a scholastic scholarship to Dartmouth College. The scholarship only included tuition, but not room and board. He had saved enough money from his part-time jobs he had worked after school and could make up for the funding he would need to attend the prestigious college.

About the same time my grandfather died a premature death from a heart attack. My grandmother was devastated, suddenly left alone with two children to support. She was a housewife and had not worked for many years. My aunt was just starting high school, and was a great person, but still was just a kid. The social welfare net had yet to be established, so my grandmother had no means to support her family. She decided to open a bakery in town to try and make a living and fulfill a dream of owning her own business. She came to my father for a loan of all the money he had in the bank as collateral for a business loan to rent a storefront and buy the necessary equipment. My father was caught in the middle, knowing this might prevent him from attending Dartmouth but also knowing his family was depending on him. He finally gave in, and gave her the money, since he did not want her to have to depend on others for her existence. My father's dream of going to an Ivy League College would have to wait until another day. His family came before anything.

Things went well in the business for some months after the grand opening, but then business began to fall off. The quality of the product was great, but my grandmother and aunt could not keep up with the demand. They also could not run the business side of the operation well enough to succeed. My father tried to do the books for her at night, but he had his other jobs to attend to, and also had to do his homework every night. Despite their efforts, things began to unravel. Sales continued to drop . . . My father would ask my aunt what was the problem, and she would give a shoulder shrug or a perplexed look of disbelief. The landlord and the bank began to send notices. Things looked grim.

One night my father came home from one of his jobs and found my grandmother passed out on the couch with an empty pint of whiskey laying on the floor beside her. What he had suspected for many months was confirmed. The pressure of losing her husband and the financial pressures of starting a business to provide income for her family were too much to bear. It was such a terrible time, and the responsibility of helping run the household was never so obvious. After high school, he got a job to support my grandmother and aunt and went to college at night.

I got to the bottom of the cellar staircase, turned the corner, and saw my father sitting at his desk doing some work. He had invited me and my family to dinner with the caveat that he had to discuss something important with me. I walked by the hot water heater and furnace, walked over to his desk, and pulled up a chair. As I sat down he turned towards me and I noticed how old and frail he was starting to look. His hands and fingers were crooked, with a slight shake from arthritis, and some other medical issue that I was unaware of. I could tell by the look on his face that this was not going to be a fun conversation.

"Hi, son," he said to me in a defeated voice. "How did you enjoy your mother's cooking? Your mother still makes the best roast beef diner in the neighborhood."

I looked back to him in agreement, since he was right, and I always looked forward to her meals. I was fortunate, since my wife was also a great cook, and had borrowed some of my mother's recipes to duplicate. My father kept tapping a manilla folder on his desk with his finger. It was about an inch thick.

He looked down at the cellar floor, and then back to meet my eyes several times, like he did not know how to start the conversation off. I decided to get the ball rolling. "Dad, what did you want to talk about?" I said in an inquisitive manner. "You said you had something important to discuss with me."

He pondered what I had said for a few seconds, and then said "Son, it has come to my attention from your mother that I am not as sharp as I used to be. She said I are getting a little bit forgetful and missing some things with running the household and taking care of your sister's affairs." He looked down for a minute, somewhat deflated. I let the words linger for a few seconds while he regained his composure. "Your mother and I thought it would be a good idea if you could take over you sister's affairs and be a coguardian with me. That way if anything should ever happen there would be a smooth transition in her care."

He continued to tap the folder, and look for a response from me or some positive body language. I knew he never wanted to burden me with my sister's care or legal matters, but he obviously had no choice since I was the only logical person for the job. He had done such a great job of being there for her, and dealing with everything that came with taking care of a mentally ill child.

I looked back at him. "Dad, that's not a problem. I would be glad to pitch in and look out for Anne's affairs. I know it has been hard for you, and Anne and I are so close that it would not even be a burden to help out," I replied in a positive voice to make him feel good about the whole thing. His eyes went from serious to more of a joyful look. "I knew I could count on you, son," he said. You have always been there for me, and I know your sister would appreciate it." That made me feel good, but as fast as the words had come out of my mouth, my stomach dropped. I had no idea what I was getting myself into. Since I had gotten married, I had visited my sister every few months and on major holidays, but I had none of the responsibility for her care nor legal standing to look after her affairs.

My father flipped open the folder, and started to review all the paperwork and legal matters that would be fall on me as coguardian. The file had many letters from the State of Massachusetts, as well as medical doctors and psychiatrist reports on the status of my Sister's health and any medication changes. There were many letters from social workers on Anne's month-to-month progress, or lack thereof, and group outings or workshops she had been involved in. It took my father about an hour to explain every piece of paper and advise me on my responsibilities.

After he finished, he got up and went over to a big, gray steel filing cabinet. He pulled out a set of keys from his pocket. He fumbled with them for several seconds, due to his arthritic fingers, and finally found the right one. He unlocked the cabinet, pulled open the top drawer, and began flipping though many folders. I knew that this was where he kept all his clients' financial information, and tax preparation material on over 50 family members and friends. He had built up the business over many years, and soon they would have to depend on someone new for their accounting needs.

I looked at my father from the back; he seemed to have grown so old, so fast. I always thought of him as invincible, and always there for me with advice or help in whatever my problem was. How could so much time have gone by so fast? I guess I never looked at him more closely than now. It made me feel for the first time that he would not be around forever. I kept hearing that Jim Croche song "Cats in the Cradle," bouncing around my head.

He grabbed a file from the drawer, sat back down, and put it on his lap. He put his hand on the folder as if he were holding onto it for his life, and did not want to give it up. He looked back at me trying to muster the words of what this folder contained. "You know your sister is adopted, son," he said as he looked for acknowledgment.

I looked back at him and nodded my head. "Yes, I do know that, dad," I said in a perplexed way.

He continued on. "This folder contains all the information about your sister's adoption, and where we adopted her from, along with names of the agency that put us in touch with the people we needed to meet to get your sister." He sat there for a moment thinking out what he was going to say next. "If at any time the State of Massachusetts does not live up to its responsibilities, there is information in here that, if brought to a lawyer, will make them look after Anne for the rest of her life," he finished with a firm voice. "I am not saying you will have any problems, but keep this folder in a safe deposit box, or a very safe place in your house. This information is all original documents and they never could be replaced." He handed the folder to me, and then looked to me for a response.

I looked back at him and responded in as casual a voice as I could muster that I would live up to the responsibilities of looking after my sister as her guardian, and do my best to look after her. That day, I did not fully comprehend what my father meant by his warnings, but someday I would understand the true meaning of his words.

WESTBOROUGH, MASS., 1983

I was cruising down route 290 on my way home from work. It was a beautiful spring day following a long, cold winter in New England. This area of Massachusetts was called the snow belt, and usually saw more snow than you knew what to do with. The last remnants of the white stuff were gone, and hardy flowers were pushing up. I had wrapped up work a little bit early, and decided to visit my sister as a surprise to catch up with her.

I took the ramp, pulled onto I-495, and then accelerated up to sixty miles an hour and cruised. As I climbed the hill towards Route 9, I tried to switch lanes towards the exit. A big tractor-trailer stayed right beside me, so I decelerated quickly and dropped back, and turned into the exit. I cruised over the hill and headed down past many local businesses towards the hospital. In five minutes, I was pulling into the parking lot.

I had a jump in my step on this beautiful day, and took two stairs at a time heading up to the second floor. I waited a few minutes after I rang the bell, and finally the attendant unlocked the door. He look very disinterested; I followed him down the hall to the front desk. As I approached the counter, two administration officials buried their heads to look busy. I stood over both women until one looked up from her crossword puzzle. "Can I help you?" she asked in a tired, uninterested manner. I advised her I was here to visit with my sister Anne. She asked me if she knew I was coming, and I said no. The two of them looked at each other, and then the other woman came out from the desk area, and went down the hall to my sister' s room. The woman behind the counter told me to wait in the small recreation room to the left of the counter. I thanked her, and then walked into the room and sat down.

I sat at an old wooden table that I thought would be good to converse with Anne. I saw several resident meandering around the room like wind-up toys. They came in all shapes and sizes, and seemed to have an unlimited amount of energy. I'm sure the staff was happy about this since they would probably sleep through the night. I looked around at the people a little closer and noticed a few guys sitting on a couch watching the daily soap operas; one commented how the girl on the screen looked like his old girlfriend. The other two guys began to mock him, so he stormed out of the room. The other two were so proud of themselves. They then switched the conversation to the Vietnam War, and how Agent Orange and LSD messed them up. Then they tried to outdo each other on who's mind was more in disrepair. As I sat mesmerized by their little gripe session, a male attendant in a white outfit walked in with my sister.

I stood up to go give her a hug, but before I could get my arms around her she blurted out "Chris, where are we going? I'm hungry." I could tell from her body language she was either in a bad mood or just woke up from one of her many naps during the day. The attendant rolled his eyes.

"Anne, I did not call ahead to tell the social worker I was taking you out. I am just here to visit," I responded gently. I was trying to get her to back down, but she was not having any of it. Even if I wanted to take her out, I needed to give the social worker and legal people a three-day notice, which is part of the limited guardianship agreement. I did not bother explaining this to Anne, since she could not comprehend such things.

"I want to go out. I'm hungry and it's a beautiful day," she spouted. "I want to go out!"

I looked at her and pleaded my case again. Finally the attendant came to my rescue, and explained things to her again, and then directed her toward the chair on the other side of the table. She looked at him, and then back at me, and sat down with a disgusted look on her face. I sat down in my seat, and thanked the man for his help. Then it was just Anne and I looking at each other. I was so nervous that I did not notice anything or anyone else in the room. It was as if we were there by ourselves.

I tried a little small talk. She was used to giving me one-word answers, so I had to rack my brain to come up with many questions to fill in the time. The longer this battle of wills went on the harder it was for me to keep up with things. There was no ebb and flow to the conversation. The more I tried to be congenial, the more aggravated she got.

* * * * * *

I could not understand why my brother was here. I had been feeling awful all day, and the voices had been loud and competing to tell me what to do, and what to think. The more I tried to suppress them, the worse they got. My daily dose of medication had done nothing to lower the volume or chase away the voices. They were noisy and mean and relentless. I had tried to go to sleep and forget about them, but it was no use. When the resident aid woke me up, I felt terrible. I was in no mood to see anyone.

I got up from my nap and washed my face to try and shake the cobwebs out of my head. As I headed down the hallway to the recreation room, the voices grew more severe. I wanted to turn back but the aid said I had to go see my brother. He had come a long way to see me. The hallway seemed endless and the entrance to the rec room was so far off in the distance. When would we get there? By the time I was inside the room, all my friends were looking at me. Why were they looking at me?

I saw my brother seated at a table. Had he been talking to someone? What had they been talking about? Were they talking about me? I had not done anything wrong. The voices said they had been talking about me, and it wasn't good. That made me mad. I had not done anything wrong, and still people were against me. I hugged my brother, but I did not mean it. He must have been part of the conspiracy. If he took me out

I would ask him why he was talking behind my back. That way no one would be around. The aid had my forearm and guided me down into the chair like I was a little kid.

I looked at Chris, he looked back at me with a smile. It looked like an evil smile more than a friendly smile. Was he conspiring with the others to hurt me or take my special activities away? I started to get mad. Why had he come to see me? What did he want? I was going to test him and find out. I decided to ask him if he was going to take me out for a ride and see what he said. That way maybe I could trick him into saying something about him and the resident staff.

"Chris, are we going out today?" I asked calmly. He shook his head and said he had not planned on coming until the last minute, and the social worked could not give me a pass to go off hospital grounds right now. That sounded very suspicious. The staff could take me out of the building, why not my brother? I thought he might be lying. I got mad inside. The voices said he was lying, and I believed them. The noises became louder. I put my hands up to my ears and wished the noises would go away. My brother was always nice to me, and always told me the truth. Why would he come here now and lie to me? The noise was really starting to bother me. As I looked around the room everyone was looking at me.

I looked at my brother. His lips were moving, but I could not hear his voice. What was going on? Were the staff, the residents, and my brother playing a trick on me, or were they trying to hurt me? I felt more and more angry inside. It was me against the whole building at this point. The voices were telling me that people were out to hurt me. I had had enough. I had to respond.

* * * * * * *

The more I tried to ask my sister questions, the more enraged she seemed to get. I kept asking her questions about anything I could think of, including the food at the cafeteria, what she had watched lately on television, and the weather outside. All questions were met with a one-word answer or a put-off voice to repeat the question. This was very unusual for my sister. She was normally excited to see me and never rude. I had not been expecting this, and was starting to run out of energy since I had just come from work.

I sat across the table from her, trying to figure a way to make her feel better. The harder I tried, the worse she got. Her temperament was horrible to the point that I wondered if she had taken her medication. Most of the residents who were in the room at the beginning of the visit had meandered out into the hallway, or were harassing the front desk people for one thing or another. There were no distractions at this point, there was just my sister and me, and I had to make the best of it. I knew it was not that nice living in a mental hospital, and she did not have that much to look forward to on a day-to-day basis. I had to be a little more caring, and try to bring some sunshine into her life.

I started to ask about Bill, her social worker. She stopped me and said "What?" in a disgusted manner. I started to repeat myself, when she blurted out, "Why are you here? Are you working with the others to keep me in here?" Her tone was loud and shrill. Her face became madder and more contorted. It looked like her blood pressure was rising, and she was going to explode. I tried to follow up with what she had been doing in her structured workshop class, and then she started yelling at me.

She was ranting that I was out to get her. She was dropping F-bombs all over the place. I pushed my chair back a little because it looked like she was going to come across the table. I told her to lower her voice because she was disturbing other people around her. That was not true, since we were the only ones in the room. I would resort to anything to change her mood. After about thirty seconds of her screaming at me two orderlies in white outfits came in, and each stood to one side of Anne. One reached down and put his hand on her shoulder, and said "Anne, what's the matter?" in a firm, but comforting voice. My anxiety level was growing with every second. As she looked up at him, her face contorted, and it sounded like she was carrying on a conversation with some invisible person. She looked possessed and her voice was very low, as if she did not want us to know who she was talking to.

I looked up to the orderlies for direction. "It looks like Anne does not feel very well today, Mr. McGilvery," one said in an official voice. "I feel we should take your sister back to her room to get a little rest before dinner." I agreed. I stood up, and went around the table to give Anne a hug before I left. As I approached her she kept seated, and turned her head away, down towards the floor. She continued to talk to this imaginary person.

I thanked the orderlies for helping Anne and left the room. One of the orderlies followed me to unlock the security door. What had started out as a nice goodwill mission had turned into a disaster. As I walked past the front desk I could hear a faint sound of music coming from a portable radio. It was "Do You Really Want to Hurt Me," by Culture Club. The sound bounced around my head for a few seconds and I thought what an appropriate end to a terrible visit.

As I stepped out of the building into the early spring sunshine, I could not appreciate the beauty that God had bestowed on us. I could not get this whole nagging episode out of my head. I opened my car door to step in, and heard a faint scream coming through the barred windows in an adjacent building. The sunshine slipped away into a gray, depressing, hazy darkness.

WESTBOROUGH, MASS., MAY 1985

I pulled up to the front of Anne's building, and looked for a parking space. I spotted a doctor pulling out to go home. I negotiated a quick turn, and pulled into the spot, barely missing the doctor's car as he left. He looked over his shoulder with a menacing look as he pulled away.

It was a glorious day, and I was visiting Anne for her thirty-fifth birthday. I could not believe so much time had gone by since she had first been hospitalized, and it made me think of my own mortality for a moment. I opened the back door and picked up Anne's birthday gift that my wife had so carefully picked out for her. After all these years I had run out of good ideas of what to get a girl on her birthday, especially since she was in a mental hospital. The package contained a beautiful sweat suit from one of the nicer stores at the mall. It was something Anne would love and could surely use. We had already written her name on both the shirt and pants so the outfit would not disappear in the laundry.

I decided to take the elevator up to the second floor. It would be a nice change from taking the stairs and running into who knows who. As I was waiting for the car to arrive, I noticed the regular cast of characters hanging around the lobby, walking here and there, or sitting by themselves, and talking to themselves. Some of the more high-level residents could go outside on the steps and talk or have a cigarette. When you walked in they always asked for a cigarette or a light. I always said I did not have any, since I had quit smoking long ago.

The decorations in the lobby were sparse, very institutional. There were some Commonwealth of Massachusetts logo emblems on the wall, and a few very poor art pieces. A janitor was pushing his broom around trying to look busy. I gave him a friendly smile, but he looked away with a frown. I turned my head to the left, and saw a person peering out through the locked door of the adolescent ward, where the kids who had drug problems or severe mental health conditions were living. A child was looking back through the wire mesh glass; our eyes met for just a second. He looked about thirteen, with dark hair, and a sad look on his face. I looked away quickly and then looked back again. He was still staring at me, but he looked like his mind was a thousand miles away. I tried to imagine for a second what his life must have been like to have ended up here. I'm sure his parents were probably heartbroken. I could sympathize with that, since my parents had been through the mill with my sister. Their life went from being one of joy to one of misery in just a few years.

I heard the thud of the elevator and the door slowly creaked open. I stepped aside for a few patrons to leave, then stepped in and pushed the button for the second floor. No one got in with me and the door slowly shut. The car began to move slowly up to its destination. I stared at the inspection sticker to see the last time this elevator had been checked out for safety. The certificate was smudged, so I could not make out the year. The car was making all sorts of noises and squeaks and I kept thinking to myself, even if a cable breaks and the elevator free falls to the ground, I probably will live. As I obsessed about my fate, the car came to a jerking halt and the door slowly opened. I jumped out and decided I was taking the stairs from now on.

I stepped up to the main door on the ward and rang the bell. I waited for a few minutes, and then rang the bell again. I stood and waited for what seemed like forever, when finally I heard the sound of keys approaching. They kept getting closer and closer, and an aid appeared at the door. The man unlocked the door to let me in.

He gave me a blank stare as the door creaked. I stepped inside the ward and said a warm hello. He gave me a head bob and I stated why I was here. It was obvious that I was here to celebrate Anne's birthday, but I needed to always restate the case. I followed him to the front desk to see where my sister was and to check her out to take her to dinner

I asked the front desk staff to get my sister, and they smiled when they saw I was carrying a present. I tried to be friendly, and told them Anne was thirty-five years old today. They kind of looked at each other and laughed and chatted in their broken English. I signed a few authorizations to take Anne off hospital grounds, and as I finished Dr. Patel approached me from behind. I turned fast to shake his hand and greet him. He brought me up to date on my sister's care and progress, but as always there was more care than progress. Schizophrenia was a tough medical disorder to reverse, if at all. Since my sister had been in state care it could honestly be said her condition had stabilized, but had not improved. The voices came and went, and Anne's judgment was very impaired. Her long-term memory was good when it came to music, but bad when it came to everything else. Dr. Patel was always pleasant and tried to make me feel better. I tried to listen carefully to understand what he was telling me, but sometimes it just sounded like a bunch of jumbled words due to his heavy Indian accent.

As Dr. Patel finished and turned to carry on his duties, my sister came up behind me all excited. "Hi, Chris," she blurted in a bewildered sort of way. I exchanged hugs and kisses, and happy birthdays. Anne looked excited for the big day but behind it all, she probably didn't really realize what her birthday meant. I just assumed that in her mind one day ran into the next and any day in particular really didn't mean much at all. I tried to put on a happy face to make the day feel special.

"Hi, Anne," I said with a smile. "Happy birthday. Do you know how old you are today?" She looked at me and shrugged her shoulders. "You're thirty-five, but you don't look a day over twenty," I chuckled. I looked around to see if anyone laughed, but all I got was deadpan looks. I waited a few seconds for a response from Anne but

none was forthcoming. I asked the front desk person for a few cigarettes for Anne for the ride, and then we got on our way.

I pulled the car out of the parking lot, looking both ways for
traffic. The staff had mentioned that a state worker had been killed in
the same location two weeks ago crossing the street. A car had come
around the blind corner and the driver had not seen him crossing.
The staff was visibly shaken by the experience; it was sad since he
was going to retire in only a few months. As I peered across the street
there was a new sign that said "No Parking Anytime." I thought for
a moment how heartbreaking it must have been for the person's family. My mind jumped back to helping light my sister's cigarette, and
then making our way to the restaurant I had picked for her birthday
celebration.

It was a beautiful day in May. The temperature was around
70 degrees with a slight breeze. I accelerated into traffic, and Anne
turned the radio on and started pushing buttons.

I heard the sound of "St. Elmo's Fire (Man in Motion)," by
John Parr, come up on the radio. She turned the volume up full
blast, rolled down her window, and let the breeze blow through her
hair. She seemed so happy and content. I decided to go up and down
Route 9 for a while since she was she was enjoying it so much. I tried
to engage her in conversation, but she was zoned out to the music
and not interested.

I took her to a nice Irish restaurant only a few miles from the
hospital. It was typical Saturday afternoon with your combination
of single, middle-age men, along with older woman who were out
shopping until they dropped. I held the door for Anne who breezed
in and walked right past the hostess stand and into the restaurant. I
waved for her to come back and stand with me. She came back by my
side and put her hand in mine and sidled up to me to wait. A woman
in her early sixties appeared and asked how many people in our party.
I indicated two. She looked Anne up and down in a nonchalant way,
and was probably thinking that these two people do not go together.
I had gotten that look many times when I took my sister out in public. It did not bother me a bit, and it was part of trying to give Anne
an opportunity to have a little bit of a normal life.

We walked into a side room off the bar area. I noticed a lot of Irish mementos on the walls, which made the atmosphere seem great. Everyone was relaxed and having fun. I slid into a booth and Anne sat across from me. The woman placed the menus in front of us, and then she was gone. I looked at Anne as she struggled to take her coat off and get herself situated. She picked up the menu and brought it up to her face like she knew what it said. I'm sure she was just looking at the pictures. I glanced down at my menu to look it over for something she might want. It was usually the same thing for her, hotdog with French fries, hamburger with French fries, fried clam roll, or grilled cheese and tomato.

"Chris, read the menu to me, so I can make up my mind what I want," Anne asked. She looked determined to pick something nice. I recited the menu to her with things I thought she might want. As I went down the list Anne would shake her head what she thought. I read off ten items, and she didn't like any of them. I started to get nervous, so I started to repeat myself. As I finished up the suggestions a second time, a waitress approached and greeted us. She was young, in her twenties, with long blonde hair, and was chewing bubble gum. I thought to myself, is that how they do it over in Ireland? She welcomed both of us, and took our drink orders. I asked Anne what her final choice was, and she said steak and potatoes. I thought that was a good choice.

After the waitress returned with our soft drinks and took our orders I tried to engage Anne in conversation to pass the time. It was like pulling teeth. I talked about anything that came into my head. I talked about my job, sports, the weather, and how she was doing at the hospital. As usual I got my one-word answers, and no more. I tried to compliment her and the restaurant, and still nothing. Then I asked her if she knew how old she was. She shook her head, took a long sip of soda, swallowed and then let out a big burp. I told my sister to excuse herself, and then she let out a nervous laugh. She looked around at all the people. She came out of the McGilvery mold of being a people watcher.

My sister and I looked at each other as the time passed. Once in a while I would look away and check out what was playing on all the televisions hung around the restaurant. The walls separating the rooms were mostly glass, so you could look around. After several minutes, the waitress came back with Anne's steak and my hamburger. She placed each meal in front of us, and then asked if we wanted anything else. I asked the waitress for another soda for my sister. She acknowledged my order and turned and walked away.

Anne began to eat like she had not eaten in a week. I reminded her to chew her food, and she shook her head in a positive fashion. I started to eat, and it tasted very good. The burger was cooked to perfection. Anne was chewing and gulping soda, and seemed very content for the moment. Without warning she started to fidget around in her seat like she was itchy. I asked her what was the matter? "Nothing," she said loudly. I went back to eating. After a few moments she started with the same thing. I asked if she was all right, and she said, "No!" She blurted out that she had to go the bathroom. In a quiet polite voice I told her she needed to go to the ladies room. She looked back at me. "I can't. I want to go back," she said nervously.

I tried to reason with her that this was her birthday celebration, and she had only eaten half her meal. I had only taken a few bites. She kept shaking her head. I said I needed to pay for the meal first and she said "Okay." I got up and walked over to the hostess and asked her to send our waitress right over. She said she would go get the waitress from the kitchen. When I got back to the table Anne already had her coat on, and was ready to jump up and run out of the restaurant. I was thinking to myself, How am I going to get her back in time to relieve herself? I kept thinking of worst-case scenarios, and none of them were pleasant to think about.

Finally the waitress appeared, and I asked for the check. "Is anything wrong with the food?" she asked nervously, as if we had found glass in our meal. "No," I said. "My sister is not feeling well, and I want to take her outside to get some fresh air." She looked at me with an air of suspicion, and then retrieved the check. I pulled some money out of my pocket so I could settle the bill as soon as she came back. I looked at Anne and she was jumping around in the booth like a little kid. I looked around for a quick moment and many people were looking up from their meals and looking at us. It did not bother me, because I had bigger things to think about.

The waitress returned and handed me the check. I looked at it for a second to get the total and handed her the money with a generous tip. She said "Thank you," in a generic way, and was off to wait on another party. Anne and I breezed out of the restaurant and got in the car. I had to go west on Route 20 and pull a U-turn. I sped up as if I were trying to outrun the police. Anne was saying how sorry she was to ruin the meal. I tried to relieve her stress by saying it was okay. Of course when you need to get some place fast, the traffic is always bad.

I exited onto Route 9 and put the pedal to the floor. The car threw me back in the seat as the over drive in the engine kicked in. Anne was trying to reach the radio dial, and as I accelerated she strained to reach the dial. I let up on the pedal for a minute to let her tune in a station.

Anne was pushing buttons and turning dials like a well-oiled pianist, when she locked in a station. I immediately recognized the song as Bruce Springsteen's "I'm on Fire." I could hear the heavy rock 'n' roll sound of the lead guitar, and pleasant melody of all the background instruments. Anne put it up full blast, and this seemed to calm her for a few minutes. I flew down the road and went through a few borderline yellow/red lights. We finally got to the last intersection and I pulled into the left lane and put on my turn signal. There was a long line of cars ahead of us. I tapped the steering wheel with a nervous beat to the music. I could see my sister moving around in her seat, and I could feel my adrenaline pumping.

Finally, the light turned, and we were on our way. I looked at Anne, she looked tense and determined. I knew she was in pain, but there was nothing I could do for the moment. I pulled into the hospital entrance road, then into the parking lot, and flew out of my seat. I ran around to her side of the car, but she was already running towards the front door. We both ran into the lobby of her building and Anne pushed the elevator button. She was bouncing from one foot to another to stave off that awful feeling. I could hear the elevator creaking from one floor to the next, but it was taking its sweet time getting back to the lobby.

Anne ran for the stairwell. I followed her in quick pursuit, so I could assist her through security. I took two stairs at a time to catch up with her. In just a minute we were on her floor, headed to the locked unit. I quickly rang the buzzer and knocked on the door. As usual, no one came right away. This time I had no patience. I pounded on the door. It was so loud a resident came running out of the family visitation room, and began waving wildly and grunting for recognition. A staff member came scurrying to the door and unlocked it. As the door opened Anne ran by the man and was gone in a second. The attendant gave me a bewildered look, like "What is all the fuss for?"

I did not want to explain the reason for our rush. I followed him back to the main desk so I could sign Anne back in. I filled out the book, and noted the time back in, and then looked down the hallway for Anne. I waited a few minutes but she did not reappear. I asked the front desk people to wish Anne a 'Happy Birthday' for me, and they agreed halfheartedly. I waved to the same attendant that I wanted to leave, and he looked a little put off. I guess I was putting him out to walk all the way back down to the entrance door to let me out. I walked in back of him, so I would not have to come up with any small talk.

As I exited the building, I looked out over the rolling hills, and could see that the bright sunshine was now being obscured by some dark clouds. I thought to myself that Anne's birthday celebration had had a cloud descend over it. It was too bad because she deserved better. As I walked to my car, I had a flashback of Anne's childhood birthday parties when she was so happy. Those days had slipped away to despair and depression.

* * * * * * *

I was restless. It had been a normal day, but I did not feel well all day. My stomach felt upset, and I had a headache for most of the day. I had told the nurses at the pill window that my head hurt, but I'm not sure if one of those many pills I took today was for my head.

I had already woken up several times during the night. The full moon beamed in the window at me. The voices were starting to talk to me. It was a constant battle to deal with them and keep them away. At least I did not have to worry about upsetting my roommate, since I had none at the moment. Cherry had been my roommate for a long time, but she had some stomach problem and left one day and never came back. I wonder where she went? I remember all the times she talked to me. She was very nice and we hardly ever fought. She was a very heavy girl, which maybe was the reason she was jolly. The more I looked up at the window the more I dreamed about what a good person she was. Normally I was surrounded by noise, and upset people. It wore on you after a while. I was never at peace when I was out of my room. There were always threats lurking in the hallway or the dayroom.

The threats came in all shapes and sizes. Big people, small people, skinny people, fat people, white, black, Hispanic, Asian, young, old, it did not matter. Anyone could get in your face for no reason at all. The social workers and floor attendants tried to manage the turmoil, but sometimes it got out of control before they really intervened. Pushing, shoving, and yelling sometimes were the order of the day. Around the time of the full moon was the worst. Everyone came alive with their particular odd behaviors. Yesterday had been exceptionally hostile, with many people yelling at other residents, at the staff, or at themselves. Some people were taken back to their rooms for a time out, or given pills to curb their hostile behavior.

I always tried to avoid any controversy, but sometimes you found yourself in the middle of it. The television or the radio in the recreation room did little to distract people from being crazy. I never knew what was on TV. I just looked at it like a moving picture on the wall. The staff took more pleasure in it, since they could watch their favorite soap opera from the front desk, looking through the hole in the wall.

I was tired. I looked forward to sleeping soundly through the night. After I had slept for a bit, the voices had started. At first it was just one voice, but it seemed so mad. It was a man's voice, and it was deep and demanding. I rolled back and forth in the bed, with my hands over my ears to make it stop. When I put my hands over my ears the sound echoed in my head and made my headache worse. I could not tell if it was physical pain or imagined pain. Either way it was bothering me. I bolted upright and looked around. The room was dark. A dim light was coming in from the main hallway. I turned my body, and laid down face first. I put the pillow over my head. For just a moment, I thought I had muffled the sound. I lay there still, hoping the voice would go silent, but then it rose up again. "Please make it stop," I kept saying. "Make it stop."

The voice commanded me to stand and walk to the window. It was loud and scary. I wanted to go out to the hallway and get an attendant to help me, but the voice ordered me to the window. I walked toward the beaming moon step by step. It was like I was floating, and my feet were just off the ground.

I got closer to the window. My building was up high on a hill and I could see far into the distance. The moon was completely round and white, and seemed like I could reach out and touch it. The voice kept commanding me to get closer and closer. Before I knew it my face was pressed against the glass, and I was looking at the wire mesh in the glass and the steel bars just on the other side of the glass.

"Anne, you need to leave this place. You do not belong here," the man commanded. "These people are polluting your brain with drugs," he bellowed. I put my hands over my ears to stop listening, but that did not block out the voice. "You must leave now, or you will never be able to leave," he commanded loudly.

I got more agitated as he talked to me. I put my hands on the window and tried to scratch the glass. I didn't want to, but he was commanding me. Then I started to bang the glass with my palms and then with my fists. The voice kept cheering me on saying I was doing the right thing. I looked at my hands and there was red blood on my knuckles, but it didn't hurt. I hit the window harder and harder. The voice seemed happy and kept rooting me on. I kept lunging at the window while I fixated on the moon in the distance. I kept pounding on the window, staring at the moon.

I so wanted to leave now. He commanded me to try harder. I know believed it was the right thing to do. I just had to break through and then everything would be okay. I felt like I was making progress, and soon I would be free. Just as I thought I was about to break through the window, I felt a hand on my shoulder. I wasn't sure what it was at first, and then I heard another voice. "Anne, Anne, you need to go back to bed," a man said. The hand turned my shoulder and body toward the voice. It sounded different than the angry voice. This voice sounded soft and pleasant. As I turned around, I saw a young man in a white hospital outfit talking to me. He walked me to my bed. He was very gentle and said I must have had a nightmare. The angry voice was gone. As the man tucked me in, I wanted to show him my hands so he could fix them. I knew they must have been cut from banging the window. When I pulled one hand out from under the covers, I looked at it closely, and there were no cuts or blood. How could that be? I remember hitting the window with all my might, just as the angry voice had commanded.

The nice man came back in a few moments with a blue pill and a glass of water. I took the pill, and he said it was time to go back to sleep. I put my head on my pillow, and looked away from the window. I did not want to see the moon or hear the angry voice. I laid there for a minute or so, and I started to feel sleepy and had a floating feeling. It was a good feeling. I was drifting and there were no voices in my head. I drifted and drifted and then there was nothing.

WORCESTER, MASS., 1987

I was navigating the busy company cafeteria at lunchtime. People were streaming into the food court and seating area since it was high noon. I had brought my lunch, so I only needed a glass of water. I popped 50 cents into a newspaper machine and pulled out a *Boston Examiner* daily edition, and folded it under my arm. On one side of the huge seating area, there was a wall of picture windows overlooking the beautiful company grounds and the city of Worcester and beyond. The sun was beaming in, which made everything more detailed.

I looked around to see if I knew anyone I worked with, hoping there would be nobody. It had been a very busy morning with a lot of work, plenty of meetings, and several issues that needed to be sorted out. I was in the mood to rest my mind for a while and catch up on the latest news. As I meandered to my left I saw an empty table for two in the far corner of the room. I headed over, scanning to make sure no one was headed in competition for the table. I closed in on my chosen. Only ten feet to go. Finally, I was there. I plunked down my lunch and drink, and sat facing away from the crowd so none of my work friends would track me down.

I put the paper down to my left and looked at the front page. It had the latest news on things happening in Boston. This covered murders, fires, robberies, or domestic disputes. The second tier of news was a few national stories, and then politics, which in Massachusetts was a blood sport. The Republican governor was always fighting with the Senate President or the Speaker of the House to get his legislation debated and passed. The president and speaker ruled the legislature with iron fists, and told the governor what he could and could not do.

I continued to scan, and read the articles that interested me. I had grown up around Boston, gone to school in the city, and worked there for many years. So I was still interested in the goings-on there. As I read, it made me think about how the world had changed, and how it was so much more complicated than when I had grown up. My job had been done with paper and pencil for so long, and now we were on the verge of using the computer more to accomplish our daily tasks.

As my eyes went up and down the pages, I slowly ate my lunch. After I finished each article, I looked out the window to see the beautiful greenery and flowers that our company was known for. The company had been at this location for almost a century, and one of the strict bylaws from purchasing the land from a well-known Worcester family was that the company had to keep up the beautiful grounds. The family had donated millions of dollars to the city of Worcester; they were horticulturists out of the mold of Teddy Roosevelt. I couldn't imagine what the landscaping bill was, since the vast grounds spanned over many acres.

When I looked back down I flipped the page over to the Metro section. There staring me in the face was a headline that said 'Governor Purposes Closing State Hospitals.' My stomach dropped as soon as my mind could process what I just read. What was this about? I had always heard rumors of this sort of thing when state budgets got tight, but I never thought it could become a reality. There were so many residents in the state system who had no family or their families were very old. Who would take care of them if these facilities ever closed? I focused my eyes on the fine print and started to read.

The article focused on the hospitals and the excessive maintenance of the multiple buildings at each site. There was also a dwindling mental health population at those facilities, due to stricture laws on residents' rights, the use of halfway houses, and mainstreaming more children into the public school systems. The more I read, the more I could feel my blood pressure and anxiety rise. My stomach started to churn. The governor had offered a very convincing plan to the legislature of why the closures needed to happen.

In prior years when this was threatened, the families of the residents organized and lobbied their state representatives to make sure this wouldn't happen. But with the state budgets being strained for one reason or another, and the price of land going up due to the booming economy and growing high-tech industries, there was pressure to make some changes.

I looked up from the article for a few seconds and took a drink of water to try and calm my nerves. I was normally a very calm person, even in stressful situations, but with this news I kept having flashbacks to that meeting I had with my father many years in which he said the state would have to take care of my sister, no matter what. My mind jumped back decades to when my sister lived at home, when she was getting sick, and the upheaval it caused my parents and our family. Could the state really do something like this? Where would Anne go? What would my responsibility be if they said they could not take care of her anymore? My parents were well into their eighties and were very frail. I had a wife and young family, with no extra money to get my sister set up with all the help and services she would need. My mind was a mishmash of convoluted information and broken thoughts.

I read more. The legislation was called HR 4479, a study review to close Westborough and Worcester State Hospitals. The information was being put together with the government and neighborhood groups and businesses that would be affected by this action. The review period would take several months if not a few years for all public comments to be collected and analyzed. Halfway houses and other options were all on the table. The last sentence of the article said the executive branch would have the final authority to make the decision.

I could not believe what I was reading. How could this possibly happen? My sister was a threat to run away most of the time, and had to be in a locked, supervised facility to get the care she needed and to keep her safe and well. This news story read like mental health was the last thing the state cared about, and money and downsizing state government were the priorities. That was one thing that Massachusetts was famous for, the political and financial winds always steered the ship in the direction that was the most beneficial for the ruling class.

By the time I got through reading the story, my appetite was gone, and my interest to read anything else had passed. I stood up and folded the paper under my arm, and decided to go for a walk to clear my head. My mind was racing and even the fresh air did not make me feel better. My heart was still racing and the responsibility for my sister was coming into full focus. I kept thinking to myself, What did a limited guardianship really mean? I swore that when I got home from work today I was going to read the legal document and digest every word to see what my responsibilities for my sister really were.

I walked by my car, and decided to jump in and listen to the radio to see if there was anything on the news about the story I had just read. I put the keys in the ignition and flipped on the radio. I punched the dial to the main Boston station and listened for what seemed several minutes. The programming went from advertising to weather, to traffic, and then to sports. It was just my luck that when I wanted the news there was none available. A few of my coworkers walked by the car and waved to me, and I gave then a halfhearted wave back. I started pushing buttons feverishly trying to find a Worcester local news report, since the two hospitals proposed to be closed were in the central Massachusetts region. The more I pushed the buttons, the more frustrated I got. I stumbled onto a top forty station, and the volume kicked in by mistake, and "Nothing's Gonna Stop Us Now," by Starship came bellowing through the speakers. I immediately reached to turn it down, and the knob went the other way. The speakers were pulsating with sound. I reached for the radio to turn it back the other way, and noticed a few passers-by looking my way. I finally turned the ignition switch back to the off position and the sound went away.

I sat back in the seat, trying to relax for a minute and regain my composure before my lunch hour was over. I started to think of what the future held, and how my life and my sister's life would intersect more in the future. The thought of my elderly parents not being there to support my efforts with Anne only gave me more reason to be nervous and unsure of myself. I looked out the window up into a big oak tree, and noticed a mother robin feeding her little ones. I hoped I could be as responsible when my time came to step up to the plate.

WORCESTER, MASS., 1989

I dialed up the Anne's social worker at Westborough State Hospital in order to set a time to take my sister out after work or on the weekend. It had been a few weeks since I had seen her, and I knew she always enjoyed my company; I always brought her goodies and a big hug. Work was busy, and the company had put us in these new pods with low walls. The result was that the noise traveled across the office and hit you right in the face. It was not a good atmosphere in which to talk to an agent on the phone or concentrate on evaluating the medical records on a large life insurance case. The new management team was buying into a new philosophy of 'one and done.' This meant handling an insurance file the least amount of times, and putting all the decision makers and technicians in one pod to be able to collaborate.

I hated the process because it meant doing more mundane jobs that had nothing to do with my expertise. I was distracted from all the noise and overhearing other peoples' conversations.

The phone kept ringing on the other end and just before I was going to hang up, a man answered and introduced himself as Bill. It was Anne's social worker. I identified myself and asked how Anne was. Bill was out of breath, and needed a minute to recover before responding to my question. "Anne is fine, Chris," he said in a jovial manner. "She has been participating in her group therapy, and pet therapy sessions, and also attended the sheltered workshop group on a consistent basis. I see progress on some days, and not on others." He spoke with a sincere level of authority and confidence about my sister, and always put a positive spin, even if it was bad news he was giving.

Bill continued down the list of things he wanted to tell me, and events Anne had participated in. He said that she was physically healthy, and her medication was effective at keeping her mood even, and not zonking her out as some medications could. He then went over any supplies, cigarettes, or any other things that Anne might need. He asked how my mother was doing, since he knew my father had passed away a few years before. He had caught a bad cold in the winter, which turned into pneumonia, and his compromised lungs could not handle the infection. He had stopped smoking years before, but the damage to his lungs had already taken hold. He died after two days in the hospital.

My mother was lost without him, since they had been together for so long. I did my best to visit her often, but nothing could fill the void. Fortunately, she was a social person, and eventually started going back to her card games and other social groups. She was still a good driver and was able to stay in her home, which she loved.

Bill finished up his summary of things he wanted to convey to me. I heard a pause in his voice. I thought he might still be out of breath, when he said, "Chris, I have some news to tell you."

My heart dropped since I thought the news was about my sister. "Is something wrong with Anne?" I asked in a concerned voice. "Is she okay, Bill?"

"No. Nothing like that, Chris," he said. "I have some news about myself. The state of Massachusetts has come out and offered an early retirement package, and I fit the criteria to take it." His voice was both happy and sad at the same time. "I was ambivalent at first, but then my wife got her hands around my neck, and said I better take it or else," he chuckled as if he was a comic doing a stand-up routine at a local night club. "The more I thought about it, the more sense it made. I have been with the state for many years, and seen a lot. It is time to move on, and the state is making it worth my while."

There was a pause in the conversation, before he started to speak again. I became concerned again. "Bill, what is it," I asked.

"Oh, there is no problem, Chris. Sarah Jennings is going to be your sister's new social worker, and will be looking after Anne and her affairs," he said. "She is a great person, and you probably have seen her many times walking the hallways, but did not know who she was."

I thought for a minute; the name sounded very familiar. I believe I had seen her many times working in the same office as Bill, and saw her nameplate on the door when I walked by to ring the bell to my sister's medical ward.

"You will love her, Chris," he said in a comforting voice. "She is about my age, very smart, has led and started some of the best programs around the state's mental health facilities, and has been involved with all the political stuff to make sure the residents keep getting the services and programs they need. She is a real dynamo, and will make sure Anne gets everything she needs to stay happy and healthy."

"What about Nancy Bingham, your counterpart in social services," I inquired. "She is very nice also, and you two worked so well together. I remember her organizing all the Christmas parties and dances for the residents for years."

Bill said she was taking the package also and calling it a career. I was disappointed, but tried not to let him hear my feelings on the phone. "The reason I'm calling is to let the floor know I will be coming on Saturday, and taking Anne out to breakfast" I said. "Can you put that in the book, and let them know I will be there around 10:00 a.m.?"

"No problem, Chris," Bill said. "I will make sure I am there also, so we can say our good byes. The next time you come, I might not be here anymore."

"Do you have any plans after you retire?" I asked.

"Oh yes!" he laughed. "My wife has a six-month long list of things I have been putting off around the house, and then we are going to get a condo in the area, and spend a month in Florida this winter. My brother-in-law is down there, and has been hounding us to come down for many years." He chuckled in a quiet way, and then told a couple of crazy stories of his brother-in-law and his golf game. After a few minutes I interrupted and let Bill know I had to get back to work and that I would see him Saturday.

After I got off the phone I pondered the changing of the guard at Westborough, and wondered how many other employees would be taking the early retirement, and if it would affect patient care in any way. I made a mental note to myself to discuss this issue when I saw Bill so nothing would be left to chance. I sat back in my chair pondering what might come next. The state legislature had been complaining about the state budget for many years, and they were finally getting their way. I was concerned about the staffing at the hospital, the security, and level of care for my sister. I did not want Anne and the other residents to be neglected just because the state had financial issues that were mainly caused by patronage and mismanagement.

I briefly wrote down my thoughts on paper, trying to concentrate while being distracted from the overbearing noise and confusion of the new office set-up.

WESTBOROUGH, MASS., 1992

My mother had passed away a month ago, and I was still feeling down. It was not just because of her extended illness and death, but with my father's passing five years before, more responsibility now fell to me. It was up to me to sell my parents' house and personal possessions, sell their cars, and file all the legal papers with an estate attorney. The feeling that I had was one of both utter panic and overwhelming responsibility. My mother had always been able to do most things for herself after my father died, and she had a network of friends to keep her entertained and looked after. I visited her on weekends and we watched our political shows every Wednesday night. She was a transplant from Canada, and loved the way American government ran.

We always talked things over. We gave and received advice from each other that gave me the confidence to go out into the world and get a job and raise my own family. Now, all the decisions and responsibility would be on my shoulders. My mother appreciated me looking after my sister as she grew older. She would always say, "I am so thankful, Chris, that you go see your sister and look after her needs." As she got older she could not take my sister's outbursts and attacks on her. I can't say that I blamed her. I will never know why Anne was so abusive to her. My mother had done everything imaginable to keep Anne at home for as long as she could stand it, and then got Anne the mental health care she needed when the situation deteriorated.

Last week, Nancy, Anne's social worker called me. She was aware of my mother's death, and wanted to do something to present some closure to Anne that her mother and father were not here anymore. She said that Anne asked for them from time to time, especially my father. I was not in agreement since I never knew what would set Anne off, and this was one thing that I felt would do it.

Nancy kept pressing me, and as much as I tried to resist, we ended back at the same beginning. After a while I was too tired to put up a fight and agreed to bring in a picture of my parents the next time I came. I was hoping that she would forget about it, but that did not happen. A week later she called me at work, and locked in a date to come and see Anne with the picture.

The day finally arrived. I had stopped by my parents' house and selected a nice picture of the two of them in their mid-fifties. They were together standing in front of our house on a beautiful spring day. The picture brought back so many good memories of happier times. I had it in a brown envelope for safekeeping. It was a Friday afternoon. I had taken a half-day from work since the social workers worked mainly Monday through Friday.

As I stepped from my car, I reached across the seat and scooped up the envelope. I could feel the picture moving around in it. I held it tight so it would not fall out. It was a beautiful, sunny day, and the view looking across the rolling hills was spectacular. In the distance you could see some expensive neighborhoods being built about a mile away.

I turned from the view and walked toward the door. Two residents were standing in the doorway. I turned sideways to go between them. They were unkempt and had longer hair and beards. They were probably not as bad off as some, and that is why they could roam freely during the day. Just like clockwork one asked "Hey man, do you have a smoke?" in a semiconfident way. I turned my head and looked at him while I was walking past both of them and said, "No. I don't smoke."

As I continued on to the elevator I could hear him muttering to his friend what an A-hole I was. It did not bother me since I had heard crazy things a thousand times over the years.

When I stepped out of the elevator I could hear some screams coming from the adolescent unit. I looked quickly to my left, and noticed two orderlies restraining a young man in his teens who was swearing and yelling at them. They were doing their best to guide him back to his room, and not affect the rest of the residents. I turned away and walked to the social workers' office and knocked on the door. After a few raps I heard a female voice saying "I'll be right there." The door creaked open and Nancy was standing there wiping a piece of egg salad away from the corner of her mouth. In one motion she put down the napkin and stuck out her hand and I shook it.

"Hi," she said as she chewed the remains of what was left in her mouth. "You must be Chris? You are a few minutes early, so why don't you come in and sit, and we can talk about Anne." I stepped into the room and sat in an empty chair that was at a desk right next to hers on the same wall. We exchanged pleasantries and then she mentioned that she had seen my sister this morning and she was in a very good mood. She indicated that this would be a good day to break the bad news to her, and see what her reaction was.

She seemed matter-of-fact about the whole thing. I was paranoid that it was not going to go well, and this would be a bad experience for all concerned. I sat with her for a few minutes while she finished her sandwich. We went over how Anne was doing from a physical and mental standpoint. She was getting older, and some people's conditions changed as time went on. Nancy said age can affect anxiety about surroundings. She summarized the activities Anne had been involved in, and how my sister interacted with instructors and residents. She seemed to have a positive view of my sister, but I did not know what she was measuring it against.

After she finished her sandwich we walked out of her office. She pulled her keys out and we walked down the long corridor to the main desk area. I said hello to the staff, and was greeted by several residents pulling at my arms and asking who I was. I usually was friendly and conversed with them, but today I was on a mission and ignored their requests for questions and answers.

After a few minutes waiting at the front desk, Nancy looked over my shoulder and down the hall and saw Anne walking towards us. I turned just in time to see her face light up when she saw me standing there. The social worker said a cheerful hello, and patted Anne on the back. She tried to play up how lucky she was that I came to see her with my busy schedule. Anne immediately asked if we were going out, and Nancy squashed that idea in its tracks. I was glad because I did not want her in a bad mood before we broke the bad news to her.

Nancy guided the three of us down the hallway to a room I had not been in before. It was a conference room with ten chairs around a table made of dark wood. It was highly polished. The sunlight reflected off it into our eyes as we entered the room. I sat with Anne on one side of the table, and Nancy meandered over to the other side to be directly across from us. I put the envelope on the table in front of us and Anne looked down for a split second, and then back up.

"Well, Anne, you are probably wondering why your brother is here today," Nancy said with an authoritarian tone. "Some things have happened at home with your parents, and Chris wanted to make sure you knew." She looked at my sister and waited for a response. None was forthcoming. Anne just looked at Nancy, and then at me, and back to Nancy, and then looked down. Nancy spoke up again. "Anne, Chris has something to say to you about your mother and father that you need to hear." She tried to sound as empathetic as possible, but it came out very stiff and rehearsed. She looked at me from the other side of the table and gave me the go-ahead.

"Anne," I said in a hoarse voice, clearing my throat, then pulled the picture of my mother and father from the envelope. "The reason I am here today is to let you know that mom and dad have both passed away." I put the picture of them in front of her. She looked at me, then the picture, and started to giggle nervously. I continued and told her that our mother had died recently and our father had died a few years before.

I looked into Anne's eyes for some sort of recognition, but none registered in her face or body language. She just kept looking at Nancy, then the picture, then me, and giggled some more. Nancy jumped in and explained to her what death meant and if she felt sad she could show her emotion and not keep it bottled up. I put my arm around her shoulder in case she was upset, but she was as calm and cold as if she were a stranger and these were not her parents.

I thought to myself, what a waste of time. I sat there trying to encourage a response from Anne, but she was as uncomfortable as we were. Nancy walked her through the whole thing again as if she hadn't heard me. I went from being compassionate to being very frustrated, wondering why I had come at all. Nancy kept asking Anne for a response to her explanation. "Yes, yes, I understand!" she blurted out in a disgusted voice. She then stood up and tried to walk away. I tried to grab her and direct her back, but she flicked off my arm like I was a nuisance. Nancy signaled me to let her go. Anne walked out and then she was gone.

I looked at Nancy and said "So much for the plan" in a sarcastic sort of way. I'm sure she was not happy, but she kept her cool.

"Chris, you never know what your sister is thinking, and what breaks through to her subconscious. It is like someone who is in a coma, you cannot be sure what they hear and don't hear. The mind is a mysterious thing," she said. Then her eyes fixated on me waiting for a response.

I sat there and looked at her, tapping my finger nervously on the table. "Yeah, it went okay," I said to break the awkward silence. "I'm not sure what she heard or comprehended, but it is over for now."

Nancy changed the subject, seeing that I was not happy with the outcome and getting my sister upset. She had had enough upset in her lifetime and did not need more. Nancy switched gears and started talking about my sister's medication and care plan, and some sheltered workshops and dog therapy she was trying to get my sister interested in. I assured her that I would talk to Anne when I had the chance, and try to interest her in joining as many groups as possible and being included. That was the Westborough Hospital way, and they all felt it helped the residents feel part of something so that this place felt like their home.

When she was done we stood up from the table and I walked her back to her office, outside the locked doors. We said our goodbyes. I tucked the envelope under my arm and headed down the stairs to the lobby. I felt so depressed, and inside I felt like I had not accomplished what I had set out to do. As I looked out over the rolling hills in front of me, I could see the sun being shaded out by storm clouds on the horizon. It looked like I had ordered this weather to fit my mood.

* * * * * * *

I rolled over in bed and looked at the window. The sun was beaming in, reflecting off the wall and ceiling. The light magnified all the imperfections in the paint as it filtered through the dirty glass. It was the middle of the day but I was still tired from not sleeping well at night. I could always here the cries of someone in pain, or the staff walking by, making sure everyone was in bed. I laid there with my eyes transfixed on the radio on the other side of the room. It was a small transistor radio with a black leather case. It was tuned to a good station and a great song was on. I listened carefully to the melody, but I could not figure out what song it was or who was singing it. I lay there really still, but still could not figure out the song. I was very tempted to get up and turn the sound up a little, but I was scared. The radio belonged to my roommate, and she was a very moody person. We had had our run-ins over the past few years, and she would get in my face it she caught me fooling with it. I thought about it for a few seconds and decided it was not worth it.

I felt someone one tap me on the back of my shoulder. "Anne, are you awake?" a voice asked from behind. I rolled over and one of the staff was looking at me very seriously. "I have a surprise, Anne. Your brother is here to visit you, and he is waiting out in the hallway." I thought about what she had just said, and wondered, Why is my brother here? The social worker did not say he was coming today "Anne, I will take you into the bathroom so you can freshen up, and then we will go meet him," she said.

I washed my face with cold water to wake up, and the staff person made me brush my teeth. The brushing motion felt good. I also went the bathroom before we went out into the hallway. As I walked the long walk to the front desk, I could see my brother in the distance. He was standing next to my social worker talking about something. He was looking at her attentively, and looked engrossed in what she was saying. He held an envelope under his arm. As we got closer, he turned to greet me. He took a few steps toward me, and put his arms around me and gave me a big hug. It felt good to be in his arms, and it gave me a sense of security that I had not had since I had left home. He always made me feel better, no matter how long it had been since the last visit.

"Hi, Anne," the woman said with a smile on her face. "Your brother came by today to tell you some things that he thought were important." She turned to get Chris's input, but he fumbled to say something, and let the social worker talk. He just nodded his head in agreement. Then the woman turned and guided us all down the hallway in the other direction. As I walked next to Chris he held my hand, which was very odd. He never held my hand, he just hugged me when it was time for him to leave. I let him continue to hold my hand as we turned into a room with a big table in it. The woman went to one side of the table and Chris and I went to the other side. He pulled the chair out for me to sit in.

Once we got seated, I looked around and realized I had been at this hospital for a long time and had never been in this room. It was very nice. It had new furniture and the paint job looked bright and cheery. There were pictures and official-looking certificates on the walls. I did not know what they were, but they looked official. I remember seeing something like that at the police station once.

The woman started talking. "Anne," she said with a stern look on her face, "Chris is here today to show you a picture and give you some news." I saw her lips moving, but did not understand what she meant. I saw her doing more talking, and then Chris took a picture out of the envelope and put it in front of me.

It was a picture of mom and dad. They were standing in front of our house, all dressed up with big smiles on their faces. I looked at the picture intently and then started to smile and laugh nervously because it made me happy. As I looked at it my brother talked but I could not make out what he was saying. I had a flashback to an earlier time when my father was dropping me off at school. There were light tan buildings that were a few floors high and in the distance a beautiful church. It was the second Catholic school I had been in. I'm not sure why he was taking me to this new school, but we had just unloaded the car and he turned towards me to say good bye. Just as he put his arms around me to hug me, I saw a tear in his eye. Why was he sad? He said, "Anne, try and get along with your new teachers and friends, and see if you can make this work. I am counting on you to make it a success."

I tried to ask him what he meant, but he would not let me go. I heard him sobbing, and I let him embrace me for several minutes. I did not really understand what he saying, or why he was crying, but I never felt closer to him in my life. He was a good father and person, but for some reason he wanted me to live away from home.

I looked across the table at the woman. She was talking again, but I could not understand anything she was saying. I turned my head and saw my brother nodding and looking very serious. He kept holding up the picture of my parents in front of me. My head was spinning, and I wanted it all to end, but they both kept at it.

As I stared at the picture more intently, I gazed into my mother's eyes, and it took me back to the yard in the summer time. I was sitting in a sand box with a big, beautiful, green lawn around me. I saw the back of a beautiful white house, with a patio. The lawn had looked like it had been mowed recently, and it felt like I could smell the grass. The sun was in my face, and I could see my mother sitting on the edge of my sandbox, looking at me with a big smile on her face. She looked so happy with a smile from ear to ear.

I had a small pink plastic bucket and shovel. I was in a pink bathing suit with a t-shirt on. I was laughing and filling a bucket with sand. Then I turned over the bucket, and patted it with my hand. My mother would lift off the bucket, and what was left was a little sand mold. I kept doing it over and over, and I poured the sand all around me. It was like I was surrounded by these sand molds.

We were both giggling, and then laughing. We were having so much fun. We did not have a care in the world. I felt so loved.

My mind snapped back to my brother and the woman talking to me. The glowing memories faded away. What were they trying to accomplish here? What was this all about? My parents were always there for me. They would never leave me, but I did not remember the last time they had come to visit. I assumed my father was busy at his job, and my mother was busy with her social activities in her neighborhood, and town. They had so many friends and loved to entertain. Yes, that's it, they were busy at home and had not had time to come and visit. They would be here soon though. I knew they would never leave me.

I looked at Chris and he was still waving that darn picture in front of my face. Then, all of a sudden, his voice came into focus. I could hear words, but they were jumbled. He kept saying that they had gone to see God. What did he mean? I thought to myself, why would they go and see God? Then I saw myself standing in church at Immaculate Conception Parish. I was a little girl, and I was standing in line on Ash Wednesday, and the priest rubbed the ashes on my forehead and said "dust to dust." I remembered my mother had told me you come into this world as dust, and then you leave as dust before your soul goes to heaven. Then it hit me like a ton of bricks. Were they trying to say my parents were gone, that they were dead? My heart skipped a beat, then started to race. A wave of anxiety washed over me.

I kept looking back and forth from the woman to my brother. I was waiting for words of encouragement to say it was all right, or everything would be better. My heart started to beat uncontrollably. My mind swirled. I felt Chris putting his hand on my shoulder. I flung it off. I had to get out of there.

I jumped up and left the room. Then I ran. Everyone was looking at me. I didn't care. I needed to get away. I flew back to my room. It was my safe place where I could be alone and think about what had happened. Were my parents really gone, or was Chris lying to me? My anxiety was so strong with the thought of my parents gone. What would happen to me? Was I all alone in this place? Would my brother still come to see me?

I laid my head down on my pillow. I closed my eyes, and squeezed them as hard as I could. I needed to sleep, and forget about what I had just seen and heard. I could hear the sound of sweet music on the radio. It was Janet Jackson, and she was singing "Miss You Much." I closed my eyes and listened. As I concentrated on the words and rhythm I drifted off to another world.

SPRING 1993

I was lying in bed trying to catch a few more winks of sleep. I could hear the kids out in the living room fooling around, and my wife doing her best to keep them quiet. I was on my side, viewing the clock and the sunshine outside. It was 8:30 and the weather looked beautiful. It was shaping up to be a nice spring day, and I knew I had chores to do and a yard that needed some tender loving care after a harsh New England winter. As I rolled onto my back to look up at the ceiling, I heard the phone ring, and then my wife's footsteps working their way down the hallway.

The door opened. My wife had a concerned look on her face. I had no idea what could be so serious on a Saturday morning. "It's Westborough on the phone. Your sister is in the hospital." She handed me the phone as if it were a hot potato. I took it from her and planted it up to my ear and said "Hello."

A woman on the other end said her name and her title, but I was so anxious to hear about my sister I forgot her introduction immediately. She said my sister had had chest pain during the night, and she was transported to U-Mass Medical Center in Worcester. They were not sure if it was acid reflux, a gallbladder attack, or a significant cardiac condition. She had been admitted during the night and they were still running tests. The woman went on to say Anne was resting comfortably but not being very cooperative with the staff.

The doctors and nurses felt it would be worthwhile to have me come to the hospital to give Anne a little pep talk so she would listen to the hospital staff and do as they suggested.

I listened to the woman drone, but I was already mapping out in my mind what I needed to do to get ready and drive out to the hospital. After I hung up I reviewed the conversation with my wife and she helped me get ready as soon as possible. Before I knew it I was in my car and driving to Worcester. I tuned in my radio to the local sports station and pushed the accelerator down to get up to a nice cruising speed. As I drove the 25 miles to the second biggest city in Massachusetts I pondered what I was going to have to deal with to get my sister to cooperate.

* * * * * * *

The hospital doors opened automatically and I walked into the big lobby. I looked to my left and saw a security guard reading the local paper and drinking his morning coffee. He was dressed in a semi-official uniform and did not carry a firearm, just a black night stick hanging from his belt. He hardly gave me a second look as I flew into the lobby and walked up to the receptionist desk. There was plenty of activity, but not as much as there would be on a weekday. Most of the people looked younger. Even the doctors looked young, and were most likely residents or fellows. They normally were the ones stuck with weekend duty since they were the lowest on the totem pole.

The receptionist looked up as I approached the counter. She was about thirty, blonde hair, blue eyes, and dressed in a nice spring outfit. She put on a big smile, and then she asked me who I was looking for. She obviously had answered this question thousands of times and was very versed in her canned response.

I told her, that my sister was a resident at Westborough State Hospital. She gave me a little look up and down, since this was not a regular occurrence. I added that she had a physical issue during the night and they brought her here. She then brightened up again and punched a few keys of the computer. "Your sister is in room 602 west," she informed me. She then added some directions to get

there, waving her hand behind her and pointing to the closest elevator bank. I listened as intently as possible to try and memorize what
she was saying. I then thanked her and headed off past the counter
and toward the elevators.

There were a few people with me as I rode the car up to the
sixth floor. One was a nurse coming back from the cafeteria. She
was holding a cup of coffee and a bagel. There was an older man
with what looked like his daughter. They both looked upset and were
leaning on each other for support. The fourth person was a maintenance man who had a cleaning cart with him, and was trying to
blend in with the wall of the elevator so he would not have to talk to
anyone. I rode the car up in silence until it came to a stop.

On the floor, there was a maze of commotion going on. The
staff was going in and out of rooms, machines were buzzing, and
people were going about their daily activities to heal the patients they
had in their care. This was a teaching hospital, and a city hospital, so
there was plenty of activity, and a whole array of medical disorders
from broken bones, car accidents, to gunshot wounds, and serious
physical illnesses.

I walked down the long, sterile hallway and saw a nurse's station
on my left. I made the last 20 feet, and then walked up to the staff.
There were three nurses behind the counter writing and reviewing
their notes. Charts were stacked up all over the work area. I cleared
my throat so I could get their attention. After the second throat clear,
one of the women looked up, and said "Can I help you? "in an official voice. I said "Yes," and added "My sister Anne McGilvery is here.
She was admitted last night with chest pain." I finished, and looked
back at the nurse for an answer, and without looking at any paper
work, or checking any computers, she got up and said "Follow me."

She came out from behind the desk headed down the hallway.
I walked very fast to keep up to her because she was on a mission.
As I came up beside her she started talking. "Your sister is stabilized,
and the doctors have been running tests. She has been a little agitated
because she is out of her safe zone, and a little scared. The social
workers at Westborough thought you could talk to her and make her
feel at home here." She turned her head ever so slightly and looked

into my eyes for a response. I nodded my head in agreement and we made our way to Anne's room.

As we approached Anne's room, I could see a big guy dressed up in a white outfit from head to toe. I assumed he was an orderly, but he looked very stern and all business. As we went by him he said hello to the nurse, and cracked a smile, and then as I started to greet him he gave me a sneer. It was obvious he was not a big fan of Anne, and probably had his hands full keeping her under control.

We wheeled by him and into the room. It looked like any other hospital room, with two beds, white linen, a drab green chair in the far corner of the room, and a lot of hospital equipment hanging from the ceiling and mounted on the walls. Instruments were beeping and flashing, and monitors showed lines going across them. It looked like cardiac equipment, but I could not tell one thing from another. I saw my sister in the second bed, lying semiconscience watching Saturday morning cartoons. She was obviously heavily medicated, and in and out of sleep. I assumed it was because she had been giving the staff a hard time. I knew she could be a challenge if she was scared or just simply upset.

The man in the white outfit came in behind us to make sure everything was okay. He tried to engage the nurse in small talk, but she ignored him. Anne looked up at me with a big smile. The nurse saw that and said, "Anne, look who came to see you, your brother." as cheerily as she could muster under the circumstances. I'm sure she was tired from dealing with all kinds of patients, and this was the last thing she needed.

I chimed in. "Hi, Anne, how have you been? I heard you weren't feeling well." She looked back at me and tried to sit up in the bed, but could not move her arms. I saw her wrists were strapped to the bed's safety frame, so she could not move. She gave me a look of disgust as she struggled to sit up. The nurse saw what was going on and grabbed the bed remote control and pushed the button. The bed came to life and soon Anne was sitting straight up and seemed more pleased.

I started in with some small talk and asked Anne how she was feeling, and if she enjoyed her ambulance ride to the hospital. She gave me some one-word answers and asked when she was going home. For a split second I thought she meant going home to Winchester, but then I realized she was talking about the hospital where she lived. That was her real home and where she felt secure. I was just a visitor when I saw my sister, so I could not even grasp that that could be her home. Then again, it was all she had known since she was eighteen.

As the nurse, Anne, and I talked, a man in his early forties walked into the room. He was medium height and build, with short dark hair and a sinister mustache. He was carrying a clipboard, which I assumed was Anne's chart, under his arm. As he approached, he said "How is my favorite patient today," in an official but jovial voice.

The nurse jumped in before I could say anything and advised him that she was doing well and her vital signs were strong and normal. Then she went around the other side of the bed and began to puff up my sister's pillow.

The doctor stuck out his hand to me. "I'm Dr. Wanecoat, and you must be Anne's brother, Chris. She has been asking for you since she got her. I'm glad you could come way out here to see how she is doing," he said in a patient but firm voice.

I stuck out my hand and shook his, and thanked him for looking after my sister and treating her so well. I then inquired about what he thought was wrong with her.

"Well, Chris, your sister was quite a handful when she got here, and that is why she was medicated and restrained as you can see. She kept trying to get out of bed, and take out her IV. We needed to remedy the situation so we could run the proper tests to get to the bottom of her situation. I'm sorry that you had to see her like this," he said apologetically. I told him that I understood, and whatever he needed to do to help Anne was okay with me.

He told me they had run a battery of tests, and they all came back within normal limits. On Monday they would finish up an echocardiogram, and if that came back negative they could discharge her back to Westborough State. I asked why Monday, and he said that the full-time technology team was off for the weekend, and only emergency testing was authorized due to union rules. He then continued that he thought my sister had a bad case of indigestion that triggered an anxiety condition called a panic attack. This condition simulated a chest pain, which feels like a heart attack. He felt she did not have a cardiac condition even though Anne smoked. We had no way to know her family history since she was adopted.

The nurse came around the other side of the bed, and joined us in the middle of the room. She said they would keep Anne comfortable and entertained until Monday. I asked if they would give her something for the nicotine withdrawal, and they both nodded their heads that she was already on a medication for just that thing. That made me feel better, since I knew she would be bugging them for a cigarette break at some point.

As we finished up our conversation I heard a raspy voice call "Chris, come over here and sit down and talk to me. I miss you." I turned around and Anne was smiling at me. The doctor and nurse looked at me and smiled. "That is the biggest smile I have seen on Anne's face since she got here," the doctor said. Then he chuckled, and excused himself from the room.

The nurse and security attendant backed up to the door and stood at attention, conversing quietly. I sauntered over to the bed and sat down. My sister and I began to talk back and forth for a while. I would ask questions and she would answer them. This went on for about a half-hour. After what seemed like an eternity Anne started to drift off to sleep. I imagined that she had not gotten much sleep since she arrived here because she was out of her element. Her eyes closed and did not open for good. I quietly got off the bed, and walked with the nurse back to the nurses' station.

There, the floor nurse filled me in on anything the doctor had not mentioned. I asked a few more questions, and then said my goodbyes and headed off down hall. As I went by other rooms on my way to the elevator, I could hear the faint sound of a song coming from a radio in someone's room. It was Bob Dylan's "Knockin' on Heaven's Door." It had a steady beat to it, but it also gave me an uncomfortable feeling as I departed. I knew Anne would have liked that song if she heard it.

WORCESTER, MASS., OCTOBER 1994

The phone on my desk rang with its familiar tone. I was in the middle of a pile of work. It was an average morning at the company with the normal dull roar of many people doing lots of work, and a few people hanging around shooting the breeze and avoiding work at any cost. I spun my chair around, picked up the receiver in a smooth motion, and said "Hello."

On the other end I heard the voice of a woman. "Hi, Mr. McGilvery. This is Linda Parkman, Anne's social worker from Westborough Hospital. How are you today?" she asked. Her voice was meek and unsure, which raised my level of concern that something had happened to Anne.

"I am doing fine," I replied. "Is Anne doing okay?"

"Yes, yes, Chris, Anne is great, and feeling well," Linda said. "She has been participating in group and all her social activities and getting along well with her fellow residents. The reason I am calling is there have been some big changes in the state mental health group in the past few months. The people on Beacon Hill are really pressing the mental health commissioner to come up with a plan to consolidate resources and facilities." Linda paused for a moment.

My stomach dropped, waiting for the bombshell to come. Anne was doing so well at Westborough that it was too good to be true. The conversation paused for a moment, and I could hear Linda breathing into the receiver on the other end of the line.

"Westborough Hospital is going to be closed in two months, and we have to move all the residents to other facilities around the state," she said quickly. "The people in Boston said we need to save money on the budget due to fiscal realities, and every state agency will have to tighten its belt."

I started to think of intelligent questions to ask her in rapid-fire order, but as I opened my mouth I began to stammer. "Ms. Parkman, where will my sister go? She has been at this facility for so many years it is like her home." I finished with a firm confident voice.

Linda came right back with the options. "Anne will most likely have a choice between a state mental health facility in Taunton and another in Tewksbury. Both of them are similar to Westborough. The only difference is these locations have some criminally insane wards in the hospital. There are also state police barracks at the facilities to help keep the peace," she summarized. Her last statement hung in the air.

I thought to myself, Taunton was a long way from my house, and not on my way home from work. The bigger question was, did these criminals have any access to walk the building or grounds near where the other residents would be? "Ms. Parkman, I can't believe this is happening. This came up so fast, and there don't seem to be many good options," I said as I could hear my voice starting to rise to match my mounting level of concern. I tried to rein myself in, and sound somewhat businesslike, but my heart was racing with anticipation. "Why are those criminals in the same institution that my sister will be in? What have they done, and why aren't they in jail?" I blurted out.

Linda went onto say that they were there for a variety of reasons, none of which were good, of course. State-mandated psychiatric examinations had deemed these people not fit to stand trial for their actions. They were remanded to a mental health facility for the rest of their lives or until they were deemed fit to be tried for their offences. She went on to say that the state police were there for security, and this would make my sister as safe as she was in Westborough.

I told her that I would opt for Anne to go to Tewksbury because it was the closest facility to my house, and I knew the area a lot better than Taunton. She was agreeable to that, and said she would lobby for that location on my behalf. The conversation lasted no longer than twenty minutes, and my sister's fate was sealed. I thought to myself of all the options, and things that could go wrong, but I tried to keep a positive point of view to make sure Anne got the best possible situation and would be treated with respect and dignity. The last thing the social worker said to me as she finished the conversation was that another social worker from the new facility would be in contact to advise where Anne was, and when I could come and visit. She suggested that I stay away until sometime after the transition had taken place.

TEWKSBURY, MASS., DECEMBER 1994

I pulled off my exit on Route 93, and fumbled with the directions the social worker had given me over the phone. I looked up quick as the road took a quick left, and then dumped me off on a well-traveled secondary road. I stepped on the accelerator and brought the car up to 40 miles per hour. The neighborhood was a conglomeration of small restaurants, small- to midsize manufacturing businesses, and suburban homes. It was a nice drive the further I got away from the highway.

As I came around the bend, I noticed a beautiful lake to my right. The water was blue and sparkling. It was a cold winter day, but the lake had not yet frozen over. About another mile down the road I saw corn fields that had been plowed under for the season, and a few abandoned farm stands. To my left I saw the state facility, made up of several buildings up on the hill. I thought to myself, why were state hospitals always on the top of hills? Was it to make the residents and staff feel better or was it for built-tin air conditioning? I pondered the thought for a few seconds until I saw the dilapidated Tewksbury State Hospital sign on my left and the driveway just before it. I jerked the wheel to the left so I would not overshoot my turn.

As I cruised up the main driveway I looked down at my directions and the name of the building my sister had been moved to. The facility's social worker had called me a few weeks earlier and introduced herself and told me to wait a few weeks to come. That worked out great for me because I was busy with work, and Christmas shopping, and tending to family responsibilities. This first visit would be memorable because it was my first time here, and I was also going to give Anne her Christmas presents today. She always loved to get presents, and I hoped this would be a nice, festive atmosphere to have Anne and I bond at her new home.

I pulled up the long driveway, looking at buildings on my right; they had the same dreary look as Westborough State. The architect and the construction company must have been the same, I thought. As I approached the top of the hill I saw a large parking lot. I saw a sand-colored building that stood out from the other red brick buildings. According to my directions from the social worker, this had to be the place. I pulled in and grabbed the Christmas presents out of the back seat.

I veered to the left side of the building, where I saw state police cars and several troopers coming and going. As I entered the front entrance I stepped into a holding area. I looked to my right and saw a glass security window and a woman sitting at a desk with two troopers standing in back of her drinking coffee and talking to each other. I looked straight and noticed a man in his thirties looking through the glass in the steel locked door. Our eyes met for a second. He was gazing at me, like he was looking right through. He had dark hair and a Fu Manchu mustache. He looked glassy-eyed, like he was high, but I knew he could not be since he was under locked supervision. He gave me a kind of smirk and then a weird feeling came over me. I had a flashback to when I read about Charles Manson and his escapades in California. The man was giving me the same look as Charles gave his followers and victims.

I turned my head away quickly to the woman at the registration window. She was waving me over to the glass, and then she spoke through it. "Who are you looking for?" she said with an official tone.

"I am here to see my sister who is in a locked unit on the fourth floor of this building," I responded meekly The woman's voice came to life and she instructed me to go out the way I came in, and walk to the other end of the building and enter there. I did as I was told and left.

As I was heading up to the fourth floor on the elevator, I looked across at two girls talking and giggling and a janitor who was standing next to his cleaning cart looking totally bored. The elevator moved at a snail's pace and I had regretted not taking the stairs. As the door creaked open I jumped out like I thought the elevator cable was going to break. I stood in the fourth floor lobby, and looked to my left and then to my right. I saw another locked door and walked up to the window and looked in. It was like looking backstage of a three ring circus, with people coming and going and nobody knowing where they should be.

I rang the bell on the wall, and as I did I saw a check-in table about six feet inside the door. Many residents who were coming in and out of the main recreation room called back to the nurses' station, which was about 30 more feet down on the left of the long hallway. I could see several nurses and aids sitting there looking at their computers or paperwork. They looked up and waved to the residents and then went back to what they were doing. I rang the bell and knocked on the door, and the more I did it, the more anxious and excited the patients got. They looked at me through the glass and said "Hi," and then turned back to the front desk and yelled.

Finally one of the nurses yelled to someone in a back room. An aid came out walking quickly toward me. He arrived and shooed away the people at the door, and then grabbed the keys from his belt and threw one key into the door. He opened the big steel door; I slid through and stated my business. He was a man about forty years old, maybe six feet tall, with dark hair and a scruffy face stubble. He wore old clothes that made him blend in with the residents. He started to fumble with some papers that had names listed and then looked up and said we do not have your name on the visitor list. I told him that I called the social worker last week, and set up a visit for today and would be taking Anne out to lunch and giving her some Christmas presents. He continued to fumble with the papers and then gave up and said I could visit but not take Anne off the ward. I looked back with a blank stare and a frustrated feeling inside.

He walked into the great room and left me standing there, and then came out thirty seconds later. He then walked down the long corridor and disappeared around the corner. I stood there with my gifts tucked neatly under my arm. After five minutes, the man came back with Anne following right behind him. I waved down the hallway to my sister and she looked excited to see me. I hoped that I could appease her with the presents so hopefully she would not ask why we were not going out anywhere.

"Hi, Anne," I said in a cheery voice. "Are you excited for Christmas?" She looked back and nodded her head. The aid started babbling something to me, but I completely ignored him, and started walking with Anne into the great room. We sat at a big round table and I put the presents on the table. The room was total chaos, and the noise level was horrible. I tried to talk to my sister, but when the resident saw the presents it was like bees to honey. I kept looking at Anne, and then back at the residents coming up to me and asking questions. Finally after a few minutes of struggling to make this visit memorable, a social worker came over and introduced herself.

"Hi, I'm Mrs. Beauregard," she blurted out in a well-meaning hello. "I am Anne's social worker, and it is so nice to meet you. Anne speaks of you often and was very excited to see you today." I extended my hand and shook hers and was tempted to mention the screw-up with the pass to take my sister off hospital grounds for lunch. We all sat down and conversed, and Anne ripped open her presents.

Anne looked so happy when she opened her new suede coat with matching boots. She put them on to fashion them to us. I asked the woman how my sister was getting along. She looked back at me a little apprehensive and then stated "She is having some growing pains, but she will settle in after a few weeks." She looked back at me for understanding. "She is in a room with three other residents, and she is getting used to having more than one roommate. One of the girls for some reason does not like Anne, and we are trying to have them bond with each other."

I asked some questions about the other conditions on the floor in general and the food, and social life, and was satisfied with the overall program. Then she said the commissioner of mental health had mandated that all workers and residents would not be able to smoke on state hospital grounds. I was taken aback. I looked back at her, and asked, "Are you going to take them out to the edge of the grounds to have their cigarette breaks?"

She shook her head. "Oh no. The medical staff is going to issue nicotine patches to all residents who smoke." she responded She sat there waiting for a response, and a million thoughts were going through my head. My sister had only a few things that brought her joy, and one of them was smoking cigarettes. I thought to myself for a moment and then let this pass for another day. This was supposed to be a celebration for my sister's Christmas.

I switched gears with the social worker, to her surprise, and asked her about what activity programs the hospital had for the residents, how many people were on the ward, and I slid in a question about the dangerous felons who resided on the first floor. She categorically promised me that they were not a threat and were under lock and key all the time. We talked about several other issues including Anne's hygiene, food, and medication schedule. As we talked more, Mrs. Beauregard seemed to let her defenses down, and was being very nice and accommodating.

Once Anne finished unwrapping her presents and then left to take them back to her room, we stood up and I followed the social worker back out to the front desk. There were a lot of people going here and there. I stood by the counter as two aids worked on some paperwork, and then Mrs. Beauregard said her goodbyes and stepped into an office that was to the left of the counter. The noise level seemed to be quite loud for some reason and the people generally looked agitated.

As I looked down the hallway I could see Anne coming towards me and she was walking at a good clip. I thought, why was she in such a hurry? She was not going anywhere. Then I noticed another girl dressed in blue surgical scrubs and an old Army jacket; she had short brown hair and a mean look on her face. She was catching up to Anne. When my sister got to me she grabbed my arm and hugged me, and said thank you for the presents, over and over.

Out of the corner of my eye, I could see the girl coming to us, and I prayed she would pass us and go into the day room, or anywhere else. Of course, she was not going to pass us. She stopped right at my sister's side, and tried to wedge her hand in between us to turn Anne around. I spun around to have Anne on the other side of me so I was facing this woman. She had fire in her eyes and then blurted out a string of curses that brought the office staff to attention. I could not make heads or tails of what she was saying, and then Anne started to wave her off, which infuriated her even more.

I smiled at the aides behind the desk and tried to make light of it. They chirped a little at her to go away and leave us alone, but she was like a dog on a bone. She wanted to make her demands heard loud and clear. Mrs. Beauregard came out of her office, and called the girl by name, Crystal. She told her to quiet down and leave Anne alone, or else.

It was as if she had not said a thing. The girl was out of control, and even the other residents were steering clear. Momentarily, two men who looked like security appeared, but in reality they were aids also. They got on each side of this girl, and then turned her around, and headed her off down the hallway to her room. I looked back at Anne's social worker and asked "What was that all about?"

She said Crystal was not happy with the arrangements of four residents to a room. Anne was in the same room as Crystal, and she went on to say that the two of them were still working out some issues. It would be resolved as soon as possible, she promised. I was nervous inside but did not show it. After I said my goodbyes to Anne, and told Mrs. Beauregard we would talk soon, I was on my way. What started out to be a very nice day, finished as a horrible one. I had hoped it didn't ruin it for Anne.

I turned the key in my car and it fired up. The radio was already on an oldies station and Simon and Garfunkel's "Bridge over Troubled Water" came blaring through the speakers. I turned the volume knob down immediately to a more acceptable level. I looked out my windshield, gazing at Anne's building and thought, how appropriate. A troubled feeling was bouncing around in my mind. Little did I know what troubling events would appear. Soon, I would understand why my heart was aflutter and my mind was uneasy.

TEWKSBURY, MASS., APRIL 1995

‹•••••›

I raced up the hospital steps and stepped into the lobby. The security guard was juggling his coffee, daily newspaper, and looking up to check people in and give directions. I stepped up to the old steel desk and stated my business. The last few weeks had been hectic ones for Anne. She was losing weight, not cooperating with staff, and was being very erratic with her behavior, according to the social worker. I had been tied up with responsibilities at work and home, and had not been able to come sooner to see why she was so disruptive. I did not get a warm fuzzy feeling from this facility like I did from her prior residence.

The staff seemed very inattentive, the medical staff very distant and unfriendly, and the social workers seemed to be going through the motions. They acted like they were doing me a favor taking care of my sister. I felt the mandate that had come down from the state house that all state hospitals would be smoke free was very unfair for mentally ill people. They looked at cigarette smoking as a luxury they enjoyed, and it brought some sunshine into their lives. I remembered back to when the social worker told me about this new rule. She said the medical staff would give Anne a nicotine patch and she would be monitored.

From what I had seen, it seemed that mental patients associated going out of the building with drinking soda, having a cup of coffee, and smoking a cigarette. This small but important daily ritual was all but stolen away by some bureaucrat sitting behind a desk, coming up with a great idea without understanding its implication. The residents on the floor had been getting more agitated as the weeks went on, and the association between cigarettes and going outside was too big an obstacle to ignore. The workers were taking all the abuse, and the nurses had to push more pills to get everyone in line. There were stories of dayroom brawls and food fights that had not happened at this facility since the sixties. The situation with four residents to a room only made things worse. Residents could not get away from the confusion to rest their minds and shut off all the noise. Weeks of commotion had worn everyone down.

The security guard looked up and noticed me standing there. He said "Can I help you?' in a voice with very little sincerity. I jumped at the chance to ask him where the health ward was. He pointed to the end of the lobby to another locked door. It was opposite the criminally insane wing. I had a queasy feeling come over me. Were any of those crazy criminals on this ward or was it for only mental health residents, who posed no risk to the public? I pondered the thought as I thanked the guard and walked away.

As I walked the distance to the health wing I noticed another guard who was standing next to a state trooper and who was checking people in and out of this unit. My stomach dropped, knowing I had gotten my answer and it was not the one I had wanted. As I approached, I stated my business and the guard pulled out his clipboard and took my driver's license to check it against his list. My name was there, and he checked it off, and the trooper looked me up and down, just in case I was planning anything.

The guard shoved a set of keys into the big beige steel door, and opened it up. As I walked in, it slammed with its own weight, and I could hear the tumblers being turned the other way. I was looking down a long corridor, with a combination of woman and men in white outfits, just like I had remembered from other state hospitals in the sixties.

As I walked the long corridor, I saw the nurses' station about fifty feet on the left. I walked faster to get there, thinking I would be safe once they saw me. Anxious residents were coming and going in wheel chairs, some other walking around with johnnies on, but naked in the back. Some were talking nonsense, and some were staring at me with a blank stare that looked right through you.

As I approached the counter, a nice young nurse looked up, and said "Can I help you?" in a very nice, concerned voice. I was taken aback for a moment, not expecting such professional behavior. It was clear that this place was not run like the rest of the building. This floor was run like a real hospital, and the staff behavior reflected that. I said I was there to see Anne McGilvery; she grabbed her chart and said she was in room 102. She came out from behind the nurses' station and told me to follow her. I gave her a nod of my head, and we headed off together.

We exchanged a little small talk on our way down the long hallway. As we entered my sister's room, I saw it was huge, painted off-white, with only one bed, one night stand, a food tray, and no television. I saw Anne sleeping, and noticed her arms were restrained. The restraints were dressed up like bandages to not give it as much stigma. The nurse noticed what I was looking at, and said Anne had to be very medicated and restrained because she had been very disruptive and abusive to mental health personnel and residents. She said based on my sister's records it was very unlike Anne, and the psychiatrist felt that adjusting her medication in a hospital setting, and resting Anne would help her get over this little bump in the road.

I, on the other hand, felt this was more than a bump in the road, and was caused directly by her new environment and overcrowding at this facility. Anne was worn down by all the turmoil and confusion and things had to change. I conveyed my concerns to the nurse and she genuinely agreed with what I was saying. I could tell in her voice that she cared about both the physical and mental well-being of the patients, and she saw people on an acute basis versus a chronic basis. She assured me that Anne was on the road to recovery, and would be fine and be integrated with her friends on her old floor. The social workers upstairs had initiated some new programs to deal with just the issues I had raised. Once I talked to her for a while, and looked at how peaceful my sister was, I started buying in to what she was say-ing. I could tell she really cared and I think she saw the same in me.

I sat down in a chair next to the bed. We finished our conver-sation, and she intimated that Anne would be asleep for quite some time. I told her I just wanted to sit there and look at Anne for a while, and I would stop by the front desk on my way out to say goodbye. She got the message and whisked out of the room to attend to other duties.

My sister looked so peaceful. If I closed my eyes I would never believe she was in a mental hospital, and she had been in one for decades. How unfair was this to live a life with so little happiness? Anne had missed so much, but never in her own mind really know-ing what she had missed. One day was just like the next. People here were like robots or wind-up toys, walking around with no destina-tion in mind.

LAWRENCE, MASS., FALL 1996

◆◆◆◆◆◆

The old state van came to a stop abruptly in a parking lot. I looked out the window and saw an old brick building with many people going up the steps and going inside. I looked at the driver, who was listening to the radio and not paying much attention to me. My mind was a swirl of voices and a headache., I had an upset stomach from the van going over so many potholes. The van must have had bad suspension and the driver hit every hole on the way here.

I was still half asleep when the van door flew open and a lady who looked familiar to me said "Come on, Anne, we need to get out and go to a meeting we have inside." She sounded very official. She had a brown briefcase and had new clothes on. Her clothes stood out because no one at the hospital ever dressed up.

She reached in and took my hand and helped me step out onto the pavement. People of all shapes and sizes were going here and there, and just watching them got me very mixed up. The nice woman helped me to the front stairs, and kept telling me to stay with her at all times. Little did she know I certainly planned to stay with her because I was scared. I was not off the hospital grounds that much, and when I did go out the voices said people were out to get me. Today was an especially bad day. I did not sleep well last night. I took my last medication right before we left, and it had done nothing to make me feel better.

When we got to the top of the stairs we had to go through security. There were two guys there checking people on a clipboard, and making them open their things and show them. I immediately got nervous and thought they might bust me if I had some pot. I put my hands in my coat, and then my pockets, but I had nothing. I felt a brief sigh of relief, but as we got closer my anxiety began to soar. The voices got louder. They were telling me the two men were evil and they were out to get me. I gripped the woman I was with tightly under her arm and stayed close. She did not seem to be nervous or concerned at all.

I wondered if she was with them and if she was bringing me to them. I looked around to see if I broke loose if I would have an exit to safely. As I scanned the lobby, it looked like everyone was looking at me. Were all these people in on this? What had I done wrong? I stayed close and readied myself for a break. As we approached the men the woman with me called these two guys by name, and started asking them how they were doing. She opened her briefcase, and they looked down for a split second and then waved her through. I was safe. We had made it, and were climbing another set of gray marble stairs to the top.

As we rounded the top, there was even more commotion, with people dressed in suits and girls in their Sunday best, and they were talking to people with them and giving them instructions of what to do and what not to do. It seemed like such a blur and the noise level was so bad I put my hands over my ears and kept walking. The nice lady with me was saying something to me, but I could not hear her. All of a sudden a woman approached and was getting closer. I clutched my companion and used her for a shield. She came right up to us, and said hello to the woman I was with. They seemed to know each other.

"Anne, this is Attorney Prince. She is going to help us with today's proceedings. She is going to represent you to the judge in your annual meeting with the court," the nice woman said in a very official manner. The new woman was older; she smiled and introduced herself. I was immediately suspicious because why did I need a lawyer to represent me? I had not done anything wrong.

Then I saw my brother walking towards us. I was so happy, I broke away from the woman and walked toward Chris. He had a big smile on his face, and when we met I said "Hi, Chris," and he wrapped his arms around me and gave me a big hug. He said "Hi," to me, and asked me how I was, and then we walked back to the two woman. Now I felt safe because I knew Chris would protect me.

The three of them exchanged hellos and discussed some things that I didn't really understand, and then we made our way inside and all of us sat down in a very hard, uncomfortable wooden bench.

As we sat there I clutched my brother's arm and kept looking at him. He was still in his teens, but looked a little older. I knew he could be because I was a teenager also. He seemed so confident and in charge and was making some small talk to pass the time. All of a sudden, an older man in black robes came from the front of the room and sat up on a stage behind a big desk and started rapping a big wooden hammer. Everyone stopped what they were doing and came to attention. Once he was seated, people in the front of the room were standing and talking to the man in very official language. He would ask some questions, and then the people would walk up the center isle and leave though the big wooden doors. This seemed to go on over and over, and eventually Chris and the other two woman stood up and we marched up to the front row, and sat at another desk.

The lady who was dressed up went up and handed the man a folder and said a few words and came back and sat down with us. I was getting nervous. What had I done wrong to end up here? I had a flashback to many years ago at a subway station in Boston. My friends and I would go underground and steal all the fruit and vegetables the vendors had thrown out at the end of the day. We ate the food when we had no money and we didn't feel like panhandling to eat. Sometimes the police would chase us away, and we would run to the other end of the station and up the stairs into the Common. That was so long ago, I'm sure it could not be related.

A man at a desk in front of the man in the black robes stood up and read out, "This is a court-ordered wellness check for the Commonwealth of Massachusetts for Anne McGilvery, Middlesex docket number M18726 583, motion to extend treatment." As soon as he had finished I heard a woman's voice from across the aisle at another desk. She was talking to the judge about my treatment. They asked about my living situation, the substance of the monitor's meeting, the review of the court-ordered treatment, types of dosages and medication names, whether the incapacitated person remains incapable of making medical decisions, and details of the associated staff.

I got scared again. Were they trying to throw me in jail? Why was I here? What had I done wrong? My head started to hurt and I was becoming paranoid. I did not want to go to jail. I liked my home where I just came from. I did not want them to take me away. Then both the woman on my side of the row, and the woman on the other side walked up and stood in front of the old man, and it seemed like they were whispering. Why were they doing that? I wanted to hear if they were talking about me. The voices said they were out to get me, but when I looked at my brother, he was smiling and rubbing my arm and making me feel safe. I'm sure everything was okay, but I was not sure.

Then the women returned to their seats and started talking to the woman right next to me. They whispered also and seemed to be in agreement. The man in the black robe started talking to me, but the other woman kept answering the questions. This went on for a few minutes, and then he said something about renewing the state-mandated hospitalization and treatment plan and then he picked up his wooden hammer and banged it again on the desk. As soon as that happened, Chris started to get up, and I attached myself to him so someone else could not take me away.

We all walked out in one big group, and made our way down the long marble stairs, and past the two policeman near the front door. The two women with us were talking, and I could not hear anything, but it looked serious because they were not smiling. Chris kept asking me how I was and what I was up to. I gave him a few one-word answers because I could not remember what I had done lately. Every day was the same, and I tried to remember, but my mind was all mixed up. I couldn't remember any details. I just kept smiling and clutching my brother's arm as we stepped through the doors and walked to the bottom of another set of stairs outside.

I saw the white van parked in front, and the sliding door was open. I thought we all must be going for a ride. Maybe Chris was going to take me somewhere and get some food. I got excited and happy. As we got closer to the van, my brother took his arm from under mine and turned and *kissed me goodbye. The other woman took my arm and directed me into the van and sat me in my seat and latched the seatbelt. Was I a prisoner? Were they taking me to jail? I was afraid, I didn't know what had happened. Chris was talking to the well-dressed woman and looking back at me. What had I done? Where was I going? I started to get out and the driver reached back and put his hand on my knee and said, "Anne, just sit and relax and we will be back at the hospital in a few minutes." As the sliding door began to close I yelled as loud as I could for my brother. He turned instantly and looked at me and waved. Then he started for me.*

I yelled to him that I was scared and wanted to go with him. He looked perplexed and stepped up to the van and patted my arm and said, "Anne, you need to go with these nice people back to your home. They will take care of you."

I blurted out, "I don't want to go with them. I want to go with you." I was feeling upset but everyone around me was acting like everything was all right. I didn't know what they were going to do to me. Before the voice came back my brother stretched over and gave me a kiss on the cheek and said, "Anne, if you're good for the staff and do what they say, I will come and take you out to lunch and we will go for an extralong ride and listen to the radio." I was all ready to run, but my brother's smiling face and calm words made me feel safe. I believed what he said. "Okay," I said, meekly, and then the door closed and the woman jumped in the front seat and started talking to the driver.

As we pulled away into traffic the woman reached over and started punching the radio stations, and I heard a Joan Baez song being introduced. It was "Love is Just a Four-letter Word." I remembered it from many years ago, and I started humming it and smiling. The driver and the woman in the front turned and looked at me, and cracked up laughing, and they starting singing with me. They knew the song too! I was having fun, but I wanted to get back to my home. The world was too scary for me.

ACTON, MA. FALL 1996

I had just finished loading the last of the dinner dishes in the dishwasher. I closed the door and turned it on. It always started out softly, and ended softly, but in the middle the jets of water and the mechanism that made it work was as loud as a plane going right over the house.

The kids were in their rooms doing homework, and my wife was at a PTA meeting at my daughter's school. She made sure to keep informed about the latest and greatest things related to our kids' education. She would not be home for a few hours.

I made my way to the couch, and grabbed the newspaper from the end table. I looked over the front page. It had its usual assortment of murders, fires, and political corruption, and then I saw a story that caught my eye. It was the never-ending controversy about the state trying to shut down the mental hospitals, and the citizens' groups trying to keep them open. This had been going on for a few years, and Westborough State Hospital had been downsized to almost nothing except a few wards and administrative offices. My sister had been moved to another facility, but I had hoped this would be the end of the uncertainty. Anne was just settling in and I did not want any more changes to upset her or mess with her life. She did not like change, and the staff and I had to deal with the fallout from any change that could upset her.

I read deeper into the article, and it was the usual back and forth, with the governor and some state reps looking to consolidate real estate and people, or put residents in halfway houses all over the state. The Democratic reps were fighting to keep the status quo, and the governor was pushing changes that could free up money for other priorities in the state budget. I was no longer surprised by how politicians could go after such a vulnerable people who had no one to represent their interests. Fortunately, some caring citizen groups took the bull by the horns and spoke out for the residents to make sure they were treated fairly.

As I read deeper into the details, I found that the governor was winning the argument for a variety of reasons, and was getting support to carry the day. People wanted better schools, roads and bridges repaired, and lower state sales and income taxes. The money had to come from somewhere. Why not from mentally ill people? They would never know the difference. My blood pressure began to rise as I continued to read. I had had enough. I flipped to page two of the paper, and read the mundane news of the day. Then I made my way to the business section and on to sports. The stock market was booming, and my favorite baseball team, the Red Sox, were steaming along in the American League East division. Yes, life was good from my perch in the limited world in which I lived, and I could feel my muscles and mind starting to relax a bit.

I flipped back to the editorial section, and turned one page too far. I was on the last page of the first section of the paper. On the bottom of the page was a headline about a woman who had been murdered by a resident of a halfway house. My mind began to race and my pulse was ticking along with a shock of adrenaline through my body. I was instantly upset and suddenly found it necessary to focus on reading the article.

The story told about a young woman who had graduated from college a year ago with a degree in social work. She wanted to make a difference in the world, so she got a job with a halfway house in Beverly. The house was coed, and the residents a combination of recovering drug addicts, alcohol rehab, and lower-level mentally ill patients.

My pulse was beating out of my chest, I was starting to sweat, and my anxiety level was sky high. What was going on in this state? How could they be so callous about people who were defenseless? I was getting mad and upset, but I had to keep reading.

The second paragraph said an arrest had been made at a fleabag motel in some small town in western Massachusetts. The suspect was a 39-year-old male who had lived at the home. He was taken into custody by the state police and questioned. He was a drug/alcohol addict, borderline bipolar, who had spent a great deal of his life in the court and prison system. At some point some activist lawyer got him declared incompetent for his own actions, and remanded into the mental health system. I'm not sure how this could happen, since his court record indicated a long list of petty crime from breaking and entering, to robbery, to minor assault.

At some point he was sent to a mental hospital and stayed there for a number of years. The guy's parents died while he was in the hospital, and he had no other family members. Once the state started closing mental hospitals he was sent to a halfway house in Springfield and lived there for a few years. About two years ago he was transferred to a new halfway house in Beverly to be near a methadone clinic in the area that the state sponsored. I thought to myself, why does this guy need methadone if he is in a halfway house? Shouldn't he be off drugs at the moment? I pondered the thought for a few seconds, and went back to reading.

It seemed that when the guy was arrested he started singing like a bird, thinking in his own burned-out mind that he was safe from prosecution. He did not resist arrest, and gave the police a full statement. It seems the day of the murder the residents of the group home were going on a field trip to the beach because it was such a nice day, and the house had a retired school bus at its disposal. All of the residents and the staff were going to go. The young murder victim was planning to stay back at the home to catch up on paperwork, as was her way. She was always working hard, helping the residents live a somewhat normal, comfortable life. She would listen to their stories of how they fell off the track of life, and she spent her own money on supplies and small gestures of kindness for the staff and people in the home. She was well-liked by all.

The suspect was making his way to the bus when he heard the young girl say to another staff member that she was going to stay back and catch up on things. When he heard that he instantly thought about robbing the office safe so he could buy some drugs. He went back upstairs and hid in his room until he saw the bus pull away. Once everyone was gone he came downstairs, and snuck up on the resident worker. According to his testimony he came up behind her, put his arm around her neck, and demanded she open the safe. For some reason, she could not open the safe, either from forgetting the combination or being too scared to get the tumblers to line up right. She tried many times but with no luck.

Once pressed by investigators, he confessed to grabbing a big steel tape dispenser and hitting her in the side of the head. As she fell to the floor she hit her head on the safe and fell silent. The enraged man came to his senses and realized the girl was either out cold or very hurt. He panicked, picked up her limp body and carried it out the back door into the back employee parking lot, and threw her into the dumpster. He went back to the office to make things look normal and untouched. Then he fled.

The article continued that once the group got back they assumed the victim had left early, since the night crew did not see the young woman when they reported for work. No one was aware that anything was awry until they discovered the suspect was not in his room after the regular head count done by staff and the parents of the girl called and said she had not come home for dinner. A night shift worker checked the front of the resident house, and noticed the girl's car was parked on the street. That is why no one had noticed it. But she was nowhere to be found.

After some back-and-forth calls with the harried parents, the Beverly Police were called, and when it was reported one of the residents was gone the state police were called in. State police officers brought a tracking dog with them, and noted the girl's sweater was still on the back of her chair. The dog picked up the scent of the employee right away, and stuck his nose by the safe. They found a small trace of blood. The dog went through the whole house, but nothing else was uncovered.

They then took their search outside the house. It did not take long for the police dog to make his way to the dumpster in the back parking lot where police found the young girl's body stashed under several layers of trash bags and boxes. The coroner was called in, and the young woman was pronounced dead, and that this home was a murder scene.

The last paragraph of the story contained the usual comments from the parents, neighbors, and workers about what a nice young girl she was, and how all she wanted to do was help people. I read several testimonials until I threw the paper on the floor, and got up to get a glass of water. My head was spinning, and my mind was jumping ahead to my sister's welfare. What did the state have in mind for her future? I was not going to let my sister get railroaded by a huge mental health system and fall through the cracks. It could cost her her life. A thousand thoughts were going through my head all at once. I tried to calm down, but I couldn't. After a few moments, I made my way to the bedroom, and snapped on the television, and tuned to a game to distract me from the upsetting thoughts racing through my mind. The bed felt comfortable, and my muscles began to relax as my head sank into the pillow. This night's dreams would not be so comforting.

TEWKSBURY, MASS., 1997

◆ ◆ ◆ ◆ ◆

I lie awake in my bed. I had a lot of swirling emotions caused by the commotion in the hospital. I didn't know where I was. I felt unsettled. I was not as happy as I once was. The staff seemed a lot more busy, and didn't pay attention to my needs. In the daytime the floor was a mass of people going here and there, and all with different tasks and I could not make out what they were. They were all dressed differently. I would meander through the crowds with no real purpose, and people would look at me, and some would talk to me, but I could not understand what they were saying. It was like they were mute, or my ears were numb. I would ask things of the staff, but they would shuffle me off down the hallway or into the big room with all the other residents. I was like a small star out in the universe floating around with no destination.

My sleep was off. My room was cramped and the voices were worse than ever. The room had two sets of bunks, two big bureaus, and a closet in the corner. My nightstand had a lamp, and my radio was there, at least until one of my roommates smashed it on the floor. We had had a disagreement one day and when I came back from lunch, my radio was in pieces all over the floor. I was hurt. The staff gave her a stern talking to, but the disagreements did not end there. She did not like me right from the first time I met her. The woman was about my age, with short blond hair, taller than me, and had a bad case of acne. She yelled at people all the time for no reason, and swore at staff and residents. The more she was spoken too or punished, the more trouble she caused. I had an anxious feeling all the time, and my stomach hurt more than ever.

I was lying in my bed looking out the window, I dreamed about floating up in the sky, and going all the way to the moon. It looked so bright; I was sure it would be a happy place. I had been so unhappy and frustrated for so long, I wanted to feel like I felt when I was little. I could not remember why I was happy before, but I know I was. It was distant, and far off, but I felt it in my mind and heart. My mind had been jumbled and disorganized for so long that it hurt my memory. The only thing I could remember was sitting on my piano stool and playing songs in someone's house and feeling very happy. I sensed there was a woman there standing behind me, and encouraging me to play. I loved music and songs, but could not remember why or when I had developed that love. The past was a haze. It seemed like another life.

As I looked up at the moon, I heard a sound. I looked down and locked eyes with my mean roommate. She was awake and looking right at me. She did not look happy, and her look was one of disgust. I immediately closed my eyes and tried to dream of good things, but the voices came back. They were telling me to watch out and be careful. There were evil forces lurking nearby and I should be on my guard. I could feel my heart beating fast, and I put my sweaty hands on my chest to try and make it stop. I slowed my breathing, and hoped that my roommate would go back to sleep.

After a few moments, I assumed she had rolled over to ignore me, but suddenly I felt a sharp slap to the side of my face. I immediately put my hand to my face because of the pain, when another blow came down on the back of my hand. I opened my eyes, and her face and evil eyes were looking through me like a laser beam. Why was this woman hurting me? I had never done anything to bother her. I raised my arm to block her next blow, and threw off the covers and tried to swing my feet around to sit up. I needed to get up to defend myself, but she was holding me down, and I could not get any leverage to sit up. This beast was holding me down, and bashing me at will.

My other two roommates had woken up, and were yelling at the other girl to stop it. I was fending off her blows as best I could, and wished that the staff would come in and break it up. Things like this had *happened over the years, but this place was the worst. This was making the voices sprout up. I swung my arms and tried to protect my face. The woman was possessed and swearing up a storm. Finally, two of the night staff ran into the room. They grabbed her from behind, and pulled her off me.*

Once she was off me I sat up, pulled the covers up to my face as I shivered. The orderlies asked me if I was all right. I nodded. I didn't want to be difficult, and they seemed relieved I was not hurt. My roommate continued to make a scene, and they kept telling her to lower her voice. They kept asking her what was wrong, but she could not calm down enough to tell them.

Finally the staff had had enough. They did not want the commotion to spread to the rest of the floor and wake up all the other residents. That would be the last thing the night staff would want. They had better things to do. The orderlies dragged her kicking and screaming out of the room. I could hear the swearing fading away as she was dragged further down the hallway. I looked at my other roommates with a look of relief, and they gave me the same look back.

I looked back out the window, and fixed my eyes on the bright moon. I wished that someone would take me away. The voices started to go away, and I began to drift into a subconscious state. I kept wishing for happy dreams and a life like I had long ago.

TEWKSBURY, MASS., SPRING 1997

◆◆◆◆◆◆

I was sitting at my desk at work, thinking about all the things I had on my plate. My company was busy with work, I was coaching my daughter's softball team, my son was away at college, and my wife was working full-time. We used the weekend to catch up around the house, and fit in social occasions with family and friends. I was staring at my cubicle wall when I started thinking about my sister. It had been a while since I had called and checked in with her, and I thought I should give the hospital a call and talk to the social worker about Anne.

I dialed the number, which I had burned in my memory, and after several rings a female voice picked up. The woman answered saying "Mary Jo speaking," in a very formal bureaucratic voice, but with a heavy Boston accent.

I identified myself, and asked for Anne's social worker. The woman said to hold on, and put down the phone to go find the person. I could hear background noise from many feet away from the desk. It was a conglomeration of staff talking to one another, residents speaking their piece to staff or among themselves, and a few people who I couldn't identify speaking in another language. I listened carefully to pick up the country, but it was too faint to make out. The noise coming through the phone was a cacophony, but just another day at the hospital for everyone concerned.

I waited for a few minutes, praying that my own work phone would not ring. Then I heard a woman's voice came on the line. "Hello, this is Nancy Drake speaking," she said with a faint southern drawl. It sounded strange for someone in the Boston area to talk like that, but she was obviously a transplant or married to a Massachusetts resident. She sounded middle aged, and her English was something to be desired.

I spoke up and introduced myself to the woman, and then asked how my sister was doing. As she was talking, I could hear her fumbling for something, which I assumed to be my sister's file, because she didn't seem to know much about Anne or what she was up to. I could hear her wince while we were talking, and all of a sudden I could hear her flipping through pages. I thought to myself, this person must have been working at another hospital and then transferred when it closed. Since the workers were unionized they could bump someone else out of a job if they had the seniority to pull it off.

As she talked, it became obvious she did not know my sister, and it seemed she was discussing another person entirely. I let her go on for a few more minutes, and then cut in to the conversation. "Miss, I think you are talking about another resident. This does not sound like my sister from how you are describing her," I said. I was puzzled, and then I said in a confident voice, "Her name is Anne McGilvery. Are you sure you are talking about the right person?"

I could hear her flip the file over, and then she let out a loud, exasperated "I'm so sorry, sir, I pulled another person's file out of the drawer. I am new here, and just getting settled, so you are going to have to bear with me for a few moments."

Then there was the sound of more papers and folders crunching, and I could hear the woman asking the front desk people where my sister's file was. There was a lot of muffled sounding discussion. I still had the same feeling about this place as I did from the first day Anne got there. They were not being as attentive as the people in Westborough, and there was a lot of movement with mental health staff from one facility to another, due to facilities being closed, early retirements, and everyone getting used to each other. The residents seemed to be getting lost in the shuffle with all this going on.

The woman's voice came back on the line. She apologized again for being so disorganized, and stated the obvious that she was new to this place, and she was getting up to speed on all the residents. She finally had the right file, and started reading the file and chart to me. I really did not want to go over my sister's history, but I felt bad for the woman because she was embarrassed enough, and I didn't want to add to it. I let her keep reading, and have her say for a few more minutes, and then I asked how Anne was doing today. She paused for a few seconds, and then I heard her hand go over the phone receiver, but I could hear her asking the day staff how Anne was today. I knew she was getting an update of my sister's goings on so far today.

"Have you seen Anne today? How is she doing? Has she been eating well?" I inquired as if I were cross examining someone at trial. "I have not talked to anyone at your office in a month, and the last time I talked to someone, Anne was not getting along with her roommate. How is that situation going?".

"You don't have to worry about a thing, Mr. McGilvery. Anne is doing just fine and she is happy as a lark. Ms. Smith, the day coordinator saw Anne a little while ago, and said she had just got back from her workshop, and had a big smile on her face," she said trying to convince me.

I could tell from the tone in her voice that she was talking right off the top of her head. The day staff had no idea how Anne was doing, and I'm sure she was in the dayroom stuffed in a corner looking at the television, like a drone.

I asked myself if I was getting the true update from this woman or getting the party line that they gave any guardian or parent who called to check on their loved one. The staff had a big job running a whole floor full of patients, and the coordination, medication, food, and workshop and education programs must have been difficult to organize and pull off on a daily basis. I had no idea how hard this job was, and I had never spent any more than two hours on a floor at one time. These people spent eight hours a day there, five days a week, and they worked under some very difficult conditions.

As I reflected on this, the woman on the phone explained what had been going on today with Anne, and that she was settling in just fine. She reiterated that the overcrowding situation had been smoothed over, and everyone for the most part was getting along. It was like she was reading my mind. Every point she touched on was something I was thinking about. I started to come around with this person and even got comfortable with her.

Our conversation moved from a very formal conversation to more of a personal exchange. I was right about her background. She had been raised in the South, and came to Boston to go to college where she met her husband. She still had a drawl, even though she had been here for many years. The woman continued to tell me about her family, how many kids she had, where she lived, and how long it took her to commute to work. As she talked I felt better about her and my sister and began to feel that she truly cared about the residents and their needs.

After she had finished her biography, she started to ask me some questions about Anne, my relationship with her, and my family. The flow of information, and the back and forth seemed natural, and broke the ice from how my normal visits or phone calls usually went. At one point I must have mentioned a family cottage in Maine, and that someday I would like to sell my home in Massachusetts and move up north.

Then the most unbelievable thing happened. After I talked about summers in Maine, she said, "That place you have sounds great, and Maine is such a nice place. I have been up there on day trips before, and we always enjoy it. Have you ever thought of moving your sister up to Maine?"

The free-flowing conversation came to an abrupt halt. I thought I had misheard what the woman said. And then she continued. "I've heard Maine is a nice state, and I bet they have superior mental health facilities compared to Massachusetts," she offered.

I was shocked, not just because Maine was one of the poorest states in the country, and its mental health system could not compare to the system in Massachusetts, but she clearly did not understand that Anne was committed by the state to its facilities for the rest of her life. I was a limited guardian, and had no formal responsibility for her direct care or shelter.

I thought for a few seconds and then blurted out, "Excuse me, excuse me, what did you say?" in an exasperated voice. "What do you mean, I should move Anne to Maine? I don't understand what you mean by that statement? Anne has been committed by the court to be in the state's care for the rest of her life. I have only very limited responsibility for her care and well-being. It's the state that has the major responsibility for her welfare." I finished my statement with as much authority as I could muster.

"I, I did not mean anything by what I said, Mr. McGilvery," she said in a very meek and humble voice. I could tell from her response that she knew she had said something she never should have.

I sat stewing on the other end of the phone, still in shock over what she had just suggested. I'm sure there were many people in state custody that were there under a variety of circumstances and legal remedies, but how could she have gotten this far off base? I asked for her name twice before she gave it to me, and then I asked to have her supervisor come to the phone. At that point she knew she had created a grave error in judgement.

When her supervisor came to the phone, she was already in full retreat, and knew exactly what the other woman had said. She went on and one trying to assure me that she misspoke, and that Anne was safe and secure at this facility and everything was fine. I went over with her the way I understood the situation and the court order, and my limited guardianship, and she agreed with it all and said I was correct. She couldn't have been nicer, and I tried to lighten the mood at the end of the conversation, because she was so nervous not know-ing if I was going to hang up the phone and call my lawyer.

Little did she know that that was the furthest thing from my mind. I was happy overall with the care Anne was getting, and I was the kind of person who did not want to rock the boat. I assumed if you were nice to the staff, and tried to be upbeat, the staff would appreciate it and Anne would be the benefactor. I finished up the conversation with a heartfelt goodbye, and thanked the woman for all she did for my sister.

After I hung up the phone, I sat there for a while pondering what the social worker had said, and if she was aware of any information that would affect my sister's situation at Tewksbury State Hospital. I tried to think of only positive things, but the negative side of things kept creeping back into my head. My heart began to race a little and my anxiety started to pick up. My parents were gone, and I was the sole person responsible for my sister's well-being. I had to be her advocate and make sure she was getting good care and would not get lost in the system. Hopefully, my fleeting concerns were just that, only baseless concerns. I sat there tapping my computer keyboard, just looking at my reflection on the monitor, thinking about what had just unfolded, and hoping the future would be okay for Anne.

PART III

ACTON, MASS., 1997

◆ ◆ ◆ ◆ ◆ ◆ ◆

I was sitting at the kitchen table on a beautiful Saturday morning. My stomach had been off for a few days, so I had asked my wife to run the kids to their religion class and dance practice so I could rest. I wanted to get myself back into game shape so I could bring my trash to the dump, which closed at 3:00. I started flipping through the local paper. As I turned the pages, I could tell I was not concentrating on the news of the week, or anything else due to my anxiety and stomach issues. As I looked around the kitchen, I could see a number of home projects and updating that needed to be addressed, and that made me even more anxious. I hadn't the money or the time to accomplish the projects.

I decided to meander over to the couch in the living room. I lay down and rested my eyes. My wife had left strict orders to rest and drink flat ginger ale until my stomach came back into shape. I lay on my back on the soft white couch, and gazed out the picture window. The sun was shining and I could hear the morning traffic zipping by outside. Everyone was doing their Saturday morning chores or taking their kids here and there. As I looked up in the large trees I could see several squirrels running and jumping from branch to branch playing like they did not have a care in the world. As I looked up in another tree I saw a robin tending to her little ones in her nest. She was standing guard over them, waiting for the right time to go out and search for food.

As I was lying there, being lulled in and out of sleep, I heard the phone ring in the kitchen. I thought about not answering it, due to my health and laziness, but elected to get up and answer it. It could have been my wife having car trouble or needing me to bring something to her or the kids. I stood up and started for the kitchen. As the phone rang more I picked up speed, came around the corner, and grabbed the receiver. I put the phone up to my ear, and said "Hello;" in a sleepy soft voice. There was a moment of silence on the other end and then a woman's voice perked up.

"Hello, is Mr. McGilvery at home?" the woman said in an official manner.

I responded with a questioning "Yes. Who is calling?" The caller paused for a minute, and then she responded.

"This is Mrs. Prince, Anne's lawyer from the state. It has been a while since we've seen each other. How have your been, Mr. McGilvery?" she said with a sincere tone in her voice.

I responded back that I was under the weather, and was not sure if I was getting sick or if I had eaten some bad food.

"I'm sorry to hear that. There is a lot going around these days, so it could be anything . . . I hope you feel better soon though."

"I'll be okay," I said in a pathetic manner. "I can rest over the weekend, and hopefully by Monday, I will be feeling better." I was curious why Anne's lawyer was calling. I had not received any notices in the mail that I had to do anything or that an important legal date was coming up. I racked my brain for a few seconds, but nothing came to mind.

"I'm sorry to bother you on the weekend, but an urgent change for Anne has come to my attention, and I thought the earlier you knew and the more information you had, would be better than not," she said. "Anne's social worker called me yesterday, and said they are closing your sister's floor at Tewksbury State Hospital and sending all the residents to group homes around the state."

I sat there with a feeling of anxiety mixed with shock. For so long all the people in charge of Anne had said she would never go off a locked ward, and she would be always taken care of, no matter what. Now the statement that I had just heard blew away all the rhetoric and promises, and let out a genie from the bottle that I could never get back in. I had had lawyers, social workers, doctors, nurses, and everyone else telling me that my sister would be safe and not able to wander, and now that had just been thrown all out the window. "How could this happen, Ms. Prince?" I blurted out with a tone of concern.

"Well, Chris, the state has been closing facilities over the last ten years, and rumors have circulated for months that Tewksbury could be next on the list. Group homes are the wave of the future and the doctors, nurses, and social workers all feel Anne would thrive in that environment. They have assured me that your sister would be safe and secure as if she was inside the hospital, and it will open up so many other possibilities for field trips, walks around town, and real human interaction with the general public."

I was too stunned to speak. My mind kept going back to what Anne's social worker said about moving her to Maine, and the news reports about that poor girl in Beverly who had been murdered by another resident in a group home. My stomach already was upset, but thinking about my sister's future made it churn even more.

"Chris, are you still there?"the lawyer said in a low tone.

"Yes, I'm still here. I am just trying to digest all you have told me. This has come completely out of the blue. I know it has been all over the papers the past few years, but I tried to convince myself that this wouldn't affect Anne," I responded with a defeatist sound in my voice.

"Don't worry, Chris. This is just at the beginning. The wheels of progress with the state move very slowly, and there will be plenty of time to ask lots of questions, and tour many new group homes to make sure they are up to our standards. No one will push you or Anne into a situation that is not a good fit and not safe."

I continued my conversation with Ms. Prince and asked what I thought were appropriate questions, and she gave me a series of safe answers and was noncommittal about several items, because even she did not know the details. The newspapers had been filled with this news for months, and of course it was tied to a cutback in state jobs and an early retirement program to save the state millions of dollars in the budget. Things were moving fast. The land where the old Met State building was, and where Anne lived many years before, had already been sold, and was being developed under a three-town shared agreement. I had to get out in front of this thing before I lost control of the situation. As I listened to Anne's lawyer drone on for what seemed like forever, I pondered my next move. I needed to come up with a counterstrategy to slow down the hospital . . .

Long after the conversation was over I lay on the couch thinking about what I needed to do. Anne's life and well-being were hanging in the balance, and I needed to step up and be my sister's protector. I thought about my options, and a game plan, and fortunately this took my mind completely off my sore stomach. Hopefully, I could save my sister from being lost in the state system.

As I drifted in and out of sleep, I could hear the radio on faintly in the kitchen. The song sounded familiar, but I had to strain my hearing to make out what the song was. After a few moments I figured it out. It was "To Sir with Love," by LuLu. It was a huge hit back in the sixties. As my mind drifted in and out, I had a flashback to my sister coming home from the local music store with the forty five. The British invasion was in full swing. As I passed her on the stairs going out to the back yard to play football with my friends from the neighborhood, she was running upstairs two steps at a time. The look on her face was one of true happiness.

I thought back to what happened next and why it colored my thought process now. I was out in the back yard playing with my friends when a group of older kids from down the street strolled into my back yard and challenged us to a game of football. We knew this was going to be a problem, but we did not want to back down and look chicken or hear about it at school the next day. As soon as the game started these guys forgot all about the football game, and were going out of their way to knock us down at every turn. We tried to hang tough, but it was a losing battle. After about a half hour of getting schooled, one of the kids who had taken a dislike to me really zoned in on kicking my butt. I put up with it for a while and then dropped him with a hard tackle. He came up swinging. He was breathing fire. I tried to talk my way out of trouble, but he was having none of it. He started pushing me backwards, taunting me to take a swing at him. I knew if I did, it was all over.

Both groups of guys started to get on both of us to take the first swing. I had seen my mother leave in the car an hour earlier to go shopping, so I knew I had no fallback plan. It looked as though I was going to get an old-fashioned whooping. Just when I thought there was no tomorrow for me I saw my sister bounding across the yard. She hit the kid on his blind side, pushed him with all her might, and he went flying to the ground.

All the kid's friends cracked up laughing, and my sister went off on this kid. He did not know whether to look at her or me. I stood there relieved, as my sister unleashed a barrage of four-letter words, and said she was going to go to school and tell everyone that he was picking on little kids to get his jollies.

She told him when the word got around with the girls at school, and downtown at the local ice cream shop, he would not be able to get a date for a thousand years. They shouted at each other for a while, but he knew my sister had an advantage on him. His friends started pulling him away, and she told all of them to clear out of the yard or she would have my mother give their parents a call. That was it. The bigger kids went into full retreat, and my friends and I stood there amazed.

My friends all thanked Anne for saving the day, and as fast as she came, she was gone back into the house. We stood around the yard for few minutes talking about how we could spin the story to make us look good, but I knew my sister had just saved my bacon.

She had always been there for me growing up, and it was time I stepped up to help her as best I could. I did not know what I was going to do, but I knew it had to be good. Time was of the essence.

* * * * *

I scurried up the library steps and opened the door for a young mother who was trying to negotiate the stairs while guiding her three little children inside. I smiled as they went by, and the woman made sure all three of the little ones said "Thank you." Once they were by I made my way inside, and vaulted up the stairs two at a time to get to the top. I wanted to find a little desk cubby where no one would disturb me.

As I looked around for a spot I saw students doing research with books or computers, and as I walked further, there were several other kids sitting at a big table making themselves look busy, but they really were just talking. I'm sure they told their parents they wanted to go to the library to study, but they had other things in mind. I gazed over at the magazine rack, and thought to myself, they have every magazine known to man. There were a number of older men and women sitting around in comfortable chairs reading their favorite periodical, and some were totally engrossed. It was their version of recess away from their families.

I turned a corner and saw a young couple making time, so I turned back the other way and went deeper into the other side of the floor. Eventually, I came across an empty wooden desk. I put my cardboard folder down on the desk, took my jacket off and hung it over the back of the chair. Then I sat down, and looked at the folder. I had dug the folder out of my strongbox in my bedroom closet. I remembered back to that day when my father turned the responsibility for Anne over to me, and said, "If the state ever gives you any problems with your sister, make sure you use this to have them live up to their promise." I didn't know what that meant then, but I was upset about the future of Anne's care, and I had to see what this folder contained that might help me convince the state to keep her safe.

I sat back, took a deep breath, and flipped open the folder. It contained a lot of old, official documents, some with the seal of Massachusetts, and some with the Catholic Charities seal. The writing and the ink had faded, but it was still legible enough after all these years. I picked up documents, and then put them down without really digesting them. My heart was racing and it was affecting my ability to concentrate.

After a few minutes, I decided to take another approach. I flipped through the stack of records and found a birth certificate. It was issued by clerk Russell Osner of Worcester, Mass. It was dated May 3, 1950. It said the mother was a woman by the name of Joan McNulty. I quickly looked down for the father's name and it said "Unknown." It had the time of the baby's birth, and a few other particulars, but I pondered why the father's name was left off.

The next document I picked up was Anne's baptism certificate. It was issued by pastor Paul Demone of Saint Margaret's Parish, also in Worcester. It was dated May 9, 1950, and said the mother was Joan McNulty and the father was unknown. It was signed by the pastor, and stamped with the bishop's signature.

The next form I came across was from the Commissioner of Health, Department of Public Welfare. The person's name was Patrick Snelling, and it authorized six months of prenatal care for Joan McNulty. It was dated December 20, 1949. It had an addendum at the bottom that ended with normal live birth.

I flipped over the form. Next was a beige piece of paper with a doctor's office logo on it that certified that Anne McNulty was given all the appropriate vaccinations for her age, and she was a healthy female child. It was dated December 1951. I thought to myself, that was strange. Everything I had been reviewing up to this point was dated in 1950, and this record was from more than a year later. Wouldn't a pediatrician see a new baby for a checkup, and newborn vaccinations within a few months from birth? I thought it odd, but I wanted to continue through the file, so I put the piece of paper down and went on.

As I turned the next document over I saw an official state seal of the Probate Court of Massachusetts/Worcester County. It was the adoption papers from when my parents adopted my sister. My spirits brightened, because I remembered back to happier days, and how my mother said it was the best time of her life when they adopted Anne and brought her home. When she told me the story of that day, she always had a smile in her voice. The official court records showed my parents' names, John and Patricia McGilvery. The document was dated May 3, 1950. The judge who signed it was Joseph Allen, and the book/records number was 1680, page 470. I thought for a minute, that's odd. I know my parents said they adopted Anne when she was around 18 months old. This official record made it look like she was adopted at birth. I thought for a few seconds about it, and then looked out the window. My eyes strained to get a view of the parking lot to see my car. All I ended up seeing was my reflection looking right back at me.

I heard a woman behind me trying to coax her two children that it was time to go, and to figure out which books they wanted to check out. The woman walked away while the kids kept debating to each other why they wanted to take home each book. I looked back at the folder, and pondered what I would find next in this stack of paper and what kind of story it would tell about my family.

The suspense was building as to what I would find in this folder, and as much as I was interested in its contents, I was also afraid as to what I would find. My father was adamant that this information could help me through any bad times with Anne. I took a deep breath, and looked down and began again to sort through the various documents.

There were many pieces of paper I could not make out too well, but one was a piece with scribbled notes. The blue ink was lighter than the original writing, and it was not in my father's handwriting. It said 'found all forms backdated to 5-3-1950.' It said Anne was born to a Joan McNulty (mother) and a Samuel Jenkins (father). Adoption was processed by Gertrude Flavin of the Commonwealth of Massachusetts.

I looked at the notes, fixated on the two names. I had never heard my parents talk about my sister's real parents, and I always wondered where they came from. Here they were in plain English, and then a second thought came to my mind. If they were a couple, why would they give a beautiful, healthy baby to Catholic Charities to be adopted? Back in the 1950s no one gave up a child, and most people were ecstatic to bring a new addition into the family. The only time someone gave up a child was when a teenage girl found herself pregnant. The girl's parents would pull her out of school during the later stages of the pregnancy. Then after the baby was delivered, it was left at the hospital for some loving family to adopt, and the young woman would all of a sudden reappear back in school. The real story was never spoken about so the family could save face. An unwed mother in the 1950s could ruin the reputation of any family at that time.

My mother worked for a society in town that did fundraising to support a resident house for girls who became pregnant and who had been kicked out of their home because the parents were so embarrassed by the circumstances. I remember my mother going to bake sales, book sales, and even a town fair to raise the funds to help fund the house. Volunteer social workers coordinated the teenagers' care and well-being until the baby was born. Then the home would coordinate with the state and the church to find a good home for the new arrival, and then either send the teenager back to school or arrange for a job in another town. I always wondered if my mother did this because she was so thankful to have benefited from using the adoption services to have that baby girl she always wanted.

I finished going through the folder without anything really important, and sat there flipping the folder open and closed. As I was lost in thought, someone came up behind me and startled me. I looked up and it was an older woman. She said, "Five minutes until the library closes.' My pulse jumped just a bit because I was in deep concentration. I grabbed my jacket from the back of the chair. As I stood up, I picked up the folder, and as I brought it to my side a business card fell onto the floor. I bent down and picked it up. I turned it over. The edges were frayed, but the print was legible. It said Salvatore D'Agostino, Private Investigator, Medford MA, 617-232-5693. It had some official police logo on it.

I walked down the stairs from the second floor to the first, looking at the card, and wondering why my father needed a private investigator to accumulate this information. As I went out the door into the cold night air I thought of the possibilities, and I knew there had to be more to the story. I did not know that my little adventure was just beginning.

* * * * *

It was a beautiful sunny day as I meandered my way through the Mystic Lakes, on my way to West Medford. It was a nice blue collar town four miles north of Boston. My parents had lived there for many years before I was born. As I guided the car down the winding road I noticed the lake and sail boats out for the afternoon, tacking back and forth as the wind would allow. The sun was beaming off the water and I had to keep shifting my head to keep the glare from obstructing my vision.

I had called the private investigator's number, and had gotten his son on the phone. It turned out the dad had passed away many years before. As it turned out, he was the only son, and had lived with his parents his whole life and was still living in the family home. He sounded a little put-off at first when I called, but as I summarized my father's relationship with him, his coarse personality mellowed into one of being interested in my story. I only gave him a small overview, because I did not know many facts at this point, and I figured we could see if his father's file was still on the property.

I got to the end of the Mystic Parkway, turned up to Boston Ave., and travelled up to West Medford Square. Right before I got to the railroad tracks I took a right. This looked like any typical square in suburban America, with its various shops, gas stations, and churches. As I went further down the street, I noticed Sheridan Circle on the left, and pulled down the street. I started to crawl, looking for the correct address. Most of the houses were two-family homes in good condition, painted in a variety of colors or covered in vinyl. I spotted number 22 on the front stoop of a brown two-family; it had a drive-way that led to a two-car garage with a second floor. I went down the street a few yards until I saw the first open parking space. It was a tight street with not much room, so I had to do a ten-point turn to wedge my car in between two other oversized vehicles. I popped open the door, and made sure I locked my car, since I was not sure if the neighborhood was safe. Back when my parents lived here it was just like anywhere in America: safe, no drugs, and everyone knew their neighbors. Those days seemed like a long time ago from what I saw in the newspapers and on the television news.

I walked back looking for the brown house. A woman with a baby carriage passed me by. She gave me a look up and down as she went past. I almost asked her if the brown house was the D'Agostino house, but decided against it because of her body language.

I got to the house, and walked up the front steps. The house was in disrepair compared to its neighbors. Some of the siding was rotted and the paint was peeling off the house and window trim. A faded, handwritten sign said use knocker, doorbell out of order. I gave the knocker a few good raps, and heard someone inside. I knew someone was home since there was a late model car in the driveway, but it also could have been the upstairs tenant's. I had called ahead, the son and I had agreed on a date and time, so I was hoping I did not waste my time driving the 25 miles to get here. I gave it a few more seconds and then rapped the knocker again. This time I heard a yell from inside, "Be right there." I wondered what I had gotten myself into. I did not know this guy. He could be a loser or a degenerate with a bad temper. I pondered for a split second, suppose he had a gun on him? I decided right then that I would conduct business outside to avoid any chance of a bad outcome.

Just as I was thinking over all this, the door opened with a big squeak and there was a big guy looking at me with some disgust in his eyes. "What are you selling?" he groused. I looked up at him and stated my business as fast as I could. As I referred back to my phone call with him a few days before, his personality changed, and he was more jittery; that made my heart jump a bit. Standing in front of me was a big Italian guy, about sixty, with a big stomach, and greasy black hair slicked back. But he turned out to be receptive to my plight.

"The neighborhood has changed a bit," he said. "A lot of college students live around here, and I have always been leery of outsiders." He paused and thought for a moment, and then said in a sarcastic way, "I guess it's because of my old man and his job. He busted so many criminals in his career, his mistrust of people rubbed off on me."

The man had a very thick Italian-slang accent, so I had to listen very closely to what he was saying. But it seemed he was on the same wavelength as me. Once we got the formalities out of the way, he closed the front door to the house and guided me around the side, heading towards the garage. As we walked he went over his father's story. It seems he was a Boston cop for many years, but was badly wounded in a shootout with a mob hit gone bad around North Station. From what he said, the father caught a bullet in the leg, and it affected his walking after that. He wanted to return to police work, but the police union would not let him come back and gave him a disability pension. From what the son said his father was heartbroken, and horrible to be around after that. I guess after several months of feeling sorry for himself he started a private investigation business. What with all his contacts in the police department, the business prospered, and his father became his old self. As the son told me more and more, I could sense he was proud of his father, but clearly had not followed in his footsteps. He did not look like a policeman or a success in any way. I'm sure he was a working class guy who inherited a house and a tidy sum of money from his parents and wasn't interested in working too hard.

When we got to the garage, he opened the big overhead door, laboring to push it over his head. I thought for a moment that I should help him, but then thought better about it. The last thing I wanted was to insult the man who could possibly be the key to all the questions I had about my sister and where she came from. "When did your father pass away?" I inquired, with more concern than questioning?

"Died about ten years ago from lung cancer," he sputtered. "The guy smoked like a chimney, and it finally caught up to him." He then turned to me for a response, and I quickly said, "That's too bad," with as much empathy as I could muster on short notice. I noticed a big blue Cadillac parked on the right side. It sparkled like new. "That was my father's pride and joy. He bought that once his investigation service got off the ground, and he was making a lot of money. He took my mother down to the showroom, and had her pick out any car in the lot. She thought he had won the lottery". He chucked under his breath, and was very proud of his quick wit.

We climbed the stairs to his dad's second-floor office. He unlocked the door, and we stepped in. The walls had been finished with a homemade sheetrock job covered with a thin coat of white paint. There was an old mahogany desk with several files piled on it, and on the other side of the room there were four gray, metal filing cabinets with three drawers in each. An old red bradded rug was in the middle of the room.

I walked to the center of the room, and the son followed right behind. "This is quite a place your father had here. I'll bet there are a lot of memories in this room," I said in an uplifting manner to raise the guy's spirits.

He fired back. "All I have is bad memories of this place. Every time I came up to see my father, he would shoo me away. Or he would yell out the window at me to quiet down if I was playing street hockey in the driveway. He was so engrossed in his work, he had no time for me or my mother." He looked back at me for a response, but all I could muster was a shake of my head in disgust.

I turned the other way and noticed some framed pictures on the wall. I took a step closer to get a better look. I noticed a Boston Police Department citation for bravery, with the father's badge mounted under the glass. Next to this was another plaque with the logo for the Sons of Italy Lodge, with Salvatore D'Agostino as a good member in standing. Next to that was a picture of soldiers, somewhere in Europe or Korea. I could not tell, and I surely was not going to ask.

"Are you familiar with your father's filing system?" I asked meekly.

"Hell no," he practically shouted. "Haven't you been listening to me? I was not allowed up here, and once my father died I shut the door and kept it locked until today." He stood there with his eyes fixated on me waiting for a response.

"Well, do you mind if I just poke around a little to see if I can find your father's file on my sister, and see what it contains?" I asked, hoping not to get my head taken off.

"Yeah, that would be okay I guess," he replied. "Just lock up when you are done, and put the key in my mail slot on the front porch. I am going down to the Wonderland dog track in a while to see if I can change my losing streak, and I don't want to wait around." He gave me a sly smile out the corner of his mouth.

I said that would be fine, and I would be more than glad to close up when I was finished. He gave me the head bob, and made his way down the stairs. I heard every step groan as he made his way down the staircase. I watched him walk down the driveway and around the corner, I pulled out a piece of paper from my father's file with a date on it. It was April 4, 1971. I decided to look for files with that date or my father's last name.

I worked my way over to the first gray filing cabinet. No identifying tags or stickers were on the outside. I thought to myself, this is going to take me a while to locate this file, if it was even here. How did I know that the private eye just didn't give my father the file back when he was finished? My dad was getting so forgetful when he turned over my sister's affairs to me, he could have had two files, and forgot to give me one. I thought for a moment and shrugged off the thought.

I opened the top drawer of the first filing cabinet, and it was full of manila file folders with names written on a little tab at the top in red pen. The first name was "Abbott." I flipped through the whole drawer, and it ended with Carter. I shut the top drawer, and the next drawer started with Deaver. I let out a small sigh of relief knowing this guy used an alpha system to keep his case files straight.

I moved over to the third filing cabinet, and rifled through files until I finally got to the Ms. There it was. John P. McGilvery, in red ink. The file was about an inch thick, and was very dusty. I pulled the file out, blew it off a few times, and shut the drawer. Then I stepped over to the desk and placed it carefully on the mahogany surface. I brushed the brown leather chair off and sat down. I gazed out the window and looked down the drive way, to see if the son had gotten nervous about leaving me in the office by myself. After about a minute staring out to the street, I calmed down enough to flip the file open.

The first thing I saw was a handwritten bill with a five-digit figure, and marked paid in full. I tried to guess what kind of money that would be worth today. The next several documents were the same ones that were contained in my father's file. The I saw a Commonwealth of Massachusetts, Department of Mental Health document that said

"Transfer Notice" on it. It was dated June 6, 1950, and was directed to Central State Hospital, in Indianapolis, Indiana. The name of the transfer order was Joan McNulty. My stomach dropped, and a bell went off in my head. That was Anne's mother's name. I tapped my index finger on the desk nervously, pondering what had taken place and why.

I made my way through the file folder. There were a lot of hen-scratched notes that were hard to read, but they all talked about Worcester State Hospital, the Department of Mental Health, or Catholic Charities. I was having a problem following the trail, when I turned a page and noticed an official form that was made out to Samuel Jenkins, age 55, June 6, 1950. His address was 36 Fairhaven Road, Auburn, Mass. I thought to myself, why is this in this file.? Then it hit me. I flipped back to the patient transfer form I had just reviewed and the date was the same: June 6, 1950. Both things happened about one month after my sister was born. I sat there for a few minutes trying to digest what I had just found, and then another bell went off in my head. The hospital my sister was taken to in Indiana after she ran away from home once was the same one her mother had been transferred to decades earlier. I know it sounded crazy, but the more I thought about it I became convinced it was pure coincidence.

Then my mind jumped back to this Samuel Jenkins character. Who was he, and what did he have to do with this whole situation? I took a minute to collect my thoughts, and then I decided to leave and take the whole file with me. I'm sure the son would never miss it or care, since he had not even been up here in a decade. The dust and cobwebs proved his statement. I jammed the file down my pants and zipped up my jacket to hide the folder. I locked the office door, went down the stairs, and casually made my way back to the car. As I turned the corner at the end of the driveway, I held my breath that the son would not come back out of the house to start up a conversation. Then I remembered I had the keys to the garage and house in my pocket. He told me to put them in the mail box on the porch.

I looked up the stairs and saw a black metal mailbox just to the right of the front door. My heart dropped. How was I going to get up there and down without making any noise? I thought for a few seconds, and knew I had to put the keys back. If I took them this guy had my number. I sized up the situation, and then started to head towards the stairs. I kept saying to myself, "I hope this guy is not home." As I hit the first stair, it gave a loud creak. I pulled back, and quickly looked down, and then up towards the door. I waited for something to happen. I could feel my heart beating out of my chest. As I waited, I noticed no activity at the front door.

I then started to make my way up the steps. Every time I put my foot down on a new stair, it sounded louder than the last one. I kept my eyes right on the front door window for any activity. I finally hit the landing, and tiptoed towards the mailbox. As I came up to it, I pulled the keys put of my pocket and tried to drop then in as quietly as possible. Of course they made a big bang when they hit the bottom. I looked to my left and still saw no one lurking. I turned, went down two stairs, and then jumped the other six on to the walkway and grass. I walked quickly to my car. I made one last glance over my shoulder, and did not see the man in any of the windows. I thought to myself, he must be at the race track. My pulse started to return to normal until my mind flashed back to all the new information I had uncovered. I wondered to myself, where was all this going to lead?

* * * * *

I kept dialing the phone from my desk at work and getting a run-around at the switchboard at Central State Hospital in Indianapolis. I needed proof that Joan McNulty had been transferred there from Worcester State Hospital to cover up a workplace incident between a patient and an orderly. The dates and circumstances I had uncovered were just too coincidental to not be true. My office was busy this morning, and I really did not have time to be starting some kind of investigation, but my sister's transfer to a halfway house in the near future was driving me.

I kept punching the numbers I had found, but was getting recorded messages that Central State Hospital was closed and any questions should be referred to the Department of Mental Health in Indianapolis. I did not want to go that route if I could help it, since

I knew I would get the runaround, and never get near to the place where the information was stored. I finally dialed the last number from the list I had acquired, and it started to ring without rolling over to voicemail. I sat there while the constant buzz of business was taking place all around me. I tried to tune out the background noise so I could focus. The number rang about fifteen times, and I was just about to hang up when a male voice answered. He identified himself and the name of the facility, which was exactly where I was calling.

I sat up straight in my chair, and tried to introduce myself with as much presence as possible. What came out was a garbled hello and that I needed to find out some information.

The security guard, as he identified himself, said that Central State had been closed for a few months, and they were in the process of shutting down the physical buildings and grounds. All staff had been transferred to other facilities or retired. I started to lose all confidence in my mission, and then it just came out. I told the guard that I was adopted, and I was looking for my birth mother, who had been a resident of Central State. I paused for a minute, and I could hear him breathing on the other end of the phone.

"Listen, sir. No residents are left here. They have been transferred around the state, and most have been relocated to halfway houses. I have no way of knowing where your mother went, or even if she is alive," he said gently.

I sat there on the other end of the phone, deflated, and on the verge of giving up, when it just came out of me. "Listen sir, do you have a mother?" I asked in a forceful tone.

"I sure do. She is the greatest lady in the world, and the best cook around," he chuckled lightly.

"Then you can imagine me never knowing what a great lady my mother was, and what kind of a life she had. I have a void that my adopted mother cannot fill, and I just want to know what happened to her." I tried to appeal to the guard's human side. I hoped it was working. I waited for a response, but none was forthcoming. I could still hear him breathing on the other end of the phone, and I could hear him tapping his fingers on a hard surface. Maybe he was thinking about what I had just said. The seconds keep ticking by.

"Now listen, son. I feel bad about your plight, and am not sure how I can be of help, but I do know a woman who worked here for many years and has been kept on to get all the hospital paperwork cataloged and sent to the new facilities and resident homes. I can talk to her, and see if she could be of any assistance to you," he offered.

My heart skipped a beat. I had been given a little hope that I didn't have at the beginning of the conversation. I thanked the security guard, and gave him my cell phone number, since I did not want anyone to know what I was doing. We exchanged goodbyes and I expressed my thanks several times for anything he could do for me. The phone went dead and now I just had to wait.

* * * * *

I walked quickly through the parking lot to get to my car. Both kids had sporting events in the evening and I did not was to miss a minute. My wife would attend my son's soccer game and I would go to my daughter's softball game.

I opened my car door, jumped in, and started the vehicle. I pushed the button on the radio for the local sports radio station, and then punched on my cell phone. It was a clunker, mounted on the middle boot of my car; it illuminated to life. I had just started to back out of my space when the phone rang. I let it ring a few times as I stopped the car.

I picked up the receiver and said, "Hello," fully expecting it to be my wife calling with a change of venue for my daughter's game or a last-minute grocery list to pick up at the supermarket. Instead, I heard an unfamiliar voice.

"Hello, is this Chris McGilvery's number?" a meek older woman's voice asked. "This is Emma Jean Smith from Central State Hospital calling. I got a message from security you were looking for someone."

My heart dropped. It had been a week since I had called the hospital, and the security guard's demeanor was such that I did not have confidence that he would take my request seriously and would just blow me off. I stammered for a few seconds, then blurted out,

"Yes, this is Chris McGilvery, and I was looking for the whereabouts of my mother who was a resident of Central State."

There was a long pause on the other end of the phone. I pulled back into my parking space and shut off the car engine. "Well, Mr. McGilvery, I have been working at this hospital for a long time, and I was in charge of administration and record keeping for the institution." She went on to tell me this was her first job out of high school, and she was scared to death to be exposed to people with mental disabilities, so the human resources manager put her in the administration office and away from the patients. It took her months to get used to the place, she said, and then it took a few more months to get used to encountering patients as she went to her car at night after work. As the years rolled on she became comfortable with the residents, and even let them in her office if they wanted to kill time during the day.

"I was not sure anyone would call me back," I said with thanks in my voice. "I am searching for what happened to my mother Joan McNulty, who was a resident of your facility around June 1950." I knew that she was not my mother, and I had told a white lie, but I did not want to make the story sound more complicated than it had to be.

"Well. I worked for the state for 47 years, and I was not here then, but we would have had a record of any patient who were here at any time," she replied. "The facility is officially closed, and I was kept on to coordinate and dispense of all records and files."

My confidence dropped when I heard her say she was getting rid of the records. The date of Anne's mother's transfer was so long ago I assumed the files would have been transferred to an off-site warehouse or destroyed, since the facility was in the process of being shut down.

"How much longer is the state going to keep you on to finish the processing and packaging of the records?" I asked with an inquisitive tone in my voice.

"Oh dear, I am only going to be here for one more month, and then the doors will be shut, and the windows and doors will be boarded up," she said. "All the residents are gone, and the state wants to sell the property."

I talked more with her, trying to elicit as much empathy as possible to have her go the extra mile to locate Joan's records, if any existed. I knew I had to make a bold move to get the evidence I would need to make the state keep Anne where she was and not move her to a halfway house.

"Well, Chris, I can continue to poke around, and see what I can find with the time I have left here. But when I leave, nothing will be left in the administration office, and no records will be left on the property."

I started to panic. "Emma, can I come out to Indianapolis and meet with you?" I blurted out. I could not even believe I said it. She was an elderly woman who had worked for the state for a lifetime. She was looking forward to a nice retirement. Why would she want to go out of her way to help a perfect stranger? I waited for some kind of response. The dead air was making my stomach burn.

"Well, dear, I have many things to do in the next month, and Indiana is so far for you to travel from Massachusetts to just see little old me," she said. Her voice was high and fragile. She repeated her concerns, but I put her mind at ease that I needed to see her, and see where my mother lived for a period of time. We agreed on a date and time to meet at Central State.

After I hung up the cell phone in its cradle I pondered how I was going to tell my wife where I was going, and what this road trip was all about. I was somewhat optimistic about my mission, but had no idea why. I started the engine, and the sports radio station came to life. I had a ray of hope I would get to the bottom of this mystery.

SOMEWHERE IN INDIANA

———————— ◆◆◆◆◆◆ ————————

It was an overcast day. I was cruising west on I-70 between Columbus, Ohio, on to the Indiana state capital. I had left home many hours before. I had decided to drive straight through from Massachusetts to Indiana to meet Emma Jean at Central State Hospital and get the proof I needed to blow the lid off things.

I had told my wife I was going on a three- day business trip to the Midwest and did not want to fly in case bad weather came in and left me stranded at some airport far away from home.

But the truth would come out if I had to charge more expenses away from home on my own personal account. I told my boss at work I was taking three days off to attend to some family business, which was sort of true in the whole scope of things.

I had been making good time and cruising at a fairly high rate of speed for hours. The only time I stopped was for a food break or to go the bathroom. I was accompanied by truckers along the way; the state police had been invisible in Indiana, at least so far.

I was out in the middle of nowhere in farm country. There was field after field of mostly corn and soybeans, with some fields mixed in that looked like vegetables. From my vantage point I didn't know what they were. All I knew is the farms were beautiful and went on for many miles. As I drove along I noticed some of the farmhouses must have been empty, as there were no vehicles in the yard. I knew someone was working the fields because I could see heavy machinery going back and forth.

The radio signal started to fade from the last station I had tuned in, so I looked down for a few seconds and started trying to find some music that suited my taste. I hit scan and let the radio run through several stations. After a couple of minutes I heard something that sounded good, so I locked it in. The artist was John Mellencamp, singing "Rain on the Scarecrow." It was a classic song about the farm crisis in the late 1970s and early 1980s.

At the time, farmers in the Midwest saw an opportunity to expand their crops to sell to Russia and third-world countries. They needed new tractors, combines, grain storage, irrigation, and other technologies to try to meet ever-expanding demand. During the mid-seventies interest rates were low, so farmers borrowed heavily, and went in big to make more money and grow their family business.

In the 1980s when the Soviet Union invaded Afghanistan, the U.S. slapped an embargo on exports to the Soviets. Meanwhile, other countries around the world had fallen on hard times. The net result was the grain export business tanked, and farmers were caught in the middle. They could not sell their crops, and local bankers started calling in the loans. Many farmers were forced to sell farms that had been in their families for over 100 years. Some despondent farmers felt the only way out was to commit suicide and have the life insurance help their families get through to the next boom period.

It was an ugly time for family farms and this song captured the mood of the time. I felt it was ironic that it came on as I crossed into Indiana. I was listening to the beat, and the road ahead was straight as an arrow. I was blowing by cars and trucks like they were standing still. I did not think anything of it, and then on the side of the road I spotted a state trooper sitting in his car; he had radar pointed at oncoming traffic. I quickly looked down and realized I was going close to ninety miles an hour. I took my foot off the accelerator. I dropped my speed, aimed for a break in the right lane between two cars, and slid myself right in.

I cruised on, fully expecting to be pulled over and cited for speeding, but I didn't get stopped. After that I kept up a decent but lawful rate of speed, and watched as the miles ticked by. I crossed onto I -65 and by night fall banked off the ramp and down into the city of Indianapolis. The lights of the city looked beautiful.

I went down the exit ramp into a commercial area. It looked familiar. I kept looking for the orange roof of the Howard Johnsons where my father and I had stayed many years ago, but I could not see anything with orange. Then I spotted it up on the right. It was the same motel, but had been painted a different color and renamed. I did not recognize the name, but I did notice this part of town was pretty run down. I started to second guess myself about staying here, but I thought about my budget and the fact that I was dog tired, so I pulled in.

There were a few cars in the lot, so I parked my car and went in to get a room. As I stepped in a bell rang, and an old man came out from a back room and asked if I wanted a room. I nodded my head in agreement, and we exchanged money and keys. He was a pretty low-key guy in his mid-seventies, and didn't really want to get into a big conversation. I asked him where I could catch a bite to eat and he pointed to the fast food joint across the street. I put in a wakeup call for seven and then was on my way.

After a burger and some fries, I settled in my room and zoned out to cable TV until I fell asleep.

* * * * *

I was in a serene dream state, but I kept hearing a noise in the back on my mind that wouldn't quit. I could hear scraping and scratching, and when I came to and looked around, I was disoriented. It took a second for me to realize I was in a strange room. The clock next to the bed said 1:56 in red lettering. I sat up in bed for a moment to get my bearings, and then that same sound started up again. I jumped out of bed in my underwear, and made my way across the room to the door. I had left the bathroom light on in case I needed to go the bathroom.

As I listened at the door the sound started up again, and at that point I realized it was coming from the other direction, outside my window. I walked over to the other side of the room, and pulled the shades back ever so slightly. The window was open. I crouched down on my knees to take a look. I looked out over the parking lot and saw a man trying to break into a car. He was dressed in ragged clothes. He had something in his hand, like a wire or stick, and kept trying to jam it into the opening in the door seam. It must have been a wire coat hanger. He was methodically pushing it in and pulling back, trying to catch the door lock to pop it. I made sure I was very quiet because I was on the first floor, and only about 25 feet from where the man was standing.

After some more unsuccessful attempts, he backed away from the car for a minute, and then the street light fully illuminated the car he was breaking into. The man was breaking into my car! I knew I should have stayed in a different part of town. I started to rethink my choices, but then I had to focus on the situation at hand. Should I call the office, or maybe I should call the police? I had no idea if the motel manager was on site or asleep, and who knew how long it would take for the police to respond to a car break-in over on the bad side of town.

As I thought about my options, I saw the man pick up a rock from what passed for landscaping. He made his way back over to my car. Panic set in. I quickly yelled "Get away from that car, or I'll call the police." I crouched back down on the floor, out of view. The man hesitated and looked back over his shoulder. The glare form the street light spread across his face, and I could see how glassy his eyes were. He was totally stoned and most likely looking for something to steal and trade for some cash for drugs.

He looked in my direction, and then turned back towards the car like he was not sure if he heard anything. I suddenly remembered that my briefcase was in the car; it had all my documentation on my sister and her mother. If the crook stole that or the whole car, I would be out of business, since I had never made copies of the documents.

I jumped up from my spot on the motel floor and paced nervously back and forth. I had only seconds to do something before the window in my car was smashed. I had no time to think. I had to react right away. I went to the window and yelled as loud as I could, "Hey you, get away from that car, I'm calling the cops right now!" I waited for a response from the man. I prayed he would turn away.

The man looked back at my window; I'm not sure if he could make me out. He stood there with the rock in his hand. Then he turned and walked through the parking lot, and dropped the rock along the way. I let out a huge sigh of relief as he moved further and further away. I wanted to go out to my car and get my briefcase, but thought better of it. I was still in a bad part of town and if the guy doubled back I could be in real trouble.

I decided to turn on the TV, sit on the floor, and stand watch over my car until the sun came up. My body and mind were completely awake, so I had no problem staying up the rest of the night. I turned the channel to cable news, and sat back with a view of the parking lot.

In the morning I showered and dressed, then left the motel. I double-checked my directions and headed out for my appointment with Emma.

I drove until I found my way to the hospital entrance. I went to look in my outside mirror to take a left-hand turn to get into the correct lane to enter the driveway. I was startled when I realized that druggy had broken the mirror off. I immediately turned my head to the left, and entered the next lane and put my blinker on. Once the traffic cleared from the other direction I turned into the long, winding driveway to the grounds and made my way to where the administration building was, and where I had my appointment with, hopefully, someone who could help me.

As I drove up the hill I could see how much the grounds and the buildings were run down and in disrepair. The road had cracks and pot holes, the grass was overgrown, and the buildings were dingy, with paint chipping off the old wire mesh windows. The whole atmosphere made it more spooky than it really was.

I passed a worn-out sign with the names of all the buildings, with arrows pointing the way to each one. The paint had faded from the sign, so you couldn't really figure out what the names and directions were. I remembered where the administration building was from years earlier when I came here with my father. I was like my father in that way. Once I had been somewhere, I never forgot how to get there.

At the top of the hill I saw the administration building on the right. There were two cars parked on the left, so I pulled into a space next to them. I pulled my briefcase from the back seat, jumped out of the car, and made my way up the steps. I walked up to the big brown doors and tried to turn the big brass handle. It did not turn, so I just gave the door a big pull and it creaked open.

I stepped into a huge entryway looking across a red and white linoleum floor that went all the way to the other side of the building. Every ten feet or so, there was a smoked glass mahogany door with the name of an official person or department. It was so quiet you could hear a pin drop. I yelled "Is anyone here?" and my voice echoed throughout the large open space. I heard nothing back. Then I repeated my yell again, and I waited for a response.

Then I heard a toilet flush, and some water running for a few seconds. After that, I could hear the shuffling of feet. An old man emerged from the men's room. He had gray hair, with a neatly pressed state security uniform and a nice shiny, silver badge on his chest. He looked to be in good spirits, and when he saw me he smiled. "Sorry to keep you, son, but mother nature was calling," he said in a quaint Midwestern drawl. "I could hear you yelling, but I knew you weren't going anywhere in a hurry." He let out a chuckle under his breath.

"Miss Emma Jean told me you were coming today, so we both have been expecting you. She has been going through wads of paper and files the past few weeks trying to get organized here before the final shutdown day. We are the only two left," he belted out with a proud affect to his voice. "I been here almost forty years, and never had a sick day. Can you believe that?" His face broke into a sly smile, and I was not sure if he was pulling my leg. I kept nodding my head agreeing with everything he said, hoping it would lead to Emma Jean sooner rather than later.

As we passed the time I could hear the echo of footsteps coming, but I could not tell from what direction. The noise bounced around because there was no furniture or drapes or anything to absorb the sound. After a few seconds of guessing which direction the steps were coming from, an older woman appeared from the opposite end of the lobby from where we were standing. This had to be Emma Jean. We both turned and walked towards each other. The security guard walked step-by-step in unison with me towards the woman.

As we got closer her features became more apparent. She looked about 65. She had short gray hair, and was of average size and weight. You could tell looking at her face that she must have been a beautiful woman in her youth. I'm also sure that is why the security guard paid so much attention to her. I bet this guy had had a crush on her for years.

As we closed the last ten feet she stuck out her hand, and said "You must be Mr. McGilvery. I am so glad to finally meet. I can't believe you came so far to find your mother." I put my hand in hers, and she shook it with a very tender touch. I had pangs of guilt about the story I had told her to gain her confidence and have her help me. "You have come so far to unlock this little mystery of yours, I'm sure you always wondered what happened." She looked straight into my eyes and gave me a disarming smile that made me melt.

We stood together and listened to the security guard tell us a few war stories of being on the front lines in this place when it was in its heyday. Then he switched subjects and told us all the plans he had made for his retirement. After he touched on fishing, hunting, and drinking down at the lodge, it reinforced my theory that he was a bachelor and had a crush on Emma Jean. I listened to his stories politely, and then Emma Jean pulled me away and told the man we had to get to work before the electric company shut the lights off. We actually backed up 20 feet with the man still talking to us before we turned and disappeared into another office.

As we walked away I could still hear his voice telling us to call him if we needed anything. Emma told me "George is a great guy, and a good friend. I have worked with him for years, but once he gets to talking, you just can't get away." She gave me a nice smile while we walked, and I explained why I was here, and what I was hoping to find. She said she understood completely, and was more than willing to wade through files to find out if my mother, well, my make-believe mother, had been in this institution.

Her office was outfitted with old-style furniture and decorations, and adorned with many awards and plaques from the state for good work and going above and beyond. I looked at one picture right behind her desk and it looked like a higher-up with her in an official photo. He was giving her a silver bowl with an inscription on it. He looked like either the head of this facility or the secretary of mental health for the state of Indiana. In the background there were some residents in the picture. I pondered if she had wanted the residents in the picture or the politicians wanted a good photo op. I did not approach the subject with her because she looked so proud on the picture and it was in a key spot behind her desk.

The rest of the office was pretty run of the mill, with several chairs, a small photocopy machine, several filing cabinets, old style drapes that framed out the window looking down the hill to a beautiful view of the Indianapolis skyline.

She sat down behind her desk looking very proud, looked at me, and waved me over to sit in a chair that was facing her. I hung my coat on the back the chair, and put my briefcase on the floor beside me and exhaled. "It won't be long before me and George walk out that door for the last time. We had a lot of good years here, but mental health philosophy has taken a different path and dinosaurs like us have been left behind," she said. She looked at me for a response and I nodded my head politely. "I suppose my husband will be happy. Now we can travel in the camper around the country. That was his dream. This layoff has forced my hand. It's funny how a job you anticipated not liking could turn out to be so fulfilling." An uncomfortable silence fell on the two of us.

"You have come a long way, sir, and I'm sure you have a million questions to ask. Your story intrigued me on the phone," she said in an inquisitive way. "You said your mother was a resident here back in the fifties. Do you have any idea what date you think she might have come here?" She sat back in her chair, and folded her hands on her lap.

I sat bolt up in my chair and picked up my briefcase, and took out a file and flipped it open. I did not want to give it to her, in case she discovered my little white lie. So I acted like I was flipping pages to find the date. I told her I thought it was around May or June of 1950. I waited uncomfortably for a few seconds, getting ready for the obvious question.

"What was your mother's name, Chris?" she asked. I hesitated for a few seconds and then said, "Joan McNulty." She looked across at me with a suspicious look on her face. "How did you end up with a different name that your mother?"

I should have had a canned answer, but with the long trip and being so upset about the whole situation I never thought to come up with a cover story. I sat there looking across the desk in an awkward silence. Then it came to me. "Well, I believe when the Massachusetts hospital sent here out to this facility, they changed her name to cover up a situation they needed to put to bed. It is very complicated, and I'd rather not get into it, if I can help it."

I sat there nervously thinking that either Emma Jean was going to ask for more information, or she was going to flat out turn me down, thinking I was a reporter trying to get information to write an expose about the mental health system in the past and how unfairly patients were treated. I sat there fidgeting in my seat waiting for her response.

"So that's an interesting turn of events. You believe your mother was transferred from one mental health facility to another to cover up some misdoing by the facility?" she sat there rubbing her chin thinking about what I had just said, and then said "Many disturbing things happened everywhere at many facilities across this country that many states would be embarrassed to have become public. I know exactly what you mean. I sat in this office, so I could justify looking the other way, but honestly I knew the residents were not always treated humanely by all the attendants, and it broke my heart." She sat looking down, tapping her fingers on the blotter of the desk. "Thank goodness those days are over, and it's a new beginning with mentally challenged patients, and they are treated much better"

I agreed with her, since it was not her fault for any of the misdeeds of the past. As our conversation went along and she asked questions, and I gave guarded answers, Emma was writing everything down in a tablet of white paper. When she finished she looked at me, and said, "This is a very interesting turn of events. Now it's time for us to get to work," she said in a commanding voice. She stood up and walked by me with her pad of paper. "Follow me," she ordered

I jumped up, leaving my briefcase and coat and trailed on behind her. As we walked we engaged in conversation about the state facility and Emma's personal life. She had a wealth of knowledge and I tried to absorb as much information as she was giving out. We strolled down one corridor and onto the next. As we passed room after room, I looked in and saw some rooms with just the bedframes left behind. Some rooms also had an old bureau or dresser. Some rooms were empty, and you could see across the emptiness and look through the old smoked glass with cold metal frames.

It gave me a strange feeling thinking about how many broken men, women, and children had come through this place. If only the walls could talk, I'm sure they could tell me so many heartbreaking stories.

We turned the corner and walked down a flight of stairs to the basement level. Emma opened an old steel door, and we entered a huge room with all the furniture from upstairs, along with rows of gray metal filing cabinets. When I let go of the door it slammed with an unforgiving thud. Even though it was daytime, little light came through the windows. Emma walked to a big light with a sting hanging; she pulled the string and the section of the basement we were in came to life.

"Well, hopefully the filing cabinet we need is still here," Emma said in an unsure voice. "The people contracted to store our records have been coming in here for months removing cabinet after cabinet. It's got to the point, they don't even include me with coordinating the removal anymore. They just check in with George and do their thing."

She looked down at her pad of paper, and she started walking up and down the rows of old filing cabinets. We walked very slowly, and at each one she looked at each of the three drawers, peering at the white label that indicated names and dates. She worked her way along methodically, not wanting to miss a faded label, and giving it her best shot. We did not say anything for about fifteen minutes. I could tell we were getting to the end of the line, and I started to have a sick feeling about what was coming next.

"Well, Mr. McGilvery, it looks like we are out of luck," she sighed. It looks like all the filing cabinets from the 1950s and 1960s have been removed. They are now with a professional storage company, and if you don't have legal authority or have a lawyer and a court order you are not going to get any cooperation." She looked disappointed, but not as disappointed as I started to feel. Here I had come halfway across the country on a wild goose chase and was going to leave with nothing.

"Emma, I appreciate that you have even taken the time to meet with me," I said with as much enthusiasm as I could muster. "You have gone way out of your way to try and help me, and that's all I could ask for."

"Don't give up just yet, sir, I still have a couple of tricks up my sleeve," she smiled. She started walking and I followed along. As we went by the overhead light I pulled the string and the blackness filled the room again.

After another long walk we ended up back in her office, and I was back in my seat. She sat behind her desk, and pulled out a set of keys from a side drawer. Then she opened the middle drawer, and pulled out a larger set of keys. She got up, walked over to a very big wooden cabinet, stuck a key from the chain into the lock and turned it ever so slightly.

I was looking at her the whole time, not knowing what she could possibly be doing. I heard a click, and she pulled the doors open. The cabinet was filled with plastic bins, each one with a file label.

"I plum forgot about this little beauty," she said in a sly way. "I can't believe this did not cross my mind until we were downstairs. I must be really losing it. Maybe the state was right when they said I should retire and enjoy myself." I could hear a cute little chuckle from under her breath. She turned back and looked at the containers, reading the labels very carefully. Then she pulled a bin out from the bottom level, walked over, and placed it in the middle of her desk.

I sat there peering at it still wondering what was inside. She popped the top off the bin, and then pulled out a bunch of what looked like old microfiche. I instantly remembered this storage format from doing research in the library. In the seventies many companies started converting paper files to this, in order to save space, which in turn saved money. "What is on the microfiche?" I asked in a hopeful, inquisitive voice.

Emma held the blue plastic in her hand as if she had found a rare diamond. Then she held it up to the light. Then I heard her say as she turned her back to face the window, "The same thing that was in all those filing cabinets in the basement. All the records on every patient and resident that ever passed through this facility." She held up the packet of blue plastic, letting the sun light pass through.

I sat bolt upright in my seat, and felt a shiver of hope run through my entire body. Could this be the break I was looking for? I saw Emma place the plastic down on the desk, and make her way over to another piece of furniture. She started going through the key chain in a methodical way until she found the key she was looking for. Then she jabbed it into the lock and turned the key and pulled open both doors. "I was wondering, good sir, if you could pull that machine out of there and place it over there on that big table?" she commanded.

I jumped right up and hurried over to her. There was a 1970s, state-of-the-art microfiche reader. I had not seen one of these for at least 20 years. What a relic. It was gray metal, covered with dust, but looked to be in perfect condition. I reached under with both hands and pulled it out, then stood up straight. It was heavier than I thought, but I tried not to let Emma see that I was struggling.

"Now, now honey, don't go hurting yourself on my account. Make sure you lift with your knees," she ordered. She followed behind me over to the table. After it landed, I pulled a handkerchief out of my pocket and began dusting it off. She took the cord, stretched it over to the wall, and plugged it into the nearest outlet. She came back to the table and flipped the switch. The machine came to life, except for one thing: No light. A strong light should have come on to project the image up on the screen.

"Well, well, lookie here. It looks like the light is not working for some reason," Emma said. She walked back to her desk, while I fiddled with knobs and switches. After a few minutes, she walked up behind me and handed me a letter opener. I looked at her with a curious look, and she said, "Turn those two screws over there, so we can pull the bulb out and check to see if it's good"

I took the letter opener from her, and jabbed it into the top of one of the screws to get some traction. I pushed down, and finally I got one screw spinning. As I pulled it out, I jimmied with the plate, which helped get the second screw to come out easier. I removed the plate. I turned the bulb a few revolutions and I popped it out carefully so as to not drop the precious commodity on the floor. As I removed it, I brought it up to my ear, and shook it. My heart sank as I heard the filaments rattling around inside. It was broken. I held it up for Emma to see, and shook it. She could tell from my expression what had happened without saying a word.

"Now honey, don't get all your britches in a bunch. I still have a few more tricks up my sleeve," she said in a playful manner. Then she strolled over behind her desk, sat in her chair, and started flipping through more keys until she found the one she was looking for. She impressed me with her memory, and could out-duel any janitor with a string of keys on his belt. She walked over to yet another filing cabinet and opened the lock. She pulled open the middle drawer and reached in. I was curious as to what she was looking for, and then her hand came back up with a new box of lightbulbs for the microfiche reader. I could not believe my eyes. "Where did you ever get those bulbs, Emma? Those have to be two decades old, and the box is not even open, I exclaimed.

"Well, she said, I never had any need to open them. Up until we put that fiche machine in the closet, the bulb which came with the unit was still working. I'll bet one of the office workers or janitors banged it around enough to break it." She paused for a moment, and then said, "Now that you mention it, I think I paid for these out of my own pocket. I was always trying to plan ahead in the event a situation came up. Well, it's too late now anyway to claim it. This dam state doesn't have any money anyway," she said, chuckling.

I took the box from her hand, opened it, and pulled out a fresh, new bulb. They were in perfect condition, and in the back of my mind I prayed she got the right size for this machine. I compared the new one with the old one, and they looked the same. I started to thread the new one into the socket. Suddenly the light illuminated, and hit me in the eye like a laser. I turned my head fast, but all I could see was stars. I continued to screw the bulb in tight while my vision came back to normal, and Emma hit the off switch just as I was searching for it like a blind man.

After a few moments, my sight was back to normal. I put the plate on, and put the screws back in place. Emma went back to her desk and grabbed the box of microfiche. We sat down at the table, and she started to look at the dates printed on the pouches holding the fiche. As she was doing that she said, "What was that date again son, May of 1950? That sure was a long time ago."

I nodded my head in agreement, and she kept going through the box, flipping through the even rows of fiche. That one bin had over 50 years of admission records, and court material. I sat back in my chair and let her do her thing. I did not want to make her feel I was peering through her, but I was so excited to find out the truth about Anne's mother, I felt like jumping out of my skin. If I could only get some additional proof of this tragedy, I would have the leverage I needed.

Emma removed stacks of blue fiche and inserted films one by one into the machine, and then directed the travel guide to line the pictures up on the screen. As she did this, I sat up at attention and looked at the screen from about two feet away. Our heads were probably only six inches apart, and I was busy looking over the same prints that she was looking at.

She methodically went through reams of fiche and I was astonished how many residents had come through this facility.

After we had looked through many, many records, I started to lose my focus, and slumped back in my chair. My back was hurting from the old wooden chairs, but I tried to look interested. Emma still had the same intense look on her face, and was determined to find the file. I felt as if this was her final official act, and when she accomplished it she could retire with a clear conscience.

I saw the sun setting and I looked at my watch. It was almost 7:00 and we had been at this for most of the day. Neither of us had had anything to eat, and we hadn't even gone the bathroom. I started to feel guilty, since I had not even offered to run out to a fast food restaurant and get us something to eat.

Emma had gone through so many fiche pouches, I could not even keep count them. She was working like a well-oiled machine, and you would never know that she was a woman of an advanced age. She could put me to shame.

As I sat back contemplating if I should offer to get some food or call it quits for the night, I saw a smile emerge across her wrinkled face. She kept looking at the various pictures lined up on the screen, and then she sat back for the first time in hour, put both arms behind her head, and that big smile just got bigger.

I looked at her once more, and then back at the screen, and lo and behold I saw nine black and white pictures of official state documents up on the screen. I could tell by her expression we had struck gold. As I peered closer I could see the name on one form that said Joan McNulty, and her date of birth. At the top of the form was a transfer notice from Worcester State Hospital to Indiana State Hospital dated May 10, 1950. It had a copy of her birth certificate, social security card, health records prior to her transfer, Indiana Central State official paperwork, and a number of other documents. My heart was jumping with joy, but I did not want to show my elation, so I played it cool.

Emma explained all the forms to me, and what they meant, and then finished putting the other fiche back in the plastic bin. She handed me the pouch with the documents I needed. I gave her a look that said, can I have these to keep, and she put them in my hand and said, "I didn't see a thing." Then she let out one of her familiar cackles, shut off the machine, and stood up.

As she drifted across the floor, I raced after her to grab the fiche container out of her hand, and neatly put it back in it cabinet. I locked the cabinet and handed her the key. I put the pouch in my briefcase, closed it, and began to ask her if I could take her out to dinner. She cut me off in midsentence.

"Just a minute, Mr. McGilvery, we are not done yet. I have one more thing to show you before you go on your way." She took me by the arm and guided me out of the administration office, and down a dark hallway headed for the back of the building. We went past many empty offices and rooms that had housed so many troubled souls. I held on to her arm partly to hold her up, and partly because I was getting the creeps. Emma kept the conversation going with a history lesson on the facility, and eventually we came to an old steel door. She told me to push it open. I pushed down on the bar and nudged the door with my shoulder to open it. It started to open ever so slightly with a loud, scary creak.

Emma directed me out through a patio where the residents must have congregated to get fresh air, talk, and smoke their cigarettes. There were still hundreds of cigarette butts in mounds along the edge. She grabbed my arm even tighter as she led me down a long walkway, and on to a grass lawn and up a hill. As we approached the top, I could see a black, wrought iron fence outlining a small graveyard.

Once I figured out what this was I pulled on Emma's arm, and said "You really don't have to show me this Emma. It looks like sacred ground." She looked back and assured me it was important. I continued to walk.

We walked through the open gate and into the gravestone area. The sun was just setting, and the shadows were reflecting on us, which made it even more eerie. The gravestones all had the same surname. I asked Emma who all these people were and she said that these were members of the family that owned the land before the state purchased it from them. I looked at every headstone, and then we came to a large statue, at least twelve feet tall, made of white granite. It had turned dark over the years, and had hundreds of names inscribed on it.

Emma stepped forward and peered very closely at the names and went up and down the rows of names, and then her finger stuck on one name. She put her arm behind me and directed my head down to look at the name. As my eyes adjusted to the diming light, I could see the name Joan McNulty inscribed in small etched letters.

I tuned to Emma, and asked her when Joan had died, and she said "I'm not sure, but it is in the paperwork you have now. A death certificate is all part of the paperwork that goes in the resident's file. The family that owned this land had a son with Down syndrome, and he is buried here, and the family wanted residents who died here to be cremated and buried with him. They were so devoted to the mental health community because they understood the heartbreak of having a child with mental disabilities."

I looked into her eyes, and she was so solemn. We looked away in the other direction, paid our respects, and then Emma sent me on my way. I begged her to go to dinner, and could I pay her for her trouble, but she would not hear of it.

As I was driving back to New England I thought about how nice she was, and how much she cared for the residents, and how much pride she had in her job. I thought to myself that she was one-of-a-kind, but then I realized a lot of people from the Midwest were just like her. I sat back in the seat of my car, and accelerated onto the Interstate to travel back home, wondering what Anne's future would hold.

PART IV

ACTON, MASS., WINTER 1998

◆◆◆◆◆

I kept rubbing my hands after many hours of shoveling snow. A nor'easter had come in like a lion and stuck around for more than a day. It had disrupted the Boston area and its suburbs, and I was not able to make it to work. The kids were home from school, and my wife was doing her best to keep them entertained with movies and games.

The neighborhood looked like winter wonderland, and most people near my house were out doing the same thing. It seemed like I had been outside for hours shoveling. The storm had dropped more than twelve inches of snow, with another six inches forecast for tonight. I wanted to keep ahead of it, since I lived on a busy street and the plows kept coming up and down the street filling in my driveway. The cold had really settled into my body and the bone chilling wind kept me frozen. I wanted to keep the driveway as clear as possible so I would not have as big a job shoveling in the morning.

The hard pack was starting to freeze up at the end of the driveway, and I exchanged my aluminum shovel for an old steel shovel that penetrated the hard layers of snow. The going was tough, and progress was slow, but I was determined to get the whole driveway done. I was losing what light there was, and the temperature was dropping every hour, so I bore down on my task. I could feel myself breathing heavy since I was out of shape from working an office job for the past 25 years.

I saw a stray car working its way down the street. I wondered if they were a medical person who had to go to work, or a poor parent who had run out of food and had to go to the store. Either way it was not a good day to be on the road. After another few minutes of stabbing at the snow, I heard a car horn blow as it went by. It must have been one of our friends from around town. I gave the one-handed salute, and went back to what I was doing.

After about an hour, I finally broke through to the main street, and worked the pile over to both sides. I could see the finish line to what I was doing, and for a moment I wondered if I would be able to see any traffic as I pulled out in the morning. The piles of snow were five or six feet high, and sitting low in a car, I knew it would be difficult to see to pull out onto a busy street. As I was thinking this, I heard that fateful sound. It was a plow coming down the street, spraying mounds of snow into the air, aiming to ruin my just-completed job.

I stepped back about 15 feet as the big state plow bore down on my driveway. He was totally clueless as what he was about to do to my handiwork that I just spent three hours on. I was dog tired, and not in the mood to start over. I was looking forward to going in the house, warming up, and having something to eat or drink.

The sound of the truck got close and closer. I could see the plow closing in on my driveway. I braced myself as the driver went rushing by with what I thought was a smile on his face. The plow and the wind blew a white cloud into the air, and just like that I had another two feet of white slop in my driveway. I cursed at the driver as he disappeared into the distance. I threw my shovel into the snow in disgust. I started swearing up a storm, and started stomping around the driveway like a crazy person. Even though I knew I was acting like an idiot, I could not help myself.

As I was walking around acting foolish, I could hear the faint sound of someone's voice carrying in the air. I looked around but could not see where it was coming from. I started to get concerned that my elderly neighbor across the street had fallen, and could not get up from the slippery snow and ice. I tried to look over on the other side of the street, but could see nothing. The visibility was poor, I started to make my way to the end of the driveway to cross over to the other side of the street, when I heard the sound again. It was coming from behind me. As I turned, I could see my wife in the door, waving to me to come in. I was so glad to see her, I guessed that she had made me a nice cup of cocoa to warm my frigid body. My mood began to improve once I saw her, and I waved back to her, only to realize she was holding the phone in her hand and was signaling me to come into the house because I had a phone call. My mood dropped again, wondering about the reason for the call.

I made my way up the steps and into the house. Once in, I took my coat, hat, and gloves off, and then sat on the stairs and pulled off my boots. I tried not to make a mess, and then looked up at my wife. She said it was my sister's lawyer, and she needed to talk to me. My heart sank at that point. I was hungry and tired, and I knew this phone call was not going to be anything but trouble.

I grabbed the phone from my wife, and she gave me a peck on the cheek, as I made my way down the hall into our bedroom to have a little privacy. In the other room I could hear my two children enjoying their vacation day from school. As I entered the room, I made a conscious effort not to sit down on the bed because my pants were wet. I peeled off my damp socks, and put on my slippers, which was a vast improvement to help warm up my frostbitten toes.

I put the phone up to my mouth, and tried to give a cheery "Hello." It came out very dull and rehearsed. I heard a female voice say "Hi, Mr. McGilvery. This is Ms. Prince from the Department of Mental Health. How are you today?" she said in a nice demeanor.

"I have been okay. Just trying to get through the winter, I suppose," I lied. I knew I had to go back out and shovel the slushy mess in my driveway before I went to bed, or it would be hard as rock in the morning. "What is the reason for your call Ms. Prince? Is my sister okay?" I questioned.

"She is doing just fine. Anne has been doing well, and been attending her day programs every day. My call is to discuss something else with you today. I won't take too much of your time."

I waited for what was coming, and a sick feeling started to form in the pit of my stomach. I wasn't sure if it was hunger or from what I was about to hear.

"You remember what we talked about some time ago, Mr. McGilvery? About Anne being transferred to a resident home?" she inquired. "Well, one has come available for your sister that would meet her needs."

"Yes I do remember that, unfortunately, Ms. Prince. I was hoping this day would never come," I replied in a sarcastic voice. I felt guilty about my tone, but I was so upset, and protective of my sister, I couldn't help it.

"I know," she said in a comforting tone. "We have to make the best of the situation, but on the positive side, your sister could make great strides in a group home. I have heard good things back from some of them."

My mind drifted back to the group home where the social worker was murdered, and I could feel my anxiety level start to climb. I wanted my sister to be safe, and I had the feeling the controls would be very lax, and my sister would be able to run away.

"The state called yesterday," Ms. Prince said. "They have a group home that is in the early stages of being remodeled, and should be ready by May or June at the latest. It is in a town called Foxwood, down on the South Shore of Boston. It was donated to the state by an estate, and it suits all the needs and criteria to be a group home. The people in Boston seem to think it will be a good fit for Anne."

I was half listening while Anne's lawyer went on, and my mind drifted in and out of focus. I was focused on all the negative things that could happen to Anne, and none of the good. I was letting my thoughts race away and I kept trying to catch myself and sound like an adult. I knew that this woman was trying to do the best for all involved.

"Chris, are you still there?" I heard the woman cut in.

"Yes, yes, Ms. Prince, I was distracted by my children outside my bedroom door. What was that you were saying?"

"I'd like us to go down to the site of the new group home next week and meet some people from the state and the social worker who will be in charge of the new house. You and I will be able to ask all the questions and concerns we have about the new arrangement, and I think it will be beneficial for all involved," she said.

I responded back to her that I would be interested in attending the meeting, so we made arrangements, and I thanked her for her time and concern for Anne. As I hung up the phone, I pondered what that meeting would be like, and if Anne and I were being railroaded by a state system. Only time would tell.

* * * * *

I swung off my exit on Route 128, and looked over my shoulder to merge with traffic. The volume of cars was too heavy during the midday for any normal person. I put my blinker on, and took a quick left, and pulled into a hotel parking lot. I drove around until I found a visible parking space, and backed my car in and shut it off. I was to meet Ms. Prince here at 11:00 and then drive with her to Foxwood to tour the new group home.

An old, red compact car pulled up in front of me and blocked me in. I was thinking, I probably was in a restricted space, and just when I was starting my engine to move, the window went down and Ms. Prince appeared with a big smile on her face. I waved to her to pull into my space, and then pulled out. I was sure we would have lots to talk about on our way down to Foxwood.

After a moment, the passenger side door opened, and she stepped into my car, putting her big, black legal briefcase on the floor with a thud. She huffed and puffed, then said, "I am getting too old to carry this briefcase around. I don't know why I haven't bought one of those light ones with nice colors and soft material."

I looked over at her for a split second, nodding my head. Then I pulled out on to the highway, and we made our way south to our destination. The ride itself was really just a bunch of small talk about my family and life, and Ms. Prince's family and life. She had a very impressive record of achievement with the state and in her private practice. She was not much different than me; she had grown up in a suburban town close to Boston, and her occupation was really the same as it always was. She used to be employed by state Mental Health Department to represent residents. Now she was still representing them, just not for the state, but for the families of the residents. She made the ride pleasant, and the trip down to the South Shore took no time at all.

As we drove she read off directions to me. We entered the town, and made our way through the town square with all its shops and stores and its quaint charm. As we drove through the main intersection, my spirits began to rise. This didn't seem like such a bad place. As we drove further I noticed the many nice Victorian homes in all shapes, colors, and sizes.

"Pull in over there," Ms. Prince suddenly ordered. I put on my left blinker and moved over to the middle of the road to wait for a break in traffic. As I looked over, I could see a dark brown, run down, old home. A big dumpster was in the back of the driveway.

I pulled in and parked the car. Two other newer model cars were in the driveway. They must have belonged to the two people from the state we were meeting today to go over the transfer of Anne to this home. As I shut off the engine, I looked over at Ms. Prince. She had a look of doubt on her face, just as I did. I tried to not show my cards, but my expression must have said it all.

I jumped out of the car and ran around to open her door. I escorted her inside. As we stepped onto the porch, I almost broke through the floorboards. I stepped over a few good cracks, and advised which way for Ms. Prince to go, as if we were walking through a minefield. I reached for the door, turned the knop, and pushed as hard as I could. The door weighed a hundred pounds, and was very creaky. I held it open as best I could for my companion to enter into the main house.

When we got in, all I could see was a run down, dilapidated, home in need of major repair. How could Anne live in this place? I could not see a good outcome with any amount of money involved. I knew the state did not have unlimited financial resources, and mental health had even less.

As we walked in, two women came out of a side room that had been made into a makeshift office, with two desks pushed together and a filing cabinet in the corner. It was very sparse and the walls were a dingy, grayish white. You could see where some holes had been covered up, but not sanded before being painted over.

"Hi," one woman said. "You must be Ms. Prince and Mr. McGilvery. It is so nice to finally meet you." The woman was of good size, with short blond hair, and an outdated blue pantsuit. She stuck out her hand to both of us and we each shook it. "I'm Ms. Atwood, the regional director of all the resident homes in the South Shore district.

Another woman who was much younger, maybe in her late twenties, stepped up from behind Ms. Atwood and introduced herself as Lora Durfer. She was meek and mild. She had brunette hair, was small and thin, and dressed in style for the times. She was carrying a clipboard with lots of hen scratching on it. She was very nice, and tried to lower the anxiety level, which must have been written on our faces when we walked in.

We exchanged pleasantries, then they invited us into their office. They opened up a couple of old steel folding chairs, and pushed them closer to the two desks so we could sit down and talk. Ms. Atwood opened her folder and got down to business.

"I am sure you two have a lot of questions about Anne's transition to a group home from Tewksbury State Hospital. I know you both have reservations because Anne has been in a locked unit setting for most of her adult life, and my boss said you have security concerns about the group homes in general. Is that what I'm hearing?" She moved forward in her chair to make a commanding presence.

I looked over at Ms. Prince, and was ready to speak when she decided to give the opening volley. "Ms. Atwood, as you well know from our phone calls and e-mails my client Mr. McGilvery is very concerned for his sister's safety being out of a locked unit. She has a history of running away in the past. I was wondering if you could go over those safety concerns, and what the group home would do to keep a safe environment for their residents?" Ms. Prince sat back in her seat and waited for Ms. Atwood to reply.

"Well, Ms. Prince, this remodeled home will have state-of-the-art locks on all outside doors, which will be wired with buzzers when they are opened. The main office will be near the front door so we can see whoever enters the premises, and if a resident tries to open any door without supervision, an alarm will go off to alert the staff. The day and evening shifts will consist of two well-trained social workers, and the night shift will be staffed by a male social worker. We are confident that once the house opens, and we have all staff on board, the resident home will be as secure as a locked unit with all the comforts of home," she concluded. Ms. Atwood sat back in her chair very pleased with herself when the younger woman spoke up.

"Mr. McGilvery, our staff are very experienced and all have advanced degrees in social work and psychology. They are young, but very professional. There will be a day program, field trips, and lots of social occasions. At least once or twice a week, there will a field trip down to the shops in the center of town. That way Anne can interact with the town folks and shop owners," she finished with a smile.

The two of them continued to go over all the detailed plans for the house. They also brought out plenty of paper work to review and sign. Ms. Prince carefully read every piece of paper, and gave me the ones that needed to be signed.

After there was a lull in the conversation, I interjected, "How much work will go into this house before its ready for residents? It looks like there will need to be tens of thousands of dollars of work done. I would hope it is up to code, and has all the things the residents will need to be comfortable."

"Oh," Ms. Atwood jumped in. "The house was given to the state by the Azinger family, who had a child involved in the mental health system her whole life. They were so happy with the devotion of all the mental health workers over the years so they left this house to us in their estate. This house will be as nice as a new home, and it will be completely up to code and handicap accessible. I know you will be pleased with the final product." She looked over to Ms. Prince for reassurance.

Ms. Prince looked at the woman and asked, "May we have a tour of the house while we are here?"

Ms. Durfer sat forward and said, "The house is in the middle of being stripped out, and being readied for remodeling. I don't think it is totally safe, and we would not want to be responsible if something fell on you, or you tripped and fell. I think it would be better if you wait to see the finished product."

Once I realized the meeting was wrapping up, I felt nervous how fast things were changing, and had to ask a few more questions. I looked over at Ms. Prince, and she had finished with all her questions and comments. I looked back at the two state workers, and said, "Ms. Durfer, my sister has a history of running away and disappearing. Can you guarantee me that this will not happen under your watch?" She looked surprised and somewhat stunned.

"Mr. McGilvery," she said carefully. "We try to address all safety measures for taking care of residents, but no amount of planning can guarantee Anne will never run away or drift away from a social worker in public."

"We are confident that your sister will be safe, and you will be happy with her care, Ms. Atwood added.

"You mean like that social worker's safety in Beverly. Do you mean that kind of guarantee?" I snapped. As soon as the words came out of my mouth I could not believe I had said them. I had all this nervousness and anxiety built up inside me from worrying about Anne's welfare, but they did not deserve that comment.

I looked around the table at everyone, and all three women were staring at me. I was just about to try and smooth over my stupid comment, when Ms. Atwood came at me with both barrels. "Sir," she said testily. "Our number one priority is the residents of the state facilities and resident homes, and our workers are tireless and devoted to them. We will care for your sister as though she is being looked after by yourself. You can count on that." She had a look on her face that could kill.

I felt bad for my inconsiderate comments, but I just had to leave that thought with them for the future. We wrapped up the meeting with very formal goodbyes. The ride home was quiet. I knew Ms. Prince was upset with me, since she worked for the state for many years, and could sympathize with their position. I felt I had to protect my sister's welfare, but still had a thread of embarrassment about what I had just done.

As I drove along, my thoughts raced, as I was still worried about the future. I still had many questions and so many doubts about Anne leaving a locked unit for a resident home.

ACTON, MASS., EARLY SPRING 1998

I fiddled with the phone in my hand for several minutes, trying to collect my thoughts before I made the call. I had my file folder laid out on the kitchen table, with organized piles of documents in chronological order. I had been thinking about this day for quite some time, as my frustration and anger built up over the past several weeks about my sister's impending transfer from the hospital to a resident home. I had thought about the pros and cons of the situation, and I still could not get comfortable with the state's plan to move Anne. She was so fragile, and the administration's track record on mental health was not as good as it claimed. With such a large bureaucratic system, things just got lost in the cracks, and every once in a while someone got hurt or disappeared.

I told my family I had an early morning dentist appointment. That way I could make the call from the comfort of my own home. My wife had gone to work and the kids were in school. I would have quiet and privacy to make my points.

As I looked over some of the Commonwealth of Massachusetts official documents, I decided to try to call one of department's legal staff. As I started dialing, and heard the rhythmic beeping as I pushed the numbers, my pulse began to pick up steam, and as it did my collective thoughts began to get jumbled up. I wanted to have a constructive conversation with someone to plead for my sister to stay in a locked unit due to my safety concerns. I tried desperately to calm down and get my thoughts in order when someone picked up the phone.

"Department of Mental Health legal department, how can I help you?" a young female voice spoke.

I tried to come off as forceful as possible. "This is Chris McGilvery, and I would like to speak to a legal representative in your office about my sister. Anne McGilvery."

"Can I ask what this is about, sir?" the woman asked in an official tone. "I need more information so I can transfer you to the correct person."

I tried to sound professional and under control, but I was jumping out of my skin. "I will talk to any lawyer in your office who deals with the state mental hospitals." I knew I sounded abrupt, but I needed to get someone with authority on the phone who could listen to my plight.

"Hold on, sir," the woman said with a deep Boston accent in her voice. Then the hold button went on and quaint, tranquil music started playing through the receiver. I sat back in my chair for what seemed like an eternity when an older man's voice came on the line.

"This is Dell Barry, assistant legal counsel for the director of mental health. What can I help you with, Mr. McGilvery?" he said in a very confident manner.

"Well, sir," I stumbled with a frog in my throat. Then it cleared. "I am calling about my sister Anne, who is a resident of Tewksbury State Hospital, and is scheduled to being transferred to a resident home in June of this year. My sister has lived in an institution nearly her entire life, and I am very worried that this transfer has not been thought through, and could put my sister is a dangerous situation, due to her history of running away."

"Mr. McGilvery," the man said in what I thought was a condescending voice." I'm not about to minimize your concerns, but this resident program has been thought through with a lot of input from mental health professionals, along with many administrative people who are professionals in this sort of thing."

My dander was getting ramped up as I heard him pontificate about the details of the program, and how much I did not understand the finer points of the resident house, and all it had to offer to people with mental illness and their quality of life. "I know that all sounds good," I told him, "but the number one thing is Anne's safety and welfare. There have been some security concerns with these houses in the past, and my sister's safety is paramount to anything else the house has to offer. Can you guarantee my sister's safely no matter what?" I finished with a forceful stamp on my statement.

There was dead space at the other end of the phone. All of a sudden the man said, "Look, sir," in an angry tone. "You can rest assured every aspect of this program has been thought out, and thought out again. Many people have addressed all the safety concerns, and the homes are acceptable, and adhere to state standards."

My blood was boiling. This guy was giving me the party line, and I wasn't having it. This guy was going to make this program work come hell or high water. He did not know my sister or care to know her. He did not know she was a flight risk, and heard voices in her head that told her what to do. He just wanted to check off another box on his list of things to do, in order to get this program off the ground and so be it if there were a couple of casualties. The more I thought about it, the more I got worked up.

"Mr. Barry," I said. "What you're saying is all well and good, but the bottom line is you cannot guarantee my sister's safety. She is a flight risk because of her schizophrenia, and if she gets out of that resident home in Foxwood, she could get hit by a car or disappear altogether. I want a second review of her file and have your people reconsider keeping her at Tewksbury in a locked unit."

The lawyer shot back at me almost immediately. "Look, Chris. May I call you Chris," he said. The state hospital is closing except for the criminally insane, and no residents will be left there or at any facilities in Eastern Massachusetts. I could not even comply with your request if I wanted to. It's just not possible." He finished with a sense of exasperation in his voice.

I thought about what he said for a few seconds, and then my frustration got the better of me. I took a deep breath, and launched into my sister's life story. I took about twenty minutes to complete my summary and Mr. Barry did not interrupt me once. I finished my diatribe with a threat that if he did not find another option that guaranteed my sister's safety, I was going to go to the newspapers with the whole story. Once I finished, my blood pressure was back to normal, and I felt like I had a thousand-pound weight removed from my shoulders.

I couldn't hear Mr. Barry talking on the other end of the phone, but I could hear his breath. I'm sure he was thinking carefully about his response. Lawyers always dotted the I's and crossed the T's before they jumped in and said something that could be used against them. "Well, Mr. McGilvery, that is quite a tale you have told me, and I assume you can back it up with proof," he said. "The state does not take too kindly to threats in any fashion, and we have been more than generous taking care of your sister all these years. If I were you, I would think long and hard before you take this situation to the next level, and end up regretting your choices." He finished with a high level of confidence in his voice.

"I can back up everything up that I have stated," I said confidently. "I would hate to put the state in a bad light, but my sister's welfare is the most important thing to me, and I will do anything to assure her safety and well-being. Don't pat yourself on the back about what a good job you have done. You and your department put my parents through hell for years until they passed away, and they died with broken hearts because of you and you cronies in the mental health department."

The voice at the end of the line was mute, but I could hear some faint breathing through the line. I waited for him to respond to my last statement. "Well, Mr. McGilvery," he said. "I am not in charge of that aspect of the changes that are taking place around the state, but I can assure you this plan has been very well thought out and reviewed by many mental health professionals, as well as advocates representing the residents. We have been very forthright and up front with the families throughout the process over the last few months, and we have not heard from many people who have reservations about the program."

I did my best to think about my rehearsed speech, but as soon as I started talking I knew the conversation was going to go downhill. "Well," I blurted. "I don't feel like this situation has been vetted or been conveyed in a forthright way to the parents and relatives of these patients who have been hospitalized for many years. The way I see it is you and your department have made a management decision to push vulnerable people out of professional state care, and put them in group homes where they will not get the attention, the programs, or the safe environment that people who are mentally disabled need. I see the state in financial trouble and my sister and her friends are the pawns to make your bottom line look better."

The lawyer came right back at me. "Mr. McGilvery, there is no reason to get upset," he reassured me. "We are all trying to accomplish the same thing for your sister. We want what is best for her, and the people in our department hold the residents up as our number one priority, and we feel resident homes will give them a chance to thrive in a somewhat normal environment. I'm not sure what your reservations are."

I was starting to get flustered, and I was losing my train of thought. I needed to say something constructive that would make an impression. "I am not impressed with your safety plan at the group homes and feel there needs to be either more supervision or locks inside that the residents cannot mess with," I blurted out. "The overview that Ms. Atwood gave me a few weeks ago was shabby, and she could not guarantee my sister's safety. The resident home is on a busy street, and if Anne gets out, she could walk right into traffic or get picked up by who knows who." I tried to sound as dramatic as possible, and I thought I was succeeding.

"Chris, I know you have reservations," he said reassuringly. "But the hospital is closing in June, and only the criminal insane will be left there and the state police. Otherwise the facility will be shut down. That decision has been made and it is out of our hands. We are just trying to make the best of the situation and have a smooth transition in June. I'm sure everything will work out."

I sat back in my chair, and stewed for a moment. I repeated my threat to expose the state's actions in pulling a fast one on my parents, and the resulting cover-up. I played it up as best I could, and threatened legal action. My anxiety and heartrate were off the charts as the dead air continued at the other end of the phone.

"Mr. McGilvery," the lawyer firmly. "Stop making idle threats; the state has provided excellent care to your sister. As I said, her welfare and safety are paramount to anything."

We went back and forth for another few minutes on the phone, but it was useless. This guy and the state had already made up their minds. I did not have the resources to take care of Anne myself, and she was a ward of the state, so I had run up against a brick wall. I finished the phone call by saying I was not going to take this lying down, and hung up the phone.

I was frustrated with the way the phone call ended. The state was not going to budge and customize my sister's care. I tried to stay positive that things would be all right, but doubt was seeping into my mind. I wanted to keep my promise to my parents that I would look out for Anne, but I kept getting the feeling that there were other forces at work that were competing with my promise.

ACTON, MASS., MARCH 1998

I raced in the house from work around five. I remembered we had a PTA meeting at my kids' school, and there were important issues that were to be discussed. My wife and I tried to be proactive and involved with our children's education.

As I breezed in I saw my wife cooking in the kitchen. She gave a quick "Hello, how was your day?"

I said "My day went well," gave her a peck on the cheek, and whisked out of the kitchen, down the hallway into our room. I took off my business clothes, and put on my casual clothes to get ready for the evening. I grabbed my business clothes to put them in the closet. When I opened the door, I noticed my steel filing cabinet was open, and two file folders were on the floor. What was this? I hung up my pants and shirt on the hangers. Then I bent down and picked up the file folders. They were two folders of legal documents for two home equity loans I had taken out a few years ago. What were they doing on the floor? Who had been in my filing cabinet? This is where I kept all my important documents, and if my wife went in there she would have told me, and also would have put the folders back in their rightful place.

I pondered the situation for a minute, and then let out a roar. I yelled to my two children to come upstairs. I was abrupt, and starting to get paranoid. A few seconds later I heard the patter of little feet racing up the stairs, my two children came into the bedroom, and stood at attention in front of me, not knowing why I was yelling. My daughter and son were young, but knew not to go into that filing cabinet under any circumstances.

They both looked nervously at me, wondering what all the hoopla was about. I had the two folders in my hand, and I kept slapping them in the palm of my other hand to get their attention as to what I was questioning them about. "Were either of you two playing in my room today?" I questioned them. "My filing cabinet was opened, and these two important folders were on the floor in the closet."

They stood there looking back at me with blank stares. Then they looked at each other, and then back at me again. "Dad," my son said in a quiet voice. "We were playing downstairs all afternoon. We have not been up here at all."

I looked back at them, studying their body language to see if they were telling a white lie because they thought they would get in trouble. "Listen you two," I scolded. "If you were playing in this room today you better both tell me the truth, and I will go a lot easier on you." I tried to be firm, and give them a chance to change their minds.

"Dad, we are telling the truth. We have been downstairs, and have not been in your room at all," my son repeated. My daughter did not say a word but looked at my son, and then back at me shaking her head with an agreeing glance.

I was getting upset. If my children had not opened my closet door and gone in there, who had? I started huffing and puffing and threatening them that if they were not telling me the truth, the punishment would be worse.

My wife breezed into the room. "Chris, why are you raising you voice to the children? You are going to scare them," she said in a comforting voice.

"I found these folders on the floor of the closet," I said. "The file drawer was open when I went to hang up my clothes. Did you go into the file cabinet today?"

My wife shook her head. "No. I was the only person here today, and when the kids came home, I sent them downstairs, because I was cleaning up here. I did not go into the closet at all since this morning."

"Did you go out today to do any errands?" I asked.

"Yes" she said. "I went to meet the girls for coffee this morning for a couple of hours, and then I came right back here. Otherwise, I have been here all day."

I kept looking at everyone, and they were looking back at me with questionable looks on their faces. They never really saw me upset, and were probably wondering why I was getting myself so worked up. I looked back at my wife, and said I was sorry, and she dismissed the kids and went back to the kitchen.

I put the folders on the bed, and went into the bathroom to wash my face and clean up for dinner. I splashed soap and water on my face. I noticed the window was open a half-inch, which I thought was odd since it was late winter and the chill was still in the air. I dried my face, and looked back at the mirror, and noticed a look of confusion written across it.

I opened the window. As I studied the silver storm window I noticed the screen had been pulled down, and looked like it was somewhat out of its track. That looked strange to me, because I always had the storm windows down in the winter. I did not remember switching them up yet, since spring had not arrived. As I reached up to pull down the storm window again, the screen fell out of the window to the ground below. This startled me, and I opened the window, and stuck my head out to see where it had fallen. I saw one of my patio chairs wedged up against the window, with a muddy shoe print on it. To me, it looked like someone had used the chair to boost themselves up and climb in the window.

My blood pressure shot up and anxiety raced through my body. What was going on here? Had someone broken into our house and stolen something? This was always a possibility in suburbia, where most people worked and the houses were empty all day and were sitting targets. I raced back into the bedroom closet, and pulled out the folder with all the documentation on my sister's life. Had someone broken in here to steal these important papers to cover up what I already knew was a cover up by the mental health agency? Had they gone to this extent to cover their tracks on what they had done?

I put Anne's folder on the bed, and started going through all the papers and documents. My mind was racing and I could not exactly remember all the important papers that were in the folder. Suppose one or two pages with incriminating information were removed? How could I be sure I had what was originally in the file? I could feel my armpits getting moist from nervous perspiration.

I heard my wife calling me and the kids for supper, but I was at my wit's end. The situation was spinning out of control, and I had no idea what to do about it. My mind was racing and I felt like I had let this go too far. I needed to get on top of things and make sure my sister was going to be treated fairly. As my anxiety rose, I reached down on the bed and picked up the home equity files and threw them across the room. As they flew to the other side of the bed, they hit the clock radio, which fell off the bedside stand and hit the floor.

It immediately came on with blaring music. The volume was up really loud, and I could hear Peter Townsend and the Who playing "Won't Get Fooled Again." I froze, not being able to decide if I should hit the wall switch and shut it off or run to the other side of the bed and turn it off. The song took over my mind, and started to get me infuriated. I needed to do something to shake up the state and make it keep its promises to my mother, father, and my sister.

BOSTON, MASS., APRIL 1998

◆◆◆◆◆◆

I stood out in the parking lot of the *Boston Examiner*, staring at the old, three-story red brick building. It was a cloudy, cold day, with charcoal gray winter snow still melting on the ground. As I looked passed the building, I could see the inner Boston Harbor with the outer islands in the distance.

I was leaning against the bumper of my car, a manila folder tucked under my arm. I was trying to figure out what to say to the people, contemplating how to tell them what it all meant. I had a swirl of facts in my mind, and I wanted to somehow present it to get the maximum impact of my story. My heart was pounding, since I felt like a fish out of water. I never had done anything like this in my life. Finally, I got my gumption up and walked towards the front door.

As I entered the front door, I was met by a receptionist sitting there looking as important as possible. To the right was a security guard looking more interested in watching the television on the wall than paying attention to me or the woman at the front desk.

I introduced myself to the woman behind the desk and stated my business. She asked me a few questions, and I felt at ease that I was not the only person to walk through those doors who had a big scoop that would help sell their newspapers. The woman asked me to sit in the reception area and make myself comfortable. I sat down and picked up a current copy of the newspaper. As I sat engrossed in my reading a young woman came out from a door across the room and began walking towards me. I stood up and waited for her to close the distance. She had blond hair, a conservative brown pantsuit, with matching patent leather shoes. Her glasses even matched, and made her look very studious.

"Hi, Mr. McGilvery. How are you?" she stated in an upbeat manner. "Sarah tells me you needed to talk to us about something that has been on your mind? My name is Marilyn Steinberg, the assistant editor of the newspaper."

"Yes, you're correct," I said, clearing my throat. "I have a story that I thought you might be interested in." My confidence level was starting to build. "I have documentation in this folder that will back up everything I am saying." I waved the folder for her to see it.

"That's great, Mr. McGilvery," she said. "Why don't you follow me up to the second floor, and we can talk in a conference room and see what you have to say. I will get you a drink or a cup of coffee, and you can make yourself at home."

She put me in a long conference room with a wall of windows. The other walls were wallpapered with multiple literary awards and photos of famous Boston and Massachusetts people, pictured with what I assumed were the newspaper's reporters. It looked very impressive, and raised my level of confidence in these people and what I was about to do.

I sat there tapping my finger on the table and scanning the room. Ms. Steinberg walked back into the room carrying a yellow tablet of paper and a tape recorder. She had a cup of coffee in her hand, and placed it on the table in front of me, then sat down at the corner of the table facing me.

After a few minutes of general conversation I launched into my story. I started at the beginning of my sister's life, and as I talked Marilyn became very animated and more engrossed by what I was saying. As I continued with my story, I pulled out supporting documents from my folder and showed them to her to prove what I was saying was the truth. After a half-hour of talking, the woman stopped me and said she was going to bring her boss into the room to be part of the conversation. I knew from the look on her face that I had just given her an important story, and one which would be on the front page and cause a lot of state bureaucrats a lot of anguish.

I pulled over her yellow legal pad, and tried to read it, but her handwriting was hen scratching. I pushed it back just in the nick of time as she came back with a man in his sixties; he had a balding head with gray hair on the sides. He had on a nice blue shirt, with matching pants and a colorful wool vest. I stood up to shake his hand.

"This is Mr. Rosen, Mr. McGilvery," Marilyn said. "He is the head editor of this newspaper, and my boss. I thought he would be very interested in what you had to say."

"Nice to meet you, sir," he said in his official Boston Brahmin manner. I immediately felt guilty thinking that and pushed it out of my mind, and stuck out my hand. We exchanged hellos, and then he said, "Marilyn tells me you have a very interesting story to tell us. I thought it would be best if I sat in and listened."

The assistant editor sat down, and she recapped what I had already talked about. She showed him multiple documents from my folder, and he studied them with a high level of concentration, and asked some questions of me. Once he had an overview, I continued with my story, while showing both of them additional documentation to support everything I was saying. As we progressed they asked some probing questions to fill in any gaps of details they did not understand. The whole meeting took about three hours, and when we were finished I was mentally and physically exhausted. They asked me if they could copy all the documents in my folder, and I agreed under the condition that none would be printed in the newspaper. They said they only wanted them for their files to back up their story. I knew there would be significant backlash from the state, and I could see their point that they needed proof in hand.

They said my story was very compelling, but did not seem all that shocked while I had been telling it. I'm sure after covering stories of murder, rape, fires, and car accidents, this story seemed tame by comparison. They said they would turn the story over to one of their reporters, who would research the details, and also give the state a chance to tell its side. Once that was accomplished their team would decide if the story was going to be run, and what day of the week it would run in the newspaper.

I agreed to all of what they said, and told them I was not selling the story for money, I just wanted it to get out there in case other families had the same experience. I felt a little guilty because my driving force for releasing this exposé to them was to get the leverage I needed to keep my sister in a state hospital setting. As I walked out the front door of the building, I could hear the drone of rush hour traffic on the expressway. A feeling of doom settled in. Had I just let out a genie that could not be put back in the bottle? How would the state react to this story being released to the public? Only time would tell.

ACTON, MASS., APRIL 1998

I was driving on the backroads of Acton, meandering through rush hour traffic. The weekday commute never got any easier. Acton was a nice town, with a good school system, and the home office of a computer giant right down the road. A lot of people wanted to live here, but the roads had never been upgraded to absorb all the additional citizens and traffic.

I accelerated onto Main Street, and made my way across town to where I lived. The sun was still up, but setting in the sky, the snow had finally melted, and a hint of spring was in the air. The weather made me feel somewhat upbeat about the day, and I was looking forward to getting home and relaxing a little.

As I turned the corner and was headed down the street to my house, I could see the flashing blue lights of a police car in the distance. I did not think much about it until I got farther down the street and saw the police car was in front of my house and a policeman was in the street directing traffic. My heart sank; I had a sick feeling of doom. Then I noticed television news vans in front of my house, their TV antennas up in the air, and people swarming around the driveway. I stopped the car, and rolled down my window to ask the policeman what was the matter. As I slowed, he kept waving at me in a wild manner. I knew he did not want traffic to stop, so I drove by him and pulled into my neighbor's open driveway. I flew out of the car, and as I moved toward my house all I could see were news people, reporters, and interested neighbors.

I walked through the throng of people without anyone stopping me; they must have thought I was another reporter. I walked by the TV reporters setting up for live broadcasts. As I moved closer to my front stairs, some reporters started to look at me funny. They probably thought I was a cub reporter trying to get a big story. I began to push and shove to get up the stairs. The front door was open a crack, and I could see my wife standing at the top of the living room stairs, with the phone planted in her ear and a look of fright on her face.

As I hit the top of the stairs, a neighbor shouted out, "Chris, what's going on?" I looked back to her, and saw her standing there with her little girl, a perplexed look on her face. I shrugged my shoulders, but then the news people swarmed me. Microphones were stuck in my face, spotlights turned on, cameras began to roll, multiple questions came flying at me from all directions. I lunged up the final steps, got through the door, and then slammed it and flipped the lock. The noise was dulled for a second, and I looked up the stairs and saw my wife glaring at me. Our children were standing behind her, cowering.

"Chris," my wife said in a frustrated tone. "Mr. Rosen is on the phone from the *Boston Examiner*. He wants to talk to you. What on earth is going on?"

I was about to respond with some quick line, and then she shoved the phone in my face and took the kids to their rooms. I put the phone up to my ear and shouted into the receiver, "What is this all about Mr. Rosen? My driveway is filled with news people and reporters. All hell is breaking lose around here. You said you were going to call me a day before the story was going to be in the paper. I thought we had a deal?" I was angry.

"Mr. McGilvery, I'm so sorry, but we moved up the date of the release, and I could not get in touch with you today," he apologized. "You told me to call you, but I did not have your work phone. I called your home, but the phone just keep ringing, and I didn't want to leave a message with such important news. I wish I could have held back the story one more day, but as we researched your story, our reporter hit a real nerve with a few state reps and some people over at the department of mental health. It turned into a real thunderstorm. Once we started asking questions, the department went on full information blackout, and then important people started calling the newsroom making threats to us"

Then I got really nervous, because it sounded like this article had pissed off a lot of people, and made the state start circling the wagons. "What type of threats were they making?" I asked.

"Oh, they demanded to see the proof, where did we get this information, and then started saying they were going to sue the newspapers for slander. When that starts to happen you know you have a hell of a story. We put it on the front page of today's newspaper. The buzz is going through the roof" His voice was one of compete satisfaction with himself, and he was not that concerned that he just caused a shit storm in my life.

As I listened to him say how big this story was, I looked out the front door, and heard people yelling through the door to come out for an interview. I shook my head and waved them off. They began to lean hard on the front storm door. I was afraid it was going to break. I ran down the short flight of stairs, and slammed the wooden front door in their faces. There must have been fifty people in my front yard and driveway. I never thought this would ever happen this way. How would I explain this to my friends and family? I wanted to use the story for leverage, but now it had gone way beyond its intended purpose.

I stayed on the phone with Mr. Rosen for a few minutes, and went over the follow-up articles that would come next, and the paper's planned interviews with state employees and representatives in the coming weeks. A few liberal officials from certain districts were already asking the governor and the commissioner of mental health for an investigation into these allegations. The more he talked, the more my heart sank. All I had wanted to do was help my sister be safe, and now I had created a big mess.

After I got off the phone, I turned to go into the bathroom. Standing there was my wife tapping her foot on the hardwood floor. She had that look. I knew the rest of the night would be spent explaining all I had been up to, and trying to convince her that everything would be okay. She had a soft spot in her heart for my sister, and I hoped that was my ace in the hole.

BOSTON, MASSACHUSETTS

─────── ✦✦✦✦✦ ───────

As I walked up the state house steps, I looked up to the top of the gold dome. A chill went down my spine. It was a gray day in Boston, and I was feeling anxious and melancholy. To my right was Ms. Prince, dressed up a blue blazer and matching shirt, and carrying her usual huge black legal bag that seemed to weigh more than she did.

The preceding weeks had been filled with accusations by the state, legal maneuvering, multiple articles in local newspapers, and threatening phone calls. Just trying to keep my life on track had been a major struggle. I was getting hit with questions from many of my friends, family, coworkers, newspaper reporters, and offers from attorneys to go after the state with lawsuits totaling millions of dollars. I did not want any of it. I had opened a can of worms, but now I wanted to get all the worms back in the can.

Thank goodness for Ms. Prince. She was my legal counsel to the stars. She had looked out for my sister all these years, making sure she got what she needed and was well taken care of. Now she was helping me put out this huge fire I had started. She had never been aware of the whole story, of my sister's history and beginnings, but she was so accommodating and caring. She had done a great job dealing with a huge bureaucracy. She was now keeping me from getting sued for slander. She had had many phone calls with me and the powers that be in the state over the past few weeks. She had given me an over-all idea of what would take place today, but once you got deeply entrenched state employees and lawyers in a room, who knows what would happen.

As we walked up the balance of the granite stairs and went through the huge brass doors, Ms. Prince was in my ear coaching me on what to say and what not to say. I was so nervous that I only heard half of what she was telling me. I tried to look attentive. Up until now, I did not have a good track record of handling things in an exemplary way. I had really done the opposite. I had not consulted with people who knew this business, and my strategy had not worked. In fact, it had gone off the tracks, hurting a lot of people and bringing up old wounds about mental illness and care in Massachusetts that many people would just as soon forget.

The state house was a beehive of activity on this Tuesday morning. I was always in awe standing in the lobby, thinking about how much history had happened here and how many historic people had walked in these hallways.

After we showed our identification and stated our business to the capital policeman, he checked us in and then directed us to the second floor of the building. Ms. Prince was yessing the policeman, due to the fact she knew every square inch of this building, and could not understand why this old timer did not recognize her. I silently got a chuckle out of the whole back and forth, and then we made our way up the huge gray marble stairs to the second floor. As we walked up the stairs I looked up and saw many murals painted on the ceiling. Most were scenes from famous battles of Bunker Hill, Breeds Hill, and Lexington Green. The paintings were bright with detail, and looked like they had been touched up very recently. It reminded me how much history this state and city had, and were part of what made me proud to be a citizen. As I walked, I started to become dizzy, and jerked my head down to regain my equilibrium.

As we crested the top of the stairs the long hallway stretched for several hundred feet. We walked slowly, taking it all in. We went by the Senate chambers on one side and the House chambers on the other. Then came the Speaker's office, the President of the Senate's office, and then the Cabinet secretaries' offices. They all had huge oak doors with a smoked glass window and a big brass door knob. Of course, they all had impressive black lettering on the glass. We came to the office we were looking for, and Ms. Prince grabbed the door knob and started to turn it. Written in big letters across the glass was Secretary of Mental Health with the commissioner's name underneath. The man's name was Mr. Phillip Jackson. He was a well-known official; he had served several terms as commissioner under several administrations. He was a Democrat, but he had worked for Republican administrations in the past because he was a good commissioner and did a good job. That also made me feel bad, as the last month had probably been hell for him trying to do damage control and limit the fallout from what he thought was going to be a big mess and maybe even his downfall. He had not done anything wrong, and his stellar name was being tarnished. It was all because of me.

As we swung into the office we first encountered an administrative assistant. She had on a bright, yellow dress, her red hair done up in a bouffant hairdo, and wearing retro glasses. She looked like a throwback to fifties or sixties. Ms. Prince and I walked over, and she introduced us and said we had an appointment with the commissioner. Once the assistant knew who we were, a cool look came across her face. The last few weeks had been hell around here, and local talk show hosts across the radio dial had had a field day with her boss and the state agency in general. I could tell from her demeanor I was not on her 'A' list.

The woman came out from behind her desk and acted professional, even though I knew it must have been killing her inside. She directed us into a big conference room, and said her boss would be with us in a few minutes. Then she offered us coffee or a soft drink and of course we both refused, not wanting to be any more trouble than we already had been. As soon as we refused any service she vanished as quickly as she came. We both looked at each other with a visible sigh of relief.

I sat back in the nice red leather chair and looked around the room. This room looked so historic, I wondered how many famous state employees or politicians had sat right here where we were. The walls were covered with historic pictures and artifacts. The paint on the wall was an awful blue green that did not match anything. The ceiling was scrolled plaster, with several designs that I didn't quite understand.

Ms. Prince began to pull out a few legal folders and place them on the mahogany conference table. In those folders were photocopies of the historical proof of my sister's history. It was all the damaging evidence that the state had wanted to suppress for so long, and now the jig was up.

Just as we were starting to get our composure the commissioner walked in accompanied by a small man in a very expensive blue suit, white shirt, and black leather shiny shoes. He was carrying several folders under his arm. He looked about 45 years old, and had a tan complexion with black, slicked back hair. He looked like a lawyer and sure acted like one.

We both stood up, and Commissioner Jackson came over and shook both our hands and said good morning. He said how glad he was to get together and hash out this misunderstanding to an equitable agreement. He put on an air of not being upset in the least. I had tarnished his reputation, but he was as cool as could be. I guess that is why he was part politician and part executive. You had to be like this to survive working in such a political state.

I shook his hand. He had a firm grip. He was on a first-name basis with Ms. Prince, which surprised me, but I knew she had been a patient advocate for many years and had probably had many conversations with him in this very room. That gave me added confidence that we were in a good bargaining position.

"Well folks, the reason we are here today is to settle the case of Anne McGilvery vs, the State of Massachusetts once and for all," Mr. Jackson said in a formal manner. "I know there are not any legal suits pending against the state, but we want to make Mr. McGilvery feel like we are treating his sister fairly and will provide all the things she needs to be safe and secure." The lawyer on the other side of the table pushed a brown folder across between the two of us, and Ms. Prince flipped it open

My jaw almost dropped. It contained copies of many of the same documents that I had. As the lawyer started going through each one and what it meant I knew I had been on the right path all along. The state had known the truth about Anne and tried to suppress it. As we went through every document, I could only think about how much time and effort had been used to cover up this injustice and how much pain it had caused my parents. There were several documents that I had never seen and that were important to Anne's history of being packaged as a beautiful little girl who would be a treasure for anyone to adopt. One document was a state retirement and pension form for one Samuel Jenkins, Anne's biological father.

We sat there for an hour going though paperwork, and both the lawyer and Mr. Jackson commented on several points and how certain information affected the overall situation. The story started in Worcester and Metropolitan State, then continued in Indianapolis, then back to Westborough State Hospital, and finally finishing at Tewksbury State Hospital. It had been an almost 50-year adventure filled with deceit, cover-ups, pain, and now the day of reckoning. As we got to the end the lawyer pushed a piece of paper over the table to us. It was an agreement between the state and my father that the Department of Mental Health would find my sister incompetent by a court of law, and would take care of her for the rest of her life. My father would be a limited guardian to oversee some of her care in regard to basic things, and would help bring her extra things like new clothes with up-to-date fashions, cigarettes, electronics, and anything deemed outside the state guidelines. For this consideration, his limited guardianship would not constitute food, shelter, or medical care in any way. In consideration of this care, my father would not sue the state, and would drop any pending lawsuits. It was signed at the bottom by the then-commissioner of mental health and my father, and dated so long ago. It took my breath away to just see the document, and I felt proud that my parents had not let the state get away with this injustice.

I sat back in my chair, just starting to feel composed, when the lawyer slid another document over to us. As my eyes gazed down on the print, I noticed it was another codicil to the original one my father had signed. It was almost identical to that one except it had my name on it, and guaranteed the same things with my sister and the same shared responsibility. The lawyer went through all the language, and the commissioner jumped in to clarify anything I did not understand or questioned. I felt good about how things were going, and when Mr. Jackson said if we both signed it, then we could put this whole affair behind us. Anne would be taken care of for the rest of her life. No questions asked.

I looked over at Ms. Prince and she coaxed me to sign. She said this would benefit Anne, and that I would be happy with her care. Just as I was about to put the pen to paper the commissioner mentioned how nice the new resident home was and how happy Anne would be there.

I was skeptical about his smooth style and confidence. He seemed like this message he was sending me had been told many times to many family members of patients in the state system, and he had it down pat. I was not buying it, since I had seen the outcome of some of mental health's failed policies. This was a big step for Anne, and I had doubts about the monitoring and the level of care she would need to be safe. I played around with the paper, and made it look like I was reading the fine print. Then I put pen to paper, and signed and dated the document and pushed it back across the table to the lawyer.

They both smiled, and seemed content with themselves. Then they pulled the ace out of the hole. The lawyer pulled out another official piece of paper, and as he was pushing it over to Ms. Prince, Mr. Jackson started describing what was on it. I was totally taken by surprise.

What could this all be? I thought the official business was all concluded. As he began explaining himself, Ms. Prince was reading and nodding her head as if she were all on board with what he was saying. From what I could understand, this document would absolve all responsibilities for any past treatment of Anne and any future treatment of her, as long as the state gave her medical care, shelter, and food. I could not ever come back at them for the abuse of public trust they had perpetrated on my parents and me. As the lawyer explained the details my head began to cloud up. What was going on? Why did I need to sign an additional document? As they all talked to each other, it was like their lips were moving, but I could not hear the words that were coming out of their mouths.

I pushed my chair back and stood up. The other three looked perplexed. I was not going to put up with this. I knew they were trying to pull a fast one on me. I could not understand why my sister's lawyer was going along with it. As I moved towards the door, the voice in my subconscious grew louder. I still could not make out what anyone was saying. I just kept walking out the door, and through the outer office, and into the main hallway on the second floor. My mind was starting to clear, and as I shut the door I saw a stampede of reporters and news people coming at me.

What was happening? No one was to know about this meeting, and everything was to be held in the strictest confidence. Why would they have leaked this meeting to the press? This would not help their cause, since the public would think they were trying to buy me off. I was perplexed and nervous. As I backed up to the door I had just come out of, the gang of reporters and camera people were only a few feet away. I had no idea what I was going to say, and for a split second, I thought about running back into the office.

But the pack blew right by me, as if I was invisible, and continued down the hallway to the door of the Senate chamber where they set up their cameras. I stood and watched as the Senate President came out of the door, and the lights went on and the reporters' questions started to fly. There must have been an important vote today that I was not aware of.

I turned and made my way down the hallway and stairs to the outer lobby and out the door. I did not want anyone to catch up with me and start to harass me for my sudden departure. As I started down the steps of the state house, the sun peered out from behind the clouds, and I looked down the hill over the Boston Common. As I walked further down Beacon Street, I could hear and then see a gang of high school kids walking through the Park.

One of the kids had a boom box on his shoulder, and was strutting his way down to Park Street Station. I could hear an old sixties song, "Time Has Come Today," by The Chambers Bothers blasting out of the radio. The song caught my ear, and I could hear the signature tap of the drum start snapping like the tick of a clock. I could not stop feeling that my time had come today, and I would not be crushed by the state bureaucracy. I would stand tall and protect my sister from any future act or deeds that could jeopardize her safety or security. I felt confident that I had made the right decision.

FOXWOOD, MASS., MAY 1998

+‧+◆◆◆+‧+

I was on the last leg on my journey to Anne's new resident home. The past months' events had been fast and furious. Ms. Prince had cleaned up all the legal details of Anne's new home and care with the state, and Anne had been officially moved to her new residence in the suburbs. I had relented on my disagreement with the process, and everything seemed to be in order for Anne's next stop on the tour. The state had gotten the message that it had to keep Anne safe, and any breach in that trust would be met with the harshest penalties.

I approached the driveway of the home, and put my left blinker on and waited for the oncoming traffic to pass. As I waited for a break in the traffic, I noticed that the old, run-down house had been restored into the beautiful Victorian it once was. It looked like it had just been built. The driveway had been repaved; there were new gardens and beautiful spring flowers. It looked like a professional horticulturist had done the work.

This was to be a big party hosted by the state to celebrate the opening of the newest resident home in the area. I wasn't sure who would be there, but the main reason I came was to make sure my sister was settled and secure in her new surroundings. As I parked my car I saw that some of the cars already there had official state license plates. That tipped me off that some higher-ups from the state would be in attendance. I hoped I would not get any daggers shot at me, since my recent behavior was not to their liking.

As I stepped from my car, I could hear the faint sound of people talking and music wafting in the air from the back yard. I stepped up on the front porch, and before I could put my hand on the knob, the door magically opened. A nice young woman in a blue party dress met me, and gave me a big "Hello" and handshake.

"I am Nicole," she said in an enthusiastic voice. "I have heard so much about you, and have looked forward to meeting you. Anne has also been asking for you." She shut the door behind me and led me into what looked like an office space. She gave me an overview of the day. She seemed genuinely happy to see me, and had nothing but good things to say about my sister.

We walked out of the office and stepped into a kitchen area. The house inside was brand new, and such a contrast from my earlier meeting just a few months before. Several people stood at attention as we came into the room. They were introduced to me as the staff of the new house, and each of them introduced themselves, were upbeat, and answered any and all of my questions. As I looked around I saw a lot of great food, party platters, and drinks. Once the formalities were out of the way, they guided me upstairs to see Anne's new bedroom.

On our way upstairs, I saw that the antique banister and stairs had been restored by sanding and being treated with several layers of varnish. They looked so shiny, I was practically blinded by the sunlight streaming in through a skylight.

We walked about halfway down a long hallway, going by a beautiful full bath that was spotless, and then into a bedroom. The room was beautiful, filled with natural light. It had a view of the backyard and side yard. The walls and ceiling had a fresh coat of paint, and the hardwood floors had been sanded and highly varnished. The house employees all stepped in and lined up against the opposite wall. They all looked so happy to be there, and as I scanned the room, I noticed the beautiful pink window drapes, matching Anne's pillow and bedspread. It looked perfect for a girl's room. There was a white dresser in the corner, with a nice mirror over it. Nicole opened the closet door, and as I peered in I noticed all new clothes hanging in an orderly fashion, and several pairs of shoes placed neatly at the bottom of the closet.

After we were finished with the upstairs tour, the staff bought me down to the first floor, and through a beautiful open living room that had a few couches, a television, and a piano, which I assumed must have been donated to the house. I was guided to the back door, and out onto a farmer's porch with several nice white rocking chairs lined across the back of it.

The backyard was full of people, and over to the right a few employees were cooking on a barbecue grill, and handing out beverages to the guests. I could not get over how beautiful the yard was. The nice, colorful plantings from the front were wrapped around the back of the house. The grass had grown in very green for so early in the season, and it was cut to resemble a highly manicured golf course.

Nicole passed me off to another house worker named Jeff. He escorted me around the backyard, and introduced me to everyone including the contractor and his staff who did the work on the house. I met several higher-ups from the mental health department, but the commissioner was not there, which pleased me to no end, since I was embarrassed by how our last meeting ended. After several more introductions, I was reunited with my sister, who was dressed to the nines, with a nice yellow dress, matching shoes, a new hairdo, and even earrings. She looked so happy and promptly introduced me to her new housemates, in her usual introverted way. They began peppering me with inappropriate questions about Anne and my personal life, a phenomenon I had gotten acquainted with over the years of visiting Anne.

After several minutes with my sister, Nicole came over with a soft drink for me, and walked me over to the back porch. We sat down, and talked about a variety of subjects from my life, to her life and background. The conversation flowed naturally, and there was no overriding agenda from either of us. After some time one of the social workers brought over a plate of food for me. I was famished and appreciated the gesture.

As I gazed over the yard I noticed a stream in the back of the yard which was flowing briskly. A gaggle of ducks was making its way down the stream. The mother led the way with the baby ducks following closely behind. It was a sign of spring and new beginnings. I started to daydream and reflect about how far my sister had come after all her trials and tribulations.

The last time I had seen Anne at Tewksbury State Hospital she was a beaten woman who had been a product of the state mental health system for almost 30 years. There had been so many ups and downs for my parents and myself. I was not happy with the way things unfolded in the past few months, but seeing how happy Anne was today, the uplifting new residence she would be part of, started to make me feel better.

The day was turning out to be such an enjoyable event. I knew that the staff was trying so hard to make me feel at home, and I'm sure an order had come down from the higher-ups. In any case, I was happy that the house was open, and I was impressed with the caring of the staff. Anne had only been here five days, but with her new dress and new hairdo she looked like she had already made huge strides.

As the party progressed, I noticed many of the patrons had moved inside, even though it was still such a beautiful day. Nicole was talking to a coworker, and I was taking it all in. After a few quiet moments, I heard the distant sound of the piano. One of the young volunteers stuck his head out the back door, and said excitedly, "You guys need to come and see this." We all got up from our chairs and made our way inside.

The living room was packed with guests and workers. I could hear the piano, and heard the familiar sound of a song I had remembered from so long ago. It was "Amazing Grace," a song my sister heard for the first time at her first communion. She talked about that song for weeks. It struck her as so meaningful and the melody was one that she could not get out of her head. My mother could not find the sheet music at the local music store, so she ended up asking the music director from our local parish if she could take it home and copy it. The people at the church agreed, and my mother copied it by hand, drawing all the notes and words on blank sheet music bars.

She surprised my sister with the hand-done sheet music when she came home from school one day. Anne persisted in practicing that song until she memorized it to perfection. I thought she had a photographic memory, but my parents said it was just sheer determination.

Some folks were singing along, others were humming the tune with enjoyment. The room was buzzing, and people were nodding and whispering how talented this girl was. I continued to make my way through the crowd to get to the other side to and see who was playing. I sang the words as I walked.

When I got to the right of the room, the piano player came into full view. It was my sister, playing as if she had never stopped playing. She looked so pretty sitting on the bench, her fingers dancing across the keys. It was so appropriate that she would play this song. She was like the Prodigal Son; she had been lost, and now she was found.

In my mind, a kaleidoscope of a thousand pictures of Anne appeared. They cascaded through my memory. The places and times I visualized were happy, and none of the bad crept in. As I looked at Anne, she turned her head ever so slightly, and her eyes met mine. She didn't smile, but I could see that little twinkle in her eyes that I had seen a thousand times before when we were young. She was in her comfort zone, and for the first time in a long time, I felt Anne had finally come home.

The End

ABOUT THE AUTHOR

C hris is a graduate of Northeastern University with a bachelor of science degree.

He has worked in the life insurance industry for over 40 years.

Chris has had a lifelong love of writing and reading.

Chris lives with his wife and family in southern Maine.